Praise for

The Realtor's Curse

"Alligators, snakes, sharks, amorous manatees, psychotic Florida realtors and bodies turning up everywhere. But never fear. Intrepid, neurotic US Food and Drug Administration functionary and part-time private investigator, the Walter Mitty-esque Dr. Jason Longfellow is on the case. If Miami humorist Dave Berry wrote a book about quixotic, goofball PI's, it'd read like The Realtor's Curse." *--Joe Palmer, Author, A Mariner's Tale*

"The search for a Florida condo becomes deadly in this fast-paced and funny novel by John J Jessop. Private investigator Jason Longfellow and his wife Chelsea return to action for the third time, bickering and butting heads as they try to solve a murder mystery and avoid becoming victims themselves. Dark comedy in the Sunshine State!" *--Henry G. Brinton, Author, City of Peace*

"In this zany who dunnit mystery/comedy Florida is the hot spot where everything that can go wrong does. Jessop brilliantly turns an innocent vacation into absurd comedy. The laughs keep coming until it hurts." *-- Benjamin Berkley, Author, Against My Will and In Defense of Guilt*

THE REALTOR'S CURSE

The Realtor's Curse

ISBN 978-1-7358178-5-9

This is a work of fiction. The characters are both actual and fictitious. With the exception of verified historical events and persons, all incidents, descriptions, dialogue and opinions expressed are the products of the author's imagination and are not to be construed as real.

Published by:

JJJESSOP LLC

THE REALTOR'S

CURSE

JOHN J JESSOP

JJJESSOP LLC

Other Books by John J Jessop

PLEASURIA: TAKE AS DIRECTED

MURDER BY ROAD TRIP

Guardian Angel: Unforgiven

Guardian Angel: Indoctrination

DEDICATION

To my lovely wife, who decided she wanted to be a beach girl in retirement and suggested we retire to Florida. And, to my beautiful youngest daughter; thank you for your patience, your help with editing and cover design, and for co-authoring one of the books with me. I love you and am very proud of you and your success in the Big Apple.

Chapter 1

Ted and Denise Sorensen cruised through St. Augustine, Florida, headed to Anastasia Island in their shiny new luxury SUV. They were in search of a vacation property to provide a break from their successful corporate law practice back in Chicago, which had more business than they could handle. Denise knew that their expensive tastes made it difficult to turn away new clients. Exhausted from endless hours at the office, she had complained to Ted that they needed to get away. At her insistence, this was the first non-business-related trip they had taken in years.

Cars with Florida license plates flew past them on US-1, some blowing their horns and others giving Ted the one finger salute. Denise felt a little guilty for making Ted drive. He hated heavy traffic, and she could see his muscles tensing from the passenger seat. But, Ted was a terrible navigator, and she didn't trust him to direct them anywhere useful if she took the wheel.

"Where the hell are we?" He barked. "I get that you want a beach house to visit once in a while to get away and relax, but you could have chosen someplace a little less crowded. I'm gonna be pissed if I crash my new SUV in this mess."

"Calm down, Teddy Bear. I found a couple of open houses on my phone, and am trying to figure out which one is closest. Just stay on US-1 for a few more blocks until I get my bearings."

A jacked-up pickup truck roared by them on the left. Startled, Ted swerved to the right and almost ran off the road. Denise knew her husband had a temper, and she wasn't surprised when he sat on the horn and flipped the pickup driver a salute of his own.

Ted grouched, "These damn people are crazy. I don't even like the beach. It's too hot here, and whenever I've been to the beach it's taken days to get rid of all the sand. It seems to get everywhere. I just went along with your stupid idea because you think our hearts are going to explode from stress if we don't do something." He paused. "But, I'm not thinking of this as a vacation property, so much as an investment. I'm hoping we can make a bundle between renting it and the appreciation over the next few years, assuming scientists are wrong and Florida doesn't end up under water because of global warming."

Denise looked at her husband and frowned. He always looked at the negative side of things. Ted's dark brown hair had thinned considerably and he already looked like a puffed-up version of his younger self. All the stress had reshaped and withered him to the point where his straight white teeth were the only attractive thing left on his face.

She said, "I'm concerned about your health, and you're only thirty-five. All the stress-eating and excessive alcohol consumption have given you worry lines, and you're not the slender, athletic young man you were when I met you. And, that red tinge to your nose has nothing to do with the sun."

Ted, stressed from the heavy traffic, did not appear to take this criticism well. "You're the same age as I am, and talk about wrinkles. You've got worry lines around your eyes and on your forehead. And, that once youthful figure and long blonde hair that attracted me to you is no more. You do that stress-eating thing too, but in your case it's mainly the lower half that looks like a blown-up version of the younger you. You're doing your best to hide it by wearing that flowing tunic to hide the bulges. The flowery pattern and those bright pink Bermuda shorts might make you look like you're dressed for Florida, but those clothes don't hide the defects."

"Ouch! You really went for the jugular, hitting both a woman's age and weight. I guess I had it coming after what I said, but truth be told, our current unhealthy shapes make clothes shopping difficult and expensive for both of us. Good thing our Amex cards keep us well-dressed in tailored work attire. I'm just worried that our last doctor's visits showed we both have high blood pressure, and if we don't find a way to relax we're not going to make it to fifty. Speaking of stressing, it must be really hot out. The A/C in your new SUV is struggling to keep it cool in here."

Denise wished she hadn't brought up the subject of their unhealthy habits. She could see Ted's face getting red, suggesting his blood pressure was on the rise. Squabbling was not going to find them a vacation property, and Ted having a heart attack wouldn't help either.

Ted snarled, "Dammit, stop yammering about how we've blimped up and find us an open house, or I'm gonna drive this SUV into a telephone pole or into one of these rednecks in their big-assed pickup trucks. I'm tired, hot, stressed and you know me. I'm gonna go off if we don't find something soon."

Denise focused on her phone again. "Here's one, Teddy Bear. It's only five miles up A1A, and it's on Anastasia Island. From the photos, it's a bright yellow two-story in a small gated community just off the highway. Three-bedrooms, two-and-a-half baths, with most of the living area on the first floor. Only a single bedroom and bath upstairs. And, there's a cute little balcony off the upstairs bedroom. I definitely want to take a look."

Ted said, "Which side of A1A, beach side or west side? Beach side would be better. Easier access to the water."

"It's on the west side, so you'd have to cross A1A to get to the beach. But, looks like it's in walking distance. Just turn left on Route 206, follow 206 across the bridge, turn left on A1A and go a couple of miles. The development, called Sunny Acres, is on the left. The listing says that you'll have to call into the guard's station from the speaker at the gated entrance. Tell them we're here for the Thompson's open house."

"Sounds like a pain, but a gated community would provide some security. Probably increase the home owner's association fees though."

Ted got pinned in by two tractor trailers, one in front of him and one to his left, just a block from the turn onto 206. He was already irritated, and this wasn't good. Denise felt a jolt of fear, concerned her husband's temper was going to get them killed.

"How the hell am I supposed to turn left on 206? These two throttle jockeys have me trapped. Ah, screw it!"

Ted shoved the accelerator to the floor, and Denise was amazed that he squeezed his SUV into a small gap that opened up between the front of one tractor trailer and the rear of the other. Denise grabbed the oh-my-god-bar and held on for dear life. The trucker that Ted had cut off gave him a loud blast from his air horn. Ted made the left turn onto 206.

When they reached A1A, Denise saw wall-to-wall traffic. She had heard that Florida was becoming more and more crowded, but the constant flow of cars was surprising.

Ted said, "Dee, this traffic is nuts. You'd think this A1A was the only road in all of Florida. We'd die trying to turn left without the traffic light."

Trying to calm her husband down and avoid death by automobile, she said, "You're doing great, Teddy Bear. I'm glad I'm not driving. I couldn't do it. You're amazing."

Ted had to turn left again, and cross the other side of the divided A1A highway to enter the development. This time there was no traffic light. After ten minutes, a very brief break in oncoming traffic appeared. He closed his eyes and floored it again. Denise grabbed the oh-my-god bar and squealed as he successfully negotiated their SUV into the entrance road. He followed her directions regarding the entryway, and the gate opened. She saw that the neighborhood consisted of a single street, a total of twenty-two houses lining either side.

Denise said, "Oh, Teddy Bear. Look at the bright colors; pink, blue, green, yellow. Looks very Florida-ey."

Ted said, "I'll bet these places glow in the dark. I think that's the house just up ahead on the right. Bright yellow. There's a 'For Sale' sign on the front lawn."

Ted parked at the curb in front of the house. They walked up the steps onto a large wooden porch. Denise thought she might pass out from the intense heat and humidity. Ted, already sweating profusely, knocked on the door. The house looked like it had been recently painted, the porch deck boards newly stained. On the third knock, the door opened and a blast of delicious cool air hit Denise in the face. A tall, slender brunette with bright blue eyes invited them in. She offered Ted her hand.

"Hi. I'm Laura Donovan. I work for *SellItQuick Realty*."

Ted shook her hand. Denise noticed that he did not smile or look particularly friendly.

"I'm Ted Sorensen, and this is my wife, Denise. We're looking for a property to use as both a vacation home and a rental and thought we'd come to your open house."

Then Denise took Laura's hand. Denise was impressed that the realtor's curly hair seemed tamed and her floral bodycon dress showed no signs of sweat stains. The same could not be said of her and Ted.

Shaking Denise's hand, Laura said cheerily, "It's a pleasure to meet you. You've come to the right place. As you can see, the owners have taken excellent care of the house. And, it comes with a solid record of rental income. It's only been on the market for a week, but there's been lots of traffic at the open house and I'm expecting at least one offer by the end of the day."

Denise saw the flash of anger on her husband's face.

Ted snarled, "I get it. If I don't make you an offer within the next ten minutes someone else will beat us to the draw. Can we at least look at the property first?"

Denise was well acquainted with her husband's temper and realized this realtor had gotten off on the wrong foot. This was bad; Denise had fallen in love with the house the moment she walked through the front door. The open layout, bright interior, and unusual red mahogany vaulted ceiling appealed to her expensive tastes.

"Ted, I'm sure Laura didn't mean anything by her comments. It is a nice house, and if there has been a lot of traffic today, she might be right. Let's take the tour."

Laura said, still cheerily, "Sorry. I didn't mean to offend. I just wanted you to know the situation, in case you really like the place. As you can see, this is the living room. Notice the vaulted mahogany ceiling, with two ceiling fans. Makes the space feel open and roomy."

Denise said, "Yes, it's quite beautiful. I love all the windows. And, the two skylights really brighten up the room."

Denise could see that Ted was still angry. He grouched, "The tile floor isn't all that comfortable underfoot for a living room, and there's a couple of cracks over here by the wall."

Laura's smile disappeared momentarily. Denise thought she detected some frustration in the realtor's voice. She knew Ted could be annoying.

Laura said, "Mr. Sorensen, no house is perfect. Even new construction has its flaws. I assure you, this is one of the nicest houses I've shown in a long time."

Ted had the last word. "It's my job to find the problems before signing on the dotted line."

Laura led them through the main level. "This is the master bedroom suite. There's a full bathroom, with a large jetted hot tub and separate shower."

Denise said, "Oh, Ted. This is beautiful. That hot tub would be great for your bad back. I love the colors, the dark blue tile and light blue walls. What a peaceful place."

Ted complained, "Some of the grout's missing from tiles in the shower. Probably leaks. The toilet's also in the wrong place; too close to the hot tub."

Laura said, still trying for cheery, "I would love to have this master bath in my own home. It's beautifully designed, and built with quality. You're not going to find anything nicer in this price range in St. Augustine."

Denise noticed that the realtor's smile and pleasant demeanor had become forced. They finished the tour, with Ted and Laura sparring the entire time.

Laura said, "Now that you've seen the house, I'll walk you up the street and show you the community center and swimming pool, also very well maintained."

Denise said, "That sounds lovely. With this small community, I'm guessing the pool's never crowded. That would be an improvement over all the people we have to deal with back home."

Ted couldn't resist. "I hope the pool's in better shape than the house. I did like the floor plan, but the cracked tile in the living room, that warped closet door, and the color of the paint they used in the upstairs bedroom are definite problems. Then there's the difficult access to the HVAC system in the attic."

"Oh, Teddy Bear. It's one little ol' crack in a floor tile, a bent hinge on the closet door, and I liked the color of the upstairs bedroom. Access to the air handler… that's the service guy's problem."

Ted shot her a dirty look, and Denise thought she might have heard him growl.

Laura opened the front door and walked out ahead of Ted and Denise. Denise cringed when the realtor slammed the door shut after they came through. She saw Ted smile. Knowing her husband, she figured he thought he was winning by getting under the realtor's skin.

Laura led the way as they walked up the sidewalk towards the swimming pool, past other brightly colored homes surrounded by neatly trimmed shrubbery and yards. Denise noticed that the realtor was barely sweating. She and Ted were huffing and puffing. With no breeze at all, she felt like she was baking and drowning with the intense sunshine and ninety-percent humidity.

Clearly no longer cheery, Laura said, "I'll warn you now, Mr. Sorensen, the pool house and community center building need a new coat of paint, which is scheduled for next week. The pool was just repainted two weeks ago."

Denise thought, *Aren't realtors usually sickeningly sweet, at least until they get their commission? But, Teddy is being really annoying. I know this is his way of trying to gain some negotiating leverage. I just hope it doesn't backfire.*

Denise said, "I don't see very many cars, and most of the houses look empty. There doesn't appear to be anyone at this end of the block. Is everyone at work?"

Laura said, "No. All the owners in this neighborhood are retired. It's August, and most of them go somewhere else this time of year to escape the heat. Some also leave for a couple of months during peak hurricane season, which is August and September."

As they approached the gated community pool on the right, Denise saw a fenced pond on the left, adjacent to the pool.

"Laura, what's that area? It looks pretty, like a small park. The online description didn't mention a pond in the neighborhood."

Ted and Denise followed Laura to the right, up the sidewalk towards the pool gate. "Oh, that's a little shaded park area. I was saving it for last. I'll show it to you after we look at the pool and community center."

They walked over to the Olympic size pool, complete with swim lanes and a small diving board at the deep end.

Denise said, "Look, Teddy. The pool is immaculate, newly painted, just like Laura said."

"Yeah, Dee. But, she's right about the pool house. It could use a coat of paint." To Laura. "You said that's scheduled for next week? And, I wouldn't call a room with a ping pong table and a few chairs an actual community center."

Laura answered, "Yes, Mr. Lawyer. As I said, weather permitting, the pool house will be painted next week. There's also a small air-conditioned room in the back with exercise equipment, treadmills, exercycles and an elliptical. But, I doubt it would impress you."

Denise intervened, "Laura, please show us the cute little park. It looks like a great place for a picnic."

They followed Laura through the pool gate, across a small stretch of neatly cut grass. Laura opened the gate to the pond area, the couple entered, and she followed them down a fairly steep incline towards the water's edge. Denice notice that the grass here contained dead patches and the plants were not as well-maintained as the rest of the property, but maybe it was more difficult to maintain because of the steep slope down to the water.

Denise said, "Oh, Teddy Bear. What a peaceful little park. We've got the place all to ourselves. I could see myself sitting on the bank, sipping a glass of iced tea and reading a book."

Ted shook his head and sighed. "It's hotter than hell, and there's no place to sit. No bench, nothing. Look at the water. It's green, probably full of mold, or algae, something nasty. It smells musty, and there's a hint of sulphur."

Denise looked over her shoulder, and noticed that Laura was hanging back from the water's edge. Denise's gaze met that of the realtor. Denise felt confusion and then fear, as the realtor, with a crazy look in her eyes and her arms extended out in front of her, started running towards the unfortunate couple.

"What the heck…? Teddy, look out!"

Laura, her voice low but threatening, snarled, "You son-of-a-bitch. You and your stupid wife have no intention of buying anything. You're just here to bitch and complain. You're driving me crazy!"

With that, Laura gave them both a shove. They landed with a splash in the green murky water. Denise managed to keep her head above water for a few moments. She saw the realtor back away quickly as the cottonmouths and alligators attacked. Denise tried to scream as the murky water around her turned red, but she choked on filthy water drawn in through her nose and mouth. A large alligator had sunk its teeth into Ted's arm and dragged him underwater. Then she saw a snake as thick as her arm swimming in her direction at the same time that she felt the searing pain of razor sharp teeth grab her by the leg and start pulling her down.

Denise struggled against the terrifying force pulling her underwater, and panic overtook her. She thought, *My God, she's murdered us, and there won't be any evidence we were ever here.* As she lost consciousness, Denise saw the realtor standing in front of a large sign on the street side of the pond fence, obscured by overgrown bushes.

The last thing she heard was Laura yell, "Lousy weekend browsers! That's what you get! You weren't going to buy anything anyhow! And, what kind of lawyers are too stupid to read a sign that says '*Warning. Beware of Poisonous Snakes and Alligators*'?"

Chapter 2

One Saturday morning in late May, Dr. Jason Longfellow and his wife, Chelsea, were sipping their coffee at the kitchen table, after a breakfast of bacon, eggs, biscuits and fried potatoes. Chelsea knew that as middle-aged working parents, they both needed that morning jolt of caffeine to get them going. The coffee gourmet of the family, she always made sure they had their favorite brands of coffee for the coffee machine. She preferred the strong, dark brews whereas Jason preferred the lighter, less bitter choices. Sometimes he even drank half-caff. She often taunted him that he might as well drink hot water.

Jason took a sip of coffee and winced.

"Great breakfast Chelse. But, what's the occasion? And, why am I drinking this dark roast mud? It's strong enough to rot a fella's innards."

"Why do you always get suspicious when I fix you a nice home-cooked meal? We ran out of your pretend coffee, so I shared some of the real stuff with you. You're welcome."

"I get suspicious because you're usually trying to soften me up for some stressful surprise. Like when you scheduled your trip to Central America to adopt Lizzy without talking to me about it first. You knew I wasn't ready for children."

"Graduate school was going on forever, and you were never going to be ready, so I just moved things along a little. You love the children."

"I gotta admit, they have their moments. But, there are three of them now. So, please no more fancy home-cooked meals, breakfast, lunch, or dinner."

"Jason, calm down. I'm not looking for another child. This was just breakfast. I have been thinking…"

"Oh, God. I hate it when you start a sentence like that."

"Stop it, Jason. It's the real reason I gave you the dark roast, caffeinated coffee. I wanted you fully awake for this. It's difficult enough to get you to pay attention to me, let alone when you're half asleep."

Jason sighed. "Oh, God. Now what?"

Chelsea watched as Jason took another sip of coffee and choked on the strong brew. He stood up and started clearing the table, his hands shaking noticeably. She actually felt his anxiety level rise. Maybe she had overdosed him on caffeine.

"Calm down. It's no big deal. I've just been thinking that the kids are almost out of school for the summer, and we haven't planned our vacation yet. After last year's travel debacle, I've been afraid to bring it up, but we're running out of time."

"Oh, that's all. That's why you're trying to dissolve my innards? No worries, Wife of mine. After last year's trip cross country, I don't want to travel for vacation. I've been thinking we should find a place to rent for a couple of weeks, someplace nice where we could enjoy our time off. Maybe we could rent a house in Florida."

"I like the Florida part, but I was thinking more like we should *buy* a vacation home. We could go there anytime we want and it might be a good investment. We could go to Florida for vacation this summer and combine it with shopping for a condo."

"So, that's what the full English breakfast was about. You *were* trying to soften me up for one of your ideas. I don't think we can afford a vacation home right now, although I have always wanted to spend Christmas on the beach."

Chelsea knew it terrified Jason to spend a lot of money, unless it was something he really wanted; cars came to mind. A large bank account gave him the illusion of security. She took a last bite of bacon, washed it down with a large swig of the strong brew and forged onward.

"I know you believe that having a large savings account gives us security, but I think we could afford a condo near the beach. That's if you keep your promise to hang onto your day job with the FDA. If you decide to quit your government job and do the PI thing full time, it won't matter anyhow. You won't need a vacation home, cause I'll kill you."

Jason sat back down at the table, which Chelsea interpreted as a sign of submission. He was clearly trying to think this through.

"Let's see. If we bought a vacation condo, it would cut into our savings. I'm not entirely comfortable with that, and I would have to keep working for the FDA. If we don't buy a vacation condo, I might be able to afford to do the PI thing full-time, but you said you'd murder me. That's one murder I wouldn't get to investigate. So, it's either being uncomfortable buying a vacation condo to please the wife or doing the PI thing full-time and *murder by wife*?"

Chelsea knew she had him on the ropes. She took another large drink of coffee and went for the jugular.

"So, oh great private eye, where should we buy this vacation home? My sister, Jeanette, used to live in St. Augustine, Florida. She loved it there; America's oldest city. She raved about the food, the history, the wide sandy beaches, calm ocean surf and the fact that it's an artsy place. She tried them all looking for her passion; painting, pottery, jewelry, crocheting, even music…the guitar. Unfortunately, her husband found himself a sweet young musician while my sister was busy in her studio, and his passion turned out to be of a different kind. The lady musician got knocked up, my sister got his money in the divorce and moved to California to get as far away from her ex as possible."

"St. Augustine sounds great, but your story's on the depressing side."

"Not really. Jeanette loves San Diego. She met a young stud of an actor, and she and her ex-husband's money are having the time of their lives. She's invited me for a visit; says her new actor friend has a couple of good-looking roommates. But, I never have the time. Another thing I might be tempted to do if you quit your day job, or refuse the vacation condo thing."

Jason began tapping his foot on the floor. Chelsea recognized this as one of his many nervous habits.

"Well, California's definitely out. And, my day job's in. So, America's oldest city it is."

Jason's hands were resting on the table, and Chelsea placed her hands on top of his in an attempt to comfort him. She knew she was pushing him into uncomfortable territory, but she really wanted a vacation home. She thought they could make some great family memories with their daughters, perhaps to replace the not-so-good memories she had of her own childhood.

Chelsea said, "Then it's settled. But, don't you want to do a little research before we decide on St. Augustine? Check out the weather, population, traffic, crime statistics, is it safe for children? We are going to take our three young daughters on vacation with us, aren't we?"

Jason just smiled and shrugged.

"Jason, aren't we? They're our children, and they kind of have to go where we go."

"Were you on the same trip as me last summer? They spent the entire time plugged into their laptops, tablets, and other techy stuff, watching movies, listening to music, on social media. They wouldn't even notice if we left them here. Especially if they were with a grandmother they love oh so much. Do you think your mother might like to keep the little angels for a couple of weeks this summer, while you and I go to Florida?"

"Jason Bartholomew Longfellow! They're our children. We couldn't possibly leave them with Mom-Mom for two or three weeks while we go to Florida! Could we?"

"Well…your mother seems to like the children. The girls hate riding in the car, and Florida is a long drive. They'd be bored and miserable as hell looking at property, especially in the summer heat. And, when they're miserable, they like to share the wealth, if you get my drift."

"Maybe you're right. They might prefer staying home with Mom-Mom. I'll talk to her first. She still seems really lonely, and Dad's been gone a long time. She might love to have their company. If it's okay with her, we'll tell the girls, and see what happens."

Chelsea poured herself a third cup of coffee, and took a large drink. The caffeine was really starting to kick in.

"I don't know how you gulp that strong stuff down so fast. That much caffeine gives me the shakes. Anyhow, how is your mother? You used to talk to her on the phone all the time. I've heard the two of you reminiscing about your dad. I'll never forget the story of how you and he tried to bake a cake when you were little, and he caught the oven on fire. Your Mom made him sleep in the car that night, if I remember the story correctly."

Chelsea smiled. "Then, there was the time he bought me the hockey equipment. I always suspected he wanted a son. We were playing in the living room, and he broke her glass coffee table with a slap shot. He was always getting carried away, like a big kid. I think he slept in the car that night too. I do miss him. Mom totally freaked out when we found out he had pancreatic cancer, and in his mid-forties. He went pretty fast, and so young."

"I'm sorry, Chelsea. You've told me the story before. Didn't mean to bring it all up again and make you sad. That rough patch she went through with the heavy drinking after he died must have been hard on you. You were still a kid and had to take care of her. Kids that go through that kind of thing often grow up to be caretakers. Is that why you chose to become a nurse?"

"That, and the fact that Dad was a doctor. He told me that the doctor's got all the credit, but it was the nurses who actually provided the medical care. Remember, I started out as an intensive care nurse, and at first I loved it. But, I began having nightmares from the horrible stuff that happened in the ICU, especially with the children. So, I moved into hospital administration."

Anxiety from old memories raised its ugly head, and she changed the subject. "Speaking of family stuff, what about you? Your childhood wasn't exactly all lollipops and rainbows."

Chelsea loved Dr. Jason Longfellow, now a drug reviewer for the US Food and Drug Administration. Second-generation Dutch, he was forty-seven, with a slim frame. She liked the fact that he stood six-foot-seven, and was protective of her. That made her feel safe. She teased him about the smattering of gray in his straight, sandy-brown hair, as well as his crooked nose, broken in childhood. His clear blue eyes, sharp smile, and glowing white teeth distracted from those physical flaws, and she found his combination of intelligence, clumsy charm and innocence to be very attractive. Her father had numerous affairs when Chelsea was a child, and she got crazy jealous when Jason even looked at another woman.

"What do you mean, family stuff? I'm solid as the Rock of Gibraltar."

"Yeah, right. An FDA drug reviewer who gets bored and decides he wants to be a part-time PI and investigate murder cases, on the weekends no less. Most people would think that's nuts. Speaking of that caretaker thing, that's probably why I was so drawn to you. You're a big ol' teddy bear, but a very high maintenance teddy bear."

Chelsea knew Jason as a man of integrity who loved his family, and was successful at his government job. But, he had his issues—difficulties dealing with stress, indecisiveness, a lack of understanding of the female gender, and a whopping midlife crisis. Neurotic, OCD, and an introvert, it was clear to her that he often preferred his own company. It drove her a little crazy when he carried on conversations with himself, sometimes in his head, and often mumbling aloud. She was aware of his stressful life—a tedious government job, a long, daily commute on the Washington Beltway, and raising a family with three young daughters – Lizzy, fifteen, Lilly, thirteen and Lucy, seven. Friday nights were the worst. When he got home from work, he often drank a couple of martinis to calm down before he could deal with the girls. Chelsea did not like the drinking at all.

Jason said, "What do you mean *high maintenance*? I'm a manly man. I can handle anything this old world throws at me."

"By high maintenance I mean *crazy person*, but with good reason. When you were a kid, you tried to protect your mother from your abusive alcoholic father. He back-handed you and broke your nose when you were nine. In a blackout drunk, he tried to beat you to death when you were ten, but passed out before he succeeded. Wasn't it shortly after that he ended up in prison for killing a man in a road rage incident? He died in prison when another prisoner killed him in a fight. Your mother was a nervous wreck and a chain-smoker who died from lung cancer when you were in your late teens. Isn't that pretty much the story? No wonder you never feel safe. I probably was drawn to you because I'm a caretaker. But, you're also every bit as goofy as my dad was, like a big kid; that's probably part of it too."

"Hey, now. How'd we get on the subject of my parents? There's no reason to dredge up all that stuff. I'm not afeard of nothin'. I do like the fact that you take good care of me, but don't tell anyone I said that. Bad for my rep as a hard-boiled PI."

"Jason, *all that stuff* is the reason I love you so much. It made you who you are. You might be a little neurotic and OCD and your counting things or checking door locks can be annoying. But, I know how much you love me and the girls. And, you are kind of goofy. I love the way you let Lucy dress you up and put makeup on your face. You played with the girls when they were little, just like my dad. You dressed up as Santa and the Easter Bunny; a six-foot-seven Easter Bunny was actually kind of scary. And, you took them on that cross-country trip with us in the RV, and were very patient with them. I also know that you'd give your life to protect us. You're middle-age, and prone to checking out other women's assets, but you'd never do anything to hurt our family. So what if we both have *interesting* pasts?"

"Yeah, I'd never do anything to hurt my family, and then there's that *you'd murder me* thing. You wouldn't really murder me, would you? You just said you're a nurturing nurse."

"Well, there can be two sides to a nurse. There's the nurturing side, and then there's Nurse Ratched."

Jason cringed. "That's a comforting thought. So much for wandering down memory lane." He paused in thought. "What were we talking about?"

Chelsea said, "Try to keep up. We were discussing when to travel to Florida to buy a vacation home. What do you think?"

"Middle of August is probably best for me. The government practically shuts down in August. Everyone heads out for vacation."

"I can make that work. Most of my team is taking off in June and July, so I'll have coverage for August."

Chelsea talked with her mother and the girls and got back to Jason later in the week. They sat at the kitchen table again, this time with Chelsea drinking her strong coffee while watching Jason sip his preference, hot tea with buckets of sugar.

"I don't know how you drink tea with that much sugar. You're going to give yourself diabetes. Anyhow, I'm happy to announce that it's all set. Mom-Mom is willing to watch our little darlings for the last three weeks in August, and the girls are onboard with the idea. Lizzy was relieved that she won't have to miss any pool parties this summer. My mother has agreed to take her. I must warn you, though. Lilly and Lucy were very unhappy at the prospect of spending Christmas in Florida. You need to convince them Santa will find them there."

"Or, I could just tell them the truth…no such thing as Santa. I'm sure the two older ones have figured it out by now anyhow."

"Jason, wipe that grin off your face. That's just mean. You assure them, especially Lucy, that Santa will find her, no matter where she is."

"Oh, all right. But, that Santa suit's gonna be hotter than hell in Florida." He grinned. "This thing in August, the girls staying with your mother, really is great though. Wow! Three glorious weeks alone with you, doing adult things…I mean, I'm really going to miss the girls. It's a shame they don't want to go, but I get it. We'll just have to make do the best we can. We'll champion on, and find a vacation home that'll be perfect for all of us. So, do we have to take the children on all our future vacations?"

She rolled her eyes. "If I have to keep choosing between you and the girls, maybe I'll just take the kids and leave you home with Mom-Mom."

Chapter 3

That Sunday, Jason kept an eye on the kids while Chelsea searched online for a rental condo in St. Augustine. She called him into the living room, where they sat on the couch while she reported her success. He left the girls downstairs in the playroom, telling the older two to keep an eye on Lucy. Chelsea told him she had rented a place within walking distance of the beach for three weeks in August. As part of this conversation, Jason discovered that she had planned for them to take her mid-size SUV on their trip. He threw a fit. Sitting on the opposite end of the sofa, he waved his arms dramatically while he talked.

"Come on, Chelsea! This is an awesome opportunity to get some time behind the wheel of my midlife crisis car, my convertible roadster, the red rocket. Top down, wind in our hair, get a great suntan…"

"Yeah, with bugs in our teeth, and you with cramps in your legs. Sounds great. And, where do you suppose we put our luggage? Then, there's the rain…my sister used to tell me about serious thunderstorms in Florida. Calm down. You'll scare the children if they hear you yelling."

But, he had held firm.

"Florida and my red rocket are made for each other. A convertible, the Sunshine State. What more could you ask for?"

"A car that'll carry more than a set of underwear on the trip? The condo has a washer/dryer, but we do have to pack enough clothes for at least a week. I need my makeup, a hair dryer, toiletries, bathing suits, clothes, shorts, tops, a couple of dresses, some hats to protect me from the sun, several pairs of shoes, sunglasses, that lingerie you like so much…you know, the basics. That should fill up your cute little car. I don't know what you're going to do."

"No worries, Woman. All I need is one pair of pants, one shirt, one pair of underwear and a bathing suit. Like you said, there's a washer/dryer. I can use your toothbrush, buy a cheap razor in Florida, and I'm good. That'll all fit in a small travel bag."

***

When August arrived, Jason and Chelsea packed for the trip. Early on Friday morning, he waved as Chelsea left in her SUV to drop the children off at Mom-Mom's house. Jason stayed behind to load the luggage into the red rocket.

A little while later, Jason saw Chelsea pull into the driveway. He was busy attaching the last of the bags to a luggage rack on the back of his little roadster.

"My mother sends her love. The girls also said to tell you they love you. They weren't happy getting up so early."

"They were kind of grouchy. Lucy's the only one that gave me a hug and a kiss. I'll miss them, but this way we get to spend some time together, and I get to drive my car."

"Speaking of your car, where is it? All I see is a pile of luggage and a couple of backpacks. Is there a car under there? And, where'd that rack thing come from?"

Jason walked over to his car and proudly patted the pile of luggage sitting on the rack on the back.

"One more great thing about this sports car. It might be smaller than your SUV, but you can buy a luggage rack that attaches to the trunk; holds three or four pieces of luggage. I bought the rack, knowing your idea of packing light means ten bags or less. I also jury-rigged extra hooks on the sides to attach the two backpacks."

Chelsea grinned. "A girl's got needs; some hot new beach wear, several changes of clothes and plenty of clean underwear. Where's your luggage?"

"I have a small bag in the trunk; it's all that would fit. But, no worries. Everything's fastened down tight."

"Yeah, just so long as it doesn't rain. I doubt that luggage is waterproof."

Jason rubbed his hand over one of the suitcases, feeling the sturdy material.

"It's supposed to be water-resistant. That'll have to do. If it rains, we're gonna need to be water resistant, too. Remember, I can't put the top up on this thing. My head doesn't fit."

"Jason, you're an idiot. We're also going to miss the A/C in my SUV. A convertible in Florida in August?…we're going to cook. I don't know how I let you talk me into these things."

"Stop with all the praise, Chelsea. Let's hit the road. It's starting to cloud up, and hopefully we can outrun whatever's coming. There's an umbrella and a couple of plastic ponchos on the floor of the passenger side, just in case."

Jason turned off the water, locked up the house and headed for I-95 with Chelsea stuffed in the passenger seat. She didn't fit all that well in the red rocket either.

As Jason cruised down the road towards I-95 and Florida, he turned and looked at Chelsea. He loved this woman, in her mid-forties, of Swedish ancestry with her long natural blonde hair blowing wildly in the wind.

When they first met, he had told her he'd been drawn to her deep blue eyes, cute little nose, and kissable lips. But, truth be told, it was really her cute little ass that had sealed the deal. He felt grateful that she worked out every morning to stay slim and fit. Jason had met Chelsea at Georgetown University Medical School, with him in the graduate school of pharmacology and her in the nursing school. She had been a strong and independent woman, traits that Jason had admired in her—except when she turned it on him. Later, when she had moved from an ICU nurse to hospital administration, her confidence had been shaken. It had taken a while, but it had finally come back with a vengeance.

"Jason, stop staring at me. Do I have a smudge on my face or something? Pay attention to the road and drive faster. You need to put those storm clouds behind us. I felt a few drops of rain."

Jason saw dark clouds off in the horizon behind them. He could see the rain and lightning headed their way.

"I'm driving as fast as I can. We're going uphill, and this car isn't designed for hauling or towing. The weight of all your luggage is slowing us down. Maybe we should toss a piece of luggage or two overboard. Is there anything you can do without?"

"Just keep driving. If anything's going to be tossed overboard, it's you. If we cut your head off and threw it out, at least we could put the top up. We could have been comfortable, safe and dry in my SUV. You and your hare-brained ideas."

"It's called an adventure. Once we get over this hill, I'll put the pedal to the metal and we'll outrun the storm. Also, there's always the umbrella."

"You've already got the pedal to the metal. Maybe you should pedal faster. Those squirrels under the hood of your little clown car need some help."

"Hey, now. Don't make fun of my ride. Scrunch down some. Your hair's catching too much wind and holding us back."

Chelsea growled, "Jason…"

They outran the storm, and were rolling down I-95. Jason was driving in the right lane at sixty-five, because the car wouldn't go any faster with all the extra weight. A tractor trailer passed them on the left.

"Jason, I was so focused on rain I forgot about all the trucks on I-95. That guy just about blew us off the road. Maybe you should drive under one of the tractor trailers for protection."

"My driving skills are outstanding, but I'm not a freakin' stunt driver. At least, I don't think I could do it. Well, maybe?"

"Oh God! I forgot who I was talking to. You're doing just fine, Dear. Everything will be okay."

"You're right, Chelsea. I didn't think about all the trucks either. I'm not so convinced that everything'll be okay. One false move, and we're bug splat. Twenty-seven, twenty-eight, twenty-nine…"

"Jason, stop counting trucks and pay attention to driving. Counting won't keep us safe right now."

"I know. But there's something comforting about it. Helps me to stop thinking about scary things, you know, like being crushed to death."

Jason pulled out into the left lane to pass a tractor trailer moving even more slowly uphill than the red rocket. He saw a second truck come barreling up behind the rocket, tail-gaiting inches from his rear bumper. Jason's stomach knotted up as he floored the accelerator, moved past the slower truck and cut him off, pulling quickly into the right lane to avoid being crushed.

"That guy almost ran over top of us! Chelsea, you need to learn to drive a stick shift, so you can share in this fun."

"Jason, the red rocket was your brilliant idea. Let's talk about something else. And, talk loud. I can barely hear you for all the road noise."

Jason raised his voice. "I'VE BEEN THINKING ABOUT ALL THE FUN WE'LL HAVE…"

"Don't you yell at me. I hate it when you yell at me."

"But, Chelsea. You told me to raise my voice so you could hear me. It's deafening with all this traffic."

"Oh, all right. What were you saying?"

"I've been thinking about how much fun we'll have in Florida. We can get a boat, go fishing, rent a Jeep and run around in Ocala National Forest. And motorcycles…there are motorcycle dealerships all over Florida. You can drive a motorcycle all year around."

"Jason, I was thinking about different things, like visiting downtown St. Augustine, the history, museums, arts and crafts and great food. They have one of the oldest forts in the country. You should like that…you know…guns, cannons, swords, the silly stuff you seem to enjoy. You also like seafood. My sister raved about the seafood when she was there."

"Doesn't sound like we agree on much, as usual. Maybe I could at least rent a motorcycle to drive downtown. They're easier to park."

"Now you're getting the idea Jason, although this thing we're riding in isn't much bigger than a motorcycle. You could probably park it on the sidewalk."

"Stop making fun of my ride, Woman."

"Then, next time you buy a midlife crisis car, don't go for the clown car."

Jason got stuck behind a long line of trucks in the right lane doing sixty miles per hour. As he started to pull into the left lane to pass, a very large SUV flew by, forcing Jason back into the right lane. A whole line of cars followed the SUV, trapping the clown car in the slow lane. Neither the conversation nor the driving was going well, so Jason changed the subject again.

"Chelsea, I know you're excited about buying a vacation property. What d'ya think? A condo or a single family home? Near the beach?"

"I was thinking, with three daughters we should look for something with three bedrooms and two to three baths."

"Jeez Chelsea, I'm not Mr. Moneybags. I did some research online, and a two-bedroom, two-bath condo can run two-hundred-thousand, considerably more if it's close to the beach. I'm afraid any more than that will stretch us to the breaking point, and I don't wanna break."

"Don't worry, Jason. I've done my homework too. You can find a three-bedroom, two-and-a-half-bath condo for around two-hundred-fifty to three-hundred-thousand if you look in the right place. I've already talked to a couple of realtors, and I've got one lined up to show us some properties."

"Chelsea, there's one other thing I haven't mentioned. You know I'm a manly man, and not afraid of anything. But, I can't help wonder what would happen if we got caught in a hurricane. I read online that a category five can carry winds up to one-hundred-eighty miles per hour. I don't wanna get blown away. And, what about the children? Should we put them in that kind of danger?"

"You worry too much. Hurricane season is July through October, with peak season in September. The girls will be in school back home in Virginia in September. By the time they've graduated, we'll have learned how to deal with hurricanes. Maybe we'll even move to Florida full-time. Besides, I can always increase your life insurance, in case something happens while you're protecting us."

Jason's stomach started to spasm, and he tensed up. *This trip we'll be there in late August!*

His cramped driving position was also stressing him out. Chelsea couldn't drive a stick shift, so he had to drive the entire trip. He hadn't thought that through very well. He managed to pull out to pass the trucks, and a black sports car immediately started tail gaiting him, worsening his attitude. *We're going on a three-week vacation and home-buying trip, and we apparently don't agree on anything. I'm just gonna have to put my foot down. We're only looking at two-bedroom, two-bath units, to limit the cost. And, I'll rent a motorcycle if I want. It's like my private eye thing. She thinks she's letting me do it. But, I wear the sweatpants in this family.*

Jason was lost in thought, driving on autopilot, when he came to a work zone.

Chelsea said "Jason, you better slow down. It's forty-five here and if you get pulled over, they double the fine."

Jason hit the brakes, rapidly decelerating from sixty-five to forty-five miles per hour. At the same time, two gigantic trucks with double trailers blew by him on the right doing seventy-five. The blast of wind caught him off guard. He lost control and the little roadster careened off the road to the left, just missing a center cement barrier. Jason saw several workmen scatter as he struggled to stop the car, dirt flying in all directions. He felt a hard jolt as the roadster rolled into a large, shallow hole.

"Jason, what the hell! You drove us into a hole in the middle of a construction site. I hope you didn't break anything on your little clown car. Get us out of here, NOW!"

Jason looked around, stunned. He pointed at a large cement mixer sitting nearby.

"It looks like they intend to pour cement into this hole to form the base for the support pillar of an on ramp. No worries, I'll just back us out of here and we'll get back on the highway." He sat there, looking around. "Wow. All this construction equipment's really cool. I always wanted to drive a bulldozer. Probably not as much fun as being a PI, though."

Chelsea, panic in her voice. "Jason, what's that giant piece of equipment doing?! I don't think they see us, and that large scoop shovel full of dirt is headed our way!"

"Chelsea, stop yelling. I can't think straight when you yell at me."

"But, that shovel thingy has a bucket full of dirt. I think it's about to fill in this hole, with us in it. Help!"

The power shovel moved its bucket over the top of the clown car, opened the chute and started dumping dirt on top of them.

Sputtering, Chelsea said, "Jason. Do something! They're trying to bury us alive!"

"Don't worry, Darlin'. My detecting skills tell me they dug this hole in the wrong place, so they're filling it in. They don't know we're here. I'll get their attention."

Jason started blowing the horn. It wasn't a very loud horn, being a clown car and all.

Chelsea said, "The horn on this thing sounds like Tweety bird. They'll never hear that."

Chelsea started to scream at the top of her lungs, choking on the dirt as it hit her in the face.

"Help! Help! My idiot husband drove into your hole! Stop trying to bury us alive!"

Jason was relieved to see that the power shovel had closed the bottom of its bucket half-way through the second dump. However, the car was already buried in sand and dirt up to the top of Chelsea's passenger door; the interior was filled with the stuff. Jason and Chelsea were both trapped, their arms, legs and torsos buried to the point where they could barely move.

The power shovel's giant diesel engine cut off, and a pudgy workman in his early fifties emerged from the cabin and ran towards the half-buried roadster. At five-eight, he looked to Jason like the stereotypical construction worker, with a sunburnt face, peeling skin, a large nose, graying moustache and an unkempt beard. He was dressed in the typical uniform, blue jeans and a T-shirt covered with bright orange bib overalls to make him a more visible target for the speeding vehicles. He wore a matching orange safety helmet that clashed with the mostly gray, brown hair that hung out from under it. He held the remnants of a cheap cigar crushed between his teeth. As he approached Jason's side of the car, he finished the cigar and tossed it.

"Howdy, Mister. The name's Ben. I'm the foreman on this here site. What the *hell* are you doing in my hole? This ain't no damned rest stop. We almost buried you and the Misses there alive. Now, I gotta get some of my men to come dig you out."

Jason was so overwhelmed by the stench of dirt, auto exhaust, and diesel fumes from the heavy duty equipment that he could barely breathe, let alone concentrate on Ben's words.

He turned and yelled up the hill behind him. "Jake! Bring some of the boys with shovels. We gotta dig this damned fool and his Misses out of this here hole and send them on their way." To Jason and Chelsea. "Just sit tight, folks. We'll have you out in no time."

Jason managed to work his arms free. He started removing dirt from his side of the car, attempting to dig himself out by hand.

"No worries, Chelsea. I'll free myself, and then rescue you. I got us into this mess, and I can get us out."

Chelsea's face was beet red. Jason heard her scream over the roar of trucks and cars speeding by on the interstate.

"Jason Longfellow, I'm going to kill you in a most unpleasant manner! First, you insist on driving this stupid clown car. Then, you drive us off the highway and into a hole. And, that's not enough for you? You land us in a place where they try to bury us alive. ARE YOU INSANE?"

Four additional workmen with shovels had started to approach the partially buried car as per Ben's instructions. Jason saw them all freeze in their tracks when they heard Chelsea.

"Chelsea, please calm down. You're scaring the workmen, and we need them to dig us out."

Chelsea started to cry. "I am buried in dirt. My hair's filled with dirt. My clothes are covered in dirt. My shoes are full of dirt."

Jason did his best to assure the workmen that Chelsea wasn't an immediate danger to their lives, and they eventually climbed down the hill towards the car, shovels at the ready. Meanwhile, Jason had managed to dig himself out of the driver's seat and climb out of the car, and the hole. He walked around to Chelsea's side of the car. Since the car was buried in dirt up to the top of the doorframe on her side, he was positioned above his wife. He got down on his knees and started digging her out with his hands.

One of the workmen, a small man in his mid-thirties, approached Jason, holding out a shovel in front of him. At 160 pounds with a wiry body, sinister looking dark eyes, a thin face and coal black hair, Jason thought that he looked like a pirate.

"Here, mister. This might help."

Jason checked the guy out further. *Those are some mean looking tattoos on this guy's face and arms, and with those scars over his right eye and on his left cheek he looks like he just got out of prison. If he didn't have on that orange construction worker's outfit, I'd suspect maybe he was gonna whack me on the head with that shovel. No such luck. That'd put me out of my misery before Chelsea gets free.*

Jason took the shovel, but sat it on the ground next to him and continued to dig Chelsea out with his hands.

"No worries, Chelsea. I'll have you out in no time. Then they'll dig the car out, and we'll be on our way. This is just a minor blip in our adventure to the sunny state of Florida. It's actually kind of exciting."

Jason had finally removed enough dirt that Chelsea could stand and climb out of the car. He noticed that her face was no longer red with rage, but she still didn't look all that friendly.

Chelsea continued to brush dirt off of her clothes, and out of her hair. "Thank you, Jason. I'll just sit on the ground over here and wait for you and your friends to dig your freakin' clown car out, so we can be on our way. I'm going to need to stop somewhere to get the dirt out of my blouse, pants and…well…you know. This is very uncomfortable."

"I know, Chelsea. I've got dirt everywhere, including my ass-crack. Don't wander off. Stay here where I can keep you safe."

"Keep me safe? You just tried to bury me alive."

He picked up the shovel and began to dig the car out on the passenger's side.

"One shovel full. Two shovels full. Three shovel's full. Four shovels full…Hey, what's that?"

Jason put down the shovel, got down on his knees and began to dig with his hands again.

"This is strange. It looks like the top of a human head, but how's that possible? We didn't run over anyone on the way into this hole, did we Chelsea? I think I'd know if I hit a person. Maybe it's just a head. Not attached to anything."

"Yes, Jason, I'm sure you just found a head. Not a strange way to begin a trip to Florida at all. And, no, I don't remember hitting anyone when you drove us off the road. You just aimed for the nearest large hole, and here we are."

Chelsea stood, walked a few feet further away and sat down in a patch of grass in the middle of the construction site. She looked to Jason like she'd rather be virtually anywhere else in the world. Jason dug the head out a little further. It had short brown hair filled with dirt. He took hold of the head and gave it a pull.

"Nope, it's definitely attached to something."

Two of the other workmen moved to Jason's side of the car and began digging with their shovels. In a few minutes, they had uncovered the body of a man, clearly another workman based on his orange outfit.

One of the men, a Hispanic fellow, yelled up the hill, "Hey Ben, sorry to say this, but I think we found your son-in-law Bert. He don't look so good."

Jason saw Ben, the foreman, come running back down the hill.

"What the hell are you talkin' about, Roberto? I sent Bert to get us some sandwiches a couple hours ago. He never came back. What's he doing in this here hole?"

Ben looked at Jason. "Mister, you better not have run over my son-in-law. My daughter's gonna kill me. She didn't want old Bert here to take this job, but he begged me, so I hired him. Now, it looks like he's dead."

Jason walked over to Ben and put his hand on the man's shoulder reassuringly.

"Ben…can I call you Ben? Ben, I'm positive we didn't hit anyone when we blew off the road and fell into this hole."

"Well, your fuckin' little foreign car appears to be sittin' on top of Bert. How d'ya explain that?"

Jason withdrew his hand and stepped back from the angry man.

"No worries, Ben. I'm a private eye, and I'll figure this out. My car's not actually on top of Bert…more like Bert's near the front bumper."

Jason looked up the hill to a grassy spot where Chelsea was sitting a few feet away, staring off into space.

"Chelsea, can you please come here? We seem to have a problem. This body's name is Bert, and he's the foreman's son-in-law. Might be good if we could figure out what killed him. I know I didn't run over him, but Ben here's not convinced. He's getting all agitated."

Chelsea stood up and walked back down the hill towards Jason. He saw a confused look on her face, like she still wasn't entirely sure what was happening.

"Jason, I already told you, we didn't hit anything or anyone. You just drove us into this hole. Is it possible this Bert was already in the hole when you landed on top of him?"

"Excellent thought. See, that's why I keep you around? Even though I'm the expert PI, you have a helpful idea once in a while."

"WHY YOU KEEP ME AROUND?!"

Both Ben and Roberto recoiled at the tone in her voice. Jason thought, *They look like they're afraid she's going to kill one of them, or me, and they might be right.*

The men kept digging until the roadster, and the dead body, were completely free of dirt and debris. Jason kicked into full on PI mode and started inspecting the body.

"It's obvious that Chelsea's right. The body was already in the hole, and my red rocket landed on it when we went into said hole. The question now becomes, who murdered Bert here? His body was probably partially covered by someone who knew that the hole was about to be filled in with dirt. Add a load of dirt, some cement, and voila, Bert's body is gone forever."

Chelsea said, "Sounds like an inside job."

Jason looked around. "Chelsea, what's wrong with you? We're obviously outside, at a construction site."

She shook her head. "No, Jason…Maybe one of the workers…Oh, never mind."

Jason began examining the scene more carefully. He got into the car, started the engine and backed it up so the body was free for closer examination. He turned off the engine, exited the vehicle, and knelt next to the body. He rolled Bert over onto his back.

"Well, this is an interesting development. Bert here appears to have a hole in his forehead. From the size of the hole I'd guess it's from a thirty-eight caliber revolver."

Chelsea perked up. "Jason, don't you have a thirty-eight caliber revolver?"

"Chelsea, hush. Mine's packed in my suitcase in the trunk. Must be some other revolver."

Roberto spoke up. "Mr. PI, Sir. Should you be messin' with the body? Ain't this a crime scene? And, your wife says you have the same kind of handgun that killed Bert. Don't that make you a suspect? Maybe you should just go, before the cops get here."

Jason looked at Roberto. "That only applies to civilians. I'm a licensed PI, and I know what I'm doing. I'll have this crime solved by the time the cops get here. And, don't listen to my wife. I'm the PI."

Ben said, "You better hurry. I called the cops ten minutes ago."

Chelsea's face was red again. She looked to Jason like she was about to explode.

"Don't listen to me? You're the PI? You're the idiot that drove us into the hole in the first place. I'm gonna strangle you!"

She started towards Jason, Jason stepped back and Ben stepped between them. "Please, stop it! We already got one dead body, my son-in-law. We don't need another one."

Jason said, "Yeah, Chelsea. We don't need another body. Besides, you can't drive a stick shift. If you strangle me, who's gonna drive you to Florida?"

Jason saw Chelsea relax, and he started examining the body again. "Look. There's a lipstick stain on Bert's shirt collar. Ben, I thought you said you sent your son-in-law to get sandwiches."

"I did. But, I never saw him come back."

"I suspect that he snuck off for a nooner, probably with someone's wife."

Jason looked at the four workmen standing around Bert's body. All of a sudden he pointed at Roberto.

"J'accuze."

Chelsea frowned. "To be clear, Roberto is not French. I don't think anyone here is French. How do you know he's the killer?"

"I just have a gut feeling, and he's the only one who's concerned that I disturbed the crime scene. He's trying to get rid of us. Why is that? Maybe it's because he's afraid I'll find something before he has a chance to flee the scene."

Roberto spoke up. "That's crazy, man. Are you on something?"

Jason said, "Ben, check Roberto's pockets. I'll bet he has a photo in one of them."

Roberto turned and started to run up the hill. Ben hit him in the back with a shovel, knocking him to the ground. One of the other workmen helped Ben subdue him, while Jason went through his pockets.

"Aha! What do we have here? I believe this is a photograph of Bert in a compromising position with a pretty young Hispanic lady. Your wife I'm guessing, Roberto?"

Chelsea said, "Jason, that's amazing. How'd you know he'd have that picture in his pocket?"

Jason pulled a piece of paper out of his own pants pocket with writing on it.

"Elementary, my dear Watson…I mean Chelsea. When I examined Bert's body, I found this note from a woman named Rose. In it she warned Bert to be careful, because Roberto was carrying around photos of the two of them in bed together. She found out that Roberto knew she was having an affair with Bert. So, I just figured Roberto for the killer and that he'd have a photo or two on his person."

Roberto turned nasty. "She's my *sister*, Rose. Not my wife. This bastard Bert's married, and he's been screwing my sister. I hired a private eye, who followed her and took some pictures. This is one of them. If Mama ever found out about this, it would kill her."

Jason responded. "So, you killed Bert? Wait. What? You hired a private eye to follow her? I'm a private eye. That's a good idea. I could take cases like that. Was it very difficult? How much did you pay him?"

Chelsea, frowning again. "Jason, focus. That's hardly the point. How did Roberto kill him with all the workmen around?"

Ben spoke up. "I think I can answer that. I know for a fact that Roberto carries around a thirty-eight special revolver. I've seen it in his truck. We took a water and bathroom break a couple of hours ago, we all left together, and I didn't see Roberto in the truck with us. I just figured he'd taken a separate truck. Bert must have come back while we were gone,

Roberto saw the lipstick on his collar, shot him, and partially buried him in the hole. Is that about right?"

Jason said, "Yeah, what he said. But, for the record, I'm the one who figured out it was Roberto. I'm the PI. What d'ya think Chelsea? Pretty good, huh?"

Chelsea sounded exasperated. "Much to my surprise, you managed to clear this up and catch the killer in record time. And, not to my surprise at all, you didn't have a client for the case. So, you don't get paid anything for your trouble. Maybe you should take cases from people that suspect their spouses, or sisters, of having an affair. Then you'd have a client, and maybe get paid. Oh God! Won't this day ever end? We're never going to get to Florida."

Roberto tried to escape from the men holding him. Jason watched as one of the workmen got some rope out of his truck and gave it to Ben, who tied Roberto's hands behind him. Then, he kicked Roberto's legs out from under him, forcing him onto his knees.

Ben said, "Speaking of Florida, you had better leave before the police get here. No reason for you to hang around. You already solved the case, I'm making a citizen's arrest of Roberto, and I'll turn him over to the cops. We won't even mention the two of you. The guys built a ramp out of packed dirt. You should be able to drive your little car out of the hole and hit the road. Thanks for everything. Good luck with the rest of your trip."

Jason and Chelsea got into the red rocket, Jason pulled out of the hole and they were on their way. He had trouble pulling into interstate traffic, but they made it without further disaster.

"Jason, I hope Ben turns Roberto over to the police alive. He seemed kind of perturbed at the man. More important, please stop at the next rest area so I can at least shake the dirt out of my hair and clothes. We haven't been on the road for half a day, and you get blown off the interstate and find a dead body. I swear, if we run into anymore dead bodies on this trip, I am going to kill you for real."

"Look at the bright side, Chelsea. I think I've got a way of actually getting paid as a PI. Do any of your friends at the hospital suspect their spouses of having an affair?"

"Idiot."

Chapter 4

Jason stopped every couple of hours for the rest of the trip so they could stretch their legs, pee and get gas. The first stop, Chelsea told Jason she was going to change clothes and rinse off as much dirt as possible in the rest area bathroom. Jason, only having one change of clothes, just rinsed off his face, hands and arms. Then, they hit the road again.

"Jason, I feel a little better after changing clothes, but I desperately need a long soak in a hot tub with bath salts. It's going to take a very long soak to get rid of all this dust and dirt."

"I know, Chelsea. I didn't even get to change clothes. I've still got dirt in my…"

"Jason, stop it. That's too much information. You should have packed more clothes. My grandma always told me to be sure to wear clean underwear whenever I go out. She had no way of knowing I'd marry a man who'd one day drive me into a construction hole to be buried alive."

"Again, Chelsea, I still have dirt in …"

"TMI Jason. TMI. Just hush, drive your little clown car and get us there safe."

It seemed to Jason like he drove forever. His body was tensed up the entire time, what with the tractor trailers, tailgaters and massive SUVs. He felt stiff, sore and exhausted by the time they reached St. Augustine at five o'clock. At the rental office, he parked and went inside to get the keys. He returned twenty minutes later, and found Chelsea still sitting in the little car. He stood next to the driver's door, stretching his arms, legs and back, trying to work out the kinks. The cracking and popping sounds were disturbing. Maybe he should get a bigger car.

Chelsea said, "Jason, where have you been?" The heat is sweltering, and the A/C doesn't do much good with the top down."

"Sorry Dear. You should have gotten out to stretch your legs. But, on a positive note, you'll be glad to know that I found us a realtor to help with our search for a vacation home."

"First, I'm stuck in your tiny clown car and couldn't get out without help if I tried. And, more important, what are you talking about? I already spoke to a very professional realtor from *ReallyRealty* on the phone last week. She has made plans to show us what's available."

"I know, Chelsea. But, I met Debbie in person, and she seems like a really competent realtor. She told me about a couple of places for sale near where we're staying, and I made plans with her to drive us around tomorrow afternoon. You'll have to call your *ReallyRealty* realtor and cancel."

"Jason. This *Debbie*. You met her in the rental office, not the sales office. Is she even a qualified realtor?"

"Come on, Chelsea. Give me some credit. She's kinda new, but she's young, energetic, has her realtor's license and almost sold a couple of houses."

"Jason, remind me to smack you on the back of the head once I've pried myself out of this tin can you call a car."

Jason got a faraway look in his eyes. "Debbie has blonde hair, blue eyes, a cute little button nose, and a friendly smile. She's about your height and looks like a cheerleader. Come to think of it, she's even dressed a little like a cheerleader in a cotton blouse and short swishy skirt. Reminds me of you when you were younger. And, she thinks I'm athletic looking. She asked me if I was a tennis pro, or a basketball star."

"Do you have a death wish? I was never a cheerleader, and this is not the time for one of your *cheerleader* fantasies. We're trying to find a vacation home, not film a pornographic movie. And, athletic looking? A tennis pro? Have you forgotten you're covered with dirt? Think maybe she was laying it on a little thick?"

"Chelsea, I don't know what you're talking about. We need a realtor to help us find a condo, and Debbie's a real realtor…according to her, a really good real realtor. I'm sure she'll do a really good job for us. So what if she found me attractive? She obviously has impeccable taste."

"She might not find you so attractive if I fix it so you're a few inches shorter. Maybe lop of that head? Come around here and pull me out of this seat, so I can reach you."

The tone of her voice got Jason's attention. "No need for you to get out of the car, Dear. I'll just drive us to the condo, so you can cool down and take a nice hot soak in the tub. We can play dueling realtors later." *Damn it. I'm putting my foot down. This Debbie will do fine as a realtor. And, what's wrong with cheerleaders? I'll just have to exercise my husbandly authority.*

Jason stuffed himself back into the driver's seat and drove to their rental condo. By the time they arrived, Chelsea had calmed down. Jason parked the car, walked around and pulled Chelsea out of her seat by the arms. She disappeared, and he started hauling the luggage into the condo. As he dropped off the second load in the master bedroom, he heard Chelsea running water in the tub. He looked in on her, and she was laying back in the tub, eyes closed, soaking in the steaming hot water. He didn't want to disturb her, so he finished unloading the red rocket and made the command decision to order pizza delivery for dinner. He looked forward to the perky Debbie the realtor showing them vacation properties.

***

The next day, after a long, hot bath and a good night's sleep in an air conditioned room, Chelsea navigated as Jason drove the red rocket to the nearby *ReallyRealty* office.

"Jason, the woman's name is Karen Slabotnik. She's been a realtor in St. Augustine for over thirty years, and she has five properties lined up for us to see. She's going to drive us around in her luxury SUV, so I don't have to sit in this stupid clown car all day again. I want you to be nice to her. We're depending on her to find our perfect summer home."

"This Ms. Slabotnik sounds okay. But, Debbie would have been great, all bouncy and cheerful. She would have made house-hunting fun." Jason turned his head. "Chelsea, did you just growl?"

They pulled up to a long brick building with a *ReallyRealty* sign out front. When they walked through the door, sweating from the blazing sun and stifling humidity, the air conditioning felt to Jason like a drink of cool mountain water. A short, pudgy woman in her early sixties slowly approached Chelsea and extended an arthritic hand. To Jason she looked more like someone's sweet old grandmother than a realtor. Chelsea shook her hand.

Jason could smell an overwhelming odor of Chanel. His nose twitched as he fought back a sneeze.

Debbie smelled a lot better than grandma here. Debbie also didn't have all those wrinkles, that curly gray hair and squinty eyes. I'll bet this lady can't see a thing without those coke-bottle thick librarian's glasses. She looks like a very old hippie in that loose cotton dress. And, what's with the bright pink and yellow flowers? It must be a Florida thing. This lady's got arthritis so bad, we'll be lucky if we get to one property today, or out of the parking lot.

A wry grin on the realtor's face. "Mrs. Longfellow, I presume? And, this must be your husband, Dr. Longfellow? Or, should I say PI Longfellow?"

Chelsea released the realtor's hand and stepped back. Jason turned his head slightly, and whispered, "Chelsea, what did you tell her? I think she winked at me."

Chelsea whispered in return. "I couldn't help myself. We got along fabulously on the phone, and I had to tell her a little bit about our cross country trip. Better she should wink at you than Debbie. I'm thinking this realtor's more your speed."

"Of course you got along with her. She probably reminded you of your grandma. From that grin on her face, I'm guessing I didn't come across in your conversation as the world's greatest private eye. Thanks for that."

Jason took the realtor's hand to shake it, as gently as possible, afraid he might break her.

Jason said, "So, Chelsea tells me you've been a realtor in St. Augustine basically forever? And, you have several places to show us today. That sounds nice. Sure you want to do more than one? Do you know a perky young realtor in the area named Debbie? I met her yesterday, and she was supposed to show us around, but my wife had already made plans with you."

"Don't pay any attention to my husband. He often gets confused. Thinks he's in charge of his life. Please lead us to our perfect vacation home."

"Of course. I've got some nice properties to show you. I'll go start my SUV, get the A/C running to cool it down, and I'll grab you each a bottle of cold water before we shove off. Back in a moment."

Karen Slabotnik left them alone in her office. "Chelsea. That was just mean. My realtor was all perky and energetic, and Ms. Slabotnik here looks like I might end up carrying her before the day's over. A little long in the tooth, don't you think? If she strokes out in this hot weather, it's on you. And, back in a moment? We probably have time for a nap before she gets back."

"Jason, behave or I swear, you'll be sleeping in your little clown car tonight. Besides, I think she likes you."

"But, there's no place to lay down in the red rocket. And, I think Debbie liked…"

"Don't say it. Or you'll be sleeping under your car. I hear it's supposed to rain tonight, so you might need the cover anyhow."

Jason kept checking his watch. He started counting the monogramed pens in a jar on the realtor's desk. Ms. Slabotnik re-entered her office several minutes later, obviously in no hurry.

The realtor said, "Okay, let's head out. Here's your waters. Drink lots. It's a typical August day in Florida, and you're going to need to stay hydrated. I've got a cooler with more water in the SUV."

They climbed into a very large luxury SUV. Chelsea took shotgun, and Jason was relegated to the back seat. Jason got it; this was Chelsea's realtor. Ms. Slabotnik had started the vehicle and left the A/C running. It felt to Jason like going from the desert into a freezer; a little too much A/C. They sat there chatting for a few minutes, and he started to shiver.

Ms. Slabotnik said, "Chelsea. You mentioned on the phone that you're looking for something in a three-bedroom, two-and-a-half-bath condo near the beach. I have a few lined up for today. They run mostly from two-hundred-fifty to three-hundred-fifty thousand, with a couple a little more expensive depending on location. Is that in your price range?"

"Yes, that should work okay. We have three young daughters, and I'm thinking we'll need at least that much space."

Jason, talking from the back seat, felt left out and was having trouble hearing over the humming of the A/C.

"In my opinion that's a little more than we want to spend. I was thinking of a two-bedroom, two-bath condo. According to my online search, those should run about two-hundred to two-hundred-twenty-five thousand. That's more in the ball park."

Chelsea said, "Did you hear something from the back? That must have been my husband, the one who wanted us to use the perky cheerleader realtor. I'm not sure where he thinks we're going to put three daughters in a two-bedroom unit."

Ms. Slabotnik sounded a little snippy to Jason, like maybe she wasn't comfortable being in the middle of a married couple's squabbling.

She said, "Well, for today I've arranged to look at three-bedroom, two-and-a-half bath units near the ocean. If none of these meet with Dr. Longfellow's approval, I can go back to the office and find some two-bedroom units later. There's plenty of inventory on the market right now. Also, are you completely wedded to the idea of a condo? There are some nice bungalows available in the two-hundred to three-hundred-thousand-dollar range. Maybe we'll find a dead body in one of the properties, and your PI husband can show off his sleuthing skills."

Voice from the back seat. "I really don't want a single family home. I'm quite the handy man, but I don't need the extra maintenance. I have a full-time government job, and, as my wife has apparently told you, I investigate cases as a private eye on weekends. Do you find a lot of dead bodies in your business? We already found a dead body on the trip down here, and I solved the case in record time. Didn't Chelsea tell you? I'm on vacation from the government, but I'm always on duty as a PI."

Chelsea said, "No, I haven't mentioned the dead body. I didn't want to scare Ms. Slabotnik off. I just told her about your crazy PI thing when we first talked. But, I agree. I don't want the extra maintenance either. I'd rather spend the time playing at the beach. Besides, the handy man currently sitting in the back seat doesn't know a hammer from a screw driver. Last summer he tried to build us a set of maple book cases for the living room. That episode ended with our donating a very expensive dog house to one of our neighbors."

Jason leaned forward to make sure everyone in the front seat heard him clearly.

"It was a nice dog house. Their German shepherd, Rolf, seemed to enjoy it. And, Jim invited us over for a steak dinner to repay me for the nice gesture."

"Translated…maple dog house, four-hundred dollars; steak dinner, max twenty-five dollars. And, no bodies please. Like Jason said, we already did that on the trip down here. It's not a pretty site when Jason goes into PI mode."

Ms. Slabotnik said. "You really found a dead body on your trip down here? Was it a traffic accident? What case did you solve?"

Jason, pride in his voice. "I drove us off the road and into a large hole. We got covered up with dirt, and I found a dead body while digging us out. Roberto killed the guy for having an affair with his wife. Anyhow, I figured it out in record time, and they captured and tied up Roberto. Tell her, Chelsea. Debbie would be impressed."

"Jason, quit bragging. You're going to upset Ms. Slabotnik with your rantings. We're here to buy a vacation property. Let's focus on that. And, she was Roberto's *sister*."

Jason saw Ms. Slabotnik turn her head towards him, a look of concern on her face. "Condo it is. The first one's only a few minutes up the road."

Jason hung on tight as the realtor floored the giant SUV, engine roaring, and pulled out onto the highway. She drove for ten minutes and pulled into the parking lot of a large condo complex. She parked and they exited the vehicle. The SUV was so large and high up that Jason noticed Chelsea had to jump down to get out. He was surprised, maybe even a little jealous, that this old lady drove such a manly vehicle.

Chelsea said, "So, this is a three-bedroom?"

The realtor led them up a flight of exterior cement stairs, opened a lockbox and they entered through the front door.

"Yes, three-bedroom, two-and-a-half bath. The bedrooms are upstairs."

Jason grumbled, "Debbie would have shown us two-bedroom units."

Jason saw an updated kitchen on the right as they entered, with new cabinets, quartz counter tops and shiny stainless steel appliances. He smelled the odor of newly cut wood in the cabinets permeating the air, along with the fresh, fruity aroma of a cleanser that had been generously applied to prep the place for showing. The condo was neat and spotless.

Jason preferred neat and clean. It suggested the absence of chaos. He didn't do well with chaos.

"Oh, Jason. Look at this kitchen. It's beautiful."

"But, Chelsea. You never cook, which is a good thing."

Jason saw Chelsea look at the realtor and shrug. "You cook a couple of nice meals for your husband to try to lessen the blow of stressful news, and you never hear the end of it. Besides, I don't see the purpose of cooking, when there's so much takeout available nowadays."

Jason walked into the expansive living room. "Wow, this is a large place. How much?"

The realtor said, "This one's listed for two-hundred-seventy-five-thousand. Most of the condos in this area are approaching thirty years old, and some are not in the best of condition. As you can see, these owners have fixed this one up nicely. Notice the new Pergo flooring here in the living room…a quality vinyl that looks like hardwood but wears better. The place was originally listed at two-ninety-nine-ninety-nine, and they just dropped the price last week. As I said, there's a lot of inventory right now."

They walked into the kitchen. The realtor continued her pitch. "Completely renovated kitchen, with new maple cabinets, quartz counter tops, all stainless steel appliances. This dishwasher is the most amazing thing. It's so quiet you don't even know it's running. You could sleep here on the counter, and it wouldn't keep you awake."

Jason said, "Don't give Chelsea any ideas. She already makes me sleep in the car sometimes."

Chelsea grinned an evil grin and started walking towards the stairs. "So, all three bedrooms are upstairs?"

"Yes. One master bedroom suite and two smaller bedrooms. I think there's a large soaking tub with this unit, if I'm not mistaken. And, a separate walk-in shower; very nicely done in various complimentary shades of blue Spanish tile."

"That would be nice for you Jason, since you don't fit in normal size tubs. I wouldn't have to listen to your constant complaining."

The realtor followed Chelsea up the stairs, with Jason bringing up the rear. "Another reason this unit is a little more expensive is because of its location on the eastern side of A1A. It's only a two-minute walk to the beach. There's a path through the condo complex that leads to a wooden walkway over the dunes. Very convenient, and the walk through the complex is pleasant; lots of colorful flowers, well maintained plants, trees and shrubbery. And, there's not as much flooding on this side of A1A."

Jason perked up. "Flooding? What flooding? Is there a lot of flooding in Florida? When was the last time this place flooded? Is that a problem being so close to the ocean?"

"Calm down, Jason. I'm sure it's fine."

The realtor smiled, looking at Jason. "The last time this area flooded was two years ago, when a small hurricane came up the Atlantic coast…"

Jason interrupted. "Hurricane? Flooding and a hurricane? I thought hurricanes only happened on the Gulf side of Florida. Chelsea. We can't put the girls in that kind of danger, or me either. Do hurricanes only happen on even years? That would be helpful. At least you'd know when to run away. And, even numbers are better."

"Your husband's a real worrier. Must make him a great PI, always on high alert."

"He can be a little neurotic at times. I think he was dropped on his head when he was a baby, several times. If his OCD kicks in, he'll start counting things, checking doors, that kind of stuff. Makes him feel safe. But, what about the flooding? Did this condo development ever flood?"

"Yes, some water got into the lower units. But, as I was trying to say, this unit is on the second floor, and didn't sustain any flood damage at all. You'll find that your flood insurance will be lower on the second floor. The majority of the flooding doesn't come from the ocean anyhow. It comes from the Intracoastal Waterway and marshland on the other side of A1A."

Jason, voice getting higher, headed for panic mode. "So, what about the hurricane? Were there two-hundred-mile-an-hour winds? Why didn't this place blow away? Why would anyone want to live where hurricanes roam free?"

Jason wandered into the master bathroom, and Chelsea and the realtor followed him. He started checking the closet and cabinet doors multiple times to make sure they were closed. He also flushed the toilets and made sure the faucets were not dripping, all turned off.

"He really is a nervous sort."

"Yes, he has a strong fight or flight response, more flight than fight. In one of his previous cases, he got beat up by a woman. I had to rescue him."

"Chelsea. Tell the whole story. She was a big woman, heavily armed. And mean."

"Well, it's true. She was armed with a large…well…let's just say rubber phallus."

Jason kept opening and closing the same cabinet door, making sure the hinges worked properly. He mentioned the hurricane again, still concerned. The realtor tried to reassure him.

"No two-hundred-mile-an-hour winds. The hurricane two years ago was barely a category one, with winds in the seventy-mile-an-hour range. There wasn't even any roof damage. The torrential rain and flooding caused most of the problems. The units in this condo complex are all built out of rebar-reinforced concrete. It's like living in a bunker. Please leave the cabinet doors alone, Dr. Longfellow. You're going to break them, and I'm responsible."

Chelsea walked over to him, took him by the arm and pulled him away from the cabinet.

Jason said, "Roof damage? Is it common for the roofs to blow off in a hurricane? The insurance must be very expensive. Chelsea, my PI senses are telling me that buying property in Florida is not such a good idea." He flushed the toilet again, just in case it didn't work the first time.

"Jason. Just stop it. Calm down. There's nothing wrong, and your OCD is kicking in big time. I looked online, and hurricanes hardly ever hit North Florida. The last couple of years have been a fluke, and not much damage overall. Isn't that right, Ms. Slabotnik?"

"Yes, that's right. We hadn't been hit by a hurricane for twenty years, and then we had small ones two years in a row. That's the main reason there's so much inventory. It scared people off. But, that means now is a good time to buy. The sellers are willing to negotiate."

They finished looking at the condo, and headed for the car. Once inside the SUV with the A/C running full blast, they sat and talked some more. This old lady obviously liked it cold. Jason expected it might snow inside the vehicle.

The realtor asked, "So, what did you think of the place? It's one of the nicer ones on the market right now, due to the extensive renovations."

Chelsea turned and looked over her shoulder at Jason, in the backseat again.

"I liked it. I thought it was quite nice. What did you think, Jason?"

"It was nice, the cabinet doors were all shut and none of the faucets were leaking. Not so much chaos. But there were an odd number of tiles in the kitchen floor, and it's more than I wanted to spend. And, hurricanes, high winds and high insurance rates? I'd like to see something a little cheaper, and maybe underground. What about a basement?"

The realtor smiled. "It's probably for the best that you're not interested in this one. This unit hasn't been re-piped yet. As for underground, this is Florida, you're already at sea level, and there's no such thing as underground. No basements."

"Chelsea, what's re-piping? That sounds expensive. And, if there's no basement, where do you go in a hurricane to be safe? Burrow in the sand like one of those turtles? We're gonna die."

"How should I know what re-piping is? Could you please explain, Ms. Slabotnik?"

Jason reached into the cooler on the back seat next to him, took out a bottle of water and opened it. He handed one to Chelsea, and offered one to the realtor, who declined it.

The realtor said, "I guess you're new to buying real estate in Florida. Thirty years ago when these condos were built, the builders saved some money by using cheap copper pipes from China. The copper was contaminated with flecks of other metals, and those metal flecks have started to rust, resulting in leaky pipes. To remedy this, you have to hire a plumber to re-pipe the condo with new CPVC pipes. This involves cutting into the walls to access the old pipes and adding the new ones. Not all current condo owners have had this done yet."

Jason asked, "Sounds expensive. So, how much does this cost?"

Jason took a large drink of water, intent on staying hydrated as the realtor suggested.

"For a condo this size, a plumber will charge between four and five-thousand dollars for the re-piping and wallboard repair. You have to do the painting yourself. It's really not all that bad."

Jason heard this in mid-swallow and choked, spewing water out of his nose and mouth and onto the back seat. He wiped it up best he could with his hand.

"Chelsea, that's a lot of money. And, I don't have time to paint. I need weekends to investigate my next case, if I ever come out of the basement."

"First of all, you don't have a case at the moment. Second, we just need to factor it into the price. Third, Ms. Slabotnik told you there are no basements in Florida." She took some tissues out of her purse. "And fourth, take this tissue and clean up your mess."

Ms. Slabotnik said, "No worries. It's time to wash my car anyhow. And, since I often show properties to families with children, I'm used to messes in the back seat. Why, only last week I had one ten-year-old back there that got car sick, and spewed all over the place."

Jason looked around, thinking about what she had just said. He considered asking Chelsea to change places with him.

Just then, Ms. Slabotnik pulled out onto A1A, flooring the accelerator to force her way into the constant flow of speeding traffic. Jason's went from fear of child spew to fear of neck injury. Too late, he readjusted the headrest to accommodate his height. He saw that Chelsea, being shorter, had plenty of head and neck support in the front seat.

The realtor said, "I know you're only interested in condos. But, I found a beautiful single-family home that just came on the market. It's in a new development, with brand new construction. The home owner's association fee would cover the yard work, but you would be responsible for the upkeep of the structure. However, with new construction that's not as much of an issue. What do you think? Would you like to see it? It's just up ahead on the right."

Jason sighed audibly, rubbing the back of his neck. Chelsea said, "Sure. Let's take a look. New construction might be just the ticket."

The realtor pulled into a small development. Jason saw five newly constructed houses and several empty lots, situated along an oval road surrounded by thick trees and swamp. He could tell that this development had been created by draining the swamp and removing all the trees. All that remained were the empty lots, a few new houses and lots of dust and dirt. A few small trees had been planted near the houses; future shade against the blazing Florida sun. Jason pointed out the new community swimming pool that sat near the entrance to the development. The realtor pulled into the driveway of the house with the *For Sale* sign in the yard.

"Keep in mind, we're on the west side of A1A. You're still in walking distance of the beach, but you'll have to cross the highway."

Jason said, "A1A looks like a busy road. Is crossing the highway on foot or a bicycle a problem? I'm fast on my feet, but I'm a little worried about Chelsea."

The women turned and looked at Jason in unison.

Ms. Slabotnik said, "No, Dr. Longfellow. It's not a problem. Florida drivers are very courteous, and hardly ever run over pedestrians, on purpose. What kind of detective are you? Didn't you notice I only almost got hit twice getting us here?"

Chelsea said. "Jason, first of all, you don't know how to ride a bicycle. And second, I've always been able to outrun you. That'll be especially handy when an alligator is chasing us."

As they exited the car and waited while the realtor opened the lockbox, Jason's PI senses began to tingle.

"Isn't this house made of wood? I thought concrete was best for hurricanes. And, isn't this the side of A1A nearest the Intracoastal Waterway and marshland, where the flooding comes from?"

Chelsea spoke up. "How did you do it, Ms. Slabotnik? You actually managed to get him to listen to you. I can never get him to pay attention to anything I say."

"Based on my short time with your husband, I'm guessing it has something to do with fear, and the bottom line. That's the reason I brought you here. These are single family homes, but they've managed to kept the cost down. This is a brand new three-bedroom, two-bath house, all on one floor, that sells for two-hundred-twenty-thousand dollars. It's a great deal at that price."

Jason muttered, "But, flooding, hurricanes, wood, swoosh, blow away."

"Dr. Longfellow, building a new home out of concrete is cost-prohibitive for most. This builder has solved the problem of dealing with high winds by using high tensile strength airplane grade aluminum cable to attach the roof to the ground. It's ingenious really. If you point this out to your insurance company, they will give you a better rate on your wind insurance. And, aluminum won't rust. Rust is another enemy of houses, and cars, especially near the ocean. That same wonderful ocean breeze that keeps the bugs away and keeps you cool also carries salt with it. That rusts the pipes, the metal on cars, and is very hard on the exterior of a house. Another reason why new construction is preferable; no rust yet."

Jason shook his head, a confused look on his face. "Yes, but what about flood insurance? Aren't we near the marsh land? Isn't this one of those flood zones that you mentioned? Wind insurance. Flood insurance. And rust? My cars are going to rust? My little red rocket? And the pipes, the exterior of the house? What if I get old and have a hip replacement? Will that rust too? What about health insurance to handle the stroke I'm gonna have from all the stress of buying a house in Florida, in a hurricane zone, with floods, alligators, rust? Chelsea, are our health insurance premiums paid up?"

Chelsea said, "Let's go inside. It's hot out here. Jason, you can check all the cabinet doors to make sure they're closed. Might want to flush all the toilets and make sure the faucets are turned off too. Don't want to waste precious Florida water due to dripping. Maybe count the kitchen floor tiles?" She smiled at the realtor.

As they entered the house, Ms. Slabotnik said, "Florida's a harsh environment. I haven't even mentioned the sub-tropical sun; very hard on exterior paint. You've got some decisions to make; pick your poison, if you will. Wind insurance is mandatory, since hurricanes do happen in Florida. You can mitigate that cost if you can show the insurance company that your roof is attached properly. Your flood insurance rates will depend on the elevation of the property, and a couple of feet can make a big difference. This is a flood zone. The condo that I'm going to show you next is on the east side of A1A again, and it's at an elevation seven feet higher than where you're standing now. That seven feet will reduce your flood insurance by a third. Building materials, structural integrity, wind resistance, elevation, sun versus shade. All important issues for buying property in Florida. And, you get used to the rust. People think of Florida as being full of bright colors, but truth is that's just to cover up the rust."

Jason started shaking noticeably. He felt like he was about to have a seizure, or run away.

The realtor started the tour. They entered through a small foyer that led to the kitchen on the left. Jason liked the shiny new kitchen with quartz counter tops, stainless steel appliances and expensive looking tile floors. Up the hall to the left they found a small dining area, delineated with a different neutral color, a tan and white tile floor. Jason saw a large, rectangular oak veneer table with eight wooden chairs, cushioned by foam covered with material with bright flowers, including hibiscus, Mexican heather, blue daze and coral honeysuckle; classical Florida flowers. A vase of lilies sat on the table. Then came the living room. Its floor was covered with thick neutral-colored carpet and featured a small stone fireplace at that end of the house.

The realtor said, "The three bedrooms are off the hall to the right. The master bedroom suite is here at the back of the house, and there are two smaller ones positioned in the front and center. They are all carpeted and painted in neutral colors as well, very tastefully done. In this price range, you don't get fancy hot tubs or walk-in showers, just the standard sized tub and shower combination in both bathrooms. Jason, I think you'll find that the toilets both flush. I'm betting the cabinets are all closed. I don't know how many tiles there are on the bathroom floors, but I could count them for you if you'd like."

Jason shrugged. "Any reasonable builder would use an even number of tiles. Anything else is just plain ridiculous, chaos, asking for trouble." *And, why all the drab neutral colors. I like blue, lots of blue. It's such a soothing color, like the ocean, without the sharks.*

Chelsea, said, "Jason, instead of counting bathroom tiles, why don't you go outside and take a walk around the development? Try to clear your head. I'll finish up here with Ms. Slabotnik and then we can move on to the next property. I actually like this place. The new construction is nice and the layout of the house is great."

Jason was practically catatonic, his head spinning, still struggling with all the potential hazards. This realtor was too honest, too much information; hurricane winds, flooding, high insurance rates, flood insurance, wind insurance, rusting everything, and the sub-tropical sun. *Chelsea'll have to deal with this stuff. She's the detailed one. I'm more of a high-level thinker. I see the big picture. Like, I see our vacation home flying over the Atlantic in a big blow.*

Jason walked aimlessly around the mostly empty development grounds. He ended up at the furthest point from A1A, where the clearing ended. As he approached a patch of trees, he saw a wire fence, and through the fence he saw a large drainage pond. *That's a swamp. This development really is built on a drained swamp.*

Then he saw the sign, attached to the fence at eye level. It read, *Beware of Poisonous Snakes and Alligators.* He turned and ran back towards the house. He threw open the front door.

"Chelsea! Chelsea! Don't want to live here! Run away! Snakes. Poisonous snakes, and alligators. And hurricanes, and floods, and expensive insurance, and rust! The other side of A1A. We need the other side of A1A!"

Chelsea smiled. "Jason. Calm down. We already determined that I can outrun you. We'd be fine."

Ms. Slabotnik also smiled. "He must have stumbled onto the sign. I forgot all about it. I'm from Daytona; lived in Florida all my life. This is the sub-tropics, and there are plenty of snakes and alligators around. I guess one just gets used to it. Most of this side of A1A is built on drained swampland, or marshland, as the builders prefer to call it. If you're not comfortable with this, the eastern side of A1A would be better for you. The alligators hardly ever wander across the highway. It's not safe for them to cross what with all the heavy traffic and crazy drivers. Although, there are some poisonous snakes in the dunes. They only come out among the people during heavy rains. Perhaps we should move on to the next condo."

Jason made an effort to compose himself, and take back some of the dignity that he'd just cast to the wind.

"Chelsea, you know I'll always protect you and the girls."

"Yes, Dear. I know. You have your little gun thingy."

"That's revolver. And, yes, I am armed and dangerous. But, hurricanes, and floods, and alligators and poisonous snakes, and rust?

Ms. Slabotnik grinned mischievously. "You're lucky you're not looking in Marco Island. The Everglades is full of giant pythons, up to twenty-five-foot long. When they run out of food down there, they might head up this way."

"Jeez. I'm gonna need a bigger gun."

Chapter 5

They had no luck finding a condo they could agree on. Ms. Slabotnik told Chelsea she would go back to the office to make a list of two-bedroom, two-bath condos on the eastern side of A1A to show them on the following day. Jason and Chelsea went out for seafood, and then returned to their rental unit. Chelsea had wine with dinner and was feeling frisky. She snuggled up to Jason on the couch.

"So, Jason. Here we are, on vacation without the children. Do you want to fool around?"

"I'm sorry Chelsea, but I can't get our conversation with the Slabotnik woman out of my head. I always thought the beach was a good thing. But, now I'm not so sure. There's sharks, poisonous jelly fish, and the dunes have venomous snakes that come out when it rains a lot? Plus, the hurricanes, floods, alligators, snakes, rust? It's like some twisted nightmare, as if Florida was put here to kill a person."

"First of all, the sharks are actually *in* the ocean, not on the beach. Second, you're here alone with your wife, who's had several glasses of wine and is feeling friendly. What are you going to do about it?"

She started rubbing his chest, then moved her hand further south, intent on getting a rise out of him.

"Geez, Chelsea. You shouldn't have given me that antidote after our cross-country trip if you wanted a sex machine for a husband. I'm really tired, what with walking around in the hot sun all day. I'm not twenty anymore. Let me get a good night's sleep and I'll feel better in the morning."

"Too tired, huh? Grrrrrr."

"Chelsea, did you just growl?"

Chelsea woke up with the sunrise next morning when Jason entered the bedroom. He was massaging his neck and he didn't look happy.

"Chelsea, my legs and neck are cramped up and I'm all wet. It dewed on me last night. I've gotta get a bigger car, with a top. The red rocket sucks as a bed. At least it didn't rain."

Chelsea, still angry, didn't have much to say. She just rolled her eyes at him, and was pleased when she saw that miserable look in his eyes. She limited breakfast to coffee, and she only brewed her strong stuff, which Jason choked down without complaint. Then they both got dressed and headed out for the realty office. When they arrived at the *ReallyRealty* office at ten, Ms. Slabotnik was rearing to go. They all piled into her SUV.

"I've got three darling two-bedroom, two-bath condos to show you today, all in PI Longfellow's price range. Shall we get started?"

The realtor pulled the giant SUV out onto A1A, almost taking out a shiny new BMW sedan in the process. Horns blowing, middle fingers exchanged, Ms. Slabotnik didn't seem so grandmotherly. Chelsea held on to the oh-my-god-bar for dear life. She looked in the back, and Jason had closed his eyes and rolled up into the fetal position as best a six-foot-seven man could do in a vehicle with a seat belt.

The realtor grouched. "Damned A1A. It's too dangerous, almost impossible to turn left this time of the morning…I mean…my bad. I should be more careful. It's not the traffic. I just need more coffee."

Jason said. "It must help to drive a rolling battleship. Most people will get out of the way of this thing."

"So, you like my giant SUV? I like the size and power to run folks off the road."

"Does that happen often here in Florida, running people off the road? My car's kind of small. Not much fun to sleep in."

"It happens more often than you might think. Do you sleep in your car a lot?"

Silence ensued for the next few minutes until Ms. Slabotnik pulled her SUV into a parking lot on the east side of A1A. Chelsea was glad she left the motor running, A/C on full blast.

The realtor said, "These are the Castle Keep Condos. They're all two-bedroom, two-bath, built about thirty years ago. Very solid construction with rebar-reinforced concrete and clay tile roofs. The stucco exterior also wears quite well in the Florida sun. There are thirty-two units in here, and as you can see there are two levels with upper and lower units. Most have already been re-piped. The one for sale is an end unit on the second floor."

Chelsea asked, "Also a short walk to the beach?"

"Yes, you just walk up the sidewalk towards the beachfront units. It's only a couple of minutes to the beach walkway over the dunes."

Jason said, "There are beachfront condos here? How much for beachfront?"

"I'm afraid that's out of your price range. They run four-hundred-thousand and up. They're also mainly three-bedroom units."

"Wouldn't want oceanfront anyhow. We'd be too close to the hurricanes. Right, Chelsea?"

No answer.

Ms. Slabotnik said, "This is one of the developments I told you about with the higher elevation."

Jason chimed in. "Seven feet higher elevation equals a thirty percent decrease in flood insurance."

"I can see why you're such a good PI, Dr. Longfellow. You pay attention to details."

Chelsea finally spoke. "Jason, details? Only when it has to do with the bottom line. And, speaking of bottoms, how's yours Jason, from sitting in that clown car all night?"

"It wasn't nice making me sleep in the car. I could've been eaten by alligators, or blown away by a hurricane, or died from terminal cramping, or rusted. And, what about snakes?"

"Then I recommend that you do better tonight, Husband. *Too tired* doesn't cut it."

Ms. Slabotnik turned a little red in the face and quickly changed the subject. Chelsea realized the realtor had found herself in the middle of another of their many marital quarrels.

"How about we take a look at this condo. I think you'll really like it."

They followed the realtor up the stairs to a second-floor condo. The door was open, there were helium-filled balloons tied to the door knob, and a sign stating *Open House, Fly-By-Night-Realty Company* was attached to the top of the door frame.

Ms. Slabotnik said, "I didn't realize they were holding an open house today. Those are usually on the weekend. Looks like we're the only ones here."

Chelsea had a bad feeling. "Isn't that the same realtor we're renting our condo from, Jason?"

No answer. But, Chelsea saw a big smile on Jason's face.

The realtor led them through the open door. They were greeted inside by a perky young woman. Chelsea noticed immediately that the woman wore a tight, bright-red short skirt and a blue cotton button-up with three open buttons, displaying noticeable cleavage. Her spiked heels were also red. Chelsea glared at Jason.

"Debbie! Chelsea, look. It's Debbie, the realtor I was telling you about. How about that? She's here. What a pleasant surprise! Debbie, this is my wife, Chelsea. Chelsea, meet Debbie."

Chelsea saw that Jason was totally focused on the vivacious young realtor, visions of cheerleaders no doubt dancing in his head. Ms. Slabotnik, on the other hand, took a step back, a look of concern on her face.

Chelsea shook Debbie's hand. *She does look kind of like me when I was younger, if I had been a hooker.* "Hello, Debbie. It's so nice to meet you. Jason has told me so much about you, having known you for all of fifteen minutes. He mentioned that you were a cheerleader at one time. I can definitely see that."

Debbie blushed and smiled a big smile. It looked to Chelsea like she was about to break out into a cheer. Ms. Slabotnik glanced at Chelsea and took another step backwards. Her look of concern turned to fear. Chelsea realized that her obvious anger was scaring the poor old woman.

Sometimes Jason makes me crazy!

Debbie let go of Chelsea's hand. "Thank you. It's kind of you to say that. But, my cheerleading days are over. I'm an old lady now, almost twenty-five. Your husband is a delight. He reminds me of my father; maybe a little older. We had a nice chat, and I thought I was going to show you some properties, but I guess you had already made other plans. No worries. Here we are now. Kind of ironic, don't you think?"

Chelsea fumed. *Ironic indeed.*

Jason fumed. "Older than her father?!"

When Chelsea heard Jason's reaction her mood changed abruptly, and she smiled.

Ms. Slabotnik said, "Hi Debbie. Haven't seen you for a while. Would you like to give us the tour?"

Jason said, "I sense that the two of you know each other."

Chelsea, still angry, said, "Brilliant deduction, Sherlock. Two realtors in the same town, acquainted with each other? It's almost like you have a brain."

Debbie said, "Well, didn't you get up on the wrong side of the bed this morning, Mrs. Grumpy Pants? Actually, Karen dated my dad for a couple of years before he met my mother. From what Dad told me, they were a hot item, and Karen, here, could have been my mom. But, my dad went out of town on business, and Karen ran off with some surfer guy while Dad was gone. Broke Dad's heart. He started dating Karen's best friend, and married her six months later. The story had a happy ending. Dad married Mom, and later the surfer got eaten by a great white shark off the coast of Australia. Karen moved back home to St. Augustine, and never married."

Chelsea heard Jason say, tactful as usual, "So, you and Ms. Slabotnik don't like each other very much?"

Ms. Slabotnik answered for Debbie, "Actually, both of Debbie's parents died in a car accident a few years ago, and her mother was once my best friend. Since the accident, Debbie and I have become good friends, except when we're in competition for a sale, of course."

Debbie said, "Yes, that's true. Karen and I have become besties. Now, enough reminiscing. Let me show you one awesome condo. I'm going to sell you this place. Karen here has more experience, but I'm the one who's going to convince you to buy this condo."

Chelsea said, "Does it really matter who convinces us? Don't the two of you split the realtor commission if we buy?"

Karen spoke up. "Yes, that's true. But, Debbie is a little on the competitive side. If you decide to buy, she'll want to know which of us convinced you to do so."

Chelsea thought that was kind of needy and unprofessional, and she really didn't like the way Jason was staring at Debbie. But, the condo looked nice, and since it was in Jason's preferred price range she might be able to avoid some of his whining if they made an offer.

They followed Debbie up the hallway. "This is the master bedroom suite on the right. There's a large bedroom, large walk-in closet and a great bathroom with separate shower and soaking tub."

Chelsea was surprised that Debbie failed to mention the thick, luxurious cream carpet that suited the clean, off-white walls. She also ignored the expensive granite countertop and Carrara tiles in the master bath. They gathered in the bathroom, and stood there talking for a while.

Karen, as the buyer's agent, asked, "Is the water and sewer included in the condo fee?"

Debbie looked confused. "How should I know? You're just trying to make me look bad, asking hard questions. Too sciencey. Don't worry, Dr. and Mrs. Longfellow, I'll find out and get back to you on that one. Just look at how well the toilet flushes." She gave the toilet a flush.

"Wow, that's impressive Debbie. You really know your stuff. Sounds like a good, strong, manly flush. Do all the toilets in this unit flush that well?"

Chelsea just shook her head. "Jason, you really are an idiot. Where do you think you're going to sleep tonight?"

"Be nice, Chelsea. I'm just impressed with Debbie's technical knowledge as a realtor."

"Yeah. She knows how to flush a toilet. That is impressive. Maybe I should be living with her. Why don't you go check the cabinet doors and faucets? Maybe count floor tiles or something. If you keep this up, you're gonna need to do something to feel safe."

Karen asked, "Has this unit been re-piped? If not, that'll need to be factored into the price."

Debbie frowned. "Stop asking…what'd Dr. Longfellow call them…technical questions? That's not fair. What's re-piping? How can I convince these people to buy this place when you keep asking me difficult questions?"

No one said anything.

Finally, Debbie asked, "What do you think so far? Do you like the unit? Have I convinced you to buy yet?"

Jason said, "You're doing great. I'm really interested. How much?"

Chelsea said, "We know the toilets flush. How about we move on?"

Debbie said, "I don't like to tell the buyer the price until the end, after I have dazzled them with my sales pitch."

Karen spoke up. "Debbie, Dr. Longfellow here is all about the price, the bottom line. And, Longfellows, please don't let Debbie's enthusiasm put you off. This really is a very nice unit. I assume you noticed the new carpet and freshly painted walls in the bedroom and beautiful tile in the master bath."

Debbie said, "Don't you listen to Karen. I'm the one who'll convince you to buy. She's old, and gets confused."

Debbie turned to Karen, and spoke as if the realtor were senile. "We're in a condo now, granny. That's short for condominium. Just leave the selling to me. You follow along as best you can, and feel free to sit down and rest if you need to. There's a comfortable couch in the living room."

Chelsea forgot her anger at Jason, as the two realtors appeared to be going off the rails. She whispered in her husband's direction.

"Jason. Are those PI senses of yours tingling? These realtors are starting to get on my nerves. I don't understand what's going on."

"No worries, Chelsea. Just some healthy competition."

"Didn't you hear me say there's no need for competition? They share the realtor commission if we buy this place."

They followed Debbie upstairs to the other bedroom. The realtors waited while Chelsea and Jason looked around. Chelsea liked the plush new carpet on the stairs, this time a dark blue to match the freshly-painted light blue walls.

Karen asked, "What's an average monthly electric bill for this unit?"

Debbie glared at Karen. Chelsea thought Debbie might try to strangle the old realtor.

Debbie growled, "How the hell should I know? Will you stop with all the stupid questions? I'm leading this open house. Old people should be seen and shut up."

Jason said, "Yeah, how could she know how much the electric bills are? She doesn't live here."

Chelsea and the others followed Debbie into the small bedroom. The plush carpet and wall color continued from the stairs into the room.

Debbie said, "Look how easy these sliding closet doors open and close. And, the same with these dresser drawers." They moved on into the small bathroom. "And look, when I turn on the faucet the water comes out. This one's hot, and this one's cold. Would you like to give it a try, Dr. Longfellow?"

Jason turned on the hot water faucet and stuck his hand under the stream of water.

"She's right. The faucet works, and that's definitely hot water. When you turn it off, it doesn't drip. And all the cabinet and closet doors in here are closed. You're doing great Debbie. You've convinced me. I'm interested in buying this place. How much?"

"Now, Dr. Longfellow, I already told you I like to wait until the end of the tour before mentioning anything about price. Be a good boy, and let me finish my tour."

Karen said, "Good Lord, Chelsea. You were right. Your husband really is an idiot. How about you? Do you like what you're seeing? Every realtor worth their salt knows the wife makes the final decision. This place is laid out perfectly. Most of the living space is on the first floor, and you can send your children up here at bedtime. That way you and Dr. Longfellow could spend some quality time downstairs, alone. And, the thick new carpet would wear well with young children."

"I'm not sure that quality time alone is going to be an option. If he keeps this up, he's going to be sleeping in his car on a permanent basis."

Karen continued. "Anyhow, have you noticed how well this condo has been maintained? If you don't want it, I might buy it myself." She turned to Debbie. "How old are the water heater and HVAC system?"

Debbie's frown took a turn for the worse. "I told you to stop asking me technical questions, you old hag. I'm trying to sell these people a condo."

Chelsea took a couple of steps back, wary of the tension in the room. She looked at Jason, busy trying the bathroom water faucets and flushing the toilet.

Chelsea interrupted the realtor squabble. "Debbie, how about showing us the kitchen? That's an important selling point for me."

Jason said, "But, Chelsea, you don't like to…"

"Shut up."

"Yes, Dear."

They followed Debbie down the stairs, and into the kitchen. Chelsea saw Debbie staring daggers through Karen.

"No more questions, old lady. This is my tour." To Chelsea, "So, Mrs. Longfellow. This is a nice kitchen. Look how the refrigerator door opens and closes so easily. And, it's cold in there. Even colder in the lower freezer unit. The stove has four burners. See how the vent fan over the stove turns on and off? The water faucets also turn on and off, without leaking. And, how about these cabinet doors? Look how easy they open and close. Note that they have these little cabinet door bumpers so they are quiet when you shut them."

Chelsea was afraid to ask any more questions. Debbie seemed a little unstable.

Karen said, "Yes, and notice the beautiful granite counter tops and all stainless appliances, another new addition. Everyone wants quartz or granite counter tops and stainless appliances these days."

"I was just going to say that. Stop interrupting. I'm the new generation of realtor. You're old and washed up."

Jason said, "Karen, I have to agree with Debbie. She is perky, enthusiastic, and represents the new age of realtors." To Debbie, "Debbie, I love the stick-on bumpers that make the cabinet doors quiet. I'm also impressed that all the cabinet doors were closed in the kitchen, the sink works and the freezer's colder than the refrigerator. I'm even more convinced. How much for the place?"

Chelsea realized Jason was completely oblivious to what was going on. She took several more steps backwards. The two realtors both turned towards Jason. Debbie grabbed an electric hand-held mixer that was sitting on the kitchen counter, already plugged in; someone had been using it to make cookies, probably to add a homey aroma to the place. Karen chose a large butcher knife from the knife rack. Debbie hit the mixer button, and the blades began to spin as she thrust it towards Jason's face. Karen moved towards him, the knife raised above her head.

Debbie screamed, "I TOLD YOU, I'LL TELL YOU THE PRICE WHEN I'M FINISHED, YOU SON-OF-A-BITCH!"

Karen said, "Dr. Longfellow. You suck as a detective. I guess your PI senses didn't warn you of the danger you're in. Nobody tells me I'm old and washed up. All you're worried about is the price, you cheap bastard."

Chelsea watched in horror as Jason backed up, a look of terror on his face. The two realtors had him pinned against the kitchen counter with nowhere to run.

"Chelsea! Florida realtors are dangerous! HELP!"

Chelsea pulled a large, cast iron frying pan out of a drawer under the stove, and thought whimsically, *Should I help him or let them kill him? I might not get another opportunity like this.*

Chelsea's keen eye saw that Debbie's mixer had run out of cord and pulled out the plug. Karen's knife was a serious threat.

"Stop trying to murder my husband. I know he's irritating, but he doesn't deserve to die, just sleep in his car for a couple more nights."

Jason said, in complete panic, "Debbie. Why are you doing this?! I'm on your side! I think you're the best realtor, and cheerleader, ever and I wanna buy this place."

Hearing that, Chelsea hesitated. *Little Miss Cheerleader is the best realtor ever? He wants to buy this place? I'm his wife. What about what I want? So, should I, or shouldn't...?*

Chelsea looked at the frying pan, then at Jason. At six-foot-seven, his head was almost out of her reach. She finally whacked Debbie and Karen on the back of the head. The two women lay unconscious on the kitchen floor.

Jason gave Chelsea a big hug. "Thank you, my loving wife. You saved me. Those two are crazy. Do you understand what just happened? I could've died. We should call the cops."

Chelsea smiled. *He has no idea how close to death he came.* "I'm not sure what that was about, Jason, but you can be annoying at times. You keep whining about how dangerous Florida is, ranting about hurricanes, floods, sharks, alligators, snakes, and rust. And, you always freak out about money, like spending money is going to kill you. You're such a worry wart."

"Yeah. And, now I gotta add realtors to my list."

Chapter 6

After the dueling realtor debacle, the Longfellows went back to their rental condo and Jason ordered pizza delivery. He was grateful that Chelsea finally let him sleep inside that night, in the guest bedroom. She told him she was too tired for a conjugal visit.

The next morning, after toast and coffee, Jason had a second cup and read the news on his smart phone while Chelsea phoned the *ReallyRealty* office to ask for another realtor. They were both sitting at the kitchen table, where he was trying not to spill coffee on his phone. After she got off the call, he looked up from the newsfeed.

"Have any luck, Chelse? Does *ReallyRealty* have any realtors that aren't psychotic killers?"

"The office manager apologized profusely, and introduced me to another agent on the phone. They both assured me that whatever happened yesterday was a fluke, and that their realtors hardly ever try to murder their clients, especially the buyers. Apparently, there's a lot of inventory on the market right now."

"Who's the new realtor? Is she any good? Did she sound like she knew what she's doing?"

"*His* name is Rock Handsome, and he sounded fine, very professional with a deep, sexy, masculine voice – nothing like a cheerleader. I'm looking forward to meeting him. He's going to pick us up here at one o'clock. He has a couple of places to show us today."

"Really? Rock Handsome? Sounds like a porn star. Or, an escort."

Jason looked over her shoulder while Chelsea spent the rest of the morning at the kitchen table looking at condo listings on her laptop. He wanted to make sure she only searched for two-bedroom, two-bath units. He took the last drink of coffee, thinking even the weak stuff was too bitter. He'd considered putting milk in his coffee, but not when Chelsea drank the strong stuff black. That just wouldn't be right. He was the manly PI.

"Chelsea. Look at that. There are some condos on the Intracoastal Waterway that have their own boat docks. I've always wanted a boat. I could drive us up and down the Intracoastal, and out into the ocean. Maybe I could take us deep sea fishing for marlin."

"Jason, cool your jets. You don't know anything about fishing, or driving a boat. I told you, the best thing about St. Augustine is the history, arts and crafts and museums downtown."

"Boring, boring, boring. I like excitement. What could be more exciting than gliding across the water in a fast boat, maybe one of those offshore racing boats? I read somewhere those things will do two hundred miles an hour. The girls would love it."

"You are NOT taking our children in anything going two hundred miles an hour. If you want to kill yourself, go ahead. I told you I recently increased your life insurance policy. Besides, you already bought the stupid red rocket for your midlife crisis. Then, you got a PI license. Don't get me started."

"Yes, Dear. I hear you. A guy can fantasize, can't he?"

"I know you. Your so-called fantasies can turn into disaster in a heartbeat."

They planned on leftover pizza for lunch. Jason felt confident that Chelsea could re-heat pizza in a microwave. She drank more coffee, while Jason had a diet soda and potato chips with his pizza. They finished lunch and Jason was clearing the table when he heard a knock on the door. Chelsea walked over to the door and opened it to welcome their new realtor.

Jason heard a deep male voice. "Hello. I'm Rock Handsome, your new real estate agent."

"Oh, my Lord. Please, do come in. The name's Chelsea. Chelsea…uhhh…"

Jason's back was to the door, and he turned to meet the new realtor. He saw his wife staring hungrily at a large, well-dressed man while shaking the man's hand.

Jason, amused, said, "Longfellow, your last name's Longfellow."

To Jason's surprise, Chelsea continued to stand there, holding the man's hand and staring up at him. Her expression looked like a starry-eyed young girl with a teenage crush.

Jason gave the realtor the once over, and his amusement faded. Rock Handsome stood six-five, with bronze, tanned skin and well-groomed brown hair. Jason had to admit, the guy was handsome, in a Neanderthal sort of way. That chest and those arms had been subjected to many hours at the gym. Rock…what a stupid name…was one of those guys with a permanent five o'clock shadow. He had a chiseled chin with a prominent dimple and dark brown eyes, that some women might find attractive.

Jason thought, *This guy's ridiculous. He's so perfect he looks like he was built in a lab.*

"Chelsea. Wife. Earth calling Chelsea. Would you like to introduce me to your new friend?"

Chelsea released Rock's hand. "Mr. Rock, this is my husband…"

Jason extended his hand. "Jason. The name's Jason. But, by the way my wife's looking at you, you can call me Dr. Longfellow, or PI Longfellow. I carry a gun. Well, I own a gun. I don't actually carry it. I'm afraid it might go off. But, I know how to use it. I don't work out, but I know where there's a gym, just in case I ever need it."

The realtor looked confused as he took Jason's hand and shook it. "It's nice to meet you, Jason?...Dr…PI Longfellow?"

Chelsea, still taking in their new realtor, said, "You can call him Jason. He actually has a doctorate, and he fancies himself a private eye, but Jason will be fine."

"Thanks for clearing that up, Wife."

"Now you want to get all possessive? The other night you were fine sleeping in the car."

"Chelsea. You are my wife. And, I wasn't fine with the car. My ass is still asleep from that ordeal."

Rock appeared even more confused. He looked to Jason like he might run away. Jason thought this was odd, since the man was built like a professional wrestler.

Maybe he's afraid of Chelsea. She is kind of scary sometimes.

Chelsea said, "Sorry, Mr. Rock. Jason and I have had a couple of rough days since we got to Florida. I guess we're kind of on edge. For some unknown reason, two realtors tried to kill him yesterday. You must know one of them, Ms. Slabotnik? She works for *ReallyRealty*."

"Yes, I know Karen. Although, I must say, I was surprised to hear of the incident. She never seemed to me to be the violent type."

Jason felt a need to be part of the conversation, since it was him they tried to kill.

"She didn't seem all that violent to me either. Neither did Debbie. She was the other realtor, from Fly-By-Night Realty. I liked Debbie. She reminded me of a cheerleader, right up until she tried to shred my face with an electric hand-held mixer. I could've taken them one at a time, but they both jumped me at once. Chelsea here took them out with a heavy frying pan."

Rock asked, "Do you have any idea why they attacked you?"

Chelsea said, "Mr. Rock, my husband can be quite irritating. But, enough about him. How long have you been a realtor? What does Mrs. Rock think about all the women you meet working with the public? You must have to beat them off with a stick, right? A big stick?"

"I've been a realtor for seven years, and there isn't any Mrs. Rock. I'm not married."

"If you were married, I'll bet you'd never abandon your wife and sleep in the car, would you? You'd be right there, on top…I mean, beside her, all night."

"Chelsea, you made me sleep in the car. Don't you remember? You wanted to…well…you know. And, I was tired. Don't get me wrong. I love the red rocket. It's just not much of a bed."

Jason noticed that the realtor glanced at Chelsea, then at him, appearing uncomfortable again.

Jason thought, *I don't know what his problem is. I'm the one who had to sleep in my car. I need to get one of those big SUVs like these realtors all drive. I'll bet one of those would be comfortable to sleep in. Maybe this guy won't want to work with us, and we can find a less psychotic version of Debbie out there to use instead.*

Rock said, "According to Karen's file, you guys are looking for a two-bedroom, two-bath condo to use as both a vacation home and a rental. I have a couple on my list for this afternoon, and if that doesn't work we can try again tomorrow."

Jason was feeling rebellious after Chelsea's obvious attraction to this thirty-something hunk of realtor. He walked over and stood next to his wife. *I'll show her.*

Jason said, "Mr. Handsome…Rock. Aren't you a little overdressed for house hunting in your khaki jeans and a fancy matching jacket? You also forgot to button your shirt up all the way. My wife's getting up there in age, and you might give her a stroke."

"Don't listen to my husband. He has no manners, discussing a woman's age. By the way, I just turned thirty."

Jason couldn't help but chuckle. "So, we met when I was twenty-five and you were ten? Really, Chelsea?" *The way she's looking at this guy, I better stay awake tonight and take care of business. I'll have to tough it out and drink several cups of that swill she calls coffee. Meanwhile, I'll show her who's boss.*

Jason looked at Rock Handsome. "Enough socializing. Let's get down to business. I saw a place online this morning that's not far up A1A, and they sell condos on the Intracoastal Waterway with their own docks. The development was called *Seaside Booze and Boats*, or something like that. I was just telling Chelsea this morning that I would like to buy a boat. This is

Florida, with water everywhere. It'd be a shame not to enjoy that part of the Florida experience, don't you think?"

"You must mean the *Sea Breeze Village.* There is a three-bedroom condo for sale there, with a dock. But, its three-hundred-fifty-thousand dollars, and according to Karen's notes you are looking in the two-hundred-thousand range. Of course, I'll be happy to show it to you."

"Jason, what are you doing? We don't need a boat, and when I mentioned three-bedroom condos for two-hundred-seventy-five thousand earlier you squawked."

Rock flinched when Chelsea spoke. Jason was pretty sure by the tone of her voice that he would regret this defiant behavior later in the day. But, he kept it up anyway.

"A fella can change his mind. Besides, it can't hurt to look. Rock, maybe you could show us that one first."

"Yes, Mr. Rock. Maybe you could show us that one first, and we can leave my husband's body there and move on to the two-bedroom units."

Rock said, "Okay. I'll take you to the *Sea Breeze Village* condos first. They are very nice units."

Jason thought, *Wow, he thinks I'm the boss. He's a worse detective than I am. Take that, Wife.*

They followed the realtor to his SUV. Jason realized that Florida realtors must all drive huge luxury SUVs, probably to impress their clients. Or, maybe it was to survive the traffic on A1A. This time, Jason took shotgun. When he got in, the seat was hot from direct sunlight and he burned his butt. Rock started the vehicle, turned the A/C on high and waited a few minutes for it to cool off. They sat there and chatted.

"So, Rock, tell me what it's like to own a boat in Florida. Just how much fun do I have to look forward to?"

"Well, Dr. Longfellow…"

"You can call me Jason. And, try to ugly up a little, would you? Button up your shirt. You're making me look bad in front of my wife."

Jason watched as the realtor buttoned his shirt. He struggled with the collar button, because his neck was so large from all the time at the gym.

Rock said, "Okay…So, Jason. Are you sure you want to do this? It's dangerously quiet in the back seat."

Chelsea said, "Do tell him what he wants to know, Mr. Rock. I'll just sit back here and take it all in. PI Longfellow might think he's taking a stand on this boat thing, but he'll regret it later."

Rock glanced over his shoulder into the back seat, a look of concern on his face. Jason was surprised that the realtor decided to go on, in spite of Chelsea's not-so-subtle objections. But, then, the realtor wasn't the one who was going to end up sleeping in his car, or under it. Besides, he had a big old SUV to sleep in.

Rock pulled the large SUV into traffic on A1A, headed for the first set of condos. He talked as he drove.

"Owning a boat in Florida…well…let's see. On the positive side, if you have a big enough boat there's plenty of water around. You can go all up and down the Intracoastal Waterway, with access to the ocean. You can take your boat into the Atlantic for touring or deep sea fishing. Then, there's the St. Johns River and several large lakes, like Lake George. You can boat, fish, ski, wakeboard, go tubing, swimming, all the water sports."

"Sounds like a real blast."

From the back seat. "Yeah, a blast. What's on the negative side? Gators, snakes, drowning, wife running over you with your own boat…"

"Don't mind my wife. She's in one of her bad moods. As you can see, I'm clearly in charge."

Rock said, "So, you slept in your car and you're in charge? Okay. None of my business. Boats…on the negative side, there's the salt water, which corrodes all the metal on a boat, including the engine. So, the life of a boat is half what it is in fresh water. Then, there's the tides. When you go boating on the Intracoastal Waterway, you have to pay close attention. You should be going out when the tide is coming in, and coming in when the tide is going out. There are towing services that make a fortune rescuing boats that have run aground."

"That doesn't sound so bad. In and out, in and out. Chelsea is the one who's good with details, and she'll pay attention to things like that. She'll keep us afloat."

From the back seat, "You're on your own, Sailor Boy. I'm going to be in downtown St. Augustine at the arts and craft shows and museums. Now you're talking *in and out*? Would have been nice a couple of nights ago. Maybe you could have slept somewhere besides your car."

Jason said, "Well, then, I'll just take Matilda, my trusty GPS with me."

"That's great, Jason. Maybe Matilda can rescue you from the alligators and poisonous snakes."

"Alligators and poisonous snakes? Chelsea, you don't know what you're talking about. Rock, there are no alligators or snakes in the Intracoastal Waterway or the St. Johns River, are there?"

"Well, yeah. The Intracoastal runs along swampland, and the St. Johns River is full of all kinds of nasty critters. But, not to worry, people go out there in boats all the time. You're only in danger if you get in the water."

"But, what about swimming? It's hotter than hell. And, don't you have to get in the water to ski, tube and wakeboard? What if you fall off your skis, or wakeboard, or tube? What then?"

"You silly man… I mean…Dr. Longfellow. You just need to get up on your skis, wakeboard or tube really fast. And, for God's sake, don't fall off. I did have one captain of a fishing boat tell me that most of the big alligators hide in the tall grass during the day, because there's a bounty on gators. He said that makes it safer for humans to get into the water."

"Chelsea, this boating thing doesn't sound so good all of a sudden. What if a gator or two missed the memo about hiding in the tall grass during the day? Would you go along and rescue me if I fell in?"

"Why would I want to do that? Come to think of it, it might not be a bad idea to buy one of the condos with a dock. There is that hefty increase in your life insurance I took out recently."

"She's just kidding, Rock. She rescued me from those two crazy realtors."

Rock said, "Oh, and I forgot to mention the sharks. There are sharks in both the Intracoastal Waterway and the ocean. But, don't worry. Boaters hardly ever get eaten by sharks or alligators around here…as long as you stay in the boat."

Rock floored the accelerator of the giant SUV to pass a long line of slow traffic in the right lane. The large V-8 engine roared. Jason loved the sound of the large engine.

Again from the back seat. "Mr. Rock. Thank you for explaining boating in Florida to my stubborn husband. Jason, are you sure you still want to see the *Sea Breeze Village?*

You're not winning this time, Woman. "Yes, I'm sure. I'm not going to let things like salt water, rust, alligators, snakes, and sharks scare me away. We're going to get a boat, and teach the girls how to ski, wakeboard, tube, all the fun water sports."

"Jason Longfellow, you are not going to use our young daughters to troll for deadly creatures. We can look at this condo, and buy a boat. But, you're going out in the thing by yourself, and probably will end up sleeping in it. The girls and I will stay safe and sound on solid ground."

Rock pulled the large SUV back into the right lane and flipped on his turn signal.

He said, "Well, here we are. The condo village is just up ahead on the right. We can take a look at the boat house first, and then I'll take you through the condo."

The realtor parked, they exited and followed him down a small hill to a series of boat docks. They stood on the sidewalk next to one of the docks while Rock explained the layout of the condo complex. Jason looked around, a big smile on his face.

Rock said, "These are the boat slips for the *Sea Breeze Village*. They're actually quite nice."

Chelsea said, "None of the slips appear to have boats in them."

Rock explained, "That's because it's so expensive and dangerous to own a boat here. In addition to the stuff I already mentioned, there's a lot of money in St. Augustine; lots of millionaires and billionaires. They buy a new fifty or sixty-foot yacht, and the dealer hands them the keys and a celebratory drink. He gives them a quick boating course; push the throttle forward to go forward, backward for reverse. The new owner takes a bottle of champagne and his latest version of a hot new trophy wife out on the Intracoastal, where he runs over or swamps boats the size of the one you'll be able to afford. They kill a lot more people than sharks, alligators and snakes combined."

Chelsea said. "Thank you for that. Note to self, double Jason's life insurance policy again."

Rock said, "This condo development was built in two-thousand-fourteen, only seven years old. Things are still in good shape. I'm guessing they've only had to paint and stain this dock area three or four times since they were first built."

Chelsea asked, "Who pays for that?"

"The homeowner's association covers the exterior of the condos, but not the docks. The owners are responsible for the maintenance on the docks. Those docks sit in brackish water, which is murder on any type of material."

"Hear that Jason? Maybe you could paint and stain the dock yourself while the girls and I go…"

"I know, Chelsea. While you go to downtown St. Augustine to the arts and craft shops, museums, and historic sites."

"Now you're catching on."

"Okay, Rock. Show us the condo. I'll bet it's nice. How much did you say it costs?"

"Three-hundred-fifty-thousand for the condo and boat slip, plus a five-hundred-dollar per month condo fee. You are responsible for maintaining your own boat slip and the interior of the condo."

They followed Rock up a gentle slope to the condo complex, and up a flight of stairs to the second floor. Jason detected Chelsea's eyes following the realtor's firm buttocks as he climbed. Rock punched a key code into the lock and opened the door. Jason herded Chelsea through the door ahead of him, with Rock bringing up the rear.

Rock started the tour, leading them through the first floor level. Jason kept inserting himself between the realtor and his wife as they walked through the condo.

Rock said, "This is a three-bedroom, two-and-a-half-bath unit. The bedrooms are all upstairs. It's roomy as condos go; nearly sixteen-hundred square feet in all. You enter through this hallway that leads to the dining room/living room combination, with the kitchen off to your right. The place is only seven years old. It includes granite counter tops in the kitchen, along with stainless steel appliances and beautiful maple cabinets that look like new. The living and dining room floors are tile, and there's thick carpet on the stairs, all done in tasteful whites, browns and tans. There's a small screened porch with a view of the community pool. The other side of the unit looks at a wooded area."

They finished with the main level. Jason was enjoying himself.

"Wow, Chelsea. This place's great! All this, and a boat slip for three-hundred-fifty-thousand. What a deal!"

Chelsea mumbled, "Idiot."

"What's that, Dear? It's a brilliant find? We'd never have found it if I'd listened to you?"

Jason saw the realtor flinch again. Jason felt like he needed to continue pressing the issue, pretending he was in charge. It felt good to be in charge; didn't happen often with Chelsea.

"Let's take a look upstairs. The brochure says there's a large hot tub, perfect for a man my size. My detective senses are on fire. These people have good taste, just like me. I'm sensing the master bedroom suite is done in shades of blue – my favorite color, so peaceful. If that's the case, we'll take it."

Jason charged up the stairs ahead of Chelsea and the realtor. He had already moved through the master bedroom and was standing in the bathroom by the time he heard Rock and Chelsea reach the upstairs. He heard Chelsea's voice from the bedroom.

"Jason, husband mine. Your PI senses are right on, as usual. I love the bright orange master bedroom walls with red and yellow flowers, and...you were half right…matching navy carpet. The current owners must be into psychedelic drugs, and you are a pharmacologist, so there's that. Nice detecting. Were you right about the bathroom too?"

Rock said, also from the bedroom, "I don't know what the heck happened up here. It's like a different family lived upstairs, or they let their children design the master suite."

Jason heard Rock and Chelsea enter the bathroom, but he didn't turn to look at them. He just stood there, not saying anything, his body shaking as he pointed in the direction of a large orange tiled hot tub adorned with colorful flowers.

Chelsea said, "Oh, wow! The tile in here matches the bedroom. Jason? What's the matter? It's bad, but it's not that bad."

Jason, still silent, waved her over to him, where she could see into the raised hot tub.

Jason said, "My PI senses suck. Ugly orange. Not blue. Dead body…in the tub. Chelsea, don't look, he's naked."

Chelsea said, "Oh my! He's well-endowed. I mean, oh my God, a dead body."

"Wife, I told you not to look. Someone call the police. I'm going to search the room."

As the realtor dialed 9-1-1 on his cell, Jason walked around the bathroom, looking for clues as to cause of death and who the killer might be. Jason saw Chelsea looking around, presumably also for clues. But, he noticed that her eyes kept drifting back to the tub, then to Rock.

He heard Chelsea say something, mostly to herself. "Jason, you need to do better. My mind's starting to go a'wanderin.*"

Jason pretended he didn't hear her. He was the one that usually talked to himself. He said, "I need more light in here."

He tried the light switch, but nothing happened. "What the hell? There's something plugged into this socket, and the cord leads to the tub."

Jason pulled a charred plug out of the wall socket. He reeled in the cord and removed a wet electric hand-held mixer from the tub. He turned it over in his hands, examining it carefully.

"Debbie! This is her weapon of choice. But, that can't be. She's all young, cute and perky. She wouldn't do this."

"Jason. Do I have to remind you that she tried to puree your face with a similar kitchen appliance just the other day?"

Jason paused, thinking so hard his eyes crossed. "After further consideration, my PI crime detector tells me you're right, Chelsea. Debbie must be the killer."

Chelsea said, "Oh great. You mean like when your PI senses were telling you about the blue master bedroom suite and large hot tub, without a dead body in it? Maybe it wasn't Debbie. Lots of kitchens have hand-held electric mixers in them. It could have been anyone. More to the point, who is this well-endowed man? And, what's he doing soaking naked in the hot tub of this condo that's up for sale? Doesn't that seem strange to anyone?"

Jason placed the wet hand-held electric mixer on the floor. He walked over and sat on the side of the tub, examining the dead body.

Excited, Jason said, "His nakedness could take us back to Debbie. Maybe they were having an affair, she knew this place was on the market and arranged for a bit of hot tubbing with him."

Chelsea shook her head in the negative. "I can see where a woman might arrange an affair with such a…well-equipped…man, but, he looks a little too old for the perky Debbie. I'm guessing maybe a woman in her forties." Jason saw her grin, a faraway look in her eyes. "And, *hot tubbing* is not a verb."

Jason watched Chelsea disappear into the bedroom. He heard her voice call to him, "There's a pair of pants on the floor next to the bed, with a wallet inside. According to his ID, this man's name was James Forester, MD, Specialty in Infectious Diseases."

Jason, in full PI mode, turned to Rock, who was now standing next to the hot tub.

"Mr. Handsome. Do you know this man? My wife's been checking out your ass. You're obviously popular with the ladies. Maybe you and the doc here were both sleeping with Debbie? Perhaps a hot tubbing ménage-a-trois? Did she wear a cheerleader's costume? Why did you and Debbie get together and kill him? Or, did you kill him out of jealousy and use an electric hand-held mixer to frame poor Debbie? Shame on you!"

The realtor, again with a look of confusion, said, "What are you talking about? I've never seen this man before in my life. I barely know Debbie, and I'm certainly not sleeping with her, nor do I know anything about her choice of murder weapons. I'm gay, for goodness sake."

Chelsea walked back into the bathroom just as Rock spoke. She shook her head and said, quietly to herself, "I'm sad. The hot live one's gay, the well-hung one's dead, and I'm married to the PI."

Jason said, "Chelsea, I heard that. You're being mean. That poor man's dead. Apparently Rock's not interested in the ladies. And, well, I'm alive, and I like the ladies. I've just been tired lately from all the stress. And, there's nothing wrong with being a PI."

Chelsea sighed. "You'd never know you like the ladies based on this past week. I actually think you *like* sleeping in that stupid car."

Jason had already moved on. He stood there, thinking about the pants, the dead doctor, the realtor, and Debbie, trying to process what he'd just heard. Rock, gay? He needed a new theory. In his confusion, he started counting the tiles on the front of the hot tub. Meanwhile, Chelsea disappeared into the bedroom again.

Jason heard her voice. "Jason, once your mind's done spinning, you should take a look over here. There's a man's dress jacket in the closet, with a business card in the pocket. It's a realtor's card, a Jeffrey Sellerman from *Happy Valley Realty*. If you must play at private eye, perhaps this is a clue and you should look this person up. He might be, what do they call it, a person of interest?"

Jason followed Chelsea's voice into the bedroom and walked over to the closet.

"Come on, Chelsea. Give me a break. This doc was killed by someone using an electric hand-held mixer. That's clearly Debbie's MO. She probably met him here for a little of that cheerleader fantasy, she got mad at something, and out came the electrical appliance. We need to interview Debbie again, do a background check, find out if she's ever been to this condo and if she knew the victim. Maybe she's a black widow realtor…kills her clients. Or, how about a combination black widow realtor and chef, explaining the electric hand-held mixer."

Chelsea said, "Have it your way. But, I still think he's too old for her. I'm pretty sure a *black widow realtor* is not a thing. Hard to succeed as a realtor if you murder all your buyers. And, anyone could have thrown an electrical appliance into the tub. I'll make a note of this business card. I won't contaminate the crime scene by taking it with me."

Jason looked in the closet at the coat and business card. He turned and waved Chelsea off, dismissing this so-called evidence.

"Do as you wish, Dear. But, I'm sure this is all about Debbie. Makes me sad. Ruins any future cheerleader fantasies."

"Yes, that's definitely the problem here. We can't play cheerleader anymore."

Chapter 7

Chelsea let Jason sleep in the guest bedroom again that night, a definite step up from the red rocket. She planned to give in and let him back into their bedroom eventually; she couldn't hold out forever. She needed to figure out some way to get his romantic juices flowing.

The next morning, Chelsea didn't feel like fixing breakfast, so they sat at the kitchen table drinking coffee. At least she had made Jason some half-caff, so he wasn't stuck with her *overly caffeinated sludge*, as he called it. Debbie had been released on bail, and Jason told Chelsea that he planned to interrogate her in person about the murder of Dr. Forester. He called Debbie to make an appointment to meet her, and Chelsea told him to put the call on speaker. She took a sip of her coffee as she listened.

"Hello, is this Debbie, the realtor? This is PI Longfellow, you know, the guy you attacked with an electric hand-held mixer. We need to talk. Where can we meet?"

"Dr. Longfellow? Is that you? I'm so sorry for the other day. I don't know what happened. I just lost it. I'd love to meet with you and your lovely wife, to apologize in person. Perhaps we could meet at the same condo. It's still on the market, you know."

"That's okay, Debbie. Don't worry about it. You must be under a lot of stress, what with not being a cheerleader anymore. Cheerleader to realtor is a difficult transition. We'll meet you there, say at one this afternoon?"

On hearing this, Chelsea choked on a sip of coffee. *Cheerleader to realtor is a difficult transition?*

Debbie said, "Excellent. I'll see you then."

Jason disconnected the call and turned to Chelsea. "I need to interrogate Debbie. I'm convinced she's the one that killed this Dr. Forester. I'm sure I can get her to confess."

"Jason. Do you really have to get me involved in this mess? I'd rather go downtown. There's a craft show today, with pottery and glass blowing demonstrations."

"How can you think about craft stuff when there's a killer with a foot?"

"A killer with a foot? Now you're Sherlock Holmes? And, the saying goes *now the game's afoot*. Never mind. You make me crazy."

"Just trying to sound professional."

"God, help me. So, tell me again why I'm coming with you? You're the PI. You should be able to handle one perky little realtor on your own. Also, you know that if I catch you playing cheerleader with anyone, you'll wind up like Dr. Forester, only deader."

"Make your jokes, Woman. But, I'm damn well gonna catch this killer, or my name isn't…"

"Sherlock Holmes?"

"No, PI Longfellow. Now, come along my wifely assistant. I'm gonna get a confession out of this lady realtor."

They were meeting Debbie at the same two-bedroom, two-bath condo unit as before. Chelsea liked riding around in the blazing Florida sun in a realtor's air conditioned SUV a lot more than the red rocket. Worse, a very large SUV almost ran over the red rocket on A1A when Jason pulled out in front of it. It scared Chelsea so badly she pulled the oh-my-god-bar clean off of the rocket's dashboard. Having survived the trip, Jason parked in front of the condo, and Chelsea handed him the broken car part. He looked sad and tossed it on the passenger side floor. They got out and walked up the stairs.

"Chelsea, are you okay? You broke my car. I'll have to get some duct tape to reattach the thing to the dash board."

Chelsea said, "Jason, sorry I broke your little clown car, but you almost got us killed, again. How about you? Are you okay? You seem kind of wobbly."

"I'm having déjà vu all over again. It was only a couple of days ago that I almost lost my life in this condo. Now, I'm back to catch a killer. Damn! I forgot to pack heat."

"Do you have a concealed carry permit for Florida?"

"I'm not sure. They have that reciprofication thing, or whatever it's called. But, I forgot to look up whether or not Florida and Virginia are both part of it."

"I think you mean *reciprocity*, as in the states recognize each other's CCW permits. It's probably for the best. If you'd had your little gun the other day, you might have shot me by accident, and then I wouldn't have been able to save you."

"That's true. It might have put my life in danger if I'd shot you by accident. That wouldn't have been good."

Chelsea sighed. "You don't need your little gun anyhow. If the perky realtor threatens you again, you can run her a bath and when she gets in you can toss her a toaster. Just don't forget to plug it in first."

Jason knocked on the condo door. Debbie answered and invited them in. Chelsea noticed that Debbie wore a short black skirt and tight teal and gold V-neck sweater, an outfit that looked a lot like a cheerleader's uniform.

"Do you like, Dr. Longfellow? You said I looked like a cheerleader, and I didn't want to disappoint. These are the Jacksonville Jaguars colors. I thought it might put you in the mood to buy a condo. And, you're right. The transition from cheerleader to realtor has been stressful. I'm sure that's what caused me to go off and try to kill you."

Chelsea winced. *God help us. She's crazier than my husband.*

Jason and Chelsea followed Debbie into the living room and took seats on the couch. Debbie sat in a comfortable looking accent chair across from them, a wooden coffee table in between. Chelsea frowned. Jason kept staring at Debbie's legs.

"Debbie. You look really great, and I do approve. But, we're not here to buy the condo. And, I'm only allowed to play cheerleader with my wife. Right, Chelsea? Anyhow, we found a man, a Dr. Forester, dead in a nearby condo complex yesterday. I wanted to ask you a few questions, since you turned into psycho realtor and tried to puree my face. I am a private eye, you know."

Chelsea sat there, quietly seething at the sight of Jason ogling Debbie. *Damn men. All they think about is sex, sex, sex, with other women. He'll check out her legs, but tonight with me he'll be too tired.*

Then she remembered the well-endowed doctor in the hot tub. She got a faraway look in her eyes; thought about how there must be other such men in the world, in Florida, in St. Augustine. To them, *she* would be the other woman. She returned to earth when she remembered her father's many love affairs and how badly it had hurt her mother.

Chelsea said, "Jason, please get on with it. Ask her your questions. If you get done in time, you can drop me off downtown so I can go to the craft show. This private eye stuff is your thing. I still don't know why I'm here."

Debbie looked disappointed. "But, Dr. Longfellow. I was under the impression that you and your wife were still interested in this wonderful condo. According to Karen, it's just what you are looking for; a two-bedroom, two-bath condo, well maintained. This one has an updated kitchen with new counter tops and stainless appliances, a new water heater, and a new heat pump. The colors are beautiful. It's low maintenance. Please tell me you're still interested."

Jason, looking at her legs. "Well, maybe just a little. You could show us around…"

Chelsea sat up straight, crossed her arms and clenched her fists.

"Jason, that's not why we're here. Just ask your questions and be done with it."

"But, Mrs. Longfellow. Don't you like the unit? The updated kitchen alone should be enough to sway you."

"As PI Longfellow will attest, I'm not much for kitchens, or cooking. I must admit, there is some draw to a place where two realtors tried to murder my lunatic husband. But we're just here so Jason can ask you some questions."

"Yeah, Debbie. Like, where were you all day yesterday? We hired another realtor, Rock Handsome. He took us to the *Sea Breeze Village*, where he showed us a nice three-bedroom condo, complete with dock and a hot tub full of dead doctor."

"A well-equipped dead doctor."

"Chelsea, that's not the point."

"Sorry, PI Longbottom. Ask your questions."

"You know my last name's Longfellow, just like yours."

"Okay, Sherlock. Get on with it."

"So, anyway Debbie, we found a dead doctor in the hot tub. He appeared to have been murdered with an electric hand-held mixer, like the one you tried to puree my face with. What do you know about this? Did you know this Doctor Forester? Did you arrange to meet him at that condo for a little hot tubbing? Were you sleeping with him and he refused to leave his wife, so you killed him? Or, did he ask you the price before you were finished with your tour, so you killed him? Spill it, Debbie. Did you kill this Doctor…"

"Doctor Large D…"

"Chelsea! Stop it! Doctor Forester."

Debbie stood up, looking visibly upset. She became animated as she talked. Chelsea was pleased to see Debbie distraught and defensive. It served her right for being all perky and cute.

Debbie pointed her finger at Jason accusingly and said, "Did the killer puree the doc's face with the mixer?"

Jason said, "No. It was plugged in and thrown into the hot tub with him. He was electrocuted."

"Then, see, it wasn't me. I only use a hand-held electric mixer to mess up my victim's face, like I tried to do to you, but the damned cord was too short. Throwing it in a tub full of hot water just doesn't cut it. Not violent enough. Now, are you interested in this fucking condo or not? Follow me, and let me give you the tour, again."

Chelsea was taken by surprise by Debbie's abrupt change in demeanor. She and Jason stood up and followed the realtor. Debbie led them through the living room-dining room area, outlining all the high points. Then, they followed her upstairs. Chelsea watched Jason, whose eyes were glued to Debbie's short skirt as it floated up the stairs ahead of him. Chelsea smacked him on the back of the head.

"Ouch! Woman, be careful. You'll give me a concussion."

As they walked, Jason continued to ask questions. "You're sure you don't know any Dr. Forester? He was an infectious disease specialist. You know, like malaria, mumps, meningitis, measles…Wow. That's fun. Chelsea, can you think of any more infectious diseases that begin with *M*?"

"Idiot."

"Not helpful. That's not an infectious disease, nor does it begin with *M*. Now, Debbie. Did you ever meet this Dr. Forester? Did you sleep with him? Did he give you an infectious disease, an STD perhaps? Is that why you killed him?"

Chelsea, exasperated. "Focus, PI Longfellow. Focus!"

"Yes, Dear. Come on, Debbie. Confess. You knew the doctor. You met him when you were in nursing school, or after nursing school when you were working at the local hospital."

"What kind PI are you? I'm a realtor. You know, that's why I'm trying to sell you this condo."

"Maybe you were a nurse, accidentally killed a patient, and had to go into realty to make ends meet. Confess, Woman. Why did you kill Dr. Forester? I know you did. The electric mixer gave it away."

At this point they had walked full circle, gone downstairs and reached the kitchen again. Chelsea had a bad feeling.

Debbie said, "You hardly paid any attention to my tour. You're not going to buy this condo, are you, you bastard? After all my work!"

She reached into a kitchen drawer, pulled out a metal meat tenderizing mallet, and whacked Jason above the elbow with it.

"Ouch. That hurt! Chelsea, she hit me. Make her stop."

"Are you sure you want me to stop her, PI Longbottom? This is important evidence that a hand-held electric mixer isn't her only weapon of choice. She seems to be just as happy with a manual meat tenderizing mallet. Hmmm. Those words all begin with *M* too. How fun!"

Chelsea watched as the perky realtor hit Jason again, this time on the shoulder. Debbie seemed intent on continuing until he was all tenderized and ready for the oven. When the realtor whacked him again, Chelsea took some pictures with her cell phone as evidence.

"Help! Chelsea! Stop taking pictures and do something! I don't have my gun thingy!"

"Jason, you'll be all right. Just don't bend over, and she can't reach your head."

Chelsea reached into the same oven drawer, pulled out the same frying pan, and thought the same thought as before; should she help him, or let nature take its course? She hit Debbie over her same head again. This truly was déjà vu.

Jason and Chelsea stood over Debbie's unconscious body. "Well, Jason. Share your in-depth analysis with me on the doctor's murder at this point. D'ya still think it was the perky Debbie?"

"Well, Chelsea. I can't say anything conclusive at this point. But, it does appear that I was wrong about the electric hand-held mixer being Debbie's only weapon of choice. Based on the bruises on my arm and shoulder, she's proficient with a metal meat tenderizing mallet, too."

"Maybe she's a cannibal, and she was trying to tenderize you, cook you and eat you for dinner. What d'ya think, Sherlock?"

"No, that's not likely either." He finally gave in. "Okay, Wife. You win. Maybe it wasn't Debbie. What was the name of the realtor on the business card you found in that jacket pocket?"

Chapter 8

Chelsea had told Jason the name on the realtor's business card, Jeffrey Sellerman, *Mountain Realty*. They had agreed that seemed like an odd name for a realty company in Florida.

The next morning, Jason came out of the guest bedroom after a good night's sleep. He filled his bowl with the cereal, chocked full of sugary treats, that Chelsea had placed on the kitchen table for breakfast. He added milk and ate while Chelsea sat sipping her morning coffee.

"Jason, I think you should phone Rock Handsome and ask him if he knows this Jeffrey Sellerman. I realize Mr. Handsome works for *ReallyRealty*, but they might know each other. I'd call Mr. Handsome, but he'd probably prefer to speak with you." She sounded sad.

"You bet, Chelsea. I'll give him a call, and we'll get to the bottom of this. My PI senses are at it again. I'm thinking this Sellerman fellow just might be the real murderer. Maybe he and old Rock were an item, this Dr. Forester got between them, and zip, boom, bang, Sellerman took the doc out of the picture."

"Zip, boom, bang? The guy was electrocuted. Wouldn't it make more of a sizzling sound? And, now this Dr. Forester is supposed to be gay? What happened to *hot tubbing* with Debbie?"

"Chelsea, you get too hung up on the details. Zip, boom, bang is a lot more dramatic. And, you said Debbie was too young for the doctor. So, maybe your good friend Rock was involved with the doc in some way."

Still sitting at the kitchen table, Jason called Rock Handsome at his office at nine AM.

"Hello, is this Rock Handsome, realtor? This is PI Jason Longfellow, the guy whose wife was checking out your ass the other day. Anyhow, do you know a realtor by the name of Jeffrey Sellerman? He works for *Mountain Realty*. Chelsea found his business card in the jacket pocket of that dead doctor we found in the hot tub. I no longer suspect Debbie the realtor as the killer. Last night she tried to kill me again, but this time she used a metal meat tenderizing mallet, not a hand-held electric mixer. So, there must be a different murderer, and I'm thinking it might by this Sellerman guy."

Rock paused for a few moments. "Dr. Longfellow? Is that you?"

"Yes, Rock. But, I'd prefer PI Longfellow, since I'm working a case. Just answer the question. Do you know this Sellerman guy, or not?"

"I do know a Jeffrey Sellerman. I think he works for *Mountain Realty*. I met him at the national realtor convention in Miami last year, but I don't know much about him."

"Are you sure about that? Sure you weren't having a fling with him, and old Doc Forester got in the way, so you sizzled him to death?" He turned towards Chelsea. "See, sizzled just doesn't do it. Doesn't sound very murdery."

"Dr…PI Longfellow. I haven't had a fling with anyone. I'm living with a partner, a jealous brute of a man who'd kick me across the street if I ever cheated on him. Please keep unhealthy thoughts like that to yourself. He might hear and go after you for spreading such rumors."

Kick Rock across the street? Yikes! Rock's a big guy. "Sorry. But, honestly it was Chelsea's idea. Sometimes she helps me with cases."

"Oh, PI Longfellow. My partner would never hit a woman. He'd go after her husband instead; hold him responsible."

"Of course he would. Isn't that kind of sexist? Well, nice talking to you."

Jason quickly disconnected the call. Chelsea just sat there, smiling.

"Well, Chelsea, you heard everything. Rock wasn't having a fling with anyone, and his big brute of a partner will beat up anyone who says otherwise."

"Maybe I should put in a call to him. What's his name? I'm sure Rock would be happy to share it with me."

"Easy there, Wife. I can't bed you if I'm broken."

"What's your excuse for the past two weeks?"

Jason took a drink of his now cold coffee, trying to look calm, cool and collected. He choked on it, and some came out his nose. He eventually got the coughing under control.

Jason said, "We need to focus on the case. We should pay the offices of *Mountain Realty* a visit and find this Jeffrey Sellerman. Maybe we can catch him in his office, where I can give him a ruthless interrogation."

"That's great. You could do lousy cop, idiot cop. You could play both parts."

"Chelsea. You're just mean. I'm sorry I haven't been more affectionate in the bedroom lately, but I'm tired. Buying a condo in Florida is draining, what with hurricanes, insurance, rust, alligators, snakes, sharks, and killer realtors. Then, there's all the dead bodies. This trip was supposed to be about finding a house, with some vacation fun thrown in. Now I've got a killer to catch. It makes me tired just thinking about it."

"Then stop thinking. That's not your strong suit. You're more of a…well, a worrier."

"I know. All that anxiety wears me out too."

Chelsea sighed.

Jason drove them to the offices of *Mountain Realty* in his little convertible. He and Chelsea were both sweating, their skin burning from the blazing August sun. Chelsea looked miserable, and cranky. It turned out that Jeffrey Sellerman was hosting an open house on Crescent Beach, a large oceanfront home. They had to get back into the red rocket, and Jason drove on to the open house; more heat, more misery. Jason was hungry, so he stopped for a fast food lunch on their way to Crescent Beach. He and Chelsea were sitting in a booth inside, with blessed air conditioning.

"Jason, why are we eating greasy fast food? St. Augustine has wonderful seafood restaurants; there's awesome fried shrimp and oysters, excellent fish and chips, sushi, crab, lobster; all kinds of baked and fried seafood. There's even a local rib shack with the best ribs on the planet. And, we're here at grease city, where it's anybody's guess if the meat's really meat. I don't know why I put up with you."

Jason smiled, took a big bite of his double cheeseburger, and shoved a couple of french fries into his mouth for good measure. After a couple of chews, he gulped the food down.

"Chelsea, you're eating a filet of fish sandwich. Besides, everyone knows all that seafood's full of mercury. In fact, a killer could get away with poisoning someone with mercury by simply claiming they ate too much seafood. That's like the perfect murder. I'd rather die from clogged arteries than mercury poisoning."

"Thanks for that helpful information. It's a shame I don't cook a lot. How much mercury does it take? The way you're wolfing down that burger, you're going to choke to death anyway, and I won't even have to resort to poisoning."

"Chelsea, stop screwing around. You'd never poison me. What would you do without me?"

"Have some peace? Go to an arts and crafts store? Buy a vacation condo? See fewer dead people?"

Jason wolfed down the rest of his double cheeseburger and large fries, Chelsea picked at her filet of fish, and then they were off to Crescent Beach. Jason pulled into the driveway of 1048 Crescent Beach Drive at one o'clock, and parked next to yet another gigantic luxury SUV. Jason pointed towards the house.

"Chelsea, look at this place. It's spectacular. Built up high on stilts like that, I'll bet the flood insurance is a lot lower. Can you imagine living in a gorgeous house like this, right on the beach? You could hear the waves, smell the salt water, see the ocean, enjoy the beautiful sunrises."

"Yeah, and remember what Rock said. You could also hear the rust forming and the rattlesnakes rattling in the dunes at night."

"Chelsea. You used to be so positive."

"This place must be worth a couple million dollars. I'm positive I'm going to strangle you if you even think about buying it. We could sell everything we own, including the children, and still wouldn't have enough."

"We could sell the children? How much do you think we could get?"

"Jason. I swear. We're here to talk to this Jeffrey Sellerman. I'm sweaty, sunburnt, and greasy from fast food. I don't want any of your nonsense."

Jason turned off the car. He extracted himself from the red rocket and followed Chelsea up the steps to the front door. It was open, so they went in. They found a tall, slender woman in her sixties, with the well-dressed appearance of a realtor. Jason thought her expensively styled hair was dyed a little too red, and might actually glow in the dark. He detected a strong odor of Chanel. The woman stood in a large foyer, her big brown eyes looking down at a man's body. To Jason, her face lift gone awry made the shocked look on her face appear cartoonish.

Jason walked up to her, and Chelsea followed. Jason spoke first. "Mr. Jeffrey Sellerman, I presume? Why's he lying on the floor? Is he taking a nap? Dead, perhaps? Are you his wife? Did you kill him? Come on. Tell the truth. Confess."

"Sorry. I'm Chelsea. This is my…husband…Dr. Jason Longfellow. He fancies himself a private eye, although I don't know of anyone who'd agree. We came here to speak with Jeffrey Sellerman, a realtor from *Mountain Realty*. We have some questions regarding the murder of a doctor, whose body we recently found in a condo we were looking at. Come to think of it, every time we visit a condo, a body turns up."

The woman looked at Jason, paused, and slowly blinked her eyes as if returning from somewhere else.

"My name is Joyce Connors. I'm a *ReallyRealty* agent, and I got here about twenty minutes ago. I stopped by to preview this property for one of my clients looking for oceanfront."

Jason perked up. The woman looked confused, and he had her on the rocks. He could get the truth out of her by pressing her with some clever questions before she had a chance to regain her footing. He took an aggressive step toward her.

"Aha! So you knew Jeffrey…Mr. Sellerman. Were the two of you having an affair that got out of hand? Did you kill him with an electric hand-held mixer?"

It looked to Jason like Joyce was still struggling to process recent events. Then, she stood up straight, looked him in the eye, and took an aggressive step towards him. Jason took two steps back. He saw Chelsea grin.

Joyce said, aggressively, "Do you see an electric hand-held mixer anywhere? Jeff was fine when I got here. I have no idea what killed him. We were talking about this property, when he began to twitch. Then he developed tremors, went into violent convulsions, and he fell to the floor. I felt for a pulse, but there wasn't one. I've known Jeff for ten years. Just fellow realtors, friends – nothing more. He used to work for *ReallyRealty*; that's where I first met him. It's a shame. This is such a beautiful property. If my client was interested, we could have shared a healthy commission."

Jason said, "This is an amazing house. Could you show us the place? I…we…might be interested."

"Jason, what did I tell you?"

"Chill, Chelsea. It can't hurt to look around, and we could come up with the money what with my day job, my weekend job, and your nursing administration job. That's a lot of jobs."

Joyce, less aggressive, said, "Well, I don't know. Shouldn't we call the police? It seems a little odd that Jeff should just convulse and die like that.

What if there's foul play involved? Don't we need to maintain the integrity of the crime scene?"

Chelsea said, "Yes, Jason. There's the crime scene integrity to consider."

Jason said, "Damn crime scene integrity. I wish I had slept through that hour online lecture."

"Dr. Longfellow, are you really interested in the property? It is quite nice. I guess it wouldn't hurt to show you around before phoning the police. Jeffrey isn't going anywhere, and there is that sizeable commission to consider. We can be careful where we step."

"Yeah, Chelsea. Mr. Sellerman isn't going anywhere. He's for sure not going to tell us anything about the doctor's murder. The doc was electrocuted and this realtor died from seizures, so their deaths probably aren't related. We don't even know for sure if Mr. Sellerman was murdered. I'm getting kinda used to finding dead bodies here in Florida. Come on, let's take a look at our future oceanfront home. Careful not to disturb anything."

"Idiot."

Joyce picked up a brochure. "Follow me, and I'll give you the tour."

Jason and Chelsea followed the realtor into a very large, open room.

Joyce said, "This looks like the living room. Oh my! Look at that beautiful view of the ocean. The ocean side of the house is all glass. According to the brochure, there are three bedrooms, two down here and a loft bedroom up those stairs. What a beautiful circular staircase. There's also a very large master bath with spa area, whatever that means. I guess we'll find out."

"Chelsea, just look at that view of the ocean. How would you like to get up to that every morning?"

"Jason, if we buy this place, we might get a month's worth of mornings before the bank repossesses it."

"Don't be such a negative Nellie. What are they asking, Joyce?"

Jason walked over to the large expanse of glass windows and looked out at the ocean, a big smile on his face. Chelsea sighed and shook her head.

"According to the pamphlet, they're asking two million. But, it's been on the market for a while, so you should be able to negotiate some on the price."

The realtor paused, appearing lost in thought. "You know, it's funny. Even though Jeffrey and I have been acquainted for ten years, I never really got to know him until the annual realtor convention in Miami this past year. There was a small group of us from St. Augustine that hung together. We had a blast. Miami's quite a party town. Anyhow, let's look at the master bedroom suite. I'm curious to see this *spa area*."

Chelsea sighed. "I hope this one comes without a dead body in the tub. We've already had our quota for the week."

Jason and Chelsea followed the realtor to the spa area, which turned out to be a separate hot tub, shower and steam room. Jason noted that the hot tub was large enough for his six-foot-seven frame. From there, they walked back into the living room and then out onto a large front deck.

Joyce said, "There's no screened-in area, but mosquitoes are not very strong fliers, and this beach usually has a nice breeze that keeps them away. No breeze tonight, though."

As if on cue, Jason saw the realtor swat at her arm, presumably to kill a mosquito.

"Ouch! I hate mosquitoes. Let's go back inside. This reminds me of that conference last year. I came home from Miami with several mosquito bites. I figured it was because Miami is so close to the Everglades, although I didn't spend that much time outside at night. Anyhow, what do you think about this place? Are you still interested, Dr. Longfellow?"

"What d'ya think, Chelsea? I'd even be willing to sell the red rocket to get a place like this."

"Jason, first of all, I think we need to phone the police, or we're going to end up in jail. And, second, I don't think you can do numbers in your head. How about a word problem? How many little red rockets would you have to sell to buy a house worth two million dollars? And, no, we can't sell the children!"

Chapter 9

Jason and Chelsea had spoken to the police for the third time in as many days. Chelsea had to explain what had happened after Jason started babbling that he was innocent in spite of all the dead realtors. The interviewing officer told Chelsea they weren't suspects because they had solid alibis for all the murders. Each time they had been with realtors who had vouched for them.

The morning after the visit to the oceanfront home, they were drinking coffee and eating rasher and egg brekkie pies from a cafe on A1A in St. Augustine. At Chelsea's request, Jason had fetched some. While they ate in the kitchen, they discussed how to spend the day.

"Jason. Maybe we should take the day off from condo hunting. Go to the beach. I'm afraid if another dead body turns up, you'll go to jail for sure."

"Me? But, you've been there…"

Jason was interrupted when his cell phone rang. He put it on speaker.

"Hello, PI Longfellow here."

"Hello, Dr. Longfellow. This is Rock Handsome. Have you found a condo yet?"

"No, but we're full up with dead bodies." He explained the events of the previous day.

"Well, I'd still like to find you a nice two-bedroom condo, if you're interested. But, it sounds like you need a day off."

"Chelsea and I were just thinking the same thing."

"Do you like fishing? I belong to a local boat club, and I've reserved a twenty-three-foot fishing boat for the day. Would the two of you like to go out into the Intracoastal and catch some fish? I know a couple of good places not too far from here."

Jason looked at Chelsea, who smile and nodded in the affirmative.

Chelsea said to the phone, "Sounds good to me, Rock. It might be fun to get out on the water. Take our minds off of the past few days. I'm not much of a fisherman though. You two can fish, and I'll just get some sun."

Jason said, "I agree, it sounds like a great idea. I'm a really good fisherman. Should we bring anything? Food, drinks, bait? We don't have to get in the water. Right? You know. Alligators, snakes, sharks…things that might consider us to be lunch."

They heard Rock say, "That's excellent. I've got everything we need, including fishing poles, plenty of bait, and I'll even bring lunch and a cooler of cold drinks. We'll have to stick to soda and water, though. The police are real sticklers about boating and drinking. And, no, you don't have to get into the water. How about you meet me at the marina in an hour?"

He gave Jason the address and Jason disconnected the phone.

"Okay, Chelsea. We're good to go. Get dressed and put on suntan lotion. Sounds like Rock's bringing everything else."

Chelsea pointed out that they weren't going swimming, so they both changed into shorts, cotton shirts, and caps to protect their heads. They also applied a generous amount of suntan lotion to exposed parts. Jason pulled the red rocket into the marina parking lot an hour later, with Chelsea all hot and sweaty again. Rock Handsome was waiting for them.

"Welcome. I'm glad you two could come along fishing. I figure it'll give you a chance to unwind from the stress of the last couple of days. Hunting for property can be murder."

Jason said, "Interesting choice of words. And, you're not wrong."

They followed the realtor up a flight of stairs, down another, and onto the pier. Chelsea was amazed by the large marina; dock after dock filled with everything from small pontoon boats to fifty-plus-foot yachts. There were powerboats, offshore racing boats, sail-powered yachts, gasoline-powered yachts…yachts, yachts, everywhere yachts. Rock stopped next to one of the 23-foot center-console Cobia boats.

Jason said, "My God, Rock, there must be a bazillion dollars-worth of *boatage* here. I've never seen so many gigantic yachts. I want one."

Chelsea rolled her eyes. Jason was like raising another child at times…most of the time.

Rock said, "I don't believe that *boatage* is an actual nautical term, but…"

Chelsea interrupted. "Jason does speak English, but he's been known to create his own version. He's not always concerned about the linguistic details. Just one more of the charming things about him…and by charming I mean annoying."

Rock laughed. "Interesting, a PI who ignores the details. Then, yes, the St. Augustine marina is full of *boatage*; as you can see, some really large *boatage*. More to the point…what was the point again? Oh, yes. We've got this nice twenty-three-foot Cobia with twin one-hundred-fifty horsepower Yamaha engines. I'm thinking we should avoid the ocean and stay in the Intracoastal today. It's choppy out there. So, climb aboard and let's get to it."

Chelsea was not an expert on boats, but she knew that this one was designed for fishing. It had a deep V hull design capable of handling the ocean. She climbed on board in spite of Jason, who offered her his hand and then tripped over one of the dock cleats, almost falling into the water. She sat in the three-person cushioned seat behind the wheel. Jason knocked over one of the three fishing poles resting upright on the front of the cabin, and nearly stepped in the bait bucket that sat nearby. Chelsea looked around and saw a depth meter and fish finder, radio, speedometer, anchor, a compartment full of life jackets, and a safety paddle. Her favorite part was the stainless steel hand rail put there to hang onto to keep from falling overboard.

There were also thickly cushioned seats extending from port to starboard in the stern and in the bow. Jason sat down in the bow of the boat.

Rock said, "Jason, you might not want to sit there. If we hit a wake or wave, you'll likely go flying up in the air and out of the boat."

Chelsea grinned. "I'm sure there's an alligator or shark who'd like a large lunch this time of day."

Jason moved quickly to the seat next to Chelsea. "Rock promised to keep you from falling out of the boat, so I'm going to hang next to you."

Rock smiled. "Looks like if your husband goes over the side, he plans on taking you with him. I'm not sure I can hang onto both of you."

Jason changed the subject. "What are we fishing for? I don't know anything about fishing in saltwater."

"Well, Jason we might go for some grouper, flounder, or a nice snapper. The red snapper have been biting for the past couple of days. They make for some good eating."

Rock untied the boat, climbed aboard and carefully navigated the narrow winding channel out of the marina and into the Intracoastal Waterway. Chelsea sat in the seat next to him. She was amazed that he drove the boat through the channel without hitting anything.

Jason said, "So, Rock. How long have you been fishing the waters around here?"

"I've lived in St. Augustine all my life. My father had a charter fishing business. I grew up working on the boats with him, but I didn't want to spend my life on the water. It got boring after a while. I met a lot of tourists on the job, and many of them ended up looking for vacation homes in the area. They'd often ask about St. Augustine while we were out fishing. That's how I got into real estate. I had more fun helping the tourists find the right property here in town than I did helping them catch fish. So, I took a class, the realty exam, and the rest is history."

Chelsea said, "What happened to your dad's business?

"He got old, sold the boats and the business and retired to Miami. He passed away two years ago. My mother lives in Orlando. She hated Dad's fishing charter business because he always came home smelling like fish. He also didn't earn enough to keep her happy. But, he loved being on the water and wouldn't give it up. She started drinking, graduated to martinis for breakfast, and they fought all the time. She blamed him for her drinking, and they got divorced when I was young. Mom kept on drinking; as it turned out she's an alcoholic. She and I grew apart over the years. I haven't spoken to her since I don't know when."

Chelsea said, "Sorry to hear that. Jason's dad, and my mother, had a drinking problem too. Seems there's a lot of that going around. AA must be a thriving organization."

Rock said, "Unfortunately, they don't all make it to AA."

Chelsea cringed when Rock barely made the last sharp turn without hitting a 50-foot yacht partially blocking the channel. They cruised the Intracoastal for half-an-hour. It was a beautiful day, but the sun was brutal. Chelsea kept thinking that a dip in the water would be really nice. Rock brought the boat to a stop near a small island and set the anchor.

"This is one of my favorite spots for catching snapper. Here's your pole, Jason. Just put one of these shrimp on the hook and fish near the bottom. If you feel a tug on the line, give it a yank, and hopefully you'll catch a nice big fish."

Chelsea took off her top and shorts to reveal a tiny bikini that she had added at the last minute, not bothering to tell Jason. She placed a towel on the back seat, and lay down to get some sun.

"Jason, would you please put some lotion on my back?"

Jason had already cast his line into the water. He leaned his pole up against the side of the boat, turned, and looked at Chelsea.

"I thought we weren't going swimming. If any boats go by, you're gonna cause a wreck wearing that skimpy thing."

"No swimming. Just thought I'd get some sun while we're out here."

Another fishing boat flew by, creating a sizeable wake. Jason stumbled over to Chelsea, the rocking boat making it difficult to walk. He slathered lotion on her back and more on her legs.

Chelsea said, "Jason, look over there on that island. Aren't those manatees on the beach? I thought they were larger than that."

Rock heard her. "Yes, Mrs. Longfellow. Those are manatees. They're females, which is why they're smaller. See that disturbance in the water just to the right of the island? That's several males, fighting for the right to mate with the females. When the females go into heat, they sometimes avoid the males by beaching themselves. The males are so large they can't crawl up on land. The males will remain nearby in a constant fight for dominance, to determine which ones get to mate when the females finally decide to return to the water."

Chelsea laughed. "See that big one over there by himself? He looks like he's taking a nap. That would be Jason."

"Chelsea. That's not nice. I told you, buying property in Florida is exhausting."

Jason finished applying lotion to Chelsea's back. Just as he turned to walk back to his fishing pole, the line jerked so hard that the pole was lifted up and over the side of the boat. Chelsea watched as Jason dove for the pole, tripped and fell over the side into the water.

"Chelsea! Help! I'm in the water. Alligators! Snakes! Sharks! Rust!"

"Mr. Handsome. Would you please help my husband back into the boat? I couldn't stand another dead body, and he's probably also scaring the fish. Jason, you're not going to rust."

Jason yelled. "Wife. Your concern is underwhelming. Will somebody please help me?"

As Jason swam towards the ladder, Chelsea pointed in the direction of the water.

"Jason, look. That turbulent water seems to be moving in your direction. Maybe you should swim faster."

"Dr. Longfellow. I'd recommend you hurry. You are most definitely being pursued."

"Oh, God! Is it an alligator? A hungry shark? Help me!"

Rock cringed. "It's much worse. It's a school of horny manatee."

The churning, bubbling water reached Jason, and he was surrounded by several very large frenzied manatees, some up to four-hundred pounds. Chelsea watched in awe as one of the males lowered its head, charged Jason and head-butted him in the stomach. Another raised partially out of the water and came crashing down on Jason's head. The one that most concerned Chelsea was trying to hump Jason's right leg. That one kept pulling him underwater.

Jason, coughing and sputtering. "Chelsea! Help! Horny manatee attack! Call the Coast Guard!"

Rock said, "I'll be damned. I've spent a lot of years on the water. But, this is the first time I've ever seen a male manatee try to hump anything other than a female of his own species. I've got to get a picture of this."

"Yes, Mr. Handsome. My husband has many special talents. Attracting an amorous manatee doesn't surprise me at all."

Chelsea watched helplessly as Jason struggled to escape the overexcited horde of manatees, until a couple of the females re-entered the water.

"Look, Jason. The females are coming to your rescue. You must have made them jealous."

Jason finally managed to reach the ladder. "Someone please give me a hand. That was terrifying. I thought they were going to drown me. What's wrong with them? I don't look anything like a manatee."

Rock gave Jason a hand. As Jason stepped onto the deck, the realtor winked at him.

"Are you sure you're playing on the right team? Sometimes animals detect things that humans can't."

Chelsea laughed, completely relaxed from the intense Florida sun, and a couple of glasses of wine from a bottle that she had smuggled on board.

"Rock, you may be right. I'm beginning to wonder about PI Longfellow myself. Maybe I should have jumped overboard. Those male manatees were starting to look pretty good. Jason, you need to do better."

"Wife, you know I'm playing for the hetero team. I'll show you tonight. Maybe we should stop for some energy drinks on the way home. And, I'll take a nap to rest up. One thing's for sure, I need to modify my list of dangerous things in Florida that'll kill ya. Hurricanes, alligators, snakes, rust, sharks, realtors, and horny manatees."

Rock grinned. "And, you'll have proof once I post this video on the internet."

Chapter 10

Jason was up at seven o'clock the next morning. Exhausted and sunburnt from their day on the water, he had been happy to sleep in the second bedroom again. He was too tired and sore to engage in any marital gymnastics, and Chelsea had made it clear she felt the same way. He had gone to a local French bakery with excellent pastries and strong, dark brewed coffee. He sat in the kitchen, choking down the strong coffee and eating an omelet croissant. When Chelsea finally showed up, he pointed to a paper bag sitting across the table.

Chelsea removed her own coffee and omelet croissant from the bag, spread it out on the table in front of her and began to nibble on the pastry.

"Good morning Jason. Thanks for breakfast. Did you sleep well?"

"Not really. I had nightmares all night."

"Let me guess. You dreamed that you were rusting."

"Don't be a smart ass, Wife. No, I was being chased by alligators, poisonous snakes…"

"And amorous manatees? So, that's why I heard you screaming. I hope you didn't wear yourself out running away. You need to take care of your wife tonight."

"I'll try to do better. I might have just the thing to get my juices flowing. I'm thinking we should take the day off from house hunting and do something fun again, like we did yesterday, minus the over-friendly sea creatures. I'm thinkin' something manly."

Jason shoved the remaining half of his croissant in his mouth, gave it a couple of chomps and swallowed. Chelsea took a nibble of her croissant, and washed it down with the strong coffee.

She said, "I know I'm going to regret asking, but what do you have in mind? We only have a couple of weeks left to find a place, and we haven't found a condo without a dead body yet."

"That's true, but I want to…"

"I'm not going on some bizarre search for clues. It's not your job to find out how the realtor died. You don't even know if it was murder. He could have had a heart attack."

He took a drink of the strong black coffee and choked. How could Chelsea drink this stuff?

"Cool your jets, Woman. I'm on vacation. I'll get around to solving that mystery eventually. No, I was thinking that this is Florida, where bad-ass motorcycles rules. How about we rent a chopper for the day and cruise the Ocala National Forest? It's full of trails, springs, rivers, parks…real rugged terrain. Just the kind of place a motorcycle guy might choose to roam. That should get the old testosterone flowing."

"So, now you're a tough motorcycle guy? What about alligators, snakes, and rust, Mr. Motorcycle Guy? And, what's a chopper?"

"Shouldn't be a problem if we stay on the main roads. I said there was rugged terrain. I didn't say I wanted to explore that part. A chopper's a cruising bike, with lots of power, somewhere around one-thousand cc. You'll look great sitting up on the back, hanging onto me."

Jason's cell phone rang. Startled, he spilled coffee on the table; a good thing. Less of the swill to drink. Wiping it up with a napkin, he answered the phone.

"Hello. PI Longfellow here. I've caught a serial killer, helped my wife catch a cheese thief, and even captured a monkey burglar. How can I be of service?"

Jason put the phone on speaker.

"Hello, Dr. Longfellow. This is Joyce Connors, the realtor from the other day. I thought you might want to know that I heard back from the police about Jeffrey Sellerman. They have a cause of death."

"Hello Joyce. It's nice to hear from you. I'm sorry to say that I can't talk my wife into selling the children, so we won't be able to afford that beautiful oceanfront home."

Chelsea sat there finishing her coffee and listening to the phone.

"Hello, Ms. Connor. This is Chelsea. What did the police say about the cause of death? And, on the other subject, I'd sell my husband to get that beautiful house, but I'm afraid I'd actually have to pay someone to take him."

"Chelsea, that's not nice. I'm sure there are lots of women out there that would be happy to buy me."

"I doubt that, although come to think of it, maybe I should offer you to Rock Handsome at a discount. It's a shame manatees don't deal in cash."

Joyce Connor interrupted. "If the two of you could stop trying to sell off members of your family for just a moment, I'll tell you the cause of death. According to the coroner, Jeff died from convulsions caused by the West Nile virus. They told me you get infected by a mosquito bite. Most people who get the virus don't show any symptoms. The authorities seem to think this is an especially virulent strain of West Nile, and they are sending samples to the CDC for testing. They said they found virus in Jeff's central nervous system, which is unusual, but probably explains the seizures."

Jason chimed in. "So, there's no murder to solve? Seems the killer is a mosquito. Didn't you get bitten by a couple of mosquitoes when we went out on the deck at that ocean front home?"

Chelsea chuckled. "Jason, look at you. Look how you solved this case so fast. You won't even need your little gun to catch the killer, just a can of bug spray."

The realtor was not amused. "You jest. But, Jeff died from convulsions. If there is some especially dangerous West Nile virus around here, it would be nice to know. Although I'm not sure what we could do about it."

"I know what I'm going to do. I'm going to put it on my list of things that can kill you in Florida."

"Jason, Florida's a beautiful place. I like it more and more every day that we're here. Everyone's so friendly, especially the sea creatures."

"Ha, ha, Woman. Next time, it's your turn to fall off the boat."

***

They finished their breakfast. Jason threw the bag, paper plates, cardboard cups and plastic forks in the trash can under the kitchen sink.

Jason said, "Okay, Dear. I'm off to the motorcycle dealership. I've already scoped them out online and reserved a brand new cruiser rental for the day, 1200 cc of raw power. I'll be back in a few."

"You already rented a motorcycle? But, I haven't agreed to it yet." She threw up her hands. "Oh, all right. I give up. While you're gone I'll call my mother to see how the kids are doing. We should have called earlier, but with all the excitement…"

Jason rushed out the door, trying to avoid an extended conversation about pool parties, shopping and other girl stuff. They were still children, and they could already stay on the phone with Chelsea for hours.

"Give the girls my love. Tell them I'll talk to them next time we call, and tell Lizzy to be good at that pool party."

He was out the door before Chelsea had time to argue. She yelled in his general direction.

"Jason, I'm not thrilled that you rented a motorcycle without talking to me first. This had better get your testosterone flowing. The way you drive, you should probably add motorcycle to the list of things in Florida that are trying to kill us. I can't believe I'm agreeing to this."

An hour later, Jason pulled up in front of the condo and revved the chopper engine. He was pretty sure if Chelsea heard the loud vroom she would recognize it. Jason had recorded a motorcycle commercial from TV and he listened to the sound track of a roaring chopper all the time, fantasizing about cruising down the highway.

Jason shut off the engine and entered the condo. "Hello, Motorcycle Momma. Are you ready to ride?"

Chelsea seemed distracted when Jason came charging into the condo. He surprised her, and she jumped.

She said, "I spoke to Mom and the girls. They're doing fine. Lizzy went to the pool party, and the boy we were worried about had the flu and didn't attend. I got the impression from Mom-Mom that she'd prefer we come home sooner rather than later. Our little monkeys can be a handful. Their constant bickering is enough to drive you over the edge. I gave them your love."

The she turned and looked at him. "What are you supposed to be? With the helmet, black leather jacket and pants, black shirt and boots, you look like a spaceman...or some weird ninja."

He handed her a shopping bag. "The dealership had a sale on motorcycle gear. Here's some stuff for you. There's no helmet law in Florida, but I thought it might be a good idea. The helmet and thick leather clothing should protect us from alligators, poisonous snakes and mosquito bites. Otherwise, I'd just ride in shorts and a t-shirt."

Chelsea shook her head, sighed, and took the bag. "That makes perfect sense. When riding a motorcycle on a busy highway, it's definitely the alligators, poisonous snakes and mosquitoes that are the problem. Give me a minute to change."

She came out of the bedroom ten minutes later, all decked out in tight leather pants, a leather shirt with zipper at half-mast that revealed her still youthful curves, and heavy leather boots. She carried the helmet under her arm. Jason's jaw dropped and his eyes bulged slightly.

"Oh, Babe. Those pants really show off that prize-winning ass of yours. I was hoping the motorcycle rental would get me going. I should have just bought you that outfit. If I hadn't spent a fortune on the rental, we might consider staying here and I could just jump your bones now."

"I wouldn't mind that. It would be safer, and my bones have been ready to be jumped for days. But, you're going to need a can opener to get me out of this outfit. What do you mean, you spent a fortune?"

Jason took a couple of steps back. Her tone had changed abruptly from lust to anger. Jason was a man, and could only think about one thing or feel one emotion at a time. Chelsea could change emotional states or switch conversational topics in a nanosecond, with no warning or context. He knew had no chance of ever keeping up, or understanding how she did it.

"Well…I have a motorcycle license that I got online in Virginia. I had to pass a quick driving safety test, but they just made me drive in a straight line. You know, show that I could stop and go. I thought that would be good enough for Florida, but turns out you need something called a *motorcycle endorsement*, a separate license to drive a bike. The good news is the guy at the dealership was flexible. The bad news, his flexibility required a substantial bribe, and I had to get the most expensive insurance policy. Then there was the cost of the actual motorcycle rental."

"How much, Jason?"

"Well…Let's just say I could have bought half a motorcycle for the price of the day's rental. But I thought you'd be pleased. I know you don't want me to own one."

"Idiot! Let's get this over with. If you kill me on that thing, I'll strangle you in your sleep."

Jason started to point out the flaw in her logic, but thought better of it. He led her out the door and showed her the motorcycle. It was jet black, low slung, with a raised passenger seat, cushioned seat back, an oversized rear tire and lots of chrome. Jason got on the bike, started it up and signaled for her to take her place behind him. He sat there revving the engine. After several minutes of his enjoying that manly sound, she smacked him on the back of the helmet, which was surprisingly painful. He got the message and hit the road, before she hit him again.

He had already chosen the route and set it up on his GPS. He surprised himself at how well he handled the bike, considering the high rise handlebars were awkward to control. Around noon, they stopped for fast food. They were sitting at one of the outdoor tables, eating their burgers in a bag.

"Jason, I have to admit, this is fun. To be honest, I had some doubts about your ability to drive that thing. But, you're doing great. Other than the fact that I'm sweltering in this leather getup in the August sun, I'm having a good time."

"I told you Chelse. I know what I'm doing. I aced that online motorcycle class, and I got an *A* on starting, stopping and driving in a straight line. I'm for sure a motorcycle guy."

"So, where do we go from here?"

"The Ocala National Park starts just up ahead. According to the map on my cell phone, there are several well-maintained dirt roads that run off the main highway, some of which go to Lake George. I thought we might explore a couple of those. I'll stay on the main roads though. Wouldn't want to wander off onto any of the dirt trails, where the lethal creatures hang out."

Chelsea threw their trash in a bin. They put on their helmets and mounted the bike. Jason pulled onto the highway and had to hit the gas to keep from getting run over by a tractor-trailer. Chelsea squeezed him so hard he thought she might have cracked a rib. After a couple of miles, he saw a sign for Ocala National Park. The road was well-paved, smooth and straight. They were surrounded on both sides by palm trees and endless swamp. Jason's mind wandered to eerie thoughts of swamp monsters and giant snakes. Fifteen miles into the park he turned left onto a wide, smooth dirt road with a sign that said *Lake George, 10 Miles*. He gained confidence with every mile. He liked Chelsea's arms around him. On the bike he was her rock, keeping her safe.

She's been giving me a hard time about our love life. I think she's started questioning my manhood. I'll show her how manly I really am.

Jason kicked the bike down a couple of gears and accelerated. The large engine threw them backward violently, and it felt like Chelsea might have crushed his chest.

Chelsea screamed, "Jason, what are you doing? You almost threw me off!"

He slowed so she could hear him. "No worries. I just feel like bustin' loose. Hang on. We're gonna have some real fun. And, take it easy on my rib cage."

He accelerated again, kicking up a cloud of dust behind them. He saw a small trail just ahead, off to the right. "Screw it," he mumbled. "We're going off road. That's what bikes are for."

He slowed the motorcycle slightly, down shifted, and abruptly turned onto the trail. Chelsea yelped. She squeezed him so hard he thought his head was going to pop off.

Chelsea yelled above the roar of the bike, "You said you'd stay on the main roads! What are you doing?! What's that up ahead? Jason, look out!"

She barely got the words out of her mouth, when he saw the large alligator slowly ambling across the dirt path.

"Oh Shiiiiiit! Hang on, Chelsea. This is gonna hurt!"

The front wheel hit the gator in the side and bounced up and over, the rear wheel obediently following. The motorcycle bucked like an angry bronco. Jason went flying in one direction, and he saw Chelsea go flying in the other. On his way to the ground, he also saw the bike continue forward until it slowly merged with a palm tree and fell over into a pool of murky swamp water.

Jason had landed on his head and was lying barely conscious, only a few feet from the alligator. He saw a blurry Chelsea get up, looking around frantically. She was waving her arms and pointing to something to his right.

As full consciousness returned, he heard, "Jason, get up! The gator is headed your way, and unlike that manatee I don't think he wants to hump your leg. He looks like he plans to have you for lunch!"

Jason turned his head and saw the approaching alligator. He tried to move, but his left arm was pinned under him. The gator was moving surprisingly fast for such a large creature.

"Jason, throw your helmet at the thing! Maybe that'll scare it away!"

Jason unfastened the chin strap with his free arm just as the gator started to clamp down on the helmet with its powerful jaws. He tried desperately to move, but his left arm refused to push him up off the ground.

"Chelsea! Help! He's gonna eat me!"

Chelsea tugged on Jason's legs with all her might. Jason heard the crunch as the helmet was crushed between the gator's powerful jaws, only seconds after Jason's head exited the protective device. He managed to get his right arm under him and push himself to his feet.

"Jeez, Chelsea. That could have been my head."

His knees started to wobble, and he leaned against a tree until his legs were firmly under him again. Meanwhile, the gator dropped the helmet and started looking for fresh meat.

Chelsea yelled, "Jason, pick up the bike, start it up and let's get out of here before this guy comes after us again, or worse, his friends show up."

Jason was using his right hand to support his left arm, which was dangling useless at his side.

"I think my left arm's sprained or broken. I can't move it. You're going to have to drive."

"I don't know how to drive a motorcycle. Now look what you've gotten us into."

"Wife, I warned you that Florida is trying to kill us." He started swatting at the air with his good arm. "Crap! Now I'm getting eaten by mosquitoes. Get us out of here!"

Chelsea was also swatting at a cloud of mosquitoes. She pointed at the large alligator moving slowly in their direction again. Jason was impressed as he watched her bend down, grab the handle bars and use a large surge of adrenaline to pick the motorcycle up, climb on and start it.

"Jason, get on. Let's get out of here while we're still in one piece. Why'd you have to get these raised handlebars? I can barely reach them. I know how the clutch and brakes work, but how do you shift this thing?"

He gave her a quick lesson, and she revved the engine and headed for the main road. Jason hung onto her for dear life with his one good arm. She only wobbled a little for the first few feet. Jason was surprised, and a little sad, to see how easily she got the hang of it. She drove them home like a pro, not stopping until they pulled up in front of their rental condo.

After a visit to the ER for an X-ray and confirmation that the arm was not broken, they headed to the motorcycle dealership to return the bike. Chelsea rode the bike, and Jason followed in his car, struggling to steer and work the floor shifter with his sore arm.

Outside the dealership, Chelsea said, "Jason, you're going to explain this mess to the manager. I don't want any part of it."

Jason watched her park the brand new motorcycle, full of dings, scratches and a torn leather seat, in front of the building. She dismounted the bike and climbed into the passenger's seat of the red rocket to wait. Jason went inside the dealership, his arm now in a sling, more for sympathy than out of necessity. He asked for the same manager who had rented him the motorcycle.

"Hello. I'm here to return your bike. We had a little mishap, but I'm sure the insurance will cover it. I planned to stay on the main roads, but my wife is a wild one. She coaxed me into going off road, onto a dirt path. She likes my bod, and she wanted us to find an isolated spot where we could…well…you know. Unfortunately, we went one-on-one with an alligator, and the gator won. So, there's a few dings and scratches on the bike. Nothing a little paint won't fix. Sorry about that, but if you've ever been married, you'll understand." He shrugged. "Wives. What can you do?"

The manager was not sympathetic. He threatened to tell the authorities that Jason had lied about having a Florida motorcycle endorsement. Jason had to come up with more bribery money. He returned to the red rocket, where Chelsea was waiting.

"So, Motorcycle Guy, how'd that go?"

"I apologized and told him it was all my fault. But, he said that since I don't have the proper motorcycle endorsement for Florida, the insurance policy I paid for won't cover the damages. So, I gave him some more money. I know this was an expensive adventure, but I had a blast. How about you? Did you have fun?"

"Oh yes! Crashing into an alligator on a motorcycle, much more fun than looking for a vacation home. Not to mention the mosquito bites. We'll probably get that West Nile thing. What do you have in store for us tomorrow? Perhaps we could go to Marineland and jump in the shark tank. You first. I'll chum the water."

"I know you're angry, but the good news is that I'm aroused…ready for some chica-wow-wow. How about it? You'll have to be on top though. I did hurt my arm."

"Idiot. Now you want to mess around? After almost killing me? If I hadn't pulled you out of that helmet, you'd be the headless PI. That gator wanted to rip you apart. Come to think of it, I'm getting aroused too. Come on. Drive me home and let's go up to bed. Take that ridiculous sling off of your arm. Maybe I'll use it to tie your hands to headboard."

"Uh oh. Chelsea scary, just like Florida. Jason afraid."

Chapter 11

Next morning, Chelsea was awakened by Jason shaking her shoulders. As consciousness returned, she heard the sound of wind and heavy rain. Then, she saw Jason standing over her on her side of the bed, still in his underwear.

"Chelsea. Wake up. Bad news. Florida's trying to kill us again."

Groggy, half asleep, she rolled over. "Huh? What are you whining about? Sounds like it's raining out. Good morning to sleep in. Go back to sleep."

"That's what I'm trying to tell you. According to the weather app on my phone, there's a hurricane, Hurricane Albatross, headed straight for Jacksonville…you know, the Jacksonville just a couple of miles north of here. According to the National Weather Service, it's supposed to hit land as a category four hurricane. That's bad, right?"

"That's not too bad. I did a little research online, this being Florida and all, and a cat four hurricane only has sustained winds of one-hundred-thirty to one-hundred-fifty miles per hour. Your little red rocket might fly away, but this concrete condo should be fine. Our only problem would be if the local government calls for a mandatory evacuation."

Chelsea saw Jason race over to the window and look out.

"One-hundred-fifty miles per hour? Forced evacuation? We're gonna die! I'd rather rust!"

Jason walked over and stood next to his side of the bed. Chelsea, now fully awake, sat up and reached for her cell phone on the bedside dresser.

"Jason, calm down. People here in Florida survive hurricanes all the time. My sister told me that the National Weather Service never gets it right anyhow. In Florida they call them the *weather terrorists*, because they always exaggerate these storms to increase their TV ratings. They're calling for…what was the name? Albatross?...to hit land at Jacksonville. What that really means is it will hit the East Coast somewhere between Miami and Nova Scotia."

A strong blast of wind blew by the front window, over the parking lot. Chelsea looked at her cell phone.

"Look, Jason. The hurricane isn't supposed to be here until tonight around midnight. It's down near Miami right now. We've been so busy with house hunting, wild creatures and dead bodies that we haven't been watching the news. As of now, there's no mandatory evacuation. Maybe a little early morning delight will take your mind off of things?"

She turned to look at Jason. She heard from under the bed, "How can you think about sex at a time like this? We're gonna blow away. I should probably chain my red rocket to the nearest palm tree."

"For God's sake. Come out from under there. You're no safer there and you could choke on a dust bunny. The building is made of concrete, and the safest place to be in a hurricane, or tornado, is in the bathroom in the middle of the condo. Hide in the tub."

Chelsea saw Jason's head pop out from under the bed.

"You and your sister, suggesting a vacation home in Florida. I had no idea there were so many ways to die here. Gators, poisonous snakes, sharks, hurricanes, pythons, realtors, rust and viruses? What the hell!? Do you have a death wish? And, I think I'm stuck."

"You need to calm down. You're the most nervous PI on the planet. You want to chase murderers, and you're afraid of a little weather? I'm going to start calling you *the Panicky PI*."

Chelsea couldn't help but chuckle as she watched Jason struggle to wiggle out from under the bed. He sat down next to her.

"Wait a minute, Chelsea. Did you say tornadoes? Why did you say tornadoes? I thought Albatross was a hurricane?"

"It's not uncommon for tornadoes to form from a hurricane once it hits land. But, not to worry. Like I said, this Albatross will probably hit Miami, or Nova Scotia. We can turn on the TV and watch the weather terrorists if you'd like, but it'll probably scare you even more."

"Great idea, Chelsea. You make some coffee, and I'll find the local weather."

Chelsea put on a robe and went into the kitchen. She heard the TV in the living room come on, and a weatherwoman began reporting on the hurricane. A few minutes later, Chelsea found Jason sitting on the sofa watching TV in his underwear. She handed him a cup of coffee.

"Holy crap, Chelsea. They're still saying this thing's going to hit Jacksonville as a cat four. The weather guy read a list of things to prepare…bottled water, paper products, eggs, milk, bread, candles, and a generator in case the power goes out. He's also been talking about heavy flooding. Maybe we should buy a canoe and leave it here in the living room. I'm gonna go out to the grocery store as soon as I finish my coffee and get us some supplies. You board up the windows and fill the bathtub with water, or not. I'm confused about that. If you fill up the tub so you have water in case the water goes out, and then hide in the tub, won't you drown? We're also supposed to go to high ground, but there isn't any.

While you figure those things out, I'll go forage for some supplies. Women just shop, but a real man forages."

"It might not be a bad idea for you to go to the store and get us some bottled water, paper products, bread, milk and eggs, just in case Albatross stays on its current course. Get a couple of flashlights and some batteries, too. But, it's not our condo, so I'm thinking no to boarding up the windows. As to a canoe, if it gets that bad we should probably just climb onto the roof. You don't want to be paddling around in a canoe with all the alligators, snakes, sharks and amorous manatee swimming by if the flooding is bad." She grinned her evil grin. "As to the tub thing, we'll just have to hold our breath. I get to be on top."

Jason looked terrified. He gulped down the coffee, grabbed his keys and headed for the door.

"Oh, PI Longfellow. You'd better put on some pants, or you might end up in jail. That'd spice up your sex life, but not in a good way."

"Might be safer there. But no worries. I won't abandon you, Wife. I'm going out to forage for hurricane supplies to take care of you. If anything happens to me, tell the girls I loved them."

"The only danger you're likely to run into is the crazy people in the grocery store fighting for what's left on the shelves. If you see any dead bodies, just ignore them and come home with the goods. You can always investigate the ones that don't blow away later."

Chelsea watched Jason out the window as he ran to the red rocket, started her up and headed for the local grocery store. *He has no idea what he's in for. Oh well. I'll just sit here and sip my hot coffee in peace. I'm feeling kind of mellow after last night. I should have tied his hands to the headboard a long time ago. At least that, and that leather motorcycle mamma outfit he bought me, finally got him going.*

Two hours later, Chelsea heard footsteps outside, on the stairs up to the condo. Then she heard Jason unlock the door and saw him enter the hallway. Soaking wet, his nose bleeding, left eye bruised, shirt ripped, the knees of his pants torn and blood soaked, he was holding a single soggy roll of toilet paper out in front of him like a precious treasure.

"My God, Jason. What happened?"

"Something else to add to my list of things in Florida that want to kill you…crazy people before a hurricane. It was horrible, Chelsea. The parking lot was a demolition derby. It was worse inside the store; people pushing, shoving, fighting, punching, weaponizing shopping carts…scrambling to fill their carts with the last gallon of milk…loaves of bread and broken eggs everywhere. Oh, the humanity! I managed to snag this roll of toilet paper when two women fighting over a twelve pack ripped it open, throwing TP everywhere. We can dry it out. At least we'll have TP when Albatross hits."

Chelsea sat her coffee cup on the coffee table, stood up, hands on her hips, and looked Jason up and down. She felt bad. He looked terrible, like he'd been in a war. She took the wet roll of toilet paper out of his hands and sat it next to her coffee cup.

"I'm sorry, Jason. You really didn't need to go through that. We already have plenty of food and paper products. I just went shopping a couple of days ago. And, the weather terrorists have changed the path of Albatross. Now, it's supposed to go south of Miami and into the Gulf. We're not going to get much more than a little rain and wind. I tried to call you on your cell, but you must have already been in the store."

Jason stared at the roll of toilet paper, and he looked like he might cry.

"So, I didn't need to run the gauntlet, or chain the red rocket to that palm tree out in the parking lot? Oh God, I'm so tired, and wet, and cold. It's only fifty-five out. I'm going to take a hot bath and dress my wounds. Are you sure Albatross isn't coming this way?"

"Yes, Jason. I wouldn't lie. I know how upset you get about stuff like this. The weather person did mention there is a tornado warning in St. Johns County for later this evening, if that makes you feel any better. But, not to worry. We're still safest in the bathroom."

Chelsea heard Jason run a bath. After two hours, he still hadn't come out, so she ventured in to see if he was okay. She found him sitting in tepid water, counting bathroom tiles and reading his phone.

"Whatcha doin'? I thought maybe you'd drowned."

"I'm counting the tiles in the bathroom to make sure they're all there. Since I'm a great multi-tasker, I'm also reading about West Nile virus online."

"That's nice. Maybe you could finish up. Your wife would also like to take a hot bath. Are the tiles all present and accounted for? More to the point, have you found out anything important about West Nile virus? I thought we decided that the realtor was death by mosquito, not a murder to be solved by a weekend PI."

"Yes, we did decide that it was death by mosquito. But, the counting and the reading thing distracts me from thinking about the blowing away thing, not to mention the flooding thing. If we die, we should sue your sister for recommending Florida. I never liked her."

"The feelings there are mutual. I never told you this, but at our wedding she threatened to swallow the ring to keep me from marrying you. For some reason I didn't listen to her, and here we are. Now, get out of that tub so I can have a turn."

"You just want the bathroom because it's safer in here."

"Well, there's that. But I also need a bath. If you don't get out, I'm coming in with you. I'm feeling frisky. Think you can handle it after last night? Maybe I should tie you to the faucet handles."

Jason hopped out of the tub, grabbed a towel and started drying off.

"Woman, you're turning into an animal. You fit right into the Florida scene. Just one more dangerous thing. It must be all that sunshine and salt air; causes rust and lust."

Jason wrapped the towel around his waist and sat on the floor in the opposite corner of the bathroom from the tub.

"I'm staying here where it's safe. You go ahead and enjoy your bath. I'll sit and read more about West Nile."

"Don't forget to finish counting the tiles."

Chelsea emptied the tub, and refilled it with steaming hot water. She undressed, climbed in, laid her head back and closed her eyes.

"Are you awake Chelsea? I found something interesting online. There's a medical biotech company in Miami working on a vaccine for the West Nile virus. It's one of those genetically engineered vaccines. The company's name is VaccinesRUs, and the President and CEO is a Mr. Mark Moneyman. It's currently a private company. The FDA is supposed to approve their licensing application next month. At that point they're planning to go public, which means someone will make a lot of money."

"I like money. Could you invest in this…what was it…VaccinesRUs?."

"I'd get fired and probably put in jail if I invested in any of the companies the FDA regulates."

"Yeah, and if you quit the FDA and did the PI thing full-time, we would barely have enough money for food, let alone investing."

"It doesn't really matter. Florida's gonna kill us anyhow."

Chelsea heard a huge blast of wind from the front of the condo, and Jason stood up and looked towards the bathroom door.

"I better go out and check on the red rocket. I chained it to a tree. I know the hurricane's not supposed to come here now, but there's still the tornadoes."

Chelsea said, "Better drop the towel and put on some pants first."

Jason hurried through the bathroom door. Chelsea assumed he put on some clothes before she heard the front door of the condo open and close. He was gone for forty-five minutes, when Chelsea finally decided she'd better investigate. She got out of the tub, covered up with a towel and looked out the front window. She saw Jason in the driver's seat of the red rocket, curled up in the fetal position as best he could in the cramped space. At least he was fully dressed. Directly adjacent to the driver's door sat a very large alligator, staring intently in Jason's direction. Chelsea dialed Jason on her cell.

Jason answered. "Hello? PI Jason Longfellow here. I caught a serial killer, and…"

"Hello Jason. This is your wife. I got worried when you didn't come back, so I thought I'd better look out the window. Who's your friend?"

"I almost stepped on the damned thing while I was checking to make sure the chain's still attached to the tree. I dove head first into the car; just about broke my neck. I thought the stupid realtors told us that there were no alligators on this side of A1A. Somebody should tell this guy. He appears to be lost."

Chelsea watched as the alligator moved closer to the driver's door.

"I think he heard you. What are you going to do? With all the rain and wind, I doubt Animal Control will come rescue you. Can't you sneak out the passenger's side and make a run for the condo? I'm going to go back to the bathroom where it's safe. I know the weather terrorists said Albatross is headed south of Miami, but that could change again in a heartbeat. Don't you want to come inside? We could take a nice warm shower together."

"After all that's happened, I think I'll stay put until this guy gets bored and wanders off. If not, I'll just sleep in the car again. I'm a manly man, and a little wind and rain won't hurt me. Worst case, my ass'll be asleep again in the morning. And, after being tied to the bed last night, I'm probably safer out here with the alligator.

Chapter 12

Chelsea, still in her pajamas, went looking for Jason early next morning. He sat at the kitchen table, drinking coffee and reading the news on his phone. She knew he had slept in his little car, and he looked wet, stiff and sore, and generally miserable.

"Good morning, Jason. How was your night, and why are you drinking coffee with cream? You usually take it black."

"Mornin', Beautiful Wife. I found some instant coffee in the cabinet. It's terrible, so I added enough milk to make a coffee milkshake. Not too bad. There's still some hot water in the pot if you want to make yourself a cup."

Chelsea got a cup from the cabinet, added several spoonsfuls of the dark coffee, poured in hot water and sat at the table next to Jason.

He continued, "It's a gorgeous day outside. I woke up early, all wet, with my ass asleep and cramped legs. I gotta get a bigger car. The good news, after all the fuss neither hurricane, nor tornado, nor flood appeared. The alligator got bored and went away. I'm thinking I'm not ready to go house hunting yet today. I want to do something fun that you can only do in Florida, something manly."

Chelsea took a sip of the steaming, muddy looking brew.

"Oh God, not more manly stuff. Wasn't the motorcycle disaster enough?"

"You can rent a motorcycle anywhere, although running over an alligator is kind of Florida-esque. I'm thinking more along the lines of kiteboarding. I did some research online, and there's a shop just up the street from us where you can rent all the gear. What d'ya say? Want to go kiteboarding?"

She put her head in her hands and sighed.

"That would be a hard no. You've never even been regular surfing, let alone *fly surfing*. You're a good swimmer, but it's not the same. I can just see you flying helplessly out to sea."

"Have a little faith, Chelsea. Almost dying in Hurricane Albatross got me thinking. I need to try new things while I'm still alive. I'm gonna do this. You're welcome to come along if you'd like. The weather's perfect; warm, sunny and there's some gusty wind out there…useful for flying around on a surfboard."

Chelsea added another spoonful of coffee to her cup. She couldn't understand why Jason bothered to drink coffee at all. He drank it so weak it lacked both flavor and caffeine.

"Jason, first of all, Albatross never came anywhere near us. Second, you're more likely to die *if* you kiteboard. And third, I'm pretty sure the point is not to fly around on the surfboard, but to surf and let the kite pull you through the water. Oh, never mind. I give up. I'll come along, but I'll just be there to pick up the pieces, as usual."

"Thanks Dear. I knew you'd want to watch your man in action."

After a quick breakfast of healthy sugar-coated cereal, Chelsea changed into shorts and a cotton T shirt. Jason put on his bathing suit. They both applied a thick coat of suntan lotion. Then, she followed him out to the red rocket, and they got in.

"Surfer Boy, you did unchain your car from the tree. Yes?"

"Of course, Chelsea. Do you really think I'm that stupid?"

"Well, let's see. You rented a motorcycle and hit an alligator, you find dead bodies everywhere and now you want to combine kite flying and surfing. So, there's that."

Chelsea watched as Jason got out of the car, went around back, unlocked the padlock and removed the chain from the rear bumper. Then, he drove them to the surf shop.

He parked in the store parking lot. The two of them went in, and were greeted by an energetic young blonde woman. She gave Jason a friendly smile. Chelsea noticed that he spent a few moments appreciating the blonde's attractive face, cute little nose, big blue eyes, gorgeous suntan and athletic body. He spent a little too long appreciating the matching dolphins tattooed on her left and right hips that were clad in a skimpy yellow bikini. Chelsea was amused when he threw his shoulders back, stood tall and puffed out his chest.

She slapped him on the back of the head. *Men are such idiots.*

"Ouch! Chelsea, what the hell?"

Jason approached the young woman and extended his hand.

"I'm Dr. Jason Longfellow. I'm a PI, here in St. Augustine to buy a vacation home and investigate the dead bodies that keep turning up during our search for a condo. But today, I'm just a carefree fellow looking for a little adventure. I called earlier to reserve the gear to go kiteboarding. Was it you that I spoke to on the phone? Oh, and this is my…wife…Chelsea. She's kind of grouchy sometimes."

The young woman shook his hand. Chelsea recognized that confused look on her face. She saw it a lot from people meeting Jason for the first time.

"My name's Jenny, and yes, we spoke on the phone this morning. I'm sorry to hear about the dead bodies. Most people look for cracks in the foundation, termites, leaky plumbing, that sort of thing. That must be some realtor you have helping you."

Chelsea couldn't help herself. "Carefree fellow? Jason, you can let go of Jenny's hand now, and stop drooling. You're probably older than her father." She turned to Jenny. "My husband has lost what's left of his mind and decided to try kiteboarding. I'm just going along to pick up the broken pieces? Do you offer extra life or health insurance?"

Jenny looked at Chelsea and took a step back. Chelsea saw the fear in her eyes. *Be afraid. Be very afraid. He's an idiot, but he's my idiot.*

"Chelsea, calm down. You're scaring this pretty young woman. And, I don't need any instruction. I watched a video on how to kiteboard. I've got this. If Jenny will break out the gear, I'll pack it on the red rocket and I'm ready to go."

Jenny, apparently trying to be kind, said, "Dr. Longfellow. You do look a bit…how should I put this…*brittle* to kiteboard for the first time. I would try to talk my father out of it if he ever got such a crazy idea into his head, but he has the good sense to avoid things like that at his age."

To Chelsea. "I would get fired if I refused to rent you the gear, so I can't do that. All I can tell you is there's a lot of wind out there today, blowing from the west at fifteen to twenty miles per hour, with gusts up to 30. Something around ten to twelve is best. The good news, it's going to be in the low eighties…so no hypothermia. I'll get the gear, wish you good luck, say a prayer for your husband and send you on your way."

Jenny and Jason carried the gear out to the red rocket. Chelsea just watched. If he was determined to break his neck she wasn't going to help him along, unless he checked out Jenny's tattoos again. It took a while to attach the gear to the luggage rack without anything dragging on the ground. Chelsea waited in the car and, finally, Jason got in and waved goodbye to Jenny.

Jason said, "That young lady was just rude. *Her father* indeed. And, I'm not brittle. I should have given her a piece of my mind."

"Jason, the way she filled out that bathing suit, I thought you were going to hurt yourself falling over your tongue. I swear, you better show some interest in me tonight, or breaking your neck kiteboarding is going to be the least of your worries."

Chelsea noticed the sign said only four-wheel-drive vehicles were allowed on the beach. The red rocket was rear-wheel-drive, but she knew Jason sometimes ignored such rules. She was relieved when he parked in a nearby lot and hauled the surfboard, kite and other gear to the beach. Still angry from the encounter with the youthful Jenny, Chelsea again watched Jason haul all the gear by himself. She walked along beside him, hands empty, ignoring his struggles.

They finally reached the beach entrance. Chelsea grinned when she saw the sweat pouring off of her flirtatious husband.

"Thanks for the help, Dear. You could've carried something."

"I thought you were a carefree manly man. Besides, I need to rest up if I'm going to haul your various broken parts back to the car. Don't break anything that you'll be needing tonight."

This particular stretch of North Florida beach included a wide expanse of white sand, lined with dunes backing up to brightly colored condo complexes as far as the eye could see. Chelsea could see where the beach gradually extended out from the dunes into the sea, and the water remained shallow for a good distance before the sand bar fell off into the ocean depths.

Chelsea said, "Look at this beautiful beach. I'll bet that most of the time the water here is calm and inviting, with just enough wave action for body surfing. But, today there's gusty wind and heavy cloud cover. The sea looks gray and angry, not at all inviting to a sane human being."

Jason dropped all his kiteboarding paraphernalia in the sand and started unfurling the sail. Chelsea watched him struggle mightily against the gusty wind.

"Jason, don't you think it's a little breezy for you to do this today? And, the temperature feels like it's dropping. I don't see any other kite boarders on the beach. In fact, there aren't many people at all. There's also a yellow flag posted at the beach entrance. Doesn't that mean something like *swim at your own risk* or *you're gonna die if you get in the water*?"

"Don't be silly. It's fine. It's the middle of the week, and everyone's at work. Follow me to the water's edge and help me get set up."

Chelsea took hold of the kite and surfboard and helped Jason haul it closer to the water. A heavy gust of wind almost pulled the kite out of their hands, and Jason dropped the board on his foot. He yelped in pain.

Jason said, "Now that I've broken my foot, help me hold this kite frame down while I hook up and then I'll blast off. Let's see, I hold onto this, put on this harness and hook the line to this O-ring. Chelsea. Hold the kite down! I'm not ready yet."

"Jason. I'm sitting on it, and I still can't control it. The wind's too strong. Are you sure you want to do this?"

"Yes, Dear. You worry too much. There, I'm all hooked up, and I've got the handle. Hand me the board, release the kite and off I go. Wait here. I'll return to this same spot when I'm done. I'll be back in an hour or two."

Chelsea shrugged, handed him the board and turned the kite loose. She watched as the kite took off, headed out to sea with Jason attached by the harness. He struggled to get his feet into the surf board straps as the kite yanked him through the surf towards Northern Africa.

As Jason bounced through the surf, one especially large wave threw him into the air. He performed a spectacular aerial summersault and the board left his feet and took off on its own.

"Aaaah! Chelsea! Help me!"

She could barely hear him over the howl of the wind, but she was fairly certain he was in trouble. All she could do was wave as the kite dragged him through the water, heading out to sea.

Chelsea shook her head in exasperation. *I knew this wasn't going to go well. But I didn't think it would so wrong so fast!*

The wind gusts seemed to be picking up speed, and Chelsea had to lean into the wind to keep from being blown over. Sand blasted her in the face. She looked up and down the beach, and there were very few people; no beach patrol or life guards. She dialed 9-1-1 on her cell.

"Hello. What's your emergency?"

"I'm on St. Augustine Beach, watching my husband fly helplessly out to sea attached to one of those kiteboard things. This is his first time, and he definitely needs help. I didn't know who else to call."

"Doesn't sound good. I'll connect you to the Coast Guard, and hopefully they can help. It's way too windy today, even for an experienced surfer. I have the Coast Guard on the line."

Chelsea heard a click as the call was transferred.

"Hello? This is the US Coast Guard, Petty Officer Gordon. How can I help you?"

Chelsea was embarrassed, but feared for Jason's life. She wasn't exactly sure what to say.

"I'm standing on St. Augustine Beach, and my husband just launched himself into the surf on one of those kiteboards. He's forty-six-years old, and never surfed a day in his life. The last I saw of him he had lost the board and the kite was dragging him out to sea. I dialed 9-1-1 and they put me in touch with you."

"Ma'am, you do realize that it's a felony to prank call 9-1-1, or the Coast Guard. No one in their right mind would go kiteboarding on a day like this. I'm going to hang up now."

"Excuse me, Petty Officer Gordon, but if my husband dies I'm going to sue you a lot. Jason is unfortunately the very definition of *no one in their right mind*, but he needs your help. Can't you send a boat to rescue him? Right now the kite is pulling him out to sea, he has no board under his feet, and he's basically a large chunk of bait trolling for sharks. Not to mention the fact that he might drown. Are you going to help, or not?"

"You aren't kidding, are you? I'm sorry. It's just difficult to believe that anyone would be so…"

Chelsea finished his sentence. "Stupid? My husband's not stupid. He's just very…enthusiastic." *Idiot. He's an idiot. But I need this guy's help, so we'll leave it at that.*

"I'll call for a rescue boat immediately. Where did you say you're located, so I know where to send the rescue team?"

A blast of wind-blown sand hit Chelsea in the face, and she put her arm up to protect herself. She was having trouble hearing the petty officer.

"St. Augustine Beach. And please hurry. He was moving fast, and if you don't get to him soon he'll be in North Africa. He doesn't have his passport with him."

"No worries. We'll find him. If he's alive and not seriously injured, he'll be dropped off at the Coast Guard Station Mayport. I'll let you know if we have to take him to a local hospital instead. Is this a good number to reach you once we've found him? Also what's his name?"

"Yes, this is my cell. His name's Jason, Dr. Jason Longfellow." *You can call him PI Idiot.*

Chelsea sat in the car to wait. A little over an hour later, her cell phone rang. The caller ID specified Coast Guard, US Government.

"Hello, Chelsea Longfellow here. Have you found Jason? Is he okay?"

"This is Petty Officer Gordon. Yes, we found him, and he's fine. He was a couple miles off shore by the time we got to him. I'm afraid he lost his kite and gear, though, and it's a good thing he's a strong swimmer. He somehow worked his way out of the harness, got free of the kite, and was treading water when we found him. They've taken him to Mayport. You can pick him up at the main Coast Guard office there."

Since Chelsea didn't know how to drive a stick shift, she had to call a taxi. When they got to the Coast Guard office in Mayport, she asked the driver to wait while she went in search of Jason. She found him sitting in the lobby in his wet bathing suit, with a towel wrapped around his shoulders. He looked cold; his lips were blue and he was shivering. She sat down next to him.

"Hi Chelsea. Wow! That was some adventure. Kiteboarding isn't as easy as you might think. Those first couple of waves hit me hard, I lost my surf board, and I couldn't get out of the harness. I thought I was a goner. I finally managed to get loose and was treading water, when a Coast Guard boat showed up. Pretty lucky, huh?"

"Jason, your so-called kiteboarding adventure rapidly turned into a trolling-for-sharks adventure. I called the Coast Guard. That's why they came along. They were looking for you."

"They didn't tell me that, but it would explain some of the strange looks, whispering and laughing. Thanks, Wife. You made me a laughing stock."

"Your welcome. I considered letting you get blown to Africa. I'm surprised you didn't find any dead bodies out there. You didn't, did you?"

Jason frowned. "No, no dead bodies. And, when I was being dragged along by the kite I really didn't think about trolling for sharks. I was worried about manatees, though, but I didn't see any."

"Yes, manatees were definitely your problem."

"Now I've got to add kiteboarding to my list of ways Florida tried to kill me."

A man sharply dressed in Coast Guard whites, grinning ear-to-ear, approached Chelsea.

"Ma'am. I'm Chief Petty Officer Keating. Are you here to collect PI Longfellow?"

"Yes, I'm Dr. Longfellow's wife."

He handed her a clipboard and pen. "If you'd just sign these release forms, you can be on your way."

Chelsea read the two forms. "According to this, we will be billed for his rescue? Three thousand dollars? Why is that? I don't understand."

The petty officer said, "Normally we don't bill people for a rescue, but in this case winds were gusting up to 30 miles per hour and there were yellow flags on the beaches. Your husband was breaking the law by kiteboarding under those conditions. So, our base Commander decided to apply a little known maritime regulation that allows us to charge for a rescue that should have never happened in the first place. I'm sorry, but I'm just following orders."

Chelsea was not happy. "Please provide me with this commander's name. I assure you that he will be hearing from our lawyer. This is unacceptable."

"Yes, Ma'am. Will do. Please sign the forms, and you can leave."

She signed, then grabbed Jason by the arm. "Let's go. I have a taxi waiting outside, and the meter's running. We're going to have to pay for all the equipment you lost, too, and that won't come cheap. How do you get into these messes? We could have found our ideal vacation home today, but instead you cost us another small fortune."

She dragged him outside, pushed him into the taxi, gave the driver the address and off they went.

"Chelsea. Why are you so negative? I'm alive, and I had the adventure of a lifetime. The Coast Guard guys were also impressed when I told them I'm a private investigator. They seemed really interested in my story about all the dead people, especially the realtors."

"Oh God. You didn't tell them you think you're a PI. No wonder they were laughing when I came to get you. Come to think of it, that petty officer did call you PI Longfellow. We're never going out in a boat again.

You're now infamous with the Coast Guard. You didn't tell them about the manatee, did you?"

"No. I still have nightmares about that."

"I know I'm going to hate myself for asking, but what did they say when you told them about the dead realtors? It is kind of a weird story."

"Strangely enough, one of the Coast Guard guys also had a realtor story. His sister is married to a guy, who knows a guy, who works for some company in Miami with an angry CEO that's suing *ReallyRealty*. It seems that the CEO has a seven-million-dollar beach front mansion, and he put it in the hands of one of their realtors to sell. It's been on the market for over two years, with no viable offers. Worse, rumor has it that the CEO's wife might be involved in an affair with said realtor, and they've been meeting at that mansion for their sexual encounters. Best we don't go looking for a condo in Miami. We might find another dead realtor."

"Jason, the whole thing sounds like a rumor to me. You can't trust third party information."

The cab driver sped up, passed a bus and made a sharp right turn. Jason and Chelsea were wearing seat belts, but Jason was still thrown up against her, pushing down on her shoulder.

"Get off of me, you big ape. Right now you need to figure out how you're going to pay the Coast Guard three thousand dollars for your rescue and God knows how much for the kiteboarding equipment that you air mailed to Africa. And, you better take care of your wife tonight. I could hire a male escort a lot cheaper than this."

"Chelsea. How can you say such a thing? You'll embarrass the taxi driver. Besides, don't worry, I'll take care of business tonight. There's something about almost dying two days in a row that really gets my blood pumping."

"If I'd known that, I'd have threatened you with a kitchen implement, say a meat cleaver or butcher knife, or maybe an electric hand-held mixer. It would have been a lot cheaper. Come to think of it, after the way you looked at that young woman in the bikini I'm thinking I might do more than just threaten. And, don't worry about the cabbie. His driving's probably going to kill both of us."

"If you kill me, I can't make mad passionate love to you tonight. And you'd get caught. With murder, it's always *cherchez l'spouse*."

"If I told them what you did today, they might give me a medal for putting up with you. Or, I could just tell the police you were a realtor. Apparently, they're used to finding dead ones everywhere, and they're not all that great at solving the murders."

Chapter 13

Chelsea had told Jason she made arrangements for Rock Handsome to show them another set of condos. Jason got up early, brewed himself some decaf coffee and a pot of that battery acid that Chelsea drank. He added toast, butter and black raspberry jelly to the mix. Chelsea showed up a few minutes later. They finished breakfast just as Rock arrived in his luxury SUV. Chelsea took shotgun, Jason obediently climbed in the back, and off they went. Rock weaved his way through rush hour traffic as he talked, making Jason nervous.

Rock said, "I've found three great condos in your price range, all located in a very nice development called *See the Sea*. It's on the east side of A1A, all the units have ocean views and are only a two-minute walk to the beach. We're supposed to meet one of our other *ReallyRealty* realtors, Sam Waterson, at the first unit at nine-thirty."

Jason said, "These are all two-bedroom, two-and-a-half bath units, second floor to avoid flood damage, in the two-hundred to two-hundred-fifty-thousand-dollar price range? No more three bedroom units and no dead bodies? No alligators, poisonous snakes, rust?"

"Jason, give Mr. Handsome a chance. The events of the past few days are not his fault. I'm sure what he has planned is fine."

Rock pulled the SUV into a well maintained development. Jason liked the fact that the grass was neatly mowed, the trees and bushes trimmed, and there were beautiful flower beds everywhere. Rock drove through the complex, pointing out the good stuff.

Rock said, "The buildings consist of two floors, with a one-story unit on the bottom, a two-story unit on top and concrete steps up to the second floor. Each floor has its own balcony. The condos are constructed of rebar re-enforced concrete with stucco exterior, with curved Spanish tile roofs; great construction for withstanding high winds. The developer positioned the condo complex in one gigantic V-shape, so that all the interior units have a small ocean view. Several more expensive oceanfront units also sit up against the dunes. There's a large community pool at the center of the complex, and a gated boardwalk leads to the beach."

Rock Handsome pulled up in front of one of the condo buildings and parked his SUV.

"It's unit eleven, in front of us on the second floor. Let's go up and see if Sam is here yet."

They exited the SUV. Jason regretted leaving the air conditioned vehicle the moment they opened the doors. In the high nineties with typical Florida humidity, sweat droplets rolled down their faces by the time they climbed the fifteen stairs to the second floor. Jason did the counting.

Jason reached the door first. "Hey, the door's part way open. Looks suspicious. If this were a murder mystery, the cops would draw their weapons and clear the place room by room."

"I'm sure it's okay, Dr. Longfellow. Sam probably just neglected to close the door all the way. He must be inside. His car's parked two spaces over from mine."

Jason went into PI mode. He gently pushed the door open further and peeked in.

"Let me go in first in case there's any danger. A good PI stays vigilant, always prepared. Wish I'd brought my gun."

Chelsea said, chuckling, "I hate to admit it, but I agree with Jason. We've found several dead bodies during our house hunting. Careful Jason. There might be an amorous manatee in the bathtub. Best you didn't bring your gun; I think they're on the endangered species list."

"Nice, Woman. Just stay behind me. My PI senses are tingling. There's something wrong."

Rock and Chelsea followed Jason through the door. Jason heard Rock closed the door behind them.

Rock said, "See, everything's fine. Sam's probably upstairs, or in the bathroom. I'll look down here." He yelled into the condo. "Sam. Are you here? It's Rock Handsome, with those clients I told you about."

No answer.

Jason went to investigate. "I'll look upstairs. Chelsea, you stay here where it's safe."

Jason reached the top of the stairs, and walked past a closet containing stacked washer/dryer units. He checked inside both units. You never knew where you might find a body, or a bad guy. Then, he walked on up the hall. He looked into a small guest bedroom with two single beds, a dresser and lamp, and a walk-in closet; no one there. He carefully moved up the hall past two small bathrooms, one with a shower and the other a tub, both empty of people. He reached the master bedroom with a large king size bed, a single dresser with small flat-screen TV on top, and a wicker chair. The sliding glass door leading to a small deck was closed, no intruder there. The walk-in closet door in this bedroom was partially open. He yelled down to Chelsea.

"Chelsea. I don't see anyone up here. Somebody left the closet door partly opened in the master bedroom. I better close it."

Jason approached the closet door and opened it further so he could peek in before closing it. There stood a man in his fifties, five-ten, two-hundred-fifty pounds of flab. Jason looked down on the man's partially bald head with a bad comb-over. The guy's face looked like a bulldog, but with bigger ears. Jason also detected that the man had crazy eyes, blood on his button down shirt and a large butcher knife in his right hand. Old crazy eyes did not move. Jason stood there, eyes locked with the man, his mind slowly processing the situation.

Jason shouted, his voice coming out in an unusually high pitch.

"Chelsea. I think I found Mr. Waterson, at least the name tag on his bloody shirt says Sam Waterson, *ReallyRealty*. He's in the closet."

Chelsea shouted back. "Did you say *bloody shirt*? Jason, what have you done now?"

"Nothing, Dear. Mr. Waterson seems to be hiding in the closet. And, my advanced observational skills detect a lot of blood and a large knife."

"Did you find another dead body?"

"Actually, this one appears to be very much alive. As soon as I can convince my feet to move, I'll be running down the stairs and out the door. Perhaps you could meet me in the car, with the engine running."

Jason's mind finally caught up with current events. He screamed, turned and ran towards the stairs. Mr. Waterson reacted by following him, knife raised above his head in the stab position.

"Chelsea. Help me! There's a crazy man chasing me with a large knife, and he looks all stabby. He is definitely not a dead body!"

Jason ran down the carpeted stairs, looking over his shoulder at the man in hot pursuit. As Jason reached the bottom step, the man tripped, fell and rolled forward down the stairs. The knife went flying, the man hit his head on a coffee table near the bottom of the stairwell and lay still. Jason watched from the front door, where he was about to flee the building.

Chelsea said, "Jason, you can stop running. The man with the knife is unconscious. He accidentally fell down the stairs."

Jason turned around and walked over to Chelsea. "I saw the crazy man fall and hit his head. That was my plan. I saw how obese he was, and I knew if I ran away he couldn't keep up with me and would fall down the stairs. Why didn't you follow me out the door to safety?"

"Well, first of all, thanks? Your concern for your wife was apparent from the way you flew past me on your way out the door. And second, Mr. Waterson *accidentally* fell over my hand when I reached up and grabbed hold of his ankle through the stair railing. So you're welcome."

Jason heard the sliding glass door to the balcony open. He turned and saw Rock Handsome walk into the living room and find his colleague Sam Waterson lying on the floor, shirt stained with blood.

"What did you do to poor Sam? I just went out on the balcony for a second. You didn't kill him, did you? He's a nice man. We're golfing buddies."

Chelsea said, "No. We did not kill your friend. He was chasing Jason down the stairs with a knife and I just helped him get to the bottom faster. He hit his head on that coffee table and went to sleep. I'm sure he'll be fine. I suggest we try to find out where all that blood came from. Perhaps we should think of Sam here as a suspect, considering the large knife and the chasing."

"Stop it, Chelsea. I'm the detective. I should be the one making the important observations, and using official words like *suspect*."

"Sorry Dear. I didn't mean to step on your toes. Just seems reasonable to think Mr. Waterson might have been up to no good, what with the knife, the blood and the hiding. Maybe we should look around for another dead body. If you have a suspect, isn't it handy to also have a body?"

"I was just going to say that. Yes, we need to do a thorough search of the condo. I can't catch a break. All these murders to investigate, and I'm supposed to be on vacation. And, this is the second time someone's tried to kill me. Florida just doesn't like me very much, what with all the killer realtors…"

Chelsea chimed in. "And alligators, and sharks, and snakes, and rust, and the manatee. Don't forget the killer manatee."

"Be nice, Wife. It seems like you're trying to kill me too, making me sleep in my car."

Chelsea walked over to a closed door in the downstairs hallway and opened it. Jason didn't like the smug look on her face.

"Jason, you missed this door. Why looky here. A dead person sitting on the toilet, with several puncture wounds in his chest. What do you think, PI Longfellow? Is this a clue?"

Jason walked over to the bathroom door. "Why are you so mean? I made you squeal last night, twice. You should be nice."

Rock Handsome walked over to the bathroom and looked inside. "Oh my God! That's Mr. Mortimer. He's one of our buyer clients. Sam was supposed to show him this condo last night. I don't understand."

"Jason, I think we should call the police. It looks like our latest realtor friend…"

"Chelsea, I'm the detective. It looks like Mr. Waterson killed this poor man while he was sitting on the toilet. How do the realtors down here expect to sell anything if they keep killing their buyers, and each other? Oh crap, we're buyers."

Jason looked suspiciously at Rock. "You don't have any plans for us do you, Mr. Handsome? Debbie already tried to puree my face, and I do not want to die on the toilet."

"I can assure you, Dr. Longfellow, you are perfectly safe. I'd really like to make a sale. It's been thin pickings lately. Now that you mention it, what do you think of this condo unit? Other than the murderer and the dead body, it's perfect for you guys. It's well-maintained with several upgrades, fits all your needs and priced right at two-hundred-forty thousand. In fact, I can pretty much guarantee that I can get you a better price after what we found here today."

Jason smiled a big smile. "Tell you what, Rock. If the seller will take two-twenty, I'll sign the papers right now."

Chelsea picked up the bloody knife and moved towards her husband.

"Jason, I swear, if you don't shut up I'm going to add another dead body. I'm not living in a condo where someone has been murdered, on the toilet? I could never go to the bathroom again."

Jason said, "Chelsea, put down that knife. You're contaminating the evidence."

Rock Handsome winced. "Jason, you're either the bravest man I've even seen, or the dumbest. Can you say *death wish*?"

Just then, Sam Waterson stood up, shook his head, mumbled something and ran out the door. Chelsea, startled, dropped the knife. Everyone ran to the front door and looked out at Waterson.

Rock yelled after him, "Sam! Sam! Where are you going? Come back! I might have a buyer!"

Waterson, running as fast as his overweight body would move, screamed, "My head…loud buzzing…can't stand it!"

He stopped in the middle of the street, grabbed his head with both hands, and his body began to twitch. He screamed at the top of his lungs, rage in his voice.

"Ahhhhh! Make it stop! Need to kill something!"

He collapsed onto the blacktop, had a seizure and stopped moving.

Jason, Chelsea and Rock all ran to the fallen man. Rock bent over and felt for a pulse.

"No pulse. I'm afraid he's dead. Phone 9-1-1. Maybe they can revive him, but it doesn't look good."

Jason, standing next to Waterson's body, looked pale. "One, two, three, four dead bodies. That's an even number." Then, his body slowly slumped towards the ground.

"That's my husband, PI Longfellow, tough as cotton candy. Rock, help me drag these two over to the sidewalk, before a car comes along and runs them over. I'm sure Jason will join us again, as soon as he takes his little nap."

Chapter 14

Rock Handsome told Chelsea that he felt he should call the police after finding yet another dead body while condo searching with the Longfellows. She worried Jason would go to jail, but she agreed. Two police detectives arrived at the scene along with a couple of CSI staff. They marked off the area with crime scene tape, searched for clues and ordered Jason to show up at the police precinct the following morning for questioning as a person of interest. That's how Jason and Chelsea found themselves in the St. Augustine Sheriff's Office, sitting in front of the desk in the office of Detective Lance Abercrombie.

Jason said, "Chelsea, where is this detective? Do they really think I killed someone?"

"Calm down, Jason. I'm sure he'll be here soon. Stop counting Detective Abercrombie's pencils and paper clips. His desk is neat and orderly and you're making a mess of it. Probably not a good idea to make him mad. They already think you're a murderer."

"I'm pretty sure I didn't have anything to do with these murders. I'm a private eye, I investigated, and I have found no evidence to tie me to any of these crimes. And, the detective has one-hundred-thirteen paper clips and eleven pencils on his desk. Maybe I should count the ones in his desk drawers too."

Jason started to stand up. Chelsea knew he was headed for the drawers of the detective's beat up old wooden desk. She grabbed Jason's arm and started rubbing it, preventing him from leaving the chair.

As she rubbed, she said, "Everything will be okay. You've been too busy trying to kill yourself to hurt anyone else, what with the horny manatees, motorcycling, and kiteboarding. I've been with you the whole time, and I'd know if you killed anybody."

"But, you have to admit, Chelsea. We have been at the scene of several dead bodies in the past couple of weeks. Something else to put on my list of ways Florida tries to kill you; murder by real estate."

"I must admit, the last thing I expected was to find a dead body in every condo. Just calm down, answer the detective's questions honestly and you'll be fine."

A tall man that looked the part of a police detective, or an ex-marine, entered the room. Detective Abercrombie had big shoulders and thick, muscular arms. He resembled Thor, the Thunder God, with blue eyes and long blonde hair. Dressed in Florida-detective-casual, he wore tan khaki pants, a light blue button-down shirt, a light brown cotton jacket and black loafers. The jacket partially hid a nine-millimeter pistol in a clip-on holster. Chelsea could see the gun when he walked around the desk and sat down. He never offered to shake hands.

Chelsea stopped rubbing Jason's arm and focused on the detective. He was definitely worthy of her attention.

"I'm Detective Abercrombie. I assume you are Doctor and Mrs. Longfellow? Sorry I'm late, but I was just talking to a Mr. Rock Handsome. He vouched for you, saying that he was with you each time you found a dead body. The only time he saw any violence from either of you was when you, Mrs. Longfellow, threatened your husband with a knife. So first of all, Dr. Longfellow, do you want to press charges against your wife for assault?"

Jason looked at Chelsea, raised one eyebrow and grinned an evil grin.

"I could press charges against my wife for assault? Well, she did make me sleep in the car a couple of nights, and she threatened to hurt me if I bought that condo. It was also her idea to come to Florida, where everything keeps trying to kill me."

"Jason Bartholomew Longfellow. Don't you dare. I don't know how you can press charges against me for assault after you crashed a motorcycle, got attacked by a horny manatee and tried to fly to Africa on a kiteboard. Need I remind you that I rescued you each time? Seems like you're more dangerous to yourself than I am."

Jason raised both his eyebrows and looked at her. "Can I sleep in our bed again?"

"Oh, all right. You can sleep in the condo. Just stop this nonsense."

"In the main bedroom?"

"Yes. In the main bedroom. But you have to do your husbandly duty."

Detective Abercrombie got a strange look on his face. Chelsea thought he looked like he'd just stepped in dog poop. He held up his hand.

Jason and I seem to have this effect on people. I can't imagine why.

The Detective said, "Never mind. Dr. Longfellow's *husbandly duties* aside, an assault charge probably wouldn't stick anyhow, since you didn't actually stab your husband. Making him sleep in the car is more like an insult than an assault. Let's just forget it?"

While the detective was speaking, Jason stood up, walked around the desk and started checking the drawers to make sure they were all closed. Chelsea saw a different look on the Detective's face, one of fear. That's when the detective noticed all of the pencils and paper clips were lined up perfectly on his desk. He stood up and pulled his gun out of its holster.

Chelsea put up her hands. "Whoa there, Detective! Jason's no threat to you. He's just OCD. He was counting your paper clips and pencils, and he's checking to make sure your desk drawers are all closed. Gives him the illusion he's safe and in control of the chaos. His mother told me she dropped him on his head when he was a baby, several times. Please don't shoot him…although…he did consider filing an assault charge against me." To Jason. "Come back around her and sit down, PI Longfellow. You're making the detective nervous."

Jason returned to his seat. "Sorry, Detective Abercrombie. I am a little OCD, but there's nothing wrong with bringing some order into the world. There's so much chaos. You must understand, what with the terrible things you see as a police officer."

The detective re-holstered his weapon. "No problem. I understand completely. My cousin spent some time in a nut house. He's out now and living a fairly normal life…as long as he takes his meds. Now, let's get down to it. According to Mr. Handsome, you are a government doctor, but you also fancy yourself a private eye. Is that correct?"

Chelsea winced. "Oh God. Do you really want to go there?"

Jason smiled. "Why yes. I prefer to be known as PI Longfellow, even though my day job is an FDA drug reviewer. I actually caught a serial killer, a cheese thief and a thieving monkey."

Chelsea interrupted. "Well, I actually solved the latter two cases, but who's counting?"

The detective continued the interrogation. "At any rate, where'd you get your PI license? I assume you have one."

Jason took his wallet out of his pocket, found his laminated PI license and handed it to the detective.

"I got it online, along with my CCW permit, although I don't actually carry a gun. Chelsea won't let me after I shot a hole in the poop tank of our RV."

Chelsea thought that Detective Abercrombie looked a little disoriented. *Did his eyes actually cross there for a moment?* Jason had that effect on people. The detective looked at the license and handed it back to Jason.

"I'm sorry I asked. Assuming you are a legitimate detective, did you see anything at any of the crime scenes to suggest who the killer might be, if it was the same killer…you know…clues…that kind of thing? Actual useful information."

Jason thought for a minute. "Well, we're in the market for a vacation home in Florida. All the bodies were found in condos or houses that are for sale. Some of the victims were real estate agents, and a couple were potential buyers. So, all the victims appear to have the theme of real estate in common. And, all the bodies were found in properties that we looked at; we actually found them. So, all the bodies have us in common. Chelsea, it doesn't look good for us. Help."

Chelsea murmured. "Idiot. And, what do you mean *us?*"

The detective grinned. "I was going to ask you if you suspect anyone in particular. So, you're saying you suspect yourself, and your wife. Should I make an arrest?"

Jason paused, clearly in deep thought. "Wait a minute. Rock Handsome was there with us when we found a couple of the bodies, and he's a realtor, consistent with my theory about a real estate theme. We were with him when we found the bodies, but we can't vouch for his whereabouts earlier in the day in each case. He could have committed the murders, and then showed us the condos later in the day. You might question him about the victims; look for some connection. He's definitely a suspect."

The detective said, "That's a terrible approach to selling real estate, but I take your point. I'll question him further. Come to think of it, either of you could have killed the victims earlier, and then gone back to see the houses later with a realtor."

Chelsea spoke up, "Great job, PI Birdbrain. After Rock had alibied us, you just blew our alibis for all these murders. Why don't you just confess and get it over with?"

"Chelsea. You know we didn't do anything wrong. Let's not forget that at the first house Debbie the realtor tried to puree my face with an electric hand-held mixer. One of the other victims was killed by a similar electrical kitchen appliance, also pointing to Debbie. Another victim was reported to have died from a mosquito bite. Then there's the case where the killer, another realtor, was still in the house and tried to stab me before dying of a seizure."

Jason made a stabbing motion with his hand to emphasize his point.

"So, PI Longfellow. It seems that you have done something to piss off a number of people. Any idea what that might be? It's my understanding you've only been in Florida a couple of weeks."

Chelsea couldn't resist. "Jason just being himself is enough to irritate most people. Especially when he's playing at PI. Lest you forget, I wanted to stab…never mind."

Detective Abercrombie had bumped the desk with his knee, and some of the pencils were no longer carefully aligned. Jason started rearranging them again. Then, he perked up.

"Hey, I just remembered. We found a dead body on I-95 in the median on the way down here, and I solved that case. Nobody there had any reason to be irritated with me, and the victim wasn't a realtor."

"Jason, you drove us off the road and into a construction site. That's how you found the body. I'm sure some of the construction workers were annoyed with you. You pointed out to the police that one of them was the killer, and the rest had to help dig our car out of the hole."

Detective Abercrombie shook his head. He had that disoriented look again and Chelsea could tell he was having difficulty processing what he'd just heard. The detective reached across the desk and handed Jason one of his cards.

"You certainly do not live a boring life. I don't have enough to hold you right now. Here's my card. If you think of anything else that might be helpful to the case, or cases, give me a call. Please be more careful, and perhaps you might want to look for a condo somewhere else, say Miami, or perhaps Los Angeles…somewhere far away from St. Augustine? And, I recommend you take the bus to get there."

Jason and Chelsea walked out to the red rocket. When they got in the car, Jason was grinning ear-to-ear.

"What did you do now, Jason? I'm not sure I can take any more today."

"Do you know when I walked around the detective's desk to check his drawers? I noticed a file folder on his desk labelled *Miami, Florida, Real Estate Lawsuit and Possible Assault*. I snatched it while you were talking to him. I've got it right here under my shirt."

"You really are crazy. What if he'd caught you? You'd be in jail right now."

"No worries. Take the file, and let's get out of here. I grabbed it because I remembered someone mentioning a realtor's convention in Miami. All these dead bodies seem to have something to do with real estate, and I thought it might be relevant."

When they got back to their condo, Jason made some decaf coffee, sat at the kitchen table and started reading the file. Chelsea didn't like weak decaf, so she had a glass of wine.

"This is interesting, Chelsea. According to this report, there was a realtor in Miami under contract to sell some CEO's multi-million-dollar mansion. It's been on the market for two years with no viable offers. The CEO signed a contract for three years and he's suing both the realtor and *ReallyRealty* to get out of the contract, plus several million for anxiety, pain and suffering. The realtor is alleged to have attacked the CEO, although the details of that part are kind of sketchy. The realtor's on the run; passing wind, as they say. The police have a BOLO out on him, but they haven't had any luck finding him. The realtor's name is not in the file, but the CEO's last name is Moneyman. Great name for a CEO."

"So, oh great PI. First, it's *in the wind*, not *passing wind*. Second, didn't one of your Coast Guard buddies mention something about a CEO and a realtor in Miami? Sounds familiar. And, more to the point, what do you think this has to do with the dead bodies in St. Augustine? It certainly doesn't sound like Debbie, the cheerleader, or Rock Handsome. Rock does work for *ReallyRealty*, but they have agents all over the country. How did the realtor allegedly attack the CEO? Any mention of a knife, or an electric kitchen appliance?"

"Chelsea, you're trying to play detective again. But, that is a good question. The file doesn't mention any weapons. It says *alleged attack*, suggesting there might not have been an attack at all. If there was he must have failed, since the CEO is still alive and suing."

"Jason, I don't understand how this has anything to do with attacks by knife and electric hand-held mixer or death by mosquito bite here in St. Augustine."

"My excellent PI intuition tells me that there's no connection between the two. Maybe realtors here in Florida are just grouchy because it's so damned hot. Or they're all hypervigilant because of all the things that want to kill them…you know…alligators, sharks, snakes, hurricanes, rust…other realtors. If I lived here full time, I'd probably be paranoid enough to make me want to kill someone, too."

"Jason, that's not comforting. We're buying a condo and will retire here someday."

"Not to worry. I'm a manly man, and I'll get used to all the danger eventually. I already survived deadly hurricanes, tornadoes, manatees, motorcycles, an alligator, kiteboards, and several realtors…"

"And rust. You haven't rusted yet."

Chapter 15

Next morning Jason woke early again, his mind whirling from all the Florida peril and dead realtors. He was sitting at the kitchen table drinking coffee when Chelsea found him.

"Jason, are you sure you need coffee? You tossed and turned all night, and you're up at five-thirty. Maybe you should lay off the caffeine for a while."

He took a large gulp from his cup. He had decided to drink the strong stuff to try to stay awake at night and satisfy his wife.

"I'm fine. I just need another day off from house hunting to relax. Is there something you'd like to do today besides search for more dead realtors…I mean vacation property?"

She poured herself a cup of coffee, and sat down at the table.

"I did see online that there's a pirate ship that sails daily out of the marina in downtown St. Augustine. It's an authentic tall ship, and they take you up the Intracoastal Waterway. I'm sure a manly man like yourself would enjoy playing pirate."

"That does sound interesting, although I'm not sure I want to be on the water. Last time didn't go so well."

"You just have to be careful not to fall off the boat. This is a large sailing ship, so even you should be able to manage that. Maybe I could tie you to the mast."

"Let's do it. And, stop with the tying-me-up-to-things stuff."

Chelsea said, "The ship leaves at noon. We have plenty of time to get ready, get there and buy tickets. I'll take a quick shower and have some breakfast. Then, I'll give Rock a call about showing us more condos tomorrow, and we can be on our way."

"Okay, Dear. I'm gonna sit here, choke down this coffee and ponder why we keep running into dead or insane realtors, and why Florida wants to kill me."

They arrived at the pirate ship, bought their tickets and boarded. Jason was impressed. The Black Raven looked like a typical tall ship, with three large sails, a crow's nest atop the mainsail mast, and a gun deck, quarter deck and poop deck. There were gun walls with fake cannons, and a large entryway that led below deck. The ship had a white skull and crossbones painted on both sides. The Jolly Roger flag flew from the mast. The crew consisted of young men and women, late teens and early twenties, dressed in pirate garb. Jason thought the owners had cheated history; the ship included a gasoline engine to allow tours in times of no wind, and to help with docking in tight quarters.

It was a very hot day, and the tour was only half full. By the time the ship left the dock Jason felt like a boiled lobster.

"Chelsea. We didn't think this through very well. It's hotter than hell. I'm going down below to get out of the sun and look for a bathroom."

"Okay. I'm hoping for a nice breeze later in the day. Be careful, and don't fall overboard."

Jason weaved his way through a small group of people on deck and headed downstairs. *Oh look. There's lots of doors down here, probably to the engine room, galley, pantry, closets...one's got to be a bathroom.*

They've left most of the doors part-way opened. Chaos everywhere. I'll just close them all. They'll appreciate that.

He walked up the hall through the lower level, closing doors, bringing order back to the universe. At the third door, he saw a tennis shoe sticking out at floor level, a woman's foot and leg attached. He opened this door to investigate.

Jason spoke to the unconscious lady lying on the bathroom floor.

"Well, hello. It's been a rough week, and I should have expected to find you here. I'm guessing that you're a realtor."

He didn't see a purse or other sign of identification, although it appeared she might have something in her pocket. He stepped into the bathroom and felt her neck for a pulse. She was alive. He reached into the pocket of her jeans, just as Chelsea arrived.

"Jason, what did you do now? I got worried, and came looking for you. Why are you fondling that unconscious woman on the bathroom floor?"

Jason jerked his head around, startled. His neck bones cracked so loud he thought he might have broken it.

"Chelsea! You scared the crap out of me! I'm not fondling. There's no fondling. I was closing doors and looking for a bathroom when I found her lying there, just like this. I felt for a pulse, and she's alive. I was checking her pockets for identification."

"You were looking for a bathroom, and you just happened to stumble onto a shapely twenty-something blonde woman in tight jeans, lying unconscious on this bathroom floor. So, you decided to feel around for some identification? I swear. I've been with you the whole time we've been in Florida, and even I'm beginning to wonder if you don't have something to do with these murders. Is this woman a realtor? She better not be a realtor, or the police are going to lock you up and throw away the key."

"I told you, I can't find any identification. She's starting to wake up. I'm sure she's not a realtor. Please don't let her be a realtor."

The woman came to, moaned, touched the back of her head where Jason could see an obvious bump, and tried to get up. Jason reached down and helped her to her feet.

She said, "Where…where am I? Who are you?"

Chelsea answered. "I'm Chelsea, and this is my husband, Jason."

"PI Longfellow, if you please. I've captured…"

"Not now, Jason. You'll scare the poor woman."

The woman, sounding groggy, said, "I remember now. I'm Anna Conway. I'm on the Black Raven with a group of realtors from St. Augustine. This cruise is one of the bonuses that *ReallyRealty* gives once a month to the realtors with the top ten sales."

"Oh my God, Chelsea! She is a realtor, a *ReallyRealty* realtor. I didn't do anything, honest. I just found her this way. Don't tell the police."

Chelsea said to the realtor, "Do you know what happened? How'd you wind up on the floor?'

Anna looked around. "Last thing I remember, I came below deck in search of a bathroom. Someone must have hit me on the head." She looked around. "My purse, where's my purse?"

"No worries, Anna. I'm a private eye, PI Longfellow at your service. I've captured a serial killer…"

"Yes Jason, and caught a cheese thief and a monkey. I said be quiet. The poor woman will think you're daft."

"That's not nice. My online course covered how to catch a thief. We need to look for clues, something we can get DNA from. If the thief has a record, his DNA is probably in the system."

"Jason, you don't have a DNA analyzer, and we're not buying one. I'm guessing that's not something you can order on Amazon anyhow. And, you don't know if the thief's a he or a she."

"Actually, if I'm gonna be serious about this PI thing, I should have a DNA analyzer. Every good PI should have one."

"Good PI? Did someone hit *you* on the head, too? Maybe we should focus on finding Anna's purse. We need to call the police."

"No police, Chelsea. Please! I don't wanna go to jail."

Anna said, "Why would you go to jail? You're trying to help me, aren't you? Or, are you the one that hit me on the head? Maybe I should scream."

Jason held up his hands, ready to fend off the impending noise.

Chelsea said, "Jason, I told you to be quiet." To Anna, "It's okay. I've been married to him for a long time, and I assure you he's harmless to everyone but himself. Perhaps we should go up on deck and look for your purse. The thief has probably taken the valuables and thrown the purse overboard by now. But, we might get lucky."

"Chelsea, you'd make a good criminal. Take the valuables out and throw the purse overboard. Why didn't I think of that?"

Chelsea said, "I'm sure you'd have figured it out, eventually. Maybe if we hurry we can catch the culprit before he empties the purse and gets rid of it. Let's head upstairs."

On deck, Jason tried to insert himself into his own investigation again. "Okay, spread out. Look for a man, or woman, or a monkey with a purse. That'll be the thief." He looked at Chelsea and shrugged. "The last thief I caught was a monkey." He looked around the ship. "Wait. Lots of women might already have a purse…"

Chelsea said, "Look, over there by the main mast. That pirate, he's carrying a purse over his shoulder."

Anna, surprised, "That's it. That's my purse."

Jason, excited, "That must be the thief. Get him, Chelsea!"

The three of them ran after the pirate and surrounded him. He stood five-foot tall, with a black beard and moustache. He wore full pirate garb, dressed all in black with matching pirate hat, and including a scabbard, complete with a sword.

Chelsea said, "He looks like the Mini-Me of pirates. Watch out for the sword, though. It looks real."

Jason took charge again. "Mr. Pirate, whose purse is that? Anna here says it's hers. Did you hit her on the head and steal it?"

Anna was angry. "Are we sure he's the one who did it? I'm five-eight, and he would have had to stand on something to hit me on the head." To Chelsea. "Are you sure it wasn't your husband that knocked me out? He's tall enough, and he was touching me when I woke up."

"Chelsea. Tell her it wasn't me. I was just feeling…I mean looking for some identification. Besides, the Mini-Me-pirate has the purse."

The pirate looked scared, like a cornered animal. He said, "You should be more careful when you enter a public bathroom. You never know who'll be in there standing on the toilet waiting to rob you."

He drew the sword and threatened them with it. "Now, leave me alone while I throw this evidence over the side."

He ran towards the railing, and Jason gave chase. Just as the pirate was about to toss the purse overboard, Jason tackled him. They both went over the railing and into the water. As the ship sailed away, Chelsea heard Jason yell.

"Chelsea! Help! I've got the purse, but alligators, sharks, snakes, manatee, rust, and a tiny pirate with a sword! Help me!"

Jason saw that the ship was already turning around to rescue him and the little pirate. Three crew members were lowering a small lifeboat to water level as the ship approached them. Jason was having trouble holding onto both the diminutive pirate thief and the purse.

Chelsea yelled, "Jason, look behind you! There's something coming your way, and I don't think it's a manatee, or rust. You should probably get out of the water."

Jason turned and screamed. "Alligator! Alligator! Chelsea! Help! Damn Florida! Damn water! Damn realtors! Damn pirates!"

The fear-induced adrenaline gave Jason increased strength, and he literally threw the small pirate and the purse into the hanging lifeboat. He grabbed the side and pulled himself into the boat. He struggled to get his long frame completely out of the water before the alligator reached him, and he lost part of his left pant-leg and his left shoe. He collapsed onto his back, exhausted.

As the crew raised the life boat to deck height Jason yelled up at his wife.

"Chelsea, Florida now owes me one motorcycle helmet, one pair of pants and one left shoe. These alligators are hard on your wardrobe. Who do I call in the Florida government to make a claim for these items?"

As the ship's staff helped Jason from the life-boat onto the deck of the ship, Chelsea answered.

"Forget the clothing. Just be glad you don't need to put in a claim for a left foot, leg and a head, although a replacement head might actually come with a brain."

"You're just mean. I almost got eaten, and you're making jokes."

"Jason, while you're whining, your thief is getting away."

Jason saw that the pirate thief had gotten into the lifeboat and was lowering it back down to the water. Jason ran over to the small man, grabbed him by the soaking wet shirt collar and pulled him back onto the deck. The little pirate was helpless, having lost his sword in the water.

"Chelsea, what should I do with this guy until we get back to shore?"

"How about you tie him to the mast? That's what the real pirates would do. Either that or make him walk the plank."

"Well, I don't see no plank, so the mast it is. Chelsea, that seems to be your answer for everything. If it doesn't do what you want, tie it to something."

Jason gave the soggy purse back to Anna. He blushed when she kissed him on the cheek.

"Thank you, PI Longfellow. I don't know what I'd have done if you hadn't rescued my purse. It has all my ID, credit cards, driver's license, health insurance cards…it would have taken me forever to get it all straightened out."

Chelsea, standing nearby. "Jason, if the shapely blonde kisses you again, you're going to need your health insurance card. And to think, I was rooting for you to get back onto the ship safely. Next time, I'll root for the alligator, or maybe tie you to it."

***

The ship's captain told Jason he had called the police, and they were waiting at the dock when the tall ship returned. They asked Jason, Chelsea and Anna several questions and then left with the pirate thief locked in the back seat of a police cruiser. The three of them stood around and chatted for a while after the police left with their prisoner.

Jason started the conversation. "So Anna, you work for *ReallyRealty*? Chelsea and I have had some interesting run-ins with realtors since we've been in Florida. Isn't that right, Chelsea?"

"That's true Jason. We've worked with a number of realtors here, looking for vacation property."

Jason continued. "I don't want to worry you Anna. But, truth is Chelsea and I have found several realtors lately that have been murdered horribly. We've seen a number of dead *ReallyRealty* agents."

"Way to not worry her, Jason. Until you ran your mouth, her only problem was a thief."

"Don't be silly, Chelsea. She's a grown woman. I'm sure she's fine. *Chelsea's just mad because she kissed me on the cheek. It's not my fault she was grateful and finds me attractive.*"

Anna, shaken, "I'm standing right here and can hear you. Dead realtors? Why would anyone want to kill realtors? I'm a realtor. Do you think the little pirate tried to kill me?" She gently touched the bump on her head and began to sob quietly.

"Sorry. My husband often makes me want to cry, too. I doubt this had anything to do with you being a realtor. This guy was just a petty thief, and your purse was handy."

Jason approached Anna and put his hand on her shoulder to comfort her.

"There, there. It's okay. Like Chelsea said, you've probably got nothing to worry about. It is true that all the dead realtors we've found worked for *ReallyRealty*…uh…sorry. Can you think of any reason why someone would hate *ReallyRealty* agents enough to want to murder them?"

Anna started to cry louder.

"Much better, Jason. Now you've really upset the poor woman. And, if you don't take your hand off of her shoulder, I'm going to break your arm."

Seeing the look on Chelsea's face, Jason pulled his hand away and stepped back from the realtor.

"It's okay, Anna. As you can see, my wife is terrifying. She'll protect you."

Chelsea spoke up, "Again, sorry Anna. He makes me crazy sometimes. I'm sure you can see why."

Chelsea paused, then said, "On another note, when we were talking to one of the few live realtors earlier in the week, she mentioned that she had gone to a realtor convention in Miami last year. She also said something strange about being bitten by mosquitoes inside the convention center. Did you happen to attend that convention? I really don't see any connection between *ReallyRealty* realtors, a realtor convention, mosquitoes and murder, but I thought I'd ask."

Anna stopped crying. "Strange you should ask. One of my fellow agents asked me that same question just last week. In fact, I did attend that convention. I got hit on by a couple of drunks, and of course the one I went off with was married. But, at least I didn't come home with any mosquito bites."

Chelsea said, "Like I said, even if you had been bitten by mosquitoes, I have no idea what it would mean. You seem fine to me…not particularly violent, and certainly not dead. It's just that the other realtor seemed to think it was unusual, so I thought I'd ask."

Jason chimed in. "Yeah. I can't imagine what a realtor convention and mosquito bites would have to do with anything. What about dead realtors? Did you find any dead *ReallyRealty* realtors while you were in Miami?"

Anna started to cry again. Chelsea gave Jason the death stare. "Jason, after your little interrogation, I think she might have mentioned that."

"Well, you were asking lots of questions, and I'm the detective. So, I thought I should ask her something too."

Chapter 16

Rock Handsome picked Jason and Chelsea up in front of their rental condo at nine the next morning. They climbed into his luxury SUV, the A/C going full blast. Chelsea took shotgun again. They talked while Rock navigated through the heavy Florida traffic.

Rock said, "I've only got a couple of condos to show you today. We can finish before noon. I know you've had a rough time in Florida, what with all the dead bodies, mainly *ReallyRealty* agents. Truth be told, I'm afraid to leave the house, but a man has to make a living."

Chelsea said, "You're a big fellow. I doubt anyone would mess with you." *I can't believe this hunk is gay, and my husband, the idiot PI, is straight. Sometimes life's just weird.*

Rock continued. "Anyhow, my brother-in-law works for one of the local boat clubs, called *Anybody's Boat*. They're trying to grow the business, and my sister suggested I recommend the club to some of my clients. If you want, I can introduce you to Hank. He's offered to take the three of us on a boat ride up the Intracoastal Waterway this afternoon. There's no obligation to join, and he'll provide lunch."

Chelsea looked concerned. "I'm not sure that's a good idea. We haven't had the best of luck on the water here…or on land for that matter. Jason has developed an exaggerated fear of manatees, it's very hot and it's not safe to swim. Not sure why we'd want to join a boat club."

Chelsea recognized the belligerent look on Jason's face. He said, "Come on Chelsea. A boat club might be just the thing for us. I'm almost over the manatee debacle. I haven't had any nightmares since…well…night-before-last. Having access to a power boat could really open up the recreational haven that is Florida. Besides, you don't get to make all the decisions. I'm the detective and I've got two jobs. So I should get two votes."

"Jason, all you've done since we got here is complain about alligators, poisonous snakes, sharks, hurricanes, manatees, mosquitoes and even rust! Now you want to join a boat club so we can go out onto the water? I'm not willing to swim here, and I'm certainly not going to allow our darling daughters to swim or be dragged behind a boat like live bait. And, I think it's cute that you believe you have two votes. I work and take care of our three daughters, which is a total of four female votes. You're lucky you get to vote at all."

Jason said, "All those other dangers are true, but if we were in a boat club, the rust would be their problem. And, if that's the way you want to count votes, we need to have four sons to counteract our daughters. I'm tired of the girls always siding with you. We need to get you pregnant, soon, because we're playing catch-up."

Chelsea chuckled. "First, Dearest Jason, I'm too old to have any more children. We'd be more like their grandparents. Second, even if I weren't too old, you would have to stay awake long enough to get me pregnant. And third, the idea of raising seven children is crazier than you're becoming a full-time PI. Focus, Jason. Rock wants us to go on a boat ride this afternoon. That's the issue here, not repopulating the planet with tiny private eyes."

Rock said, looking a little embarrassed, "I'm not sure what any of this has to do with getting pregnant. You'll have to go about that on your own time...and TMI. I'm just offering a free boat ride, free lunch and I'll even bring a couple of bottles of wine. There's no obligation to join the boat club. It's just that my sister can be quite irritating…uh…persuasive, and I'll never hear the end of it if you don't come along for the ride. Maybe afterwards you could mention the boat club to some of your friends; tell them how much fun you had."

Chelsea said, "Sorry, Rock. Jason and I are always battling for control, or at least I let him think he is. Anyhow, we'll be happy to come along on your free boat ride. You had me with *there's going to be wine*. I could use a lot of wine after the past two weeks. But, make it more than just a couple of bottles. If I get a little tipsy, you have to promise you won't let me fall in the water."

Rock held up his right hand. "Scout's honor. I promise I'll make sure you stay in the boat. I can't make the same promise for your husband, though. He's on his own."

Jason smiled. "No worries, Rock. I'll be fine. And, unlike Chelsea, in spite of all the things in the water that would like to taste me, I still think joining a boat club might be fun."

After swerving in and out through the heavy traffic, Rock pulled into the parking lot of the first condo. They spent the morning looking at the two condos, and surprisingly there were no dead realtors. Chelsea didn't like either of the units; poor layouts, original appliances, and the color schemes were all wrong.

In the SUV on the way home, Jason added his two cents. "That first condo sucked. Most of the cabinet doors in the kitchen had been left open. Too much chaos. The second condo was even worse. There were thirty-three square tiles in the kitchen floor. Who would use an odd number of tiles in a room? Was the builder insane?"

Rock dropped them off at their rental, where Jason and Chelsea went to change into their bathing suits. The realtor told Chelsea he was going to run home, change his clothes and he'd be back to pick them up in half an hour.

***

They met Hank in the luxurious air-conditioned marina office. Chelsea figured he was about five-six. Rotund and balding, he had the sunburnt face, scalp and arms of a boater. Chelsea recognized the bulbous red nose of a heavy drinker. Oversized facial features and the forced smile of a desperate salesman made him look like one of the seven dwarfs, possibly Happy. *Snow White and the Seven Dwarfs* was one of Chelsea's favorite childhood books; her father had read it to her often.

Rock introduced them. "Dr. and Mrs. Longfellow, this is my brother-in-law and manager of *Anybody's Boats,* Hank Underwood. Hank, this is Dr. Longfellow and his wife, Chelsea. I had to make them a couple of promises to convince them to join us today. First, we need to avoid manatees at all cost. And second, I've brought four bottles of wine, as per my promise to Chelsea."

Chelsea blushed. "Four? You outdid yourself."

Rock said "I know you've had an especially rough couple of weeks. I'll also keep my promise to make sure you remain in the boat at all times."

Jason interrupted. "Glad you brought wine for Chelsea. Did you happen to bring any bananas? I'm feeling low on potassium. I've also been craving a banana split all week...it being so hot and all."

Chelsea looked carefully at Jason. *Bald spot's still there. He's slept in the car several times this week, and he can't stay awake long enough for sex when I let him sleep in our bed. And, no climbing trees, either. Too bad. Maybe he really just wants ice cream.*

Hank shook both their hands. "Pleased to meet you. I'm not even going to ask about the promises…manatees and wine? And, sorry, I don't have any bananas in the office. I'm just glad you're here. I know my wife can be persuasive, and I'm guessing she worked extra hard to motivate Rock to talk you into this. The boat's ready to go."

Hank led them out of the office and onto the dock. Same St. Augustine Marina, with gigantic yachts as far as the eye could see. The club boats were much smaller, the largest a 23-foot Cobia with twin engines. Those boats were all clustered together adjacent to the monster yachts. It made Chelsea think of the kiddie rides at an amusement park, but she kept her thoughts to herself. Hank loaded them into one of the 23-foot center console fishing boats along with the food and wine. He started the engines, twin 150 HP outboards, untied the boat and pushed off.

Jason was impressed. "Nice boat, Hank. I'll bet it'll fly. Can I drive?"

Chelsea cringed. "Jason. I don't think that's a good idea."

"Come on Chelsea. I'll be fine. And, I'm not as likely to fall out of the boat if I'm holding onto the steering wheel."

Hank said, "We'll see, Jason. It's kind of windy today, and getting out of the marina is tricky. Lots of twists, turns and big boats. Maybe you could drive once we get out onto the Intracoastal channel."

Chelsea cringed harder. *Oh God, we're going to die.*

She could see why Hank had insisted on driving the boat out of the marina. The path to the Intracoastal Waterway wound around seemingly endless docks crowded with large yachts. The frequent wind gusts kept threatening to blow them into the hulls of those very expensive boats.

Jason pointed up ahead of them.

He said, "Look at the size of these boats. That one must be at least forty-five or fifty-feet long. I'll bet it's a blast to drive one of those."

Chelsea watched Hank fight the wheel to keep from blowing into another expensive yacht.

"Yep. There's a ton of money in St. Augustine. Some of these are worth a million dollars and up. And, the owners only use them once in a while. They hire full-time crews that get a lot more use out of the boats than they do. It's not unusual for a crew to sail an owner's boat down here from the Northeast in the fall, so the owner can use the boat over the winter. It's a crazy world."

Jason said, "Chelsea, I just had a thought."

"Amazing. A real, honest-to-goodness thought. Don't tell me. You want to buy a yacht and live on it instead of a condo."

"Hey. How'd you know, Chelsea? You'd make a great detective."

"Not at all. I've lived with you for over twenty years, and I know how you think. *God help me.* We can't afford a fifty-foot yacht, and I doubt they have any rooms for rent. If they did, we couldn't afford that either."

They reached the main channel of the Intracoastal Waterway and Hank opened up the throttle. They were cruising along at forty-five knots, when Jason's eyes flashed large, round and bright, a big, childish grin on his face. Chelsea recognized this look, and she was not happy.

Jason couldn't help himself. "Okay Hank. We're on the Intracoastal. Can I drive now? Huh? Can I? Please? Can I? It looks like so much fun and I like to go fast."

Chelsea looked helplessly at Rock.

Hank hesitated. He waved for Rock to come closer to him. Chelsea followed, in the hope Rock could keep her from falling out of the boat.

Chelsea heard Hank say to Rock, "You told me that this guy is a doctor, so he probably has the funds to join the club. But, he's kind of strange. You also told my sister he thinks he's a PI. I could really use a couple of new club members, but I can't afford for him to damage the boat. What should I do?"

Rock shrugged his shoulders and raised his hands, suggesting it was up to Hank. Chelsea remained quiet and grabbed Rocks arm, ready to hang on tight.

Hank said, "Oh, what the hell!"

He pulled back on the throttle and brought the boat to a stop as far to the right of the channel as possible. Chelsea had some idea of what was coming, and she held onto Rocks arm for dear life, kind of like it was the oh-my-god-bar in a car.

Hank said, "Okay Dr. Longfellow. I assume you've driven a boat before. You push the throttle forward to go forward, and the farther forward the faster you go. There's no brakes, so you need to give yourself plenty of time and room to stop. Take over for a few minutes. Stay to the right of oncoming boats. I'll point out the mile markers and explain how to navigate them as you go."

Jason jumped up from his seat and replaced Hank behind the wheel. He said, "No worries. I've got this."

With that, he squeezed the clutch and shoved the throttle forward, throwing everyone towards the back of the boat. Rock grabbed Chelsea by the arm and held on tight, and she had his other arm in a death grip. Hank landed hard on his butt on the aft seat and grabbed a railing.

Hank yelled, "Easy there, Doc. There's no hurry. We've got all afternoon. There's a place a couple of miles up ahead where we can beach the boat and have a picnic. But we have to get there alive."

From the back of the boat, Chelsea yelled over the roar of the engines, "Jason, remember the motorcycle and the alligator. Let's not have an aquatic version of that, please."

Hank frowned. "Motorcycle and alligator? Is there something I should…?

"No worries, Dear. I'm getting the hang of it."

Chelsea saw a very large yacht cruising along leisurely in front of them. It was at least 50-foot long, with the Captain's bridge several stories above their position, dwarfing their 23-foot fishing boat. The vessel was white with blue trim along the sides and heavily stained marine teak decking reflecting the bright sunshine. Black lettering on the stern announced the name of the boat; *Vacation Vaccination.*

Chelsea heard Jason say, "Look up ahead, Hank. It's one of those fifty-foot cabin cruisers. He's going too slow. Can I pass him on the left?"

Before Hank had a chance to answer, Jason shoved the throttle all the way forward and aimed the bow to the left of the enormous yacht. Chelsea saw the captain of the yacht look down from the helm at the small boat coming up on his left. He was apparently competitive in nature, because he shoved his throttle forward to prevent the little boat from passing him.

Chelsea yelled, "Jason, look out for the waves."

At first, Jason didn't appear to realize that the enormous yacht was speeding up. Much worse, before Jason had a chance to back off the throttle the yacht's wake rose several feet higher than the 23-foot boat. Chelsea hung on tight to Rock as she saw the Cobia hit the first gigantic wake; the bow of the boat flew upward. The bow hit the second wave on its way down, and the front of the boat submerged, diving much like a submarine on its way to the bottom of the ocean."

"Oh Shiiiit! Chelsea! Help me!"

A giant rush of water covered the boat from bow to stern, washing Jason and Hank overboard. As Jason floated by, Chelsea heard, "Gurgle, gurgle. Help! I'm drowning! Gurgle, choke."

Rock had an iron grip on Chelsea with one hand, and the steel seat frame with the other. She was amazed that he was able to keep his promise; they both remained on board when the bow resurfaced. After the boat righted itself, Chelsea dove forward and pulled the throttle into neutral. Then she looked around for her husband.

Rock pointed. "There's Jason, in the middle of the Intracoastal. And there's Hank, a few feet closer to us."

Chelsea pointed ahead of their position. "Look. The giant yacht is turning around and coming back. Hopefully they're not returning to finish us off."

Chelsea watched as the yacht stopped just short of where Jason and Hank were treading water, and lowered an inflatable life boat with a small outboard motor into the water. The man driving the life boat cruised over to Jason and pulled him into the small craft; then he repeated the act with Hank. He aimed the raft at Hanks's Cobia and slowly pulled alongside.

He yelled up at Chelsea and Rock. "Ahoy! The name's Orlando Cerveza. I'm first mate on the *Vacation Vaccination*. The owner, Mr. Mark Moneyman, would like to apologize for swamping your boat, and invite you for drinks. Put down your ladder, and I'll drop off these two gentlemen. We can meet back at the St. Augustine marina. Once we are docked, you can come aboard the yacht for drinks."

Chelsea turned off the engine, and she and Rock moved to the stern. Rock lowered the ladder. Chelsea gave Jason a hand climbing on board. She felt bad for Hank, who followed, eyes wide open, unable to speak, clearly in shock.

Jason spoke first. "Well, that was more excitement than I was looking for. I tried to pass the guy, but he wanted to race. I showed him. Nobody bullies me. I'm Jason Longfellow, PI."

Chelsea fought the urge to shove him overboard, for fear she might not be able to resist running over him once he was in the water again. After all, he was the father of her children.

She said, "What exactly did you show him? Did you think you were driving a submarine? I know nothing about boats, and even I know that this thing isn't built to travel underwater. Why on God's earth didn't you back off when he speeded up?"

"When I started to pass him, he hit the throttle…challenged me. I couldn't back down. I'm a man, a licensed PI, for God's sake."

Hank pointed at Jason and sputtered, "Boat. Sink. Damage. Crazy person."

"Jason, I think you broke Hank. You're very lucky his boat didn't sink to the bottom of the Intracoastal. He might still sue you. And why would you take the chance on capsizing our boat, what with the alligators, sharks, snakes? Your wife is on board!"

"I guess my testosterone kicked in and overcame all those fears."

"So your fear of losing a race overcame your fear of being eaten by alligators, sharks and snakes? And, your fear that I might murder you in your sleep?"

Jason knees turned weak, and his face paled. "When you put it that way, it doesn't sound so good. Damn testosterone! Damn alligators! Damn sharks! Damn boats! Damn Florida!"

Chelsea just gave up and grinned. "You forgot rust. What about damn rust?"

Hank managed to start the engine and drive them back to the dock, where he parked the boat in its slip and said his goodbyes. It was clear to Chelsea that he wanted no part of Jason as a member of his boat club. Chelsea, Jason and Rock walked a couple of docks over to where the *Vacation Vaccination* was now moored. The first mate was waiting for them at the steps leading up to the gigantic yacht.

"Come aboard. Mr. Moneyman is anxious to meet you, apologize, and drink…especially the drink part. He has already put away several martinis, and he was driving the boat. His new trophy wife, Gina, was sitting next to him, and he was not about to let you pass and show him up. He's sixty, she's twenty-four and he might be a little insecure, in spite of his millions. You're lucky to be alive. I didn't tell you any of this. If you try to sue him, he'll swear I was driving, and if I tell the truth my green card will go bye-bye."

They followed Orlando on board. He led them to the main cabin, where they saw a small, plump man in his sixties. Moneyman had a flat face, porcine nose, and small beady eyes. He looked to Chelsea like well-cooked pork, with his pudgy sunburnt cheeks and alcohol-induced red nose. His head was topped off by wind-blown curly gray hair and his face adorned by a matching gray moustache that looked like it had been drawn on using a number two pencil. The thickness of his glasses suggested that he might have paid extra to qualify for a license to drive any type of moving vehicle. He wore a flowered shirt and bright red swim trunks, and he sat on a plush leather circular deck couch. Chelsea noticed a very shapely blonde with the face of an angel seated next to him, her hand on his inner thigh. Chelsea also noticed Jason noticing the blonde.

Jason mumbled, "So that's what millions will buy you. Damn! I shoulda been a hedge fund manager."

Chelsea, standing next to him, "Excuse me? What did you just say?"

"Nothing Dear. I was just wondering how much this guy's worth."

The man didn't bother to stand and offer his hand. He said, slurring his words slightly, "Hello. I'm Mark Moneyman. Welcome aboard the *Vacation Vaccination*, my modest little summer boat. Sorry I swamped you, but it's not polite to pass someone and make them eat your wake."

Chelsea, irritated, "I doubt this monstrosity would have even noticed the wake from our tiny boat. But, I get the need to prove your manhood. What are you, five-six if you stand on tippy toes?" She glanced at the blonde.

Moneyman responded. "I like this woman. She has spunk. Good looking, too. Maybe we should ask her to party with us for a couple of days. What do you think, Gina?"

The blonde just smiled and looked embarrassed.

Moneyman then addressed Rock and Jason. "What about the two of you? Do you have any spunk?"

Jason was staring a little too intently at the blonde. Chelsea elbowed him in the ribs.

"Jason, focus. He asked you if you have any spunk. And, he invited your wife to join him on his boat for God knows what. Aren't you going to say anything?"

Jason grabbed his ribs. "Ouch! Easy, Wife. You'll break something."

He said, "Hello, Mr. Moneyman. I'm Dr. Jason Longfellow, PI. This is my wife, Chelsea, and our realtor Rock Handsome. We were getting a free boat ride on the Intracoastal Waterway to convince us to join the local boat club when you tried to drown us. That wasn't very nice of you. You also shouldn't be drinking and driving. You might endanger the life of that beautiful wife of yours."

He smiled at the blonde.

Chelsea elbowed him again. "What my husband meant to say is, what were you thinking? You're obviously drunk, and you almost killed us. And, I'm not interested in joining a fat little man and his *granddaughter* for anything on this oversized floating bar."

She turned to the blonde. "Does he really need a boat this big to compensate? If that's the case, I feel sorry for you."

The blonde grinned a four-martini grin and winked at Chelsea. "Honey, this boat ain't nothin'. He's got millions to make up for what he lacks in the bedroom. I could buy a whole store full of self-satisfaction, batteries included; know what I mean? Hell, I could buy the store."

Moneyman was staring so intently at Rock Handsome that he didn't appear to hear Gina. It surprised Chelsea when he stood up and started waving his arms about, obviously agitated.

"Did you say this man's your realtor? There's a realtor on my boat?! Orlando, throw these people over the side immediately!"

Chelsea looked at Jason. "That's what he's upset about? I challenged his manhood in front of his trophy wife, and he's upset about our realtor?"

Orlando said, "Come on, folks. You've worn out your welcome. Mr. Moneyman wants you off his boat, and so it's off you go."

He herded them onto the dock. As they walked away, stunned by this odd turn of events, Chelsea saw Orlando shrug an apology in their direction.

Chelsea said, "This trip to Florida just keeps getting stranger and stranger. Mark Moneyman? The *Vacation Vaccination?* Jason, didn't you say something about a company in Miami that makes vaccines? And this guy hates realtors. I feel like there should be a clue in there somewhere."

Jason just shrugged. "Vaccines, realtors, mosquitoes, and a fat little man that tried to drown us? I have no idea what's going on, but it's clear to me that Florida is trying to kill me. What did I ever do to Florida to make it so mad?"

Chapter 17

Rock Handsome picked up Jason and Chelsea at nine o'clock the next morning. Chelsea took shotgun again. Rock told her he had three properties to show them. He had brought Brazilian blend coffees from a local coffee house. He handed them out and then he pulled the large air conditioned SUV out into traffic, headed for the first property of the morning.

"Good morning Longfellow family. There's packets of cream and sugar in the bag if you want. I hope you're all recovered from yesterday's recreational disaster. Sorry it went so wrong. I'm guessing that you have decided against joining the boat club?"

Chelsea took a careful sip of the hot coffee through the small slit in the lid. She was the most awake, so she answered first. She looked into the back seat at Jason.

"Yes, I can state categorically that no matter what my insane husband thinks, we are not interested in joining a boat club. That was a disturbing experience. Don't you agree, Jason?"

Jason took the plastic lid off of his coffee, spilled some on his leg, and yelped.

"Coffee's hot. I should have worn long pants. And, I agree. No boat club. Too many ways to die."

Chelsea turned to Rock. "What puzzles me is why that awful man hated you so much. Does everyone in Florida hate realtors? Maybe that's why there are so many dead ones. He's the one that almost killed us, drinking and driving that giant yacht. He was very drunk. I still think we should call the police, or at least get a lawyer and sue him."

Rock said, "I hear you, but it wouldn't do any good. Wealthy men like that are treated like royalty down here. He could have killed all three of us, and I guarantee you it would have been ruled a no-fault accident. If he can afford that yacht, he could easily get away with murder."

From the back seat, a whiny pitch to his voice, "I just wanted to go fast, to pass him. Not my fault he was drunk. Wouldn't the police care about that? I could investigate, collect evidence, make a case against him. He wasn't very nice."

Rock shook his head. "Are you kidding? His first mate and wife would swear on a stack of bibles that Orlando was driving the boat. Even if it went to court, he'd just buy off the judge. Or, more likely they'd turn out to be golfing buddies at the same exclusive country club. Best to just let it go, and be glad no one got seriously injured."

Chelsea said, "Enough about Mr. Moneybags. What do you have to show us this morning?"

Rock grinned. "I have two condos. But, first I wanted to show you a very nice three-bedroom, two-and-a-half bath single family home that just came on the market. It's fully remodeled, with lots of room, and it's on the market for two-hundred-twenty-five-thousand. The only catch is that it's on the west side of A1A, but in a nice neighborhood. I thought it's worth taking a look, since it's in your price range. What do you think? It's just up ahead."

Chelsea looked in the back seat again. Jason was still wiping coffee off of his leg with several napkins.

"Jason, what do you think? I could live with having to cross A1A to get to the beach. You can actually drive on the beach. We could either take my SUV or get some bicycles. That might be fun, for us and the kids."

"But Chelsea. That's the side where the swamp…marsh is, with the alligators, snakes and stuff. Are you sure you want to live there?"

Rock said. "Jason, I've been to this neighborhood several times. I've never seen any ponds or water of any kind, or any alligators or snakes. The entire development is fenced in, so maybe that keeps them out. It's worth a look, don't you think?"

"Okay. But, we're just gonna look."

A few minutes later Rock turned into a large gated community. He entered a code into a key pad, and the gate raised up to let his SUV pass through. Chelsea liked the idea of this added security. Three blocks later Rock pulled up in front of a freshly painted stucco house. They exited the SUV, and Jason and Chelsea followed Rock onto the front porch.

"This is a very well maintained neighborhood, only twenty years old. The houses are all cement and stucco, very well built. The development spans twenty blocks in each direction, with sidewalks throughout so you can take a nice after-dinner stroll. As you saw, it also offers the security of a gated community."

Rock opened the front door. Chelsea entered first, followed by Jason and then Rock. They walked into a newly remodeled living room, with beautiful hardwood floors, a vaulted ceiling with cedar slats and trim and two skylights.

Chelsea was grinning ear-to-ear. "This is beautiful, and spacious. Look at the loft. I've always wanted a loft. Is that an upstairs bedroom? Show me more."

Rock gave them the tour. Chelsea really liked the kitchen with new cabinets, granite countertops and stainless appliances. A small open dining area was positioned between the kitchen and the large living room. Next, they walked into a large master bedroom off the hall to the right, with an all tile bathroom, including a separate shower and large soaking tub. Chelsea thought the shower looked like fun. It was done in white tile with an integrated blue lined pattern, and included multiple nozzles, some for showering and others for massage.

Chelsea said, "Jason, you might actually fit in that tub. Wouldn't a nice hot soak be great from time to time? And, look at that tile. Blue's your favorite color."

Jason flushed the toilet. "Well, the toilet in here flushes. That's a good thing."

There were also two smaller bedrooms downstairs. They shared a bathroom containing another large soaking tub with separate shower. Rock told them that the loft could not be listed as a bedroom, because of a local fire ordinance that prevented children from sleeping in a loft. The loft was set up as a playroom for small children, complete with built-in bookshelves and cabinets for storing games and toys. Chelsea knew the girls, especially Lucy, would love the loft.

Chelsea walked up to Jason, took his hand, looked up at him and gave him *the face.* She preferred the aggressive approach, but she loved this place, and sometimes pleading worked.

"Jason, this is perfect. I never dreamed you could get something this nice for a little over two-hundred-thousand dollars. Especially not a single family home. Please tell me you like it."

Jason said, "There's got to be something wrong. The cabinet and closet doors are all closed, so that's good. And, the toilets flush and sinks work and aren't leaking. There's also an even number of tiles in the kitchen. So, where's the dead body? Maybe someone was murdered in the house. Is that why the price is so low?"

Rock grinned. "No, Jason. No one was murdered here. I stopped by last night and walked through the entire house, just to make sure there were no dead bodies. I wanted this to be a good experience for you. *ReallyRealty* intends to please. Believe it or not, it's just a good buy, and you're in the right place at the right time. Take the win."

Chelsea agreed, "Yeah Jason, take the win. Let's make this our Florida vacation home."

Jason pulled away from Chelsea, determined to find something wrong. "What about rentals? Does the HOA allow renting? What are the restrictions? Is there a history of rental income with the place?"

Rock was prepared. "I knew you'd ask about that. Yes, the HOA allows rentals, minimum of a month. This house has an excellent rental history. You could rent it out pretty much every month except September, which is peak hurricane season, and there's even been renters in here the past two Septembers."

Jason said, "It *is* on the west side of A1A. Rock, I'd like to take a walk around the neighborhood to look for ponds, drainage control pools…the kind of places where alligators and snakes hang out. I know you said there were none, but I'd like to see for myself. Also, what about mosquitoes? Since this side of A1A is drained swamp, is there a mosquito problem at night? Mosquitoes can carry nasty viruses here in Florida."

Rock said, "No problem, Jason. We can walk around as much as you'd like. County trucks come around and spray the neighborhood for mosquitoes once a month."

The three of them exited through the front door. Standing on the front porch, Rock pointed out more advantages. Chelsea listened intently.

"There's a small yard in the front, and one in the back, so you can set up a barbeque and the kids have some room to play outside. There's also a community pool a couple of blocks away. It's a great neighborhood for families."

Jason said, "If there's going to be any wetlands with alligators and snakes to find, we should walk west towards the swampy area."

Jason led the way. They walked around the neighborhood for over an hour, and they couldn't find any ponds, gators, or snakes. Chelsea pointed out that the community swimming pool was crowded with families, with lots of children.

Chelsea said, "See Jason. Mr. Rock was right. This is the perfect neighborhood for families. I see a three-bedroom, two-and-a-half-bath stucco home in our future. No alligators, snakes, sharks…a neighborhood gate to keep out the bad guys; what more could you want? It's safer than our place in Northern Virginia."

Two blocks from the house that was soon to become their vacation home, Chelsea noticed a tall, thin elderly woman approaching them on the sidewalk. She appeared upset.

"Have you seen my Petey? He's my baby, a short-haired terrier. I opened the front door for just a second to get the mail and he bolted. He never wanders far from home, and I live on this street, only one block up. I've been looking for over an hour."

Jason started his usual rant, "I'm Jason Longfellow, PI, at your service. I caught a serial killer, a cheese thief and a thieving monkey. I should be able to find a lost dog. I get twenty-five-dollars an hour plus expenses. What does this Petey look like?"

Chelsea interrupted, "Jason, she told you he's a short-haired terrier. She doesn't need a private detective. She needs for us to help her find her dog." To the lady. "What color is he, Ma'am?"

"My name's Naomi. You can call me Naomi. Petey is mainly white, with a few brown spots; just a little fellow. He hardly ever runs away. It's not safe here, you know. I hope he's okay."

Jason looked at Chelsea, then back to Naomi. He said, "Doesn't need a PI? Who better to find a lost dog? Somebody probably kidnapped Petey for the ransom."

Chelsea watched Jason walk up and down the street a couple of times. She could hear him halfheartedly yelling the dog's name.

"Petey! Here, Petey! Naomi's looking for you. I'm a private detective. I caught a serial killer, but according to my wife I'm not qualified to find a stupid lost dog. Be a good boy, come to me and show her she's wrong."

Jason walked back to where Naomi was standing, talking to Chelsea.

Chelsea said, "Jason, stop pouting. I thought we should help find the dog to be neighborly, since we're going to be Naomi's new neighbors. Once we move into the house, maybe we'll find a dead body or two for you to investigate."

Naomi frowned. "Dead body? Do you often find dead bodies? And, you plan on buying this house and moving to my neighborhood?"

Chelsea smiled. "Sorry. I was just kidding with my husband. He fancies himself a private eye, and he's always looking for new cases. He likes to investigate murder…apparently more prestigious on the PI scale than adultery, skip chasing, or burglary.”

“Chelsea. Tell the truth. How many dead people have we found here in the past two weeks while looking for vacation property? Dare I say *several?”*

Naomi’s face changed from frown to fear. “Thank you for offering to help me find Petey, but I’m sure he’ll come home when he’s hungry. I do feel the need to warn you that this is not a desirable neighborhood to live in. There are too many noisy children, the people aren’t very friendly and I think they’d turn especially nasty if a bunch of dead bodies started showing up.”

Naomi turned and walked away as fast as her skinny little old legs would carry her.

“Chelsea, you scared poor Naomi away. How am I ever going to be a successful PI if you chase off all my clients?”

They returned to the stucco house. Chelsea and Rock stood on the front porch, discussing the property. While listening to Rock, Chelsea glanced at Jason pacing back and forth on the sidewalk out front, no doubt trying to find something wrong with the place. She looked away for a second, heard Jason yelp, and saw him pointing at something up the street.

“Chelsea! Rock! I think I know where Petey went!”

Chelsea watched as Jason passed out, his body collapsing slowly to the ground. Behind him, lumbering up the middle of the street like a parade float, she saw a very large alligator. It was obviously no longer hungry, as it walked by Jason without taking any notice.

“Oh look Rock. Jason’s decided to take a nap. And, based on the large green thing with a mouth full of sharp teeth walking by my husband’s unconscious body, I'm guessing my little stucco dream house is off the table. Maybe we should wake him up before the gator changes its mind and decides that Petey wasn't enough of a mid-day snack."

Chapter 18

Next morning, Jason and Chelsea sat at the breakfast table eating frozen waffles. Jason was not happy with his plate of burnt waffles that Chelsea had left in the toaster too long. Her nicely toasted brown waffles were covered with butter and syrup. Normally he would have squawked, but she was obviously angry about the previous day. So, he kept quiet and slathered his waffles with peanut butter to kill the burnt taste. He had made the coffee, strong caffeinated brew for Chelsea and half-caff for himself. He had finally mustered the courage to add milk to his, and Chelsea had rolled her eyes at him when she saw him do it.

"Jason, I don't know why you bother drinking coffee at all. More to the point, we found the perfect Florida bungalow yesterday, and you had to go and ruin it. Where'd you find that stupid alligator anyway? Did you bring it with you? Now, poor Mr. Handsome has to spend another day finding more places to show us."

Jason watched as she finished off the last bite of her waffles, washing it down with a big gulp of strong, dark roasted brew. He couldn't figure out how she could drink that stuff. It tasted to him like bitter mud. He gagged down another bite of burnt waffle; the peanut butter didn't help.

"Chelsea, I didn't do anything, except almost get eaten. Why would you want to live in a place where the neighborhood watch is a giant alligator? It ate poor Petey, for goodness sake."

"If you hadn't gotten all neurotic and gone looking, you wouldn't have found that monster, and we'd have made an offer on that gorgeous house.

If you really loved me, you'd have killed the thing and solved the problem."

"Be reasonable, Chelsea. First of all, where there's one gator, there's more. And second, how was I supposed to kill it? Did you see the size of that thing?"

"But, you're such a manly man, what with kiteboarding, motorcycling and all. You should have thought of something."

"Now you're just being mean."

"I suppose you're right. It wouldn't have been a good neighborhood to live in with the children. If that monster ever attacked one of our kids, Momma Bear would have ripped out its heart with my bare teeth."

"Chelsea, where were Momma Bear's teeth yesterday when the gator almost ate me?"

"Don't be silly, Jason. Momma Bear's teeth only come out when our children are in danger. That thing was humongous."

Jason was sad. He took another bite of waffle, which made him even sadder. He gave up and finished his coffee.

"So, Chelsea, we have the day to ourselves. Let's go to the beach, relax and soak up some rays?"

"Sounds like a good idea. You collect the beach chairs and towels from the closet, and I'll throw some drinks in a cooler. Then, give me a minute to put on my bathing suit and lotion and we can head out. You can figure out how to carry the stuff in your little clown car."

"No problemo. I'll strap the chairs on the luggage rack. The towels and cooler can go in the trunk."

Fifteen minutes later, Jason piloted the red rocket towards one of the entrances to Crescent Beach, straps from the beach chairs flapping in the wind.

"Chelsea, I know the signs say you need four-wheel-drive to drive on the beach, but my red rocket is so light it should glide along on top of the sand. I'm gonna give it a shot. Beats carrying all the beach stuff several blocks in this heat."

"Jason, are you sure that's a good idea?"

"No worries, Dear. We'll be fine, I promise."

"God, I hate it when you say that."

Jason drove up the road to the beach, gunning the engine to get a good start onto the sand. He turned right to follow the path marked by bright orange plastic cones, and the car slowed as it lost momentum. Then they hit deep sand.

"Jason, we don't appear to be moving. Are the rear wheels supposed to be burying themselves in the sand?"

"It's okay, Chelsea. We seem to be stuck. But, I'll just do the forward-backward-rocking thing, and we'll be on our way."

Jason spent several minutes shifting between first and reverse, trying to rock the car free of the deep sand.

"Chelsea, we're stuck. I can't believe it. I was sure the rocket would ride on top of the sand."

"Now what? Why do I let you talk me into these things?"

Jason got out of the car and walked around to the rear to assess the situation. He looked up the beach and saw several twenty-something women in bikinis walking in his direction.

"No worries, Chelsea. I'm thinking help is on the way." *This is my idea of a day at the beach.*

Chelsea got out and joined him. It became clear that she had also looked up the beach.

Chelsea said, "My God, we're being invaded by the bikini squad. Pull your eyeballs back into your head."

She kicked him in the shin, hard.

"Ouch! Be nice, Dear. We're stuck. We can't refuse help, no matter what form it comes in."

The lead young woman, a tall, curvaceous brunette wearing a black shoestring bikini, approached Jason. The rest of the young women, eleven in all, included bikini-clad blondes, brunettes, and red-heads. All sizes, all shapely, and all perfectly tanned, they crowded around the red rocket. Jason had never seen so much gorgeously exposed flesh gathered in one place in his life. The sight of it all made him dizzy. When he saw the look in Chelsea's eyes, the origin of his dizziness changed from lust to fear.

"Got a problem, Mister? I'm Janine, and we're the girls of the Delta Sigma Theta sorority, local Jacksonville Chapter. You're in luck. We all decided to come on down to St. Augustine for the day, and public service is our thing."

Jason smiled a big smile, his surroundings momentarily distracting him from his well-founded fear of wife.

He said, "Well, we're the public, and we could use some service…help. My wife didn't want to walk all the way from the parking lot, so she asked me to drive on the beach. I tried to tell her it wouldn't work. I don't have four-wheel-drive, but…well…you know how it is. By the way, I'm Dr.

Jason Longfellow, Private Eye." *That ought to impress them, both doctor and PI.*

Chelsea took hold of Jason's wrist and dug her nails in, hard and deep.

"Yow! Sorry, I forgot to introduce you to my wife. This is my wife…uh…Chelsea. Her name is Chelsea. Chelsea, this here's Janine. She and her friends are Delta Sigma Thighs. They want to help. Isn't that nice?"

Chelsea took her hand off of Jason's wrist, and wiped the blood from her fingernails onto his bathing suit.

"Jason, I believe it's Delta Sigma *Theta*…oh, never mind. Pleased to meet you, Janine. We'd be most grateful if you could give us a push. So silly of me insisting that my husband drive his little clown car on the beach. Now, we're all stuck and stuff."

Chelsea reached for Jason's other wrist, but he saw it coming and quickly moved away.

Janine said, "Pleased to meet the two of you. Wow, a doctor and a private eye. You must be a busy man. You remind me a little of my dad. He's a doctor too."

Jason frowned. *Why do women keep telling me I remind them of their dads? I'm not that old.*

Chelsea smiled a big smile. "Now, I'm even more pleased to meet you, Janine. It would be great if you and your friends could help Grandpa and me push his little clown car out of the sand. I'm thinking we should push it backwards to the entrance road, get the wheels on blacktop, and then we can park in one of the parking lots like I suggested Gramps do in the first place."

"Chelsea, you're being mean again."

"Just get in the car, steer, and let the women get you out of this mess."

Jason obediently entered the driver's seat, put the rocket in neutral and steered as the pack of bikini-clad young women, and Chelsea, pushed the car back onto the road.

Jason pouted. *Grandpa indeed. I might be in my forties on the outside, but I'm a twenty-something on the inside. I could teach these young ladies a thing or two…well, at least a thing…before Chelsea killed me. I'm sad again.*

Jason heard Chelsea yell that the car's rear wheels had found pavement, and the women stopped pushing. Chelsea got in the passenger seat, grumbling as she tried to brush the sand off of her sweaty body.

"Jason, park this thing in the lot like I suggested in the first place, and let's get in some sun and relaxation, before I kill you."

"You look like you need to relax. And, my wrist is still bleeding."

"Don't be such a big baby."

Jason, grinning ear-to-ear, waved at the young women of Delta Sigma Theta. "Thank you ladies. We really appreciate your help! Enjoy your day at the beach!"

Chelsea reached over and smacked him on the back of the head.

***

Jason drove the two blocks to the parking lot. He purchased a ticket, parked, and hauled the chairs, cooler and towels back to the beach. Chelsea walked empty handed alongside him.

"Jason, how far are you planning to walk? We're almost back to the condo."

"I want to get as far away from people as possible. I like to avoid the smokers and families with loud and unruly children."

He finally found a place with only a couple of other people off in the distance. He sat up the beach chairs, took his book from the tote bag and a cold Diet Pepsi from the cooler, and sat down.

"This is a nice spot. Sit down and feel that ocean breeze blowing through your hair."

Chelsea put her towel and sunglasses on the other chair.

"I'm going to take a quick dip to wash off the sand. Then I think I'll sit down in this comfy chair and take a nap in the nice warm sun."

She came back a few minutes later, dried off and got comfortable. Jason heard her snoring.

"Chelsea, I'm bored. Sitting around in the hot sun is no fun, and I just realized that I've already read this book. How about you bury me in the sand?"

Chelsea sat up abruptly, a dazed look on her face.

"Jason, you woke me up. I just fell asleep. Why are you such a pain in the butt?"

"Come on Chelse. Bury me in the sand. Please! I want to see if I can escape before the tide comes in and drowns me. I like to live dangerously."

"I've noticed, Jason. You have no idea how much danger you were in when the bikini squad came to rescue us."

"I have some idea, from the scars forming on my wrist. Now, please bury me."

"You're lucky it wasn't your throat. Okay, I give up. Dig a hole in the sand, climb in, lay down and I'll fill it in. Do you want your face covered up, too? At least that might shut you up."

"I have to breath, so, no sand in the face please. Cover everything else, and I'll see if I can get out. I'm kinda like Houdini, don't you think?"

"If Houdini was a moron."

"You're being mean again."

Jason dug a large, elongated hole in the sand and climbed in. He laid down on his back and closed his eyes.

"Okay Chelsea. Cover me up. I'll escape from this hole before the tide drowns me. Good PI training, staying calm in the face of danger."

Chelsea got down on one knee and began shoving sand in to cover him up. She stopped and pointed at something in the hole.

"Jason, why do you have two right hands?"

"Chelsea, stop fooling around and finish covering me up. The tide's coming in fast, and I need some time to escape."

"Jason, I'm not kidding. There's an extra hand in there with you."

Jason sat up and looked at the spot where Chelsea was pointing. "What the hell? That looks like a human hand."

Chelsea stood up and took a few steps back. Jason saw the fear on her face.

"No duh, Sherlock. That's what I've been trying to tell you."

Jason climbed out of the hole and got on his hands and knees to investigate. He poked at the extra hand, sticking out of the sand on one side of the hole. It didn't move, so he pulled on it.

"It seems to be attached to something."

Chelsea said, "You don't suppose some other idiot told his wife to bury him here, and he didn't make it out before the tide got him? She covered up his face; smart woman. We should go. I've seen more than my share of dead bodies in the past two weeks."

Jason said, "Maybe it's just a hand."

Jason pulled the hand upward, revealing an arm. The arm wore a tan sport jacket, made from a light cotton-polyester blend.

"Well, maybe it's just a hand and an arm."

"Jason, how's that any better than an entire body?"

Jason started digging with his hands, inward from the arm, until he struck something larger. Chelsea stood watching, an impatient look on her face.

Jason said, "No worries. I found the torso."

"Oh goodie. I really think it's time for us to leave, before somebody notices what's happening."

"Don't be silly, Chelsea. I'm a PI…"

"Yeah. I know. You're a PI, and you need to investigate. Well, I'm your sweaty, sandy, sunburnt wife, and I need to go home."

"Calm down, Chelsea. I'll get to the bottom of this."

Jason kept digging until he had unearthed the body of a man in his early forties. The man had brown hair and brown eyes. Removing more sand revealed a well-sculpted nose, a mouth with thin lips and straight teeth, and a long face with dimpled chin. A thin moustache that looked like it had been drawn in with a pencil was perched under the nose.

Jason said, "With that face and moustache, this guy looks a little like an undertaker. That would be ironic…no coffin. A tan sport jacket and white pants is an odd way to dress for the beach."

Chelsea moved closer and looked down at the body.

"Jason, he could be considered good looking, except for the sand in his eyes, nose and mouth. Maybe he didn't die here. Maybe someone brought the body here and buried it."

Jason struggled to get up in the loose sand near the hole. He managed to stand, facing Chelsea.

"You think he was murdered somewhere else and his body dumped here? That would make sense. It's too warm on the beach for a sport coat. I also doubt he would have asked his wife to bury him in the sand while fully clothed. My PI training tells me that in the case of murder, look to the spouse first. We should check out the wife. *Cherchez l'epouse.*"

"Jason, we don't have any idea who he is, or if he even has an *epouse*. Shouldn't you just call the police?"

"I probably should, but if they find me with another dead body, I'm gonna end up in jail…murder by association."

Jason searched the dead man's jacket.

"There's some business cards in this inside pocket."

Chelsea put her hands out in front of her as if warding off a ghost, or Jason, and turned her head away.

"Please don't tell me it's another realtor. Enough already."

Jason examined the cards. "Well…there are business cards of a number of different realtors, a couple of them from our buddies at *ReallyRealty*. Maybe this guy just collected realtor business cards as a hobby? That's a thing, right?"

"No, Jason, that's not a thing. Does he have a wallet on him with ID? Maybe a driver's license? If he is a realtor, the police are going to freak out. I doubt I'll be able to bail you out of jail."

Jason continued searching through the sand-filled sport coat. "Here's a wallet in the other inside pocket. The driver's license says…oh shit!"

"Oh shit what? Who is he?"

"His name's Rip Thornton, and he is a realtor, from…you guessed it…our friends at *ReallyRealty*. This is not good. The address of his office is in Miami. These other realtor business cards list Miami addresses, too."

"You're right. This is not good. We came to St. Augustine to buy a vacation condo, and instead we're knee deep in dead realtors. You just had to be a PI."

"What did I do? I didn't kill anybody. I like realtors. Like Debbie…remember Debbie? I can't help it I'm such an outstanding PI that cases just seek me out to be solved."

Chelsea punched Jason in the arm, fairly hard. He yelped.

"You mean the perky cheerleader who tried to puree your face? You're right about one thing, you are one heck of a crime magnet…mostly murder."

"Well, there's that."

"If you're such a hot shot PI, please tell me how a realtor from Miami ended up buried on the beach fully clothed, all the way up here in St. Augustine. There's plenty of perfectly good beaches in South Florida."

Jason gave her a friendly pat on the behind, and winked.

"No worries, Chelsea. Before all is said and done, I'll have this case wrapped up and we'll own a two-bedroom condo here in sunny, windy, rusty, deadly Florida. Now I understand why people say that Florida is the place where people go to die."

"No, Private Idiot. That's because old people come here to retire. However, maybe you're right about buying a condo on A1A. We do have children, so I'll have the side without gators, please."

Chapter 19

Jason and Chelsea stood side-by-side on the beach, staring at yet another dead realtor. Jason was in shock, speechless. Finally, Chelsea spoke up.

"We definitely need to phone the police. But, I'm going to call Rock Handsome first. Maybe Rock can shed some light on this particular dead realtor before the cops get here. They worked for the same realty company. We need some reason why they shouldn't just haul you off to jail."

Jason shrugged. "Thanks for the vote of confidence?"

"Listen, Jason. I'm your wife, I've been with you for this entire trip, and even I'm beginning to wonder if you're some sort of realtor serial killer. There's dead realtors everywhere you go."

Jason looked shocked. He shook his head and pointed at Chelsea.

"Me? You're always there too."

She poked him in the chest with her index finger, an innocent expression on her face.

"You're the PI. I'm just your wife, an innocent bystander."

"So, that's what you're going to tell the cops? Thanks for nothing."

"Someone has to stay out of jail to care for our children. I think it should be their mother."

Chelsea dialed her cell and placed it on speaker. Jason definitely wanted to be part of this conversation.

"Hello. Rock Handsome? Hi. This is Chelsea Longfellow."

Jason heard Rock's voice. "Hello Chelsea. How are you? Has your husband gotten over his shock yet? That was a big alligator. I'm here at the office putting together another list of condos to show you guys tomorrow. Other side of A1A."

Chelsea said, "Yes, I appreciate your efforts. But that's not what I'm calling about. We have a problem, and we could use your help."

"What's up? How can I help?"

Jason, feeling left out, yelled at the phone. "Hi Rock. PI Longfellow here. We've found a body, another dead realtor."

"Dr. Longfellow, you haven't started working with another realtor, have you? That's not ethical. I've been working hard for you guys."

"No. Nothing like that. I said *dead realtor*. We took the day off from condo hunting to relax and soak up some rays, and we found this dead realtor buried on Crescent Beach."

"Mrs. Longfellow? Chelsea? Are you there? Is your husband okay? People have been known to become delusional with too much Florida sun."

Chelsea smiled. "I'm here, Rock. Jason's always been delusional, but in this case we are both staring at another dead realtor. We stumbled on the body when my devil-may-care husband asked me to bury him in the sand on Crescent Beach."

Jason interrupted. "This is Jason…PI Longfellow, again. I found several business cards in this guy's pocket…he's buried in a tan sport jacket and white pants, quite fetching. The business cards are from realty companies in the Miami area, including *ReallyRealty*. Any thoughts?"

Rock spoke up. "Any ID? Might help if I had some idea who he is."

Chelsea said, "We found his wallet, and his driver's license says he's one Rip Thornton, a *ReallyRealty* realtor from Miami. Any idea who…?"

Rock gasped. "Oh my God! Tell me you didn't just say Rip Thornton. Please!"

Chelsea said, "That's right. His ID says Rip Thornton. Do you know him?"

"Tell me exactly where you are on Crescent Beach."

"We have our chairs set up about a half mile north of the Crescent Beach parking lot. But, why…?"

"Stay put! I'll be there in ten minutes."

The phone went dead. Chelsea and Jason looked at each other. Chelsea shrugged, looking confused. Jason smiled knowingly.

Jason said, "Now, that's a great realtor; excellent service. Sounds like he's on his way here to help us, and in a hurry. Although, I really don't know how this will help find us a house."

Chelsea shook her head. "Jason, I don't think it's about us. He appeared to know this Rip Thornton. They both work for *ReallyRealty*, although this guy is supposed to be in the Miami office. I wonder if this has anything to do with the other dead realtors. Maybe there's a clue in there somewhere."

Jason was becoming more and more insecure. Chelsea kept finding clues and answers to important questions. He was the detective, and he should be the one solving the case. Tired of standing and looking down at the body, he walked over to his chair and sat down. Chelsea followed him. He grabbed a bottle of water from the cooler, opened it, took a drink and offered it to Chelsea. She sat down in the other chair and gulped down half of the bottle.

"Yeah, Chelsea. I don't know why he would come all the way up here to ask his wife to bury him in the sand, and certainly not in his street clothes. Like you said, there's plenty of beaches in Miami. And, why would she just leave him here when he obviously didn't make it out of the hole before the tide came in? You'd think she'd have called 9-1-1, unless she meant to kill him."

Chelsea finished off the water, shook her head and sighed. "Jason, again, I don't think this guy died here. While Rock is on the way, why don't you lift up the body, turn it over, and let's see if there's anything to suggest a cause of death other than drowning, or being buried alive."

"Why? Don't you think drowning and being buried alive are sufficient to explain his death? I'm pretty sure nuclear weapons were not involved. And, I just sat down. Now I gotta walk all the way over there again?"

"Jason, don't be an ass. Just check the body."

"Chelsea, you said *ass*. You never curse. I think Florida's getting to you, too."

Jason walked back over to Rip Thornton's body, and Chelsea followed. Jason knelt down in front of the hole, not happy about touching a dead man. He hesitantly took the body by the shoulders and struggled to lift it up and forward. It was very hot, and he started sweating profusely. Chelsea bent down, brushed away the sand and examined the head and torso.

"Jason, I don't think this guy drowned. And, you're right, no nuclear weapons were involved. There is a small hole in the back of his head. Looks like it might be from a bullet."

"So, he was shot in the back of the head, execution style?"

"Yes, Jason. And, not only that, but the back of his jacket is torn on the left side, and the skin and muscles on his back are scratched and have been bleeding. It looks almost like someone took an electric hand-held mixer to him. Or, maybe a knife? How's that for strange?"

"Debbie? You think Debbie had something to do with this?"

Chelsea said, "It's true your friend Debbie rocked an electric hand-held mixer, and she's fond of kitchen utensils. But, she attacked your face. Ms. Slabotnik came after you with a knife. But, I don't remember anything about a small caliber pistol. I guess the cuts could also be from scavengers, like crabs or something."

"Wow, Chelsea. You said *small caliber pistol*. I didn't think you liked guns or knew anything about them."

"After you got your revolver I did some reading. I wanted to learn how to stay safe with a gun in the house, in the hands of a crazy person."

"So, you read up on guns and safety. Did you learn anything?"

"Yes. I learned that they're very dangerous, and there's no way you should have one. If I told anyone in authority how unstable you are, they'd probably take your little gun and put you away. Then what would I do? I'd have to raise the children by myself. I won't do it. You're not getting off that easy."

"Well, thanks again for the vote of confidence? Anyhow…this body's getting heavy. I'm gonna put it down."

Jason let go of the body and it dropped back into the hole, on its back as before.

Just then, a large black luxury SUV came flying up the beach, stopping near them so abruptly the tires threw sand in their direction.

"Chelsea, Rock's here. Maybe now we can find out what the hell's going on."

Rock jumped out of the car and ran to where Jason was kneeling. He dropped to his knees next to the body, took one look at the face and burst into tears."

Rock said, "Oh, Rip! Why did you have to go to Miami? I tried to tell you this wouldn't end well! But, I had no idea something like this would happen."

Jason whispered in Chelsea's direction. "Geez, I guess Rock knows this guy. He really seems to like him. I wonder if it's his brother or something?"

Chelsea looked at Jason and shook her head. She said, "Or something…"

Jason didn't know what to think when she knelt down and put her hand on Rock's shoulder.

"How long were the two of you together?"

Rock appeared to get control of himself. Apparently Chelsea was having a calming effect.

"Rip moved to St. Augustine five years ago and went to work at our *ReallyRealty* office. We met, hit it off immediately and ended up living together for three years. Then he went to one of those damn realtor conferences in Miami, met that horrible man, and that was that."

Chelsea asked. "What happened? What horrible man?"

Jason, feeling left out, put a hand on Rock's other shoulder. "Yeah. What horrible man? Did he meet someone else and run off with him?"

Chelsea intervened, empathy in her voice. "Jason, I don't get the sense that's what happened. Rock still seems to have strong feelings for this man."

Jason's arm started to cramp up, so he took it off of Rock's shoulder.

Rock said, "You're right, Mrs. Longfellow. Rip met a client in Miami, a multi-millionaire with a very expensive beach front mansion he needed to sell. Rip could come off as charming and confident. The man signed a contract with *ReallyRealty* with Rip as his selling agent. Rip moved to Miami to more effectively work the property. If he sold the place it would have been like winning the lottery. He was convinced if he could sell it, the commission would set us both up for life. He asked me to move to Miami with him, but the Miami *ReallyRealty* office didn't need any more realtors. I didn't want to live in such a large city anyhow. We had a big fight over it. I guess I should have gone with him. Maybe I could have done something."

Chelsea said, "I'm sorry for your loss. I'm also sorry to ask you questions at a time like this, but we need to figure something out before the police get here and haul Jason away. He's been found at the crime scene of too many dead realtors."

Jason chimed in, "Yeah, too many dead realtors. We gotta figure something out."

Chelsea frowned, continued, "Rock, do you know the name of your friend's millionaire client? That might be a good place to start."

"No, Mrs. Longfellow. Rip and I had a terrible fight, and he refused to tell me anything about the man. He said I'd try to intervene and screw things up. He moved to Miami and we never spoke again. Last thing I said to him two years ago was that I never wanted to see him again."

Rock started sobbing again.

Jason thought he should try to comfort the realtor some more. "Don't worry, Man. Old Rip here doesn't care anymore, what with his mouth, nose and eyes filled with sand, and a bullet hole in his head. He's probably on an all-male nude beach somewhere, where the sand is soft, the sun is warm and the men are all har…buff."

Chelsea choked, and gave Jason one of her death stares. He flinched, expecting a whack on the head.

"What? I'm trying to console him. You're not the only empathetic one in this marriage."

"No, but I'm the only sane one."

Chelsea smiled at Rock, moving her hand to his arm and giving a gentle squeeze. Jason felt it was unfair that his wife was consoling Rock, when he, Jason, was the one going to jail.

Chelsea said, "Do you think you can find out the name of Rip's client in Miami, or the address of that beach front mansion? We need somewhere to start. I can't help but wonder if your friend's death has anything to do with the murdered realtors here in St. Augustine. We need to figure out the connection. Once we've spoken to the police, perhaps you could go back to the office and check it out?"

"Sure, Mrs. Longfellow. Each *ReallyRealty* office is independent. I can't imagine anything that happened to Rip down in Miami would have such a dramatic effect up here. But, I'll look into it and give you the information tomorrow."

"Great, thanks. If you don't feel like condo hunting, take the day off and just give us a call."

Jason, feeling left out again, said, "I still can't imagine how, or why, a realtor in Miami winds up buried in the sand on a beach up here in St. Augustine. Maybe Rip met another guy in Miami, they came up here for a vacation and Rip asked his new partner to bury him in the sand. He didn't have my PI training, so he couldn't get out before the tide drowned him?"

"Jason, that wouldn't explain the fact that he's fully clothed. I also think that bullet hole in the back of his head might have something to do with cause of death?"

"You're just showing off, Chelsea. You could be wrong. Rock here said Rip went to one of those realtor conferences in Miami. Someone recently told us about attending one of those and getting bitten by mosquitoes. Maybe that's the connection. The mosquitoes got so bad in Miami that Rip and his new partner came back to St. Augustine to get away from them. Maybe it's those killer mosquitoes that came up from South America, and they got him."

"For Heaven sake, Jason. You don't let the facts get in the way of your detecting, do you? First of all, there's no evidence that Rip had a new partner. Second, they moved back to St. Augustine because of mosquitoes in Miami? I don't know if you've noticed, but there are mosquitoes here, too. This is Florida, and there's swamp and mosquitoes everywhere. And third, it was killer wasps, not killer mosquitoes. Only way mosquitoes had anything to do with poor Rip's death is if one of them was packing a pistol."

Jason laughed and smacked Chelsea affectionately on the behind.

"Good one, Chelsea. Pistol-packing mosquito. You're getting the hang of this PI thing. I see you're learning a lot from me. Maybe I should make you my partner."

Chelsea handed Jason the wallet, gave him a not-so-gentle shove towards the hole and pointed at the body.

"Jason, keep your hands off of my ass in public. Yes, I said *ass* again. Keep those business cards and put the body back in the same position as we found it before the police get here. Here, put Rip's wallet back in his pocket where we found it, too. I know we're not supposed to disturb the crime scene, but those cards could come in handy in case we need more information to get you out of jail."

"Good idea. We might need the cards to find more information to get me out of…wait...you think I'm going to jail?"

"I wouldn't rule it out. Just put the wallet and body back, and we'll see what the police have to say. I know you didn't kill Rip, and I'm pretty sure Rock knows it. But, how many dead realtors do you get to be found with before they haul you off to jail?"

***

Jason saw the police arrive in a four-wheel-drive truck a few minutes later and pull up next to the large SUV. The officers, a stocky female and thin, wiry male, approached Jason and gang cautiously. They were all standing over the body. Jason hadn't met these officers before.

The female officer spoke first. "Hello. I'm Detective Montano and this is Detective Brewer, St. Augustine Sheriff's Office. We got a call about a DB on the beach."

Jason, being the PI in the group, stepped forward and offered his hand. No one took it.

"I'm Dr. Jason Longfellow, PI, and this is my wife Chelsea and our realtor, Rock Handsome. Apparently Rock and this…wait…what's a DB?"

Chelsea said, "Jason, it stands for *dead body*."

"Oh. Of course. Police lingo. My online PI course only spent an hour on that; it was kind of boring and I think I fell asleep. Anyhow, where was I?"

Chelsea said, "Lost as usual?"

"Chelsea, you're being mean again. Stop it. I remember. Our realtor, Mr. Handsome here, was acquainted with the DB, as you call him."

Rock spoke up, sobbing. "That DB has…had a name. It's Rip Thornton, and he was my partner for three years before moving to Miami."

His emotions appeared to overwhelm him again, and he knelt down by the body.

Jason stepped closer to the police officers and launched into an explanation, moving his hands and pointing as he talked.

"My wife, Chelsea…this is Chelsea…was burying me in the sand when she saw that I had two right hands. That's how we found the body. I figured he asked his wife to bury him in the sand too, to see if he could escape before the tide came in. But then, when Rock got here, he told us that…the body…DB…Mr. Rip…was gay. So, he would have asked his partner to bury him; not his wife. But, we don't know if he has…had…a partner. And, he's buried in his clothes, which is strange. He probably didn't drown, since he has a bullet hole in the back of his head. But, we didn't do anything to disturb the crime scene, honest. Chelsea, my assistant, will explain things from here. Please tell the officers what happened, as best you can. Be brief, clear and concise like I taught you. And assure them I didn't disturb the body, and that I'm innocent. Oh God, I don't want to go to jail."

Detective Montano grinned. "I know who you are. You're the infamous PI Longfellow. One of the other detectives in our precinct has been talking about you for a couple of weeks now. You're the one that keeps showing up with dead bodies; mostly realtors if I remember correctly. Some of the detectives have started calling you the *Realtor's Curse*."

Jason looked at Chelsea. "Help me."

Detective Montano continued. "Don't tell me. Let me guess. This body that's buried in the sand, it's another realtor. Right?"

Chelsea, looking up at the sky, said, "Jason's the private eye. I'm just the innocent wife."

Jason said, "Yes, officer. He's apparently another realtor. Our realtor, Mr. Rock Handsome here, knows the man…body…person…DB. His name is Rip Thornton, and he and Rock used to work together at the *ReallyRealty* office in St. Augustine. According to Rock, they were partners for three years before Mr. Rip, old DB here, moved to Miami to sell a mansion on the beach. He was alive then. I don't know how he ended up dead and buried in the sand here. Oh, and it might have something to do with killer mosquitoes. We're not sure about that part."

Detective Brewer reached around, took his handcuffs off of his utility belt and stepped closer to Jason. Jason took a couple of steps back, looking like he was about to run away.

The detective said, "You're a registered PI? Here in Florida? I've never heard of a PI named Longfellow. You obviously disturbed the crime scene, since you dug up the body and discovered a bullet hole in the back of the head. We could haul you downtown for that alone. Not to mention, from the talk at the precinct this is the fourth or fifth time you've been found with a dead body. Can you give us a reason not to haul you off to jail right now? You've got to know you're at least a person of interest. In fact, at this point you're our only suspect."

"I admit I disturbed the crime scene. But, you weren't here, and I am a trained PI. Do you want to see my ID card that I printed off the internet? When Chelsea pointed out the guy's hand, I thought he might still be alive. So I dug him up, hoping I could resuscitate him. I was careful not to disturb anything else, once we found the hole in the back of his head." *No reason to mention the business cards or wallet. We put the wallet back and Chelsea's right, I might need the business cards to find my next lead. I'm gonna need all the help I can get.*

Detective Montano said, "So, the facts that he was completely buried, with mouth, eyes and nose full of sand and he wasn't breathing weren't enough to convince you he was dead? You had to dig him up and move the body to be sure?"

Jason felt Chelsea take him by the arm, like she was hanging on for dear life.

She said, "Like I said, I'm just the innocent wife. Jason was sick the day his online PI course taught the class on not disturbing the crime scene. All he did was dig up the body to make sure the man was dead, and move the head a little bit. Can't you please give him a break? Can't you please give me a break? He thinks he's a PI, and somehow he has come to the conclusion that this man, with a bullet hole in the back of his skull, was killed by a mosquito or mosquitoes unknown. Please, let him go and I promise to make sure he takes his meds tonight."

Chapter 20

The police felt bad for Chelsea. They told her it was clear that Jason had nothing to do with the murder of this realtor. They agreed the best thing would be for her to take Jason home and give him his meds. They had his address and could find him later if necessary.

Next morning Chelsea got up early and prepared cereal for breakfast, sugar coated fake fruit flakes for Jason and chocolate flavored balls of crunch and toast for her. To Chelsea's chagrin, Jason added three tablespoons of sugar to his cereal, along with a tiny bit of milk. He might as well just open a five-pound bag of sugar and dig in. She poured a full cup of milk into her bowl of chocolatey crunch.

Jason complained. "Chelsea, we need to get some bananas. I would love a cut up banana in my fake fruit cereal. Then, at least there'd be some actual fruit in the bowl."

Chelsea gave him a strange look. "Jason, are you okay?" *Bald spot still there; check. Hasn't been interested in sex with me for weeks; check. Maybe he has just taken a liking to bananas?*

Jason told her he had trouble sleeping the previous night, obsessing over the buried realtor. She made a pot of her high octane coffee, and he asked her for the strong stuff to keep him awake. They sat at the kitchen table crunching cereal and gulping down the strong brew.

"Jason, you need to relax and shut your mind off when you go to bed. There was nothing we could have done about Rip Thornton in the middle of the night, and yet you kept blabbering about it."

"I can't help it. I need to figure out why this realtor was buried on Crescent Beach fully clothed, and who shot him in the back of the head. Also, what do mosquitoes have to do with dead realtors? The subject of mosquitoes keeps coming up."

Chelsea poured herself another cup of coffee and took a sip.

"As usual, you're way off the rails. The most important thing at the moment is to find out who Rip Thornton's millionaire client was in Miami. That's where we'll get the next lead in the case. The man was shot in the head. The only reason the subject of mosquitoes keeps coming up is because you keep bringing it up. When you get off on a tangent like this, you're impossible. Pretty soon you'll be counting bathroom tiles."

Chelsea frowned as Jason took a tiny sip of coffee, and then put a spoonful of cereal in his mouth and continued to talk while chewing.

"That's not a bad idea. I'll take my coffee into the bathroom. Counting tiles is soothing. I do some of my best work when I'm counting. Helps clear my mind; forget the chaos for a while."

"Oh, God! When you asked me to marry you, I should have run screaming from the building."

"Silly Chelsea. I proposed to you in Virginia Beach, on the beach. We weren't inside a building. Speaking of beaches, I wonder how this guy from Miami got buried in the sand fully clothed up here in Crescent Beach and what it has to do with mosquitoes."

"Ahhhh! I can't take anymore! I should have let those cops haul you off to jail. What was I thinking?! I should have put the cuffs on you myself. We have the day off, since Rock Handsome is grieving over his old friend and partner. Let's do something, ANYTHING fun to take your mind off of this mess for a while."

"That's a great idea, Chelsea, just so it doesn't have anything to do with tying me up or handcuffing me. Since we drove my red rocket on the beach full of salt and sand yesterday, how about we get it washed? Otherwise, it'll rust. I saw one of those drive-through car washes on Route 1. I think it was called Spanky's Car Wash. The building looked like a giant steamboat."

Chelsea gulped down the last of her coffee, intent on getting the day started.

"I say I want to do something fun, and you come up with *car wash*? Oh well, I guess it's better than another motorcycle ride, or kiteboarding. I do have one minor question. How are you going to drive your little clown car through a car wash, when you can't put up the top?"

"No worries. I can put it up. I just have to duck my head. Not a problem since in this car wash you drive the car onto a track, put her in neutral, and away you go…no steering required. I wish you'd stop calling my red rocket a *clown car*. And, I thought I was going to count the tiles in the bathroom first."

"I see you've thought this through in your usual logical manner. I give up. It's better than getting eaten by an alligator, or buried on the beach, or going to jail. Oh God! We're never going to buy a vacation condo, are we? And, forget the bathroom tiles. Let's just get this latest nightmare over with."

"Chill Chelsea, and let's have some fun at the car wash. Maybe we can make out while we're passing through. Just don't tie me to anything."

Jason drove them to Spanky's Car Wash. Chelsea cringed as he sped into one of the gates, almost hitting the pay station in the process.

"Okay Chelsea, here's the plan. I'll pay with a credit card, and when the gate goes up I'll drive to the car wash entrance. I'll put the car in neutral, and then I'll put up the top just before we start through the wash. You just have to sit there…"

"And pray. I'll sit here and pray, that you get the top up in time."

Jason's plan appeared to be working. He paid, the gate opened and he pulled into the car wash entrance. Chelsea was concerned when she saw Jason checking out the tall, curvy, twenty-something brunette attendant with a bright yellow and blue butterfly tattooed at the top of her right breast. The young woman had a puzzled look on her face as she directed Jason to drive onto the car wash track. Jason yelled an explanation in her direction.

"No worries, lady. I'm about to put up the top."

With that he pulled the rocket onto the track, put it in neutral and continued to stare at the butterfly.

Jason said, "Chelsea, instead of getting a PI license perhaps I should have studied entomology, *Lepidoptera* to be more specific. Why are women so drawn to butterflies?"

"Jason, stop staring at that boob tattoo and put the top up, NOW!"

"Oh crap!"

Chelsea watched with amazement as he finally pushed the button to raise the convertible top. The top went up, reached its apex and moved downward for attachment to the windshield frame. As the top lowered itself into position, Jason's face was pushed against the steering wheel. He struggled to find the latches required to fasten down the top.

"Chelsea, help me! I can't lock the top down. I'm gonna have to hold it with my hands, and there's not much to grab hold of."

Jason blindly fought to hold the cloth top down, trying to prevent water from entering the car. Chelsea winced when she saw the contorted position of his head, neck, arms and shoulders. She grabbed the front edge of the top as well, holding on for dear life.

"Jason, I don't know why I keep letting you get me into these crazy situations. Hot soapy water's starting to get in! Maybe you could have pushed the button sooner, if you hadn't been gawking at that stupid butterfly."

The car moved forward, and the warm sudsy water continued. Then came the rinse, clear water under pressure. The water hit the front lip of the canvas top, pulling it out of Jason and Chelsea's hands. The top flew back into the full open position.

Chelsea ducked and covered her head. She screamed as the cold rinse hit her. She was pleased to see out of the corner of her eye that Jason looked up, just in time for the cold water to hit him full in the face.

Coughing, choking and gasping for breath, Jason yelled, "I was smart to choose the *no touch* option. Otherwise, we'd have been beaten to death by the roller brushes and spinning washers."

Then a second rinse came, a gentler flow of cold water with the odor of swamp gas that caused Chelsea to choke. This round came with flashing colored lights …red…green…blue…yellow…repeat.

Jason yelled over the roaring of the machinery.

"Chelsea, I've never seen a car wash with such a beautiful light show. I'm really glad we did this. It looks like Christmas lights. We should come back and do this again for Christmas. Make it an annual holiday event. The kids would love it."

Chelsea tried to answer while fending off the water with her arms, her mouth still filled with sudsy water.

"Cough. Choke. Gurgle. Jason, you're an idiot. We're going to drown, and you're ruining the interior of your precious clown car. If we survive this, I'm going to bury you on the beach, and this time I'm going to do it while the tide's still in."

They finally exited the car wash, and Jason pulled into one of the stalls with vacuum cleaners and paper towels. Jason opened the car door and Chelsea watched as water poured out onto the concrete. Chelsea found a sunny spot to lay down in the grass, patiently waiting for Jason while he dried off the dashboard and upholstery.

When Jason yelled that the interior was almost dry, Chelsea joined him.

"Thanks for the great date. A free bath and a light show. You're something else."

"Come on, Chelsea. It wasn't so bad. We got a little wet, but you look dry now. And you gotta admit, I did choose the *no touch* option, and that light show was pretty spectacular."

"Idiot."

They got into the car. Chelsea's newly dry rear end felt the soggy seat soak through her clothing. She was not happy. Jason pulled out onto Route 1.

Jason said, "Where should we go from here? How about seafood for dinner?"

Chelsea's cell phone rang. She answered. "Hello. Hi Rock. How are you? Again, I'm sorry for your loss."

Jason said, "Chelsea, put it on speaker so I can hear."

"Rock, I'm putting you on speaker. Jason's here with me. We're driving around in his little clown car. We just went through the car wash, with the top down. That's right. You heard me correctly. Yes, we're okay. It took a while, but we're all dried out."

Jason heard Rock say, "Let me guess. It was your husband's idea? He really is quite a character."

"Rock, I'll take that as a compliment. Have you ever gone through Spanky's Car Wash? The light show in there is spectacular."

Rock said, "You don't get out much, do you Dr. Longfellow?"

Jason yanked the steering wheel to the left and quickly crossed two lanes of traffic to make a left turn. Horns blared, middle fingers were shared, and Chelsea managed to grab onto the oh-my-god-bar without dropping her phone.

"So, Rock. Before Jason kills us both, did you happen to find out the name of Rip's millionaire client from Miami? I still think it's an important avenue for us to follow in solving your friend's murder."

Jason said, "Rock, ignore my wife. She sometimes interferes in my investigations. I'm the one with the highly regarded online PI license. I'll ask the questions. So, did you find the name of your friend's millionaire client?"

Rock said, "I called our Miami office this morning. Since I work for *ReallyRealty*, they answered my questions. It seems we have already met Rip's millionaire client. Remember the drunk psychopath who swamped us with his oversized yacht on the Intracoastal the other day? His name's Mark Moneyman, CEO of VaccinesRUs. Their corporate headquarters is in Miami."

Chelsea said, "Huh. Interesting that Mr. Moneyman was in St. Augustine the same week Rip Thornton took a bullet to the back of the head and ended up buried in the sand on Crescent Beach. Coincidence?"

Rock said, "There's more. According to the Miami office, the real estate market tanked about the same time that Rip signed the contract with Mr. Moneyman to sell his mansion. Rip worked his butt off, tons of open houses, following every lead, spending a fortune on advertising, but Mr. Moneyman has never received a single offer. The client was not happy. He had it out with Rip last week; they were seen arguing in the real estate office."

Chelsea said, "We've already experienced Mr. Moneyman's lack of manners and his temper. He had his man escort us off his boat after he found out that you are a realtor. At least now that makes sense. But, it seems a little extreme to kill your realtor because he can't sell your house."

Jason, feeling left out again, chimed in, "People have been murdered for less. I heard that on an episode of *Murder She Wrote*."

Rock said, "Did he just reference that old show *Murder She Wrote*? I loved that show. Mrs. Fletcher was great. But…what's an old TV show got to do with Rip's murder?"

Chelsea said, "Where do you think Jason got most of his detective training? An online class, and the box set of *Murder She Wrote* episodes."

"Oh, Mrs. Longfellow. I'm so sorry."

Jason said, "Chelsea, stop being so mean. Do you really think this Moneyman murdered Rip Thornton and buried him in the sand on Crescent Beach? That seems a little far-fetched."

"Far-fetched? Says the man who asked me to bury him in the sand so he could prove he could escape before the tide drowned him? If Rock's information is good, Moneyman had motive; he was angry the realtor could not sell his house. And, he had opportunity; he was in St. Augustine at the time of the murder. I don't know about means; whether or not he has a gun."

Rock chimed in, "Honey, this is Florida. Everybody's got a gun."

Chelsea adjusted her position, uncomfortable in the soggy seat. She had a death grip on the oh-my-god-bar. Jason was continually weaving in and out of heavy traffic. He turned into their rental condo complex, parked and turned off the car. Chelsea said goodbye to Rock and ended the call.

Jason said thoughtfully, "Interesting Chelsea, means, motive and opportunity. I remember those things from my PI class. I think we need to ask Mr. Moneyman if he owns a gun. We should also ask him what he knows about mosquitoes. Yes, the game's got a big foot. We need to find Mr. Moneyman and grill him, and his new young wife."

"Jason, the saying is *the game's afoot*. Oh God, I should have covered your head with sand when I had the chance. Maybe next time."

Chapter 21

Next day, Chelsea asked Rock Handsome to put together another list of condos to show them. Meanwhile, she and Jason went back to the marina to question Mark Moneyman. The multi-millionaire appeared to Chelsea to be a vain and angry drunk by nature, and he especially disliked realtors. But, was he angry enough to kill one? Did he own a gun? And, did Jason really know anything about investigating murder?

Jason drove them to the marina in his red rocket. He kept complaining to Chelsea about banging his knee on the steering wheel every time he depressed the clutch to shift gears. Chelsea chuckled to herself. Perhaps the little car had shrunk after the car wash debacle.

Chelsea said, "Jason, I smell mold. I think the upholstery of your little clown car is molding after our date at the car wash. I told you to park in the sun so it would dry out thoroughly."

"Oh, Chelsea. The Florida sun is way too intense for that. If I'd parked in the sun, it would have melted the upholstery. Besides, it would have burnt our butts when we got in the car."

"You'll be sorry when the mold colony grows, takes over your little car, and eats one of us. You can add mold to your list of dangerous things in Florida."

"Chelsea, stop it. You're scaring me."

Jason's driving became erratic, the rocket weaving side to side. Chelsea saw him glancing around the inside of the car.

"Jason, watch where you're going! You almost hit that parked car. What's wrong with you?"

"You've got me all paranoid about mold. I know it's probably not going to eat us, but it could get in our lungs. If Florida mold is as aggressive as everything else down here, we could be in serious danger. One car. Two cars. Three cars. Four cars."

Oh God. He's counting. We're not going to get there alive.

They arrived at the marina. Jason parked the car, and they exited the vehicle. Chelsea said a quick prayer of thanks and watched impatiently as he did a thorough search of the seats and under the dashboard.

Jason said, "I don't see any mold. But, it could be black mold, and that stuff can kill you. I'll have to sell the rocket and buy a new vehicle."

"Oh, for Heaven sakes Jason. I didn't actually smell mold. I was just yanking your chain. I know how you feel about this stupid car; a tiny scratch drives you crazy. I was just going for a little payback. Since you've started this PI thing, you've turned into some kind of murder magnet, and it's ruining our vacation and condo hunt. Your little clown car's fine."

Jason looked sad, and patted the driver's door with his hand. Chelsea wondered if maybe she should be jealous of the stupid car.

"Chelsea, that was just mean. I was ready to trade her in on something else fun; maybe a jacked up pickup truck or some other type of four-wheeler. That way we could do some serious off-roading in the Ocala National Forest, where the deer and the cantaloupe play."

"Don't you mean antelope? What is wrong with you?"

"Antelope. Cantaloupe. What's the difference? It's just a silly song."

"One's a fruit, and the other has four legs. I'm not doing any more off-roading with you. Have you forgotten your Evil Knievel disaster, trying to jump a large alligator on a motorcycle? More to the point, let's go visit Mr. Moneyman. Maybe he owns a gun."

She flashed an evil grin in his direction.

"You're the PI. You board the yacht first, and I'll follow."

"No worries, Wife, I've got your back."

"When we're boarding his yacht, it's my front I'm worried…Oh, never mind. *I'm gonna die.*"

They walked along the dock to the mooring spot of the *Vacation Vaccination.* Jason stopped at the foot of the portable boarding steps, Chelsea beside him.

"Chelsea. Follow my lead. There's a certain protocol for boarding a man's boat. You're supposed to ask permission."

"Probably a good idea, because this rich guy's a drunk. He just might shoot you if you don't ask permission first. Might shoot you anyhow."

Chelsea saw Jason reach down with his hand and pat his right hip.

"Stop it, Chelsea. I don't have my revolver with me. I should have worn it in my inside-the-pants holster on my hip."

"Why does that make me feel safer?"

Jason yelled up at the boat. "Ahoy there! PI Longfellow and his wife here! Permission to come aboard, please!"

They heard footsteps, and Orlando Cerveza walked into view around a large staircase that led to the upper deck.

"Hello again, Longfellow family. It is I, Orlando Cerveza, the first mate who pulled you out of the Intracoastal. Mr. Moneyman heard you shouting, and wants to know why you want to come aboard."

Jason said, "We seem to have gotten off on the wrong foot on our first visit, and would like to try again. I, a licensed PI, also have a couple of questions I'd like to ask the Captain."

"Well, Mr. PI, my Captain and his young wife have been drinking martinis all morning, and are in a jovial mood at the moment. I should warn you that the Captain's mood can change quickly with one too many drinks. I'll go talk to him. Back in a minute."

He turned and walked briskly towards the stairs to the upper decks. Jason and Chelsea stood waiting on the dock.

Chelsea said. "This fat little man tried to proposition me during our first visit. I don't care how rich he is, he's a disgusting pig. If he does it again, I want you to punch him in his pudgy face."

"Yes, Chelsea. But, how do you really feel about Mr. Moneyman? Must I remind you that we're here to question him as a possible murder suspect, as in bullet to the head? He might be a little pig of a man, but he's gonna look pretty big if he pulls out a gun."

"Man up, Jason. You're supposed to be a private eye. Brave. Fearless. Catching the bad guy?"

"You're right, Chelsea. Let's get him."

Orlando returned. "Captain Moneyman…I just love that name…says you can come aboard. He says he remembers Mrs. Longfellow's long legs, and wants another look. He's not too happy about answering any questions, though. I recommend you drink a few drinks with him and tell him how great he is before asking your questions. He likes it when people kiss his…well, you know."

Jason and Chelsea followed Orlando to the upper deck. Mark Moneyman and his young wife, Gina, were lounging on a large circular couch at the stern of the yacht, a half-empty pitcher of martinis on the table in front of them. Moneyman had on a bright red tank top and bathing suit with colored stripes. Chelsea was disgusted by the way the outfit emphasized his rotund figure, with fat oozing out along with his arms and legs. Gina wore a bright red string bikini.

Chelsea looked at Gina. *It's clear she doesn't need a life preserver to stay afloat. And, those things aren't store bought. No wonder she caught that old multi-millionaire's attention.* Then she looked at Jason, waiting for him to say something. He was staring at Gina, too distracted to speak. *I'm gonna kill him.*

Moneyman spoke first. "Hello there, Legs. I approve of the shorts; shows those fine legs run all the way from your ass to the ground. Did you wear those just for me?"

Chelsea whispered to Jason. "Did you hear what he just said to me? Aren't you going to do something?"

Jason continued to stare dreamily at places outlined in thin red fabric. Chelsea growled.

Moneyman continued. "I see you brought your husband with you. Can't say I'm not disappointed. Honestly, I was hoping maybe you, Gina and I could have some fun below deck. But, no matter. Have a seat and pour yourselves a martini. I'll be happy to speak with you since you had the decency to leave your realtor at home this time."

Chelsea didn't bother to take a seat, as there was no benefit to be gained by sitting and drinking with the man. It was clear that Moneyman was already in the bag. Jason was too busy staring at Gina to sit.

Chelsea kept waiting for Jason to speak up, smoke coming out of her ears. *Keep it together girl. We're here to investigate, find out if this little pig man has a gun. Need to play nice, tell him how important he is. Get him talking. Kill Jason later, make it really painful.*

Chelsea finally gave up and responded herself.

"Hello, Mr. Moneyman. We got off on the wrong foot during our first visit. We thought we'd drop by and try again. By the way, I just love your big boat. It's quite impressive." *Jesus, I'm going to puke if I have to keep complimenting this disgusting man. But, we need to get him to confess. Stay calm, Chelsea.*

Chelsea reached up and whacked Jason on the back of the head.

"Jason, stop staring at the young lady. You look like an old perve. Don't you have some questions to ask the Captain?"

"Ouch! Chelsea, what the hell?" Then he spoke, to Gina. "I must complement you on your choice of beach attire. Where did you find such a beautiful swim suit?"

Struggling not to whack him again, Chelsea said, "Really, Jason. You're asking her where she shops for bathing suits? Where's PI Birdbrain when I need him?"

Jason glanced at Chelsea. She liked the fear she saw in his eyes. He better be afraid.

"I didn't mean anything. I just liked her bathing suit, and thought I might buy you one like it. You'd look really…"

Chelsea growled again. "Give it up, Jason. Too little, too late."

"Chelsea, did you just growl at me? He's the bad guy. Growl at him."

Gina said, innocently, "Ah, that's sweet. You must be lovebirds, quarreling like that."

Chelsea's blood pressure shot up several more points. She gave up on Jason, and focused on Moneyman.

"So, Captain Moneyman, we heard you are acquainted with a man named Rip Thornton. Is that true? If so, how do you know him?"

Moneyman's mood changed abruptly. "What did you say?"

Chelsea repeated. "Do you know a man named Rip Thornton? I believe you met him in Miami."

Moneyman paused, then grinned the crooked grin of a drunk whose face muscles were no longer under his control. Chelsea was familiar with the effects of too much alcohol, both as a nurse and as the adult child of an alcoholic mother.

"I guess it won't hurt to tell you, since you probably noticed from our first meeting anyhow. I HATE realtors. Rip Thornton is the reason, so tread lightly."

This confirmed to Chelsea that Moneyman had a nasty temper when he was drunk, which appeared to be most of the time.

"Jason, would you like to join the conversation? Earth to PI Longfellow. I could use you about now."

Chelsea saw that Jason had gone back to the red bikini…and not hearing his wife.

Chelsea soldiered on. "So you knew Rip Thornton was a realtor. Is it true that you contracted him to sell your oceanfront mansion? Is it also true that he was failing miserably, and you were furious with him?"

Moneyman's face was approaching the color of Gina's bathing suit. Chelsea feared that the man might explode. He answered, his face contorted with what appeared to be rage.

"Nice legs or not, tread lightly Missy. And, tell your husband to stop staring at my wife's boobs. What an asshole!"

Chelsea, fuming herself. "Well, at least we agree on one thing. But, answer the question. What about Rip Thornton?"

He blurted out an answer. As Chelsea had hoped, once he started talking he couldn't stop.

"Yes, I know him. Yes, I hired him to sell my oceanfront property. And, yes, he sucked as a realtor! It's a beautiful place, and he should have sold it in the first month. But, he was distracted, mourning an ex-lover. He had been living with somebody up this way, and he broke it off to move to Miami. Apparently, the other person moved on, and he couldn't get over the breakup. It's all the idiot talked about. I tried to get out of the contract, but *ReallyRealty* threatened to sue. Bastards!"

Moneyman was getting more and more upset. Chelsea kept pushing, hoping for a confession.

"Did you ever think maybe it wasn't Mr. Thornton's fault? Maybe your property was actually a dump, and that's why he couldn't unload it. Based on the way you dress like a clown you obviously have no taste in clothes. Maybe the same goes for oceanfront property. By the way, my husband has a car you might be interested in."

The Captain pulled a small 0.22 caliber revolver from under the table and aimed it at Jason.

"Lady, you're really pissing me off! That damned realtor made the mistake of pissing me off. You keep it up, I'm gonna plug your husband. I'd shoot you, but you've got really nice legs, and he won't stop staring at my wife's boobs."

Chelsea looked at Jason. He was still staring at Gina, starry-eyed, like a school boy trying to think of something clever to say.

"Jason, I think I might be about to get a confession out of Captain Pig Face here. Could you please come back to earth and participate in your investigation?"

Chelsea turned back to Moneyman. "Isn't that a small caliber revolver? That's interesting, because Rip Thornton's body was found buried on St. Augustine Beach, with a small caliber hole in his head. Is there anything you'd like to say about that? Let me help. You were really angry with him. You have a small caliber handgun…need I say more?"

Jason finally spoke. "Gina, why do you think Rip Thornton had so much trouble selling your husband's property? It sounds lovely. Like you. We think your husband murdered Mr. Thornton. Maybe you could help us investigate, and also show off more of your excellent beach attire…to Chelsea. She might like one of your bathing suits, and we could get her one too."

Gina giggled, flattered and a little drunk. "Why, that sounds exciting. I'd love to help you investigate my husband for murder. You are an interesting man…a little odd…but not bad looking, for an older fellow. Do you and your wife by any chance like to swing? My Markie and I have been known to engage in such naughty behavior, especially after a pitcher or two of martinis. There's a large bedroom suite right here on his little old boat."

Moneyman stood up. Chelsea saw the rage in his eyes as he glared at her.

"You think you're smart, don't you? You think you're going to get me to confess to shooting that fucking realtor? And, now your idiot husband is trying to seduce my wife, right in front of me? Well, how's about I shoot the idiot in the head with my small caliber revolver?"

He aimed the handgun directly at Jason's head.

Chelsea, in the midst of the chaos, finally had time to process Jason's conversation with the lovely Gina.

Chelsea said, "If you aren't going to shoot him, give me the damned gun and I will."

Jason, still talking to Gina. "There's a large bedroom suite right here on the yacht? Cool. Unfortunately, I don't think Chelsea's into…wait…what…shoot who?!

Jason turned his head and saw the gun leveled at him. He panicked, rushed forward, grabbed Chelsea and carried her over the side of the yacht with him.

Chelsea screamed as they plummeted towards the water.

"Ahhhh! What the hell!?"

They both hit the water with a large splash. They surfaced at the same time, and Jason frantically started swimming around the boat towards the dock.

"Chelsea. Swim fast. Alligators! Snakes! Sharks! Crazy man with a gun! God, I hate Florida!"

Chelsea, a far better swimmer, passed him, pushed his head under water on the way by, and was waiting on the dock when he finally got there. She refused to give him a hand as he climbed up the ladder. They both sat down, their legs dangling over the edge.

Chelsea said, "What is wrong with you? Moneybags was about to confess to murdering Rip Thornton, when you up and hauled both of us into the water."

"But, he was aiming a gun at my head."

"He wasn't going to shoot you. Not in front of Gina and me. He was just trying to act like a tough guy. We could have gotten a confession out of him and called the police. Instead we're sitting here on this dock, soaking wet."

"But, he was aiming a gun at my head."

"You already said that. If you'd have stopped staring at his wife's chest long enough, you might have participated in your own investigation. This is the twenty-first century. Don't you know it's sexist to stare at a woman's breasts? And, it's insane to do it in front of her armed husband, and, suicidal to do it in front of your wife."

She tried to whack him in the back of the head; he ducked just in time.

"But, Chelsea. As a scientist and a doctor, I can tell you that it's not my fault. It's all about the testosterone. It's my testosterone that's sexist. I thought you wanted me to be interested in womanly things. Besides, I was just checking out that bathing suit and thinking how good it would look on you. Would you like me to buy you one like it?"

"Idiot. You're supposed to be interested in MY womanly things…and I'm not interested in a string bikini at my age. Oh, never mind. One of these days my head's going to explode. We suspected Moneybags of murdering his realtor, and came here to find out if he had a gun. He obviously does. Why didn't you bring your little gun with you? You could have pulled it out and gotten the drop on him."

"But, you told him to shoot me."

"Well, there's that. But, I heard something about swinging, saw the way you were looking at her like a piece of steak, and I lost it. I didn't really want him to shoot you, at least not a lot. You should have helped me get a confession out of him."

"But, he was…"

"…Aiming a gun at your head. I heard you the first ten times. You suck as a PI. We still have nothing, and the police are probably going to haul you off to jail. We can't afford bail and a vacation home. If it comes to that…let's just say the kids and I are going to enjoy our new condo in St. Augustine."

Chapter 22

After escaping the *Vacation Vaccination*, Jason and Chelsea drove home wet, soaking the red rocket's upholstery again. Jason figured that Mark Moneyman hadn't given chase because he was too drunk to navigate the stairs down to the dock.

For dinner they ordered pizza delivery, double pepperoni on Chelsea's side. Jason preferred anchovies and olives on his half. They sat at the kitchen table finishing up their pizza and soda.

Chelsea said, "I'm full up with dead realtors. I know Rock put together another list of condos, but tomorrow I desperately need to do something relaxing."

"Chelsea, I'm not sure I'll ever be able to relax in Florida. Dead realtors, a crazy drunk millionaire with a gun, alligators…"

"…poisonous snakes, sharks, hurricanes, tornadoes, manatees and rust. I know, Jason. It's a terrifying place. You should probably count something. As for me, I would just like to relax. There *has* to be something we can do. We've tried it your way…motorcycling, kiteboarding, going to the beach, boating, fishing. What would actually be relaxing?"

"Let's try deductive and logical reasoning to figure it out. I had an hour's worth of training in that in my online PI course."

"Oh God. I can hardly wait."

He took a drink of soda and began explaining. He used his expert PI voice, trying to sound confident like they'd taught him online.

"Well, here goes. The things we've done for vacation so far include motors, the beach, sea life and wind. Things with motors tried to kill us, I got buried at the beach and found a dead realtor, fishing led to my attack by manatee and kiteboarding…well, that was fun but too windy and also kind of scary. So, when you apply deductive and logical reasoning to these facts, the answer to the question of what to do to relax is obvious."

"I know I'm going to regret this, but go ahead. What is the logical answer to our dilemma?"

Jason took one last large bite of pizza and washed it down with a gulp of diet soda. After he finished choking, he answered.

"Canoeing, of course. No motors, no surf boards, no sea life if we stay in the boat and don't do any fishing, no wind required and no beaches or sand if we canoe on a Florida lake."

"Jason, I won't even pretend that I follow any of that. But, I must admit, canoeing does sound peaceful. Where should we go? I know nothing about rivers and lakes in Florida."

"Chelsea. You keep forgetting, I'm a detective. I have a foolproof method for choosing a lake in Florida. There's a dart board on the wall in the second bedroom of this here rental condo. We take the map of Florida that we've been using, tape it to the wall, and I'll throw a dart. We'll go canoeing in whatever lake I hit. I'm sure there'll be a canoe rental place somewhere in the vicinity of the lake. There always is."

"So, is this another of your deductive reasoning methods?"

"Oh God no. I'm all worn out from figuring out the canoeing thing. This is a quick way to pick a lake without having to think about it."

"I'm not sure it's a great idea to pick a lake in Florida without doing any research. As you keep reminding me, there are a few dangerous things here."

"Nonsense, Chelsea. I am well aware of the dangers in Florida. But, what could possibly go wrong in a canoe? Remember, we've been told over and over that it's safe on the water, as long as you stay in the boat."

"But, Jason, we're not talking about Moneyman's yacht. We're talking about a *canoe*. You know, a really tiny boat."

"Chelsea, you worry too much. I'll protect you. Maybe you should try counting something."

Jason knew he had her when she rolled her eyes, dropped her head and sighed.

Chelsea followed Jason into the small bedroom with the dart board, where he unfolded the map and taped it to the wall. He picked up a dart, moved to the other side of the room and threw it at the map. Then, he walked back to the map and proudly announced, "Downtown Jacksonville. Well, that sucks. No lake there. Guess I'll have to try again."

After four more tries, including Miami, Tampa, Orlando and Fort Myers, Jason looked at Chelsea and shrugged. Maybe there were no lakes in Florida.

"Jason, give me that dart. I don't know how you keep missing water. Most of mainland Florida is made up of rivers, lakes and swamp."

Jason felt sad. He watched as she closed her eyes, threw the dart in the general direction of the map, walked over and took a look.

"Jason, we're going canoeing on Jesup Lake. And, look. There's a small marina. I'll bet they rent canoes."

"Wow, you did it on the first try. I'm impressed."

Jason took the darts from Chelsea and threw them at the map again, just to prove he could hit water too. He hit Jacksonville, Tampa, Orlando and Miami, no lakes. This technique sucked.

"Jason, Jesup Lake is gigantic. Are you sure we shouldn't do a little research first to make sure it's safe for canoeing?"

"Nonsense, Chelsea. It's a fresh water lake, so no sharks. And, they rent canoes, so it must be okay. There may be an alligator or two and a few poisonous snakes, but we'll be fine if we stay in the canoe. I'll bet we see all kinds of beautiful birds, flowers and other wildlife."

Chelsea grinned. "Think we'll see any cantaloupe?"

"Probably not. They usually hang out in the woods. Can't swim. Anyhow, I can't wait. I'm going to find the name of that marina, google it for an address, and off we go first thing in the morning. I'm guessing it's about an hour-and-a-half to two-hour drive from St. Augustine."

***

Jason had set the alarm on his cell phone for 6:00 AM to get an early start next morning.

"Rise and shine, Sunshine! It's off for a peaceful day of canoeing."

Chelsea raised her head off of the pillow, growled, and threw Jason's pillow at him.

"My name's Chelsea. We've been married forever. You'd think you'd at least get that right."

"Aren't we a grumpy Gus this morning. Let's get on the road. I'll stop and get you coffee and a sausage biscuit on the way. I'm such a good husband."

"Again, the name's Chelsea. Dragging me out of bed before the sun comes up and clogging my arteries with fast food is not a great way to start the day. Give me a few minutes to get a hot shower, wash my hair, and think peaceful thoughts…like why I shouldn't strangle my husband."

They finally got on the road at 9:00 AM. Jason was now the one in a lousy mood. He gunned the engine, trying to burn rubber to show his displeasure. But, the little car didn't have the power. This put him in an even worse mood.

"Jason, you were right, it's a beautiful day for canoeing. I'm looking forward to the drive in your little clown car with the top down."

"I had to wait for you for three hours. What took so long? You were in the shower forever. I'm not in the mood for canoeing anymore."

She grinned a lustful grin. "Stop sulking. You could have joined me in the shower. That might have put smiles on both our faces."

"I get the feeling you regret giving me that cure, and you'd rather have a husband that hangs out in trees…"

"I'd prefer a husband that's more interested in pleasing his wife. Maybe another road trip?"

Jason loaded a hard rock album into the CD player and cranked up the volume as loud as the little speakers in the rocket would go. He could barely hear the blaring guitar riffs for the wind and road noise, but to his mind it sent the message that he was irritated and didn't want to talk anymore. Chelsea didn't appear to notice; she slept for the remainder of the trip.

They arrived at the *Alligator Alley Marina* at 11:00. Jason was concerned. The place didn't feel safe. An old abandoned barn had been converted into a bait, tackle and canoe/kayak rental store. A wall had been framed in to separate the barn into halves, and only the front half was finished, the old structure reinforced. Whole sections of the back half of the barn had collapsed, with large gaps in the walls. The original barn door on the front of the building had been nailed shut, and a smaller door built onto the side for customer entry. A couple of large windows had been installed into the old barn door, without the use of a level. The words *Alligator Alley Marina* were painted over the small door in blood red paint; the letters appeared to have been drawn by a three-year-old. Several canoes, kayaks and paddles sat in random piles near the side of the building. More canoes sat on the ground by a small dock extending out into the lake.

"Jason, are ya' sure you shouldn't have done a little research? We're in the middle of nowhere, this place looks like it's about to fall down and I'm listening for banjo music."

When Jason opened the screen door to enter, it threatened to come off its hinges. They went inside, and Jason was surprised to see fear in Chelsea's eyes. A large man with an even larger beer belly sat on a tall stool behind a glass counter. He had on a dirty T-shirt and dirtier overalls. His head and face were covered by greasy long gray hair and a long, unkempt gray beard, and an unpleasant odor hovered over him. The way he looked at Jason, Jason wasn't sure if it was he or Chelsea that was in the most danger. They approached the counter.

A cash register rested on the glass counter full of fishing poles, lures, and what looked like cardboard Chinese food containers, filled with dirt and presumably worms or some such bait creature. A filthy, slimy minnow tank sat on a table to their right. Jason read a sign on the wall behind the counter that announced, "*Minners $3.00/duzun, Shrimps $6.00/duzun, Wurms $1.50/duzun, Hot dogs $1.50, with chilly, $2.50, Cold beer $2.50, Crawdads $2.00/duzun, Chips $1.00, Canoe Rent $10.00/hor/$25/day, Kayak Rent $15.00/hor/$30.00/day*".

The man stood up. "Howdy there, strangers. The name's Jake…Jake Blackwater. Welcome to the middle a' nowhere. What can I do fer y'all?"

Chelsea whispered in Jason's ear. "Don't you dare ask him to rent a *hor* for the day. I know your sick sense of humor, and worse, he might accommodate. And, hurry up. There's no A/C or circulating air, and it's about a million degrees in here. I'm gonna pass out."

Jason grinned, spoke up. "My wife and I are here to rent a canoe to paddle around your beautiful lake. We would like to rent one for, say, four hours."

"I'll have to charge y'all for the full day. Do y'all need anythin' else? Fishin' equipment, live bait, food, drinks? It's pretty hot out there today, and you prob'ly ought not go swimmin'. Water's not deep enough to cool ya' off anyways. And, if the wind comes up, the lake can get right rough real fast…hard to stay in a canoe without tippin' over, and you don't wanna do that."

Jason looked disturbed. "Crap!"

Chelsea finally spoke. "What? Are you worried about the boat tipping over?"

"No. I got so upset waiting for you this morning that I forgot to pack any food or drinks."

Chelsea smirked. "Well, you could get us some hot dogs, crawdads and a couple of cold beers. That sounds good."

Jake looked amused. "I'm thinking your little lady's a might confused. The hot dogs are good, better with a little chili and maybe some mustard. But, the crawdads are raw, meant for the fish. I originally hail from Louisiana, and they do cook up a batch of crawdads there once in a whiles for lunch. They ain't half bad, 'specially with the right Cajun spice."

Jason had no idea how to respond. He could see in Chelsea's eyes that she wanted to stab this man for calling her a *confused little lady*. And, she had been a smart ass by suggesting they should eat the crawdads. Anything he said would no doubt piss off both Chelsea and Jake. Jason had never gotten the old adage that 'you usually can't get in trouble by keeping your yap shut'.

He smiled and finally said, "We'll have a couple of hot dogs with mustard, hold the crawdads…and a couple of cold beers. That ought to hold us over until dinner."

No one attacked anyone, so Jason took it as a win. He went to pick out a couple of canoe paddles and life jackets. He paid for the food and canoe rental, and they walked down to the dock where the canoes sat ready to launch.

Chelsea sat down on the edge of the dock, dangling her feet over the side.

"We should eat before we head out in the canoe. That thing's not going to be all that stable, and I don't want you rummaging around for food while we're on the water. Sit down here and let's eat and drink the beer while it's cold."

Jason joined her, and barely got his first bite of hot dog before the mosquito swarm attacked. He tried swatting at them, and his hot dog slid out of the bun and landed in the lake.

"Damn, Chelsea, these things are eating me alive. I didn't think to bring bug spray. That'd kill the little bastards."

"Grab your paddle and life jacket, and let's get this canoe launched while we still have some blood left. I'm pretty sure they'll leave us along once were on the water."

Jason abandoned his beer, picked up the paddle and life jacket, and swung the paddle at the mosquitoes swarming around his head.

"Jason, be careful! You almost took my head off. Help me get this canoe in the water, quick!"

"Sorry, Chelsea. These things are making me nuts."

They finally got the canoe launched, paddling furiously away from the shore.

As they paddled out of synch, Chelsea said, "Well, we're still alive. I was afraid the mosquitoes, or Bubba, were going to eat us. I shouldn't have made fun of his menu. And, could you please get with the program and paddle with me, not against me. Stroke. Stroke. Stroke."

"I'll try to paddle better. I don't think he even noticed you making fun of him. He just thought you were a dumb, confused woman." He added quickly, "Of course, I know that's not the case. Everyone knows you don't eat crawdads."

"Actually, I did know they eat them in New Orleans. I hear they're really good, kind of like tiny lobsters. Some people eat them with Cajun spice, and some dip the meat in melted butter. A real detective would know that. And, it was so hot in that shack the crawdads were probably cooked anyhow. Now, stop swatting at mosquitoes and paddle faster. Stroke. Stroke. Stroke."

Jason fumed. *I should've ordered her a batch of crawdads. Real detective indeed. I need to calm down, or I'm gonna have a stroke, stroke, stroke.*

Being heavier, Jason sat in the back of the canoe and steered in addition to paddling. It was Chelsea's job up front to paddle them forward and to keep an eye out for obstacles like shallow water, tree branches, rocks, and monsters. It was peaceful for the moment, no waves, wakes or mosquitoes. As Jason calmed down enough to look around, he saw a very large lake surrounded by a vast area of swamp, dense woods and vegetation that extended to the shoreline.

There were beautiful birds, including the typical Florida egrets, ducks, geese, grebes, and cranes. Jason recognized many of these birds from reading a Florida bird book before leaving for the Sunshine State. Jesup Lake was very shallow, average around six feet; much shallower in some spots. With the water so calm, he could see the bottom in most places. There were no signs of human life other than themselves. It was eerily quiet.

Jason took his shirt off. "It's really hot out here. I should have brought along suntan lotion. I put some of my face, arms and legs but didn't think about taking off my shirt. How are you doing? Aren't you cooking? And, doesn't it seem a little strange that there's no one else out here, not even fishermen?"

Chelsea said, "I agree it does seem a little strange. And yes, it is very hot. It would be nice to take a cool dip in the lake. Jake said it wouldn't be a good idea to go swimming. But, this is fresh water. I thought gators preferred brackish water. Also, didn't someone tell us that the gators hide in the tall weeds and on the shoreline during the day because they are hunted so heavily? Do you really think it would hurt if I took a quick dip? Jason? Did you hear me?"

She turned around, and Jason pointed accusingly towards the water in front of the canoe.

"Chelsea, you're supposed to keep an eye out for obstacles. Didn't you see that gigantic water moccasin that just swam in front of us? He looked big enough to swamp this canoe. He also doesn't know the rules of boating. He was coming from our left, and he should have given us the right of way. Do better."

"I didn't see any snake, but I am keeping an eye out. I think this is logging country and the stupid loggers must throw their debris in the lake. I've seen several small to medium-sized logs. But, we haven't gotten close enough to run into one yet, so I haven't said anything. Come to think of it, I did see a sign while we were driving through the middle of nowhere that warned of logging trucks entering the road."

"Chelsea, Honey. I don't want to alarm you, but you should probably have your eyes checked. You might need glasses. Several of those logs are moving, and there's no wind or waves, so they're likely moving under their own power."

"Jason, don't be silly. Haven't we had enough problems, without you making stuff up? Logs can't just move on their own."

"I'm not sure how to break this to you, Sweet'ums, but those aren't logs. Those are alligators, and you are correct. There are a lot of them. A ridiculous number of them. Too fucking many for my mind to process. And, counting them isn't going to make me feel safe. I feel like jumping out of the boat, but my excellent powers of deductive reasoning tell me that's not the solution to this particular problem."

"Don't be silly, Jason. No way those are all alligators. There's just too many. Those have to be logs. We're approaching one now. I'll show you. I'll push it out of the way with my paddle."

They moved a few feet, and Chelsea leaned forward and thrust her paddle into the water, pushing the smallish log out of the way. Jason saw a giant splash, the canoe lurched and Chelsea screamed, pulling her paddle back with a large chunk missing. Jason wanted to run away.

"Oh my God, Jason! You picked a helluva time to be right. Those logs are alligators. What have you done to us?"

"Me? You threw the dart that hit Jesup Lake."

"But, the dart thing was your idiotic idea. Where are we, alligator hell?"

"I don't know, Darling, but I'm starting to feel a little like Wile E. Coyote. If this were a cartoon, I'd escape by hopping from gator head to gator head all the way to the shore."

"Don't you dare stand up. You'll swamp the canoe. Did you bring your little gun thingy?"

"This isn't actually a cartoon, and my little gun thingy wouldn't make a dent in these monsters. It would just piss them off."

"More of your excellent deductive reasoning?"

"I'm going to start paddling back to the dock as fast as I can. You just hang onto what's left of your paddle. Maybe Jake won't charge us for it if he sees the alligator teeth marks. I think we can safely claim it as normal wear and tear for this lake."

Jason managed to turn the canoe around, trying not to crash into any more *logs*. The angry alligator had calmed down. The rest of the gators, hundreds of them, were peacefully basking in the sun on the surface of the lake.

"Chelsea, please help guide me back to the dock without bumping into any more of these *logs*. I want to get home alive. I can't imagine why there'd be so many alligators in one lake."

"Jason, slow down. Your frantic paddling is rocking the boat, and I do NOT want you to turn this canoe over. No more recreation selection by dart. From now on, I'll do the research myself."

They finally got to the dock. As soon as Jason reached out to stabilize the canoe, the mosquito swarm struck again. He watched Chelsea jump onto the dock and run for the bait shop. Jason struggled to get onto the dock without capsizing, his muscles fueled by a terror-driven rush of adrenaline. He yanked the canoe out of the water, dropped it on the dock and ran inside the building. Chelsea stood just inside the door, scratching her arms and neck.

"Hello! Jake! We're back. Hi, Chelsea, thanks for abandoning me out there. If I'm a little pale, it's because I'm a few pints low on blood."

Jake came out of a back room. He looked surprised to see them so soon, "Howdy folks. Y'all weren't gone long. Too hot fer ya'?"

Jason was speechless. Chelsea was not. Jason was concerned as she moved towards Jake, standing behind the counter.

Chelsea said, "What the hell? What's with the clouds of mosquitoes? And, why are there so many alligators? They were everywhere, barely enough room in the water for our canoe. One of them took a bite out of my paddle. Why didn't you warn us? We could've been eaten."

Jake looked confused, and concerned. "I just assumed y'all were from Florida, and knew about Jesup Lake. And, didn't y'all bring any bug spray? I guess yer not from around here, huh?"

Chelsea continued her rant. "Knew what about Jesup Lake? It's a lake. What's to know?" She turned on Jason, "And, bug spray would have been an excellent idea. Jason, why didn't your deductive reasoning come up with that?"

Jason finally spoke up. "Yeah, I'm a detective, and I should have deduced that we needed bug spray in the Florida swamp. But, I also detected there's a helluva lot of alligators in Jesup Lake. What's the deal, Jake? Did the state of Florida put this place here to control the tourist population? Why aren't there any warning signs?"

"Truth be told we hardly ever get any tourists out this far; just local folk, mostly hunters, a few fishermen and the like. If y'all go on that there internet thing, you'd find out all about Jesup Lake and how the fish and game folks catch stray gators that wandered onto people's property and bring 'em here to turn loose. We've got more gators per square foot than anywheres else on this here planet. I won't charge you for the paddle. I'm guessin' you bumped one of the gators. You're lucky you're still alive. Those gators can get downright cranky."

Chelsea said, "Jason, did you hear that? You took your wife out on the most alligator-infested lake on the planet, in a canoe! I thought you loved me. Then you told me to poke the log to get it out of our way. Are you insane?"

"Chelsea, I'm sorry. You're right. I should've done some research. But, when I did figure it out, great detective that I am, I tried to warn you. It was your idea to poke the log."

"It bit a chunk out of my paddle, Jason! I could have been killed. I was already weak from loss of blood from the mosquito attack. Next time you get the bright idea to pick a place using a dart and a map, I'm going to tape you to the wall and use you as the dart board."

Jake sat down. Jason couldn't tell whether the look on the man's face was one of fear or amusement, or perhaps both.

Jake said, "Damn Mister! Your little woman's got some temper on her. She's kinda spunky. I like it."

Chelsea, holding the canoe paddle by the handle like a baseball bat, screamed and made a move towards Jake. The rotund man ducked down behind the counter, arms above his head.

"Git that crazy lady outta my shop. I thought my wife had a temper. Your wife's just plain mean."

Chelsea, practically foaming at the mouth. "Well, she never had to live with my husband!"

Jason grabbed Chelsea's arm. "Hey, that's not fair. And, don't kill the nice man. It's not his fault you don't know anything about alligators and lakes in Florida."

She turned on Jason. He saw murder in her eyes. She yanked her arm free and swung the paddle, barely missing his head. He ran out the door, yelling back at her over his shoulder.

"Chelsea, calm down, and listen. I've solved the case. I was right all along. It's the mosquitoes. The mosquitoes have driven you mad, to the point where you want to murder your own husband. I'll bet those realtors got attacked by mosquitoes while showing properties, it made them crazy and that's why they killed each other, and their clients. Or, maybe it was those killer mosquitoes, the mosquitoes did the murders, and the realtors got blamed for it. And, you helped me solve the case! Good job!"

Chelsea screamed so loud Jason was sure even the alligators must have run away.

Chapter 23

It took several hours for Chelsea to calm down after Jesup Lake. Jason had apologized so many times she finally forgave him. That night, he drank gallons of coffee, stayed awake and made love to her. To her delight, he made her squeal, twice.

Next morning Chelsea slept in until 9:00. She took a leisurely hot shower and then followed the delicious aroma of coffee to the kitchen. She found Jason at the table blowing on a cup of very hot liquid, steam rising from the cup. He tried to take a sip, but quickly pulled his lips away.

"Good morning, Chelsea. I'm glad to see you smiling. I poured you a cup of coffee. Be careful. It's really hot."

Chelsea sat down at the table, picked up the cup and took a large drink. It didn't seem all that hot to her.

"Hey Jason. You did good last night. Attaboy!"

Jason yawned. "I enjoyed myself, although that second round really took it out of me. Not as young as I used to be. I only get one 'Attaboy'?"

"Okay. Attaboy. Attaboy. Any plans for today? Heard anything from Rock Handsome about showing us more properties?"

Jason took another tiny sip of the hot coffee. Chelsea was amused.

Jason said, "I talked to him a few minutes ago. He has a list of condos to show us, but he's busy with another client today. He's apparently doing a closing with a client who found a property without any dead bodies, so they bought it. He asked if we minded waiting until tomorrow morning to go looking again."

Chelsea took another large drink of the hot coffee.

She said, less relaxed. "What did you tell him? We need to find something fairly soon. Our time is running out."

"I told him we could take today off, but we have to go out again tomorrow. I had an ulterior motive. Since yesterday wasn't all that relaxing, I came up with another plan for today."

Chelsea cringed. "What's that? *Oh God. Now what?*"

"I called a place in Daytona where you can rent time on a circular race track. I've always wanted to run my red rocket around a track with no speed limits. I think I would've made a helluva race car driver."

Jason took a big drink of coffee and yelped. He ran to the sink, turned on the cold water and drank directly from the tap. Chelsea wondered if they were drinking the same coffee.

Chelsea said, "You want to what? To drive us in circles as fast as possible in your little clown car? Doesn't sound very relaxing to me."

"Oh please, please, please. I've always wanted to run the red rocket on a track; paddling her through the gears, wind in my hair, bugs in my teeth."

"Yeah, and no brain in your head."

"Come on Chelsea. It'll be fun, and all you have to do is sit there and enjoy the ride. We'll be safe. We'll wear helmets and everything. And afterwards, I'll take you out for a nice dinner, ice cream and then make you squeal again tonight. I promise."

Chelsea smiled, a faraway look in her eyes. "Lobster for dinner, my favorite ice cream shop for two scoops of ice cream, and I have to squeal at least twice again tonight."

"Yes, it's a deal. We might even go for three."

"Don't be silly. I don't want to kill you."

"No, Dear. I was talking about the ice cream."

***

Jason told Chelsea he had called the race track and they had a two-to-four o'clock slot open, so he booked it. They arrived at one-thirty and went to the office to register. Jason parked next to a small building located near the dirt track. Chelsea thought the exterior looked in need of repair, with warped boards, peeling paint and a broken window covered with cardboard. She hoped this turned out better than *Alligator Alley*. The sign hanging over the front door looked as if it were about to fall down. It read *Race-O-Rama*. Underneath that were the words *For Those With the Need for Speed*. Jason knocked on the door, and they entered.

Inside, a large man with what Chelsea thought of as abundant flab sat behind an old wooden counter. This looked disturbingly familiar to her. He was bald on top, with a pudgy face and a five-o'clock shadow. His eyebrows appeared so bushy that it was hard to imagine he could see anything, and his large mouth was filled with even larger teeth, except for the two that were missing in front. When he stood and approached the counter to meet Jason and Chelsea, she noticed that the man wore a dirty blue T-shirt with the words *Racing is for Lovers* stenciled on the front. As he walked toward them, a noticeable amount of bare-skin beer belly bulged out below the T-shirt and over the belt of his loose-fitting jeans; Chelsea figured there were no pants on earth that could have contained that gut.

"Hello, folks. The name's Earl. What can I do ya' for?"

Chelsea took one look at Earl and became overwhelmed by the urge to run away. *Earl definitely ate the whole thing, and washed it down with a keg of beer.*

Jason approached Earl, but neither one offered to shake hands. Earl nodded at Jason, and Jason nodded back. Chelsea assumed this was some sort of swamp man greeting.

"Hello, Earl. Pleased to meet you. I'm Jason, and this is my wife, Chelsea. I made an appointment over the phone to rent the track from two to four this afternoon. I'm going to show Chelsea how fast my car will fly around in a circle with my expert hands at the wheel. We'll be going so fast we'll have to be careful not to run over ourselves."

Earl grinned. "What kinda' car did ya' say y'all drive?"

"I have a two-seater, a sports car with one-hundred-eighty horsepower. I call her my *little red rocket*. Is there a problem with that?"

"No. Not a'tall. It's just our usual customers drive somethin' a little more…how do I put it…manly. We've had Corvettes, lots of Dodges including a couple'a Hellcats, Mustang GTs, Camaros with the Vette engine and even a 'xotic like Ferrari or Lamborghini. But, I don't ever remember a little sports car…and one-hunerd-eighy horsepower? Sounds kinda sissified. But, whatever floats yer boat."

"Jason, I think Earl here is making fun of your little clown car. And, he hasn't even ridden in it with the top down in the rain."

Jason turned to Chelsea and shook his finger at her. He reminded her of a school teacher she once had in grade school, Mrs. Dickie, a nasty old bat. She had not liked that woman one bit.

"Chelsea, be nice. My rocket is a perfectly legitimate roadster for racing."

Earl smirked. "Oh, 'scuse me. I din't unnerstand. You race *roadsters*. Sounds very Uro-pee-an, like them proper Inglishers. We generally think NASCAR 'round here, but…whatever…"

"I know, whatever floats my boat. I haven't had a lot of luck with boats, or anything fun, lately. Florida keeps trying to kill me. I'm hoping today will turn things around."

Chelsea grinned. "At least we're probably not going to sink, and no sharks or alligators to worry about?"

Jason said, "Probably? Earl, this track isn't built on a swamp, is it?"

Earl shook his head, reached under the counter and pulled out a clipboard with several forms and a pen. He placed them on the counter for Jason to sign.

"Mister, this here is Florida. Everything's built on a swamp. If yer gonna run your little red sissified car on our track, you'll need to fill out these here forms. It's just a formality, insurance and stuff like that there."

Chelsea took the clipboard and briefly scanned through the pile of papers. He eyes got wider and wider as she read, red flags popping up in her brain everywhere.

"Jason, this is an awful lot of paperwork for a two-hour track rental. These release forms are kind of scary. You're releasing the race track from responsibility for any and all damage and injuries, including damage to your car due to crash, blowing the engine and a whole list of other stuff. This list of personal injuries includes everything from fracturing your skull in a car crash to slipping and falling in the bathroom and...Oh God...alligator attack. I don't believe it. The good news, there isn't anything about drowning." To Earl. "What about liability issues related to any other cars on the track at the same time as us?"

Jason reached for the clipboard. Chelsea hung on to it and kept reading.

Jason answered. "There's not supposed to be any other cars on the track for my two-hour time period. I'm not racing anyone; just racing against my own time."

"Jason, that sounds kind of boring. But, at least I don't have to worry about us crashing into anyone else. How do I let you talk me into these crazy things?"

Earl spoke up. "No worries, ma'am. No need to get yer panties in a bunch. It's as safe as can be driving 'round our track. After all, yer just goin' 'round in circles…no obstacles to hit, no other cars; maybe a gator that wandered onto the track. But, dammit, this is Florida. Get used to it. Still safer than sittin' on the couch at home. Oh, and you don't have to worry 'bout fallin' in the terlet. They're both closed with busted plumbing."

"Why is everybody down here so worried about my panties bunching up? Does that happen often to women in Florida, and is it dangerous? Jason, maybe we should add *bunched up panties* to your list of things that are dangerous in Florida. Earl, you've obviously never ridden in a car with my husband at the wheel. And, if it's so safe, how many accidents have you had here in the past year?"

Earl scratched his head, then under his arm pit, then sniffed his hand. "Let's see. Only 'bout a dozen. Nothin' too serious."

Chelsea felt nauseous. She wasn't sure whether it was the dozen accidents or Earl's arm pit check.

She said, "A dozen? Accidents? Were there any fatalities?"

'Well, ma'am, boys will be boys. Earlier this year a young feller wrapped his new Corvette 'round a tree on the backside of the track. He died in the car fire. Then, an older feller in a Ferrari flipped it on the north turn and the car landed upside down. He got throwed from the car and broke his neck. Another feller, in his thirties, blew up his Dodge Charger when he hit the NOS button comin' out of the south turn. He…"

Chelsea finished his sentence. "Let me guess. He died with his parts spread all over the track. Were his panties in a bunch?"

Earl looked confused. "Yes ma'am, something like that. But, he weren't wearin' no panties."

"Jason, it sounds to me like when men get behind the wheel on a race track, they lose all sense of survival. You're senseless enough as it is."

"Nonsense, Chelsea. This is perfectly safe. I'm just going to take a few laps around the track and see how fast we can *safely* negotiate the curves. We'll be fine."

Jason took the paperwork from Chelsea, signed it without reading and handed it back to Earl, who glanced through the pile carefully to make sure all the forms were signed.

"Looks fine. What size helmet do y'all and your little lady wear?"

They both told him, and he went into the back and came out with two bright red helmets, which he handed to Jason.

"Here y'all are. Bright red, to cover up the blood…Just kidding."

Jason handed one of the helmets to Chelsea and they headed for the red rocket.

"Jason, I'm not sure this is a good idea."

"Nonsense Woman. Don't get your panties all…"

"Don't poke the bear, Husband. Just shut up, and let's get this over with."

They climbed into the red rocket and put on their helmets. Jason aimed the car towards the dirt road that led to the track. Chelsea, not at all happy, looked at a set of bleachers they passed on their right. Those bleachers didn't look like they'd been used in years; peeling paint, splintered and weather-worn wood. They brought thoughts of doom to Chelsea's mind. When he reached the track, Jason turned right at the bleachers, down shifted and floored the accelerator.

"We're off!"

Chelsea saw her life flash before her eyes. "Ahhhhh! We're gonna die!"

She discovered that the track was actually more oval than round. Jason pinned the accelerator to the floorboard at the beginning of each straight stretch, and the palm trees and swamp flew by them as a blur. Then he slammed on the brakes, crawling slowly through the curves. This caused Chelsea to be whipped backward and forward.

"Jason, I should have known you'd have some hare-brained approach to racing. I feel like a crash dummy."

"Nonsense. You said you wanted me to drive safely, so that's what I'm doing."

"If by safely you mean permanent neck damage. Couldn't you negotiate the transition between straight stretch and curve without crippling me? I thought your little clown car was supposed to be great on curves. I appreciate you not driving us into the swamp, but can't you go around the curves a little faster?"

"Do you want me to flip the car, Chelsea? I have to be careful how fast I enter the curves."

"There's slow, and then there's stopped. Even I could negotiate a curve better…"

Just then, Chelsea heard the deafening roar of an engine, a real engine, an exotic engine, a racing engine.

"Jason, did your rocket just explode?"

At that moment, a bright yellow supercar flew past them on the left, a yellow blur as it sped by on the straight stretch. Chelsea, startled, almost jumped out of the red rocket, but they were still moving.

"Wow, Chelsea! A genuine supercar, 789 horsepower, zero to sixty in 2.9 seconds. And, the engine roar at speed is deafening. How cool is that?"

"Jason, didn't you rent the track for two hours? I thought we were the only ones allowed out here. So, what's an airplane doing flying past us?"

"I don't know. Should I go back to the building and talk to Earl? I think not! Remember the boat? I don't like being passed. I'm gonna catch this guy and ask him what the hell he thinks he's doing on the track on my dime."

Jason floored the rocket coming out of the turn. Chelsea squealed.

"Jason, I just wet myself a little. Could you please pull off the track and talk to Earl? I think that's an outstanding idea. An excellent idea. One of your best ideas ever. I don't want to die in your little clown car, sitting in my own pee."

The last of her sentence was drowned out as the yellow flash pulled up on their left again, the supercar having already lapped Jason. This time as the supercar passed, it slowed to match Jason's speed. Chelsea saw the driver turn and glare at Jason. She gasped.

"Jason, isn't that Mark Moneyman? What's he doing here? He looks angry."

The man in the supercar reached over to the passenger's seat and picked up something shiny. Chelsea couldn't tell what it was, but she had a bad feeling in her gut. The ultra-expensive car's passenger's side window went down, and Chelsea recognized the barrel of a pistol. Jason tapped the rocket's brakes just before Chelsea heard a loud bang.

Jason said, "Chelsea. Mr. Moneyman is shooting at us. I don't think he likes you very much."

"Me? You think he's shooting at me? You're the idiot that accused him of murder. Your stupid PI thing has put your wife in danger. Do something!"

The supercar, now in front of the red rocket, sped up. Chelsea pointed out to Jason that Moneyman appeared to be planning to lap them again. She coughed and choked on the dirt that the powerful sports car stirred up.

Jason said, "No worries, Chelsea. I've got this. I'll speed up in the curves so he can't catch us. When he catches us, I'll expertly block him from passing us. When he gets around me, I'll give him the old NASCAR bump. If that doesn't work, I'll give him the finger."

Chelsea said, "Oh God. We're gonna die. That's probably the same twenty-two caliber revolver he pulled out on his boat. Rip Thornton was shot in the head with a twenty-two. This madman has a temper, a twenty-two, and he knows how to use it. D'ya think there's a clue in there somewhere, PI Dufus?"

"Be nice, Chelsea. And, yes, I'm thinking Mark Moneyman might be our number one suspect for the murder."

Chelsea felt her stomach tighten as Jason hit the accelerator, let off a little going into the next curve and then gave it the gas again. The rear end of the rocket skidded to the right, Jason let off the accelerator, the car righted itself, and then he expertly powered out of the curve. A gigantic great blue heron took flight in the swamp next to the track, disturbed by Jason's power slide. Chelsea was both concerned and impressed.

"Wow! I just drifted like in one of my racing video games. How cool was that?"

Chelsea turned around, pointing behind them.

"Jason, that giant bird scared the heck out of me. And, this definitely is not one of your video games. Here comes the crazy man with the gun again."

Chelsea watched as the yellow supercar roared up behind them on the straightaway.

Jason said, "I told you, I got this, Chelsea."

The supercar jogged left to pass. Jason jogged left. The supercar jogged right to pass. Jason jogged right. The supercar engine roared, and the red rocket took a direct hit as the yellow beast bumped it from behind. Chelsea's head bounced off of the head rest and her body off of the seat back. She felt the red rocket shoot forward like…a rocket.

Chelsea squealed, and not in a good way. She heard Jason scream as he fought the steering wheel.

"What the hell?! He just hit us with a half-million-dollar car! He's out of his mind!"

Chelsea hung onto the oh-my-god-bar with both hands, her nerve endings on fire with panic.

"What was your first clue? The gunshots? The ramming in the rear? Do something or we're gonna die!"

Chelsea was familiar with pool from playing with her father as a child. Just as a cue ball might drive the eight ball into the side pocket, the roaring yellow sports car knocked the red rocket directly into the dirt road exiting the track, headed for the office building. Jason continued to point the rocket in that direction and hit the brakes, hard. The red rocket skidded for a long distance, stopping just short of the front door. Chelsea felt terrified, her eyes the size of silver dollars.

Chelsea looked around, but she saw no sign of the yellow supercar. They exited the rocket and ran into the building. Earl came out of the back.

"Howdy, folks. Back so soon?"

Chelsea's face was bright red. "Where have you been? Didn't you hear the roar of the engine, the gunshots? How did that yellow monster get on the track? You told Jason we had it to ourselves!"

"Whoa there little lady. You've really got your panties in…"

Chelsea started over the counter after Earl. Jason grabbed her just in time. She continued to struggle against his bear hug with uncontrolled fury.

"Mr. Earl. I don't think you should address my wife's panties any more. I think she wants to kill you."

Earl said, meekly. "Sorry there ma'am. It's just a 'xpression. What's the problem?"

Chelsea calmed down a little, and Jason released her. She was speechless.

Jason said, "My wife's concerned that what appeared to be Mr. Mark Moneyman shot at us from a bright yellow supercar, and when that failed he tried to run us off the track. You told me we had the track to ourselves today."

Earl explained, "Mr. Moneyman is a multi-millionaire. He pays me a shit ton a money each month to use the track when he wants, so when he shows up I always makes a 'cepshun fer him. It's just good bidness. I also can't believe a important man like Mr. Moneyman would shoot at anybody, and he pays me so much money even if he did I wouldn't notice...if y'all git my drift. Anyhow, he got so much money if he wanted somebody kilt, he'd just pay someone else to do the dirty werk."

Chelsea finally found her voice. "So, if we called the police, you wouldn't act as a witness; tell them that you saw him try to kill us?"

"Ma'am, I didn't see nor hear nuthin'. I wuz in the back takin' a snooze. Sorry fer yer troubles. You still got a hour of yer time left. D'ya want to use it, or I'll be happy to give ya' a refund."

Jason looked at Chelsea and shrugged. "Well, no harm done. We're okay, and he didn't hit the red rocket hard enough to do any real damage to the rear end; just a gentle bump. I think I'd like to finish my time on the track."

Chelsea looked sad. "Jason. You're out of your mind."

Jason said, "Well, it looks like the crazy man has left. So, it should be safe."

Chelsea shook her head side to side. "No way. If you want to commit suicide, go for it. I already told you I increased your life insurance policy. I'll just sit in the bleachers and watch you suicide yourself." To Earl. "Could you please make sure that no one else enters the track for the next hour? Are there any other millionaires or billionaires who've paid in advance for the right to kill us?"

Earl smiled and chuckled. "No ma'am. Only other millionaire who ever comes 'round is Mrs. Roundbottom. She also pays me a shit ton of money every month to use the track whenever she wants, but she's so old I doubt she even remembers she's doin' it."

Chelsea walked up the road to the bleachers and took a seat in the front row. She watched as Jason drove by in the red rocket, turned onto the track, and slowed in front of where she was sitting.

He yelled, "How about you time me for a couple of laps? I want to see if I can beat my own time."

Florida being totally flat, Chelsea could see the whole track. Jason sped up, took the first curve expertly with just a hint of drift, and powered out of the curve onto the straightaway. Chelsea saw movement out of the corner of her eye and turned to look. She saw an old lady in her eighties, piloting a black, antique looking car up the entrance road and onto the track. The car looked like something you might see in an old British murder mystery. The engine sounded more like a sewing machine, not suggestive of a great deal of power.

Chelsea stood up and yelled, forming her hands into a mock megaphone, "Hey, what are you doing? You're not supposed to be here."

The woman had long curly gray hair blowing in the wind. Her face showed lots of wrinkles, and a pair of granny glasses rested on the end of her long, thin nose. She sneered at Chelsea and slowed in front of her, almost as if she were waiting for Jason. He rounded the curve behind the antique car and pulled up next to it, a confused look on his face. Chelsea watched as the old lady looked at him and floored the accelerator. Jason responded by flooring the red rocket, and the race was on.

Chelsea yelled, "Get her, Jason. Run Grandma into the ground!"

Chelsea watched as the antique car beat Jason to the first curve, did a perfect power slide and pulled further ahead on the straight stretch. Jason tried to catch up in the stretch, but Granny entered the next curve, did another perfect slide and powered out, leaving Jason in her dust. She waved, an evil grin on her face as she passed by Chelsea. Jason stopped on the track in front of the bleachers. Chelsea felt bad for him, even though this had been his stupid idea.

"Get in Chelsea. We're going home. I gotta say, I preferred the motor boat to this. At least I pulled up beside the yacht before heading for the bottom of the Intracoastal."

"Yeah, Jason. And, now you can add yellow supercars to the list of things in Florida that tried to kill you. You could also add granny there, but that would fall under the category of embarrassing you to death."

Jason wept, again.

Chapter 24

Jason was furious as he drove home from the track. He ranted in Chelsea's general direction.

"I can't believe that old lady outran my red rocket, IN AN ANTIQUE CAR! Everything has gone wrong since we got to Florida. It's bad enough the entire place keeps trying to kill me, but I lost a race to someone's grandmother. I'm Dr. Jason Longfellow, PI, I'm a manly man, and this just can't stand. I'm going to fix this right now. I'm tired of this *little clown car*, as you call it."

"Oh God. Now what? Jason, I don't know how much more fun I can take."

"I saw a used car dealership on the way to the track. I think it was called *Otto's Auto*, or something like that. I noticed a jacked-up camo-colored four-wheel-drive truck on the lot when we passed by. I'm thinking I should replace my clown car with a rugged off-road truck. With those huge knobby tires and that massive clearance, I could run right over the top of an alligator, or Moneyman if he shows up again in his stupid yellow supercar. I'm gonna do it!"

Jason pumped his right fist in the air in triumph at his latest brilliant idea. The rocket swerved across the center line.

"Jason. Calm down. You're going to kill us. Let's not act in haste. You love your little clown car. Plus, you need to think about whether or not it would be comfortable to sleep in this truck thing. After today, you might just end up sleeping in your car a while longer."

Jason was determined. He saw the sign and pulled into *Otto's Auto*. Before they could even exit the car, he was met by a tall, thin, balding man in a polyester leisure suit. A gust of wind did nothing to move his remaining hair, molded into a comb-over with half a can of hairspray. His thin black eyebrows, narrow dark eyes, dark moustache and goatee made him look like a vampire from a Vincent Price movie. The man offered Jason his hand.

"Hello, I'm Stan Simonson…they call me Stan the Salesman. And you are?"

Jason exited the red rocket and shook his hand. "Hello, Stan the Salesman. I'm Jason the PI. This is my wife, Chelsea, the…wife."

Stan smiled a big, friendly salesman smile. "Is Chelsea a PI too?"

Chelsea frowned, exited the car and walked around to Jason and Stan.

"I'm not a PI. I'm an ER nurse. I need to be a psychiatric nurse, because my husband has lost his mind. Do you know of any good divorce lawyers, Stan?"

Stan looked confused. Jason recognized that look. For some reason most people had it the first time they met him and Chelsea.

"I don't know much about divorce. Me and my misses have been married for twenty long years. But, I do know cars. Since you pulled into my lot, I'm assuming you're also interested in cars. Anything in particular you're looking for?"

Jason walked over to the lifted truck and affectionately touched the fender.

"I like this one. Fill me in on the details. How old, how many miles, has it ever been wrecked, is there a Carfax report, how much?"

Chelsea walked over to the truck. Jason watched as she craned her neck to look up at the very tall, lifted vehicle.

"Jason, isn't this thing a little high up there? That's quite a first step. Can you even get in behind the wheel? And, stop fondling it. It's embarrassing."

Stan reached out, pulled a lever, and Jason saw a three-step ladder unfold from the side near the driver's door, or where the door should have been.

Chelsea said, "Uh, Jason. Need I also mention that there's no doors?"

Stan said, "We have the doors. They're in the garage. We took them off to show the versatility of this awesome truck. You can remove the doors and the top, and even fold down the windshield. I'm sure your husband can appreciate the utility of such a thing."

Chelsea said, "That's nice, Stan. I can see how you might want to fold down the windshield, since all it does is protect your face from bugs, wind, rain, snow and the occasional flying rock tossed your way by one of the billion tractor-trailer's on the highway. And, if you tell me my panties are in a bunch, I'm going to hurt you."

Stan took a step back. "How about I let the two of you look over the truck together, and I'll be back in a few minutes to get your take on it. Meanwhile, I'll go inside and do some numbers so I can get you the best deal possible."

Jason saw the look on Stan's face and realized Chelsea was scaring the salesman. Maybe if Stan was afraid of the crazy lady, he'd be more willing to negotiate. Chelsea walked several steps away from Stan, and gestured for Jason to follow her. She turned her back to the salesman and whispered to Jason.

"I really don't like this guy. He's a smart-ass. And, he's already got you eating out of his hands. I can tell by the childish look on your stupid face."

Jason's face was actually aglow. "Oh, Chelsea. This thing is incredible. I could drive it on the beach, off-road, and in Ocala National Forest without worrying about running over alligators. It's manly, awesome. And, you wouldn't have to worry about me racing it. That's not what it's for. Keep scaring Stan, and maybe we'll get a better price."

"Jason. Need I point out that we live in Northern Virginia? You normally drive to work on the Washington Beltway. Granted, with this thing you could probably drive over top of the car in front of you, but I'm thinking the Virginia State troopers might take exception to that. I can't believe I'm going to say this, but it's even less practical than your little clown car."

"But, Chelsea, I could put the top up on this one."

"Fair point, I guess. But, shouldn't we at least take it for a test drive first?"

Stan showed up as if on cue, carrying a clipboard and a license plate. "Here's the keys. Dr. Jason the PI, if you'll just sign this form, you and your beautiful wife can take her for a spin."

Jason felt like a kid in a candy store. He was so excited that he started to vibrate. He took the keys, signed the form and Stan attached a license plate to the back of the truck.

"Oh, Chelsea. Let's take her for a spin. I can already tell we're going to get along famously."

"Jason, stop drooling. I swear, men are hopeless. It's not one of those top heavy woman you're always staring at. Come to think of it, that does get my panties in a bunch. Anyhow, it's only a car."

"Only a car!? That's like saying that the space shuttle is only an airplane. Come on, Woman, climb aboard and I'll take you for a real ride."

Jason climbed the set of steps. Excited to test drive his next vehicle, he agilely swung himself into the driver's seat. The steps automatically retracted.

"Come on Chelsea, let's get going. The sooner we test drive her, the sooner we can finalize the deal and take her home."

"Okay, Jason, I'm coming. But, getting into this thing's no picnic. I noticed you didn't have any trouble. You hopped up into that seat like an Olympic athlete. It's clear Stan's already got his hand on your wallet. Any chance this manly truck will at least get your hormones flowing?"

Jason grinned at Chelsea. "I see the way you're looking at me. Sorry. No craving for bananas. Just excited about my new four-by-four truck."

Jason watched Chelsea climb into the passenger seat. She said, "A girl can hope, can't she."

Jason turned the key in the ignition. The engine took off with a roar and then returned to idle.

"Jason, is the whole vehicle supposed to shake like this? It feels like there's something wrong."

"Nonsense, Woman. This is a 2006 four-by-four truck with the original straight six-cylinder engine. It's supposed to run like that. This thing's strong as an ox, and in four-wheel-drive low it can climb telephone poles. I'll bet it's even hurricane proof. We don't really need a test drive. I'll just zip around the block, go back and pay Stan, and we'll be on our way."

"But, Jason, shouldn't you have a mechanic look at it first? It is a used car. And, don't you have to trade in your little clown car? Do you know how much it's worth, and how much this monster's worth? You need to do some research online, or we're going to end up paying for Stan's kids' college educations. We have our own children to get through school."

"Don't be silly, Chelsea. I'm an expert at car stuff. I know exactly how much both vehicles are worth, and I'll get us a great deal. Now, hang on."

Jason shifted into first gear and pulled onto the road. He drove three blocks, and in the middle of the next block he took a sharp right, bounced up over the curb and onto the sidewalk. He drove several hundred feet, barely missing a row of parking meters and forcing a young couple to dive into a store front to avoid being run over.

"Jason! What are you doing?! You're going to kill someone!"

"Nonsense, Woman. I'm in complete control. I just wanted to show you how this old girl can handle driving off road. She took that curb like it wasn't even there."

Jason pulled the wheel to the left, jumped the curb barely missing a parked luxury sedan, and proceeded on down the road. He felt very pleased with himself. That should show Chelsea. He knew all about four-wheel-drive trucks.

Chelsea, hanging on to the oh-my-god-bar for dear life, said, "You've completely lost your marbles. Off road isn't the same as on sidewalk. What if you'd run over that young couple? What if a policeman had come along? What if someone took a photo with their phone? Oh God! Dead realtors, and now this!"

"Calm down, Chelsea. I just wanted to show you how tough this truck really is. Now let's go make a deal."

Jason drove back to the used car lot where he saw Stan waiting, paperwork in hand. Jason parked the truck, he and Chelsea climbed down, and Stan led the them into his tiny, dilapidated office. He sat behind a wobbly old wooden desk, and offered Jason and Chelsea seats in matching wobbly chairs. Jason wasn't worried about the truck, but he was afraid he might wind up on the floor with splinters in his butt. They sat down.

Stan handed a pile of paperwork across the desk to Jason.

"I like to make things as simple for my buyers as possible, so I've put together an incredible deal for you. I took your little roadster for a spin while you were gone, and it's in prime condition, with the exception of a moldy smell. No worries, though. I can cover that up…I mean clean up that odor. Take a look at the numbers, and tell me what you think."

Jason started reading through the papers. His expression became more and more confused and his eyes crossed. When he started counting on his fingers, he looked at Chelsea for help.

Chelsea said, "Give me that paperwork, Darling. You know you're not very good with details. That's my thing."

Jason felt better when she started reading through the numbers. Then she pulled out her cell phone and went online.

"Uh, Jason. Old Stan here has inflated the value for this 2006 truck by about forty percent, and deflated the price of your red rocket by about the same amount. There's also additional charges listed for things I don't understand; delivery fee, detailing fee, family fee, buyer's fee, convertible top fee, off-road fee, bad gas mileage fee, recreational fee, Florida fun fee, alligator protection fee, old folks fee? We're not that old. It's a great deal alright, for Stan. You, on the other hand, are getting screwed."

Stan looked at Jason. He said, "I don't know why your wife is getting her panties all in…"

Jason interrupted, "I wouldn't say that if I were you, Stan. The last guy that said that, well, I don't want to think about what she did to him."

Jason saw that Chelsea had that same murderous look on her face as at *Alligator Alley*. Her hands were balled up into fists. Stan looked surprised, and terrified.

Stan said, "Sorry, I didn't mean anything by that. It's just that in my experience wives hardly ever seem to be interested in cars. I usually just deal with the husband."

Chelsea said, "First of all, why is everyone in Florida so concerned about my panties? More to the point, this contract is ridiculous. Jason, you can't possibly go for this."

She slammed the pile of papers down on the desk. Jason winced, afraid she might break the wobbly old thing.

Jason pointed at the papers and said, "Chelsea, as you well know, I'm a crack detective. I am aware that this price is too high. This is the way real men negotiate. Stan's starting with a high number, and it's up to me to counter with something more reasonable. Right, Stan?"

Jason saw Stan smile. "Why yes, PI Longfellow. Can I call you PI Longfellow?"

"Yes, you may, Stan. And, I must say, I really like the truck. It's so masculine, the way it's lifted, and with those large knobby tires."

"You really know your trucks, PI Longfellow. It's a great off-road vehicle and I've already had seven other men in here looking at it today. One of them told me he'd be back with his wife this afternoon. He needed for her to see it before he makes an offer. Wives can be a pain that way. I'm expecting him any minute." He glanced at Chelsea and grinned. Jason thought he was just being friendly.

Chelsea balled up her fists again and tensed, ready to pounce. Jason didn't understand why she was so angry, didn't think she'd really kill Stan, and he wanted to buy this truck, a lot.

"Did you hear that, Chelsea? Several other men also think this is a great vehicle. And, he's gonna get other offers this afternoon. We don't want to lose this excellent opportunity. And, haven't we already seen enough dead bodies here in Florida? We don't need another one."

Chelsea, sounding flabbergasted, "But, Jason…There's no need to rush into anything. I'm sure there are other ridiculously tall old trucks out there that we could look at. We should sleep on this. And, we haven't found any maimed people. That would be different."

Stan looked confused, and frightened again. Jason's OCD kicked in, and he was bound and determined to have this truck, even if he had to investigate Stan's murder. Besides, that would be an easy one to solve.

Jason said, "Nonsense. I know a great opportunity when I see it. Stan, are you ready? I'm sorry to be so hard on you, but my counter offer is this. Take one-hundred dollars off of the asking price, throw in some touch-up paint, and you've got a deal."

Jason saw Chelsea stare daggers at him. She placed her hands on the sides of her head, appearing to try to keep it from exploding. Jason fought back his fear; he was determined.

"Jason, that's not a deal. My SUV didn't cost this much, new!"

"Chelsea, a 2006 lifted truck of this model is a classic."

Stan said, "PI Longfellow, you really do know your vehicles. It is a classic, a vintage 2006 four-by-four truck. We can do that deal. And, do you want the doors? I forgot to include them. They are two-hundred-dollars extra. Of course, the truck looks cooler without doors, and this is Florida where it's warm all the time, so who needs doors? Am I right? Tell you what I'll do. If you sign the current agreement, I'll throw in the doors for free…and I'll also include the touch-up paint."

Chelsea, sounding furious, "You'll throw the doors in for free? Doesn't a car usually come with doors? Jason, let's get out of here. This is ridiculous."

Jason reached out and gently placed his hand on Chelsea's shoulder.

"Calm down, Chelsea. We do need the doors, since I'm going to be driving on the Washington Beltway in winter. And, to be fair, there aren't any doors on the truck as it sits on the lot. So, they do come extra. We are getting free touch-up paint. I've always wanted a jacked-up four-wheel-drive truck. And, this one's only got ninety-thousand miles on her. Practically brand new."

Jason used that childish, belligerent look, head turned slightly down, squinty eyes looking up at her. He had decided she would either give in, or they would stay there in that used car lot until hell froze over. He could tell she knew she had lost.

"Jason, let's just get this nightmare over with. Sign the damn papers, write this schmuck a check, and take me home. I'll kill you later."

Jason finalized the deal and cleared his stuff out of the red rocket. He asked Chelsea to phone their insurance company and transfer their policy to the truck. Then they were off, Jason at the wheel, grinning like the Cheshire cat. He drove them back to their rental condo.

"Chelsea, this truck is awesome. We have to take it to Ocala National Park tomorrow, explore some of those side roads and check out what it can do. Bring on the gators. I'll drive right over top of them."

"Jason, we have to look at property tomorrow. We're running out of time."

"Nonsense. We can go to Ocala in the morning, and then wander around looking for more dead realtors in the afternoon."

That evening, Jason called Rock Handsome and told him their plans. They would meet him early afternoon at his office for another round of property hunting.

Next morning, Jason was up at the crack of dawn. "Come on, Chelsea. Rise and shine! Ocala awaits, and I've got just the thing to tame the swamp."

Jason dragged Chelsea out of the condo without breakfast. He smiled as he watched her struggle to climb into the truck. He stopped for an artery-clogging fast food sausage, egg and cheese biscuit and coffee. Then they headed for the Ocala National Forest, cruising down the highway at sixty miles per hour, top down, windows open, rear window removed.

"Jason, is this thing supposed to shake like that? I noticed it a little bit coming home from the used car lot yesterday. I can't tell whether it's the engine vibrating or the whole front end shaking. It seems to get worse the faster you go."

"Are you still mad about yesterday…that I bought this awesome machine? I don't feel anything unusual. What you're talking about is probably the knobby tires rumbling over the pavement. Just chill, Chelsea, and let's run over some gators."

It turned out to be further than Jason thought. After miles and miles of thick palm trees and endless swamp, they finally reached one of the dirt roads that Jason had wanted to explore.

"Look, Chelsea. Here's one of the side roads that goes to Lake George. I'm gonna take this one."

He made an abrupt turn to the left, almost rolling the top heavy vehicle in the process.

"Jason! For God's sake! Please be careful! This road looks well-maintained for dirt, but we are in the middle of nowhere. Not a good place for an accident."

"Chelsea, can't you feel it? The freedom of the road. The wind in your hair. This dirt road looks as good as any interstate, and there's no speed limit posted. I'm gonna open her up and see what she'll do. This thing's like a tank. What could go wrong?"

"God, I hate it when you say that."

Jason downshifted into fourth gear, floored the accelerator and up-shifted. At sixty-five miles per hour, the front end of the truck went into a severe side-to-side wobble.

"Chelsea, help! The steering's gone wacko! I can't control her!"

"Jason, slow down. We're gonna crash!"

The front wheels wobbled so badly that Jason lost control. The jacked up truck careened off of the road to the right, just missing a palm tree. Jason stood on the brakes and managed to bring them to a stop, in the middle of a shallow pool of muddy swamp water. He was sad.

"Chelsea, are you okay? The good news is that my new baby, I've decided to call her Swamp Mama, is so high off the ground that we're probably safe from alligators and poisonous snakes. The bad news…someone's got to go down to ground level to figure out what's wrong with the front end. I have no idea why Swamp Mama went out of control. I tried speeding up, but it just got worse. It's like she had a mind of her own; wouldn't do what I told her to. Maybe I should name her *Chelsea*."

Chelsea, voice eerily quiet at first, "Gee. I'm flattered. I told you to slow down. Why didn't you slow down…BEFORE we landed in the swamp?!"

"I don't know. My detective's intuition told me that the right thing to do was to speed up…make the wheels turn faster so they'd stabilize and the wobbling would stop."

"It's not exactly breaking news that your detective's intuition sucks. Now what do we do?"

Jason took out his cell phone and googled *4X4 truck shaking front end.* He found several websites discussing something called the *death wobble.*

"Chelsea, according to the internet there's this thing with older four-wheel-drive trucks with solid front axles called the *death wobble.* Apparently, if one of the front tires is not perfectly aligned, or one of them wears differently from the other, or if one hits a bump and starts vibrating, the out of whack tire can transfer the vibration to the other front tire through the solid axle. This can result in the front end becoming uncontrollable, especially at higher speeds. Doesn't that sound like what happened?"

"D'ya think? So, let me get this straight. You just spent a small fortune on an old used truck with a known defect, reported online as the *death wobble.* Then you brought us to a swamp, pinned the accelerator to the floor, and we ended up here. Some detective you are. You're supposed to catch the killer, not turn into one by killing your wife. Hopefully our Triple A policy covers *idiot crashing in swamp due to death wobble.*"

"Calm down. According to this online article, the solution to this wobble thing is to rotate the tires. I'm going to give that a try before bothering Triple A."

"You got us into this. Do what you must. I'll just sit up here where the alligators and snakes aren't."

"Sounds like a plan. I'll rescue my woman. First, I've got to check the back of the vehicle for a jack and lug wrench. Once I find those I'll get started. You wouldn't want to come down with me and keep lookout for lethal reptiles, would you?"

"You're on your own. You got us into this mess, now get us out."

Jason was sad. "Okay, Dear."

Jason climbed down from the driver's seat and walked through the murky water to the back of the truck. His tennis shoes and socks turned green as they became saturated with rotting, plant-filled, sulphur-smelling swamp water. He opened the back door and climbed up onto the rear bumper so he could reach the back seat.

Jason said, "The jack and lug wrench should be stored back here somewhere. Sometimes they're bolted under the chassis, to the back door or under the back seat. There's a spare tire attached to the rear door that I'll need to include in the rotation, since there's only one jack."

Jason struggled to find the lever to fold the rear seat forward, down and out of the way.

"There's nothing under the seat. There is one of those heavy duty rubber carpets covering the floor. I'll lift it up and see if there's anything underneath."

He managed to lift the floor cover. "Hey Chelsea. There's a small door in the floor. It has a place for a key. Please hand me the key ring that's in the ignition. There were two ignition keys and a couple of smaller keys on it. I wonder if one will open this."

Chelsea leaned over the seat back and stretched her arm to the limit to hand him the key ring. Jason tried one of the smaller keys, and the door in the floor opened.

He said, "This is strange. There's a compartment back here containing a can of bug spray, a bunch of *ReallyRealty* brochures and…oh my God…a loaded 0.22 caliber revolver."

Chelsea suddenly sounded very interested. "What kind of *ReallyRealty* brochures? Do they say anything that might help explain the dead realtors?"

"Not really. They're the usual brochures telling how *ReallyRealty* will sell your house fast and at the best possible price. Wait a minute. There's another piece of paper under the brochures." Jason reached down and dug out the paper. "It's a vehicle registration card for a 2006 4X4 truck…I'm guessing that would be this 2006 4X4 truck. The vehicle was registered to a Dr. Constance Conover. The address is in Miami. I wonder…"

Chelsea said, "We've never heard of anyone named Constance, and the last name Conover doesn't ring any bells. The bug spray isn't all that unusual for Florida. But, the 0.22 revolver is very interesting. Why would anyone sell a truck with a loaded revolver in it? Rip Thornton was shot with a 0.22, and he worked for *ReallyRealty*. Several of the other dead realtors worked for *ReallyRealty* too. Jason, is it possible that your OCD pushed you into buying a truck with a clue to these murders? That would be bizarre, like something you'd write into a murder mystery."

Jason stood there on the back bumper, struggling to keep his balance while searching through the hidden compartment. He didn't want to fall off into reptile land.

"It's not likely, Chelsea. Solving murder requires lots of thought, clever deductive reasoning and keen observational skills. No one ever just blunders into the solution to multiple murders. This Dr. Constance Conover owned this truck, and she liked to drive around in the mosquito-filled swamp, explaining the bug spray. The gun would be to kill snakes and piss off alligators; a 0.22 probably isn't powerful enough to actually kill a gator. She was probably looking for a new house, thus the realtor pamphlets. See how easy it is to explain it all away; just a coincidence. Face it, I made an awesome purchase, but it has nothing to do with the murders. That would just be crazy. And, now I have a twenty-two caliber revolver to go with my thirty-eight revolver; a two-pistol packin' PI."

Jason couldn't find a lug wrench or a jack. He called Triple A, and they came, pulled his truck out of the swamp and towed it to a discount tire store. Turned out the current tires were too worn to rotate. Jason needed to buy four new tires, pay for balancing and an alignment; total cost three thousand dollars for the same knobby, off-road tires. He was sad some more.

Jason took Chelsea out for seafood, in an attempt to make the disastrous day up to her. They were sitting in their favorite seafood restaurant, waiting for their food.

"Chelsea, I'm sorry things didn't go so well today. I still think I did the right thing buying the truck. It'll serve us well here in Florida, and it's like a tank; should be safe for me to drive on the Beltway. I'm mostly sorry we didn't get to look for property again. I'll do better tomorrow."

"What did the man at the tire store say about the death wobble? Seems like fraud to me. Can't you go to the car dealership and make them take back the truck, or at least make him pay for the new tires and alignment? We're spending so much money, we're burning through our down-payment on a vacation property."

"Unfortunately, the tire guy told me the death wobble is a well-known problem with older four-wheel-drive trucks with solid front axles. They stopped putting solid front axles in trucks to fix the problem a few years ago. He said it's highly unlikely that the dealership would be held responsible, since I should have known about the problem. The old let the buyer beware thing."

"Well, that really sucks. If you don't stop blowing through our money, we won't be able to afford to buy any property."

Trying to smooth things over, Jason said, "I know. I'll do better. There is one upside. Maybe there really is a clue in the twenty-two caliber revolver, bug spray and *ReallyRealty* brochures. Could this be some kind of good fortune; the answer to solving the case of the dead realtors? We need to find out who this Dr. Conover is."

"It's more likely you were right, Jason. The whole thing's probably just a coincidence. I can tell you one thing for sure. You better figure out how to put the top up on your new toy truck, and it's a good thing he threw in the doors. Cause after what you put me through today, that's where you'll be a'sleepin' tonight, and it's supposed to rain."

Chapter 25

Next morning, Chelsea got up early and went to look out the living room window at the condo parking lot. She watched as Jason woke up in the driver's seat of his vintage 2006 4X4 truck. He got out and stretched. He looked stiff and uncomfortable, but not as bad as it had been with the little clown car. She noticed that this time he stood up straight almost immediately. Too bad, this wasn't as much punishment. The front seats reclined and he could put the top up, so he wasn't wet either. She might as well let him sleep inside. He wasn't trainable anyhow.

When Jason came into the kitchen, Chelsea was sitting at the table finishing a breakfast bagel and sipping hot coffee. He walked over to the coffee pot and poured himself a cup of her thick, caffeinated brew.

"Good morning, Jason. How's your new off-road bed? Any improvement over the little clown car?"

"Much improved, thank you very much. I'm dry, my muscles are not completely locked up and I felt safe what with my new truck being camo colored. Those alligators and snakes couldn't even see me."

He took a sip of coffee and choked. He continued to stand near the coffee pot. She figured he was too stiff to sit at the table.

"Jason, I don't think it works like that…oh, forget it. I was waiting until nine o'clock to call Rock Handsome and apologize for not showing up yesterday afternoon. We forgot to call him, what with all the excitement. Hopefully he'll still show us some properties today."

"No worries, Dear. He's a realtor. I'm sure he wants the commission, if he's still alive. But, first I need to make a call."

"Who are you calling this early in the morning? Please, no more fun."

"No Chelsea. No more fun. It's too painful." He dialed his cell. "Hello, Gina? Yes, it's PI Longfellow. Remember? You gave me your number?"

Chelsea could feel her ears start to get hot and turn red, like the string bikini the young and curvaceous Gina had been wearing last time they saw her.

"Jason, what are you doing? Why are you calling that woman?"

Jason covered the phone mouthpiece with his hand.

"I want to find out where she got that string bikini so I can get you one. Remember? I asked for her phone number so I could call her later, after she had time to look for the receipt."

Chelsea was suspicious, but this was Jason. He was well aware she'd kill him if he ever fooled around on her.

"Oh, okay. But, hurry up. I want to phone Rock Handsome and I want you to be on the call."

Jason said into his cell, "So, Gina. I wanted to find out where you bought that beautiful red bikini, so I could get one for my wife. Have you had a chance to look for the receipt?"

Gina said, "Are we on speaker? Can your wife hear us?"

"No. I don't think so."

Chelsea was sitting close enough to the coffee pot, and Jason, that she could actually hear both sides of the conversation. For some reason he always kept the volume all the way up. Chelsea wanted to hear what was going on in this gold-digger's mind.

Gina said, "That's good. I couldn't find the receipt, and I was thinking maybe you could come back to the yacht for another visit. Mark's out of town for a few days at some stupid vaccine conference. We can share another pitcher of martinis, or two, and I'll model a couple of my other bikinis…so you can get a better idea of what to buy for your wife. You don't want to bring her along, because you want it to be a surprise. After several martinis, who knows, there might be other surprises. My husband is old, you're a big fellow, not bad looking, and I'll bet we could have some real fun…picking out bikinis that is."

Jason said, "Okay. Martinis and bikinis. And, your husband's out of town, so no firearms. Sounds good, and safe. What time works for you?"

Chelsea thought, *safe?*

"How about one o'clock? I'll have Orlando put out some munchies and a pitcher of martinis for a late lunch, set out a couple of my smallest bikinis to model for you, and we'll see where that takes us…I mean…you can choose one to buy for your wife."

"Okay, see you at one. Goodbye."

Chelsea heard the entire conversation. She knew Jason thought Gina was attractive, he was not dead after all, yet he seemed to be totally oblivious to Gina's intentions. Perhaps at his age he couldn't believe that a sexy twenty-something would be interested in him in that way, since he was not a multi-millionaire. More likely, he couldn't imagine breaking rule number one of his self-avowed code, 'always maintain marital fidelity to Chelsea, or she will kill me'. No matter. Chelsea wasn't about to sit by and let this little tramp seduce her husband.

"So, Jason, you're making plans for this afternoon? I just told you we're scheduled to look for property. What's going on?"

Jason took another drink of the strong coffee and struggled to swallow it. Chelsea recognized the nervous tic that appeared in his right eye when he was worried about something.

"I'm not supposed to tell you, Chelsea. It's a secret…a surprise. But, let's just say I have an appointment to examine some merchandise that I may, or may not purchase as a gift for my lovely wife."

Chelsea took a leisurely bite of bagel and washed it down with coffee, allowing him plenty of time to fret over the situation.

"This merchandise, might it involve the twenty-something sexy and horny wife of an old, worn out multi-millionaire and the modeling of string bikinis? Throw in lunch, a pitcher or two of martinis on the millionaire's yacht, and where do you think this is headed? This young woman has her sights on my husband. If you even think about touching her, I will run over you with your new truck."

Jason looked surprised. Chelsea assumed he had to know he was on thin ice here.

"I want to buy you a nice bathing suit, and she offered to help me pick one out for you. I know I'm a manly man, but I'm in my forties, and I'm not a multi-millionaire. Did you see her in that bikini? Do you really think that gorgeous young thing wants anything to do with me?"

"Jason, I was sitting right here listening to your phone conversation. She's a gold digger, she's hooked her multi-millionaire, he's not taking care of her…big surprise…and she's looking for love in all the wrong places. I know you intend to be faithful, but you're only human…and not too bright. You're not going anywhere, unless Rock has some properties to show us."

"But, Chelsea. I'm just trying to buy you a nice present. Besides, I figured I might ask her some questions about her husband while I'm there. You know, while she's busy focusing on modeling swimwear, I'll subtly interrogate her about her husband's role in the murder of Rip Thornton. Sneak up on her."

"Jason, I think it's the other way around. She's trying to sneak up on you. I have seen her in one of her bikinis. St. Augustine has had enough dead bodies lately, and I don't want to add yours to the mix. Besides, who'd investigate if you're dead? But, you may have a valid point. Perhaps you should go see her this afternoon, and I'll go with. That way I can be there to prevent me from murdering you, and we can interrogate her together."

Jason choked on his last sip of coffee.

"I really appreciate you wanting to prevent yourself from murdering me. That's really sweet? Your coming along will ruin the surprise, but when you weigh that against my murder by wife, I'm good with that. We'll go back to the yacht to visit Gina…Mrs. Moneyman…this afternoon."

***

That afternoon Chelsea struggled to get used to the new truck as Jason drove them to the yacht.

"Jason, I feel like I'm in an airplane. This thing is way too high off the ground. I'm glad you got the doors, or I'd feel like I need a parachute, although I still don't think the doors should have cost extra."

"I got him to throw them in for free…"

"Jason, don't go there."

"Yes, Dear."

Chelsea turned the radio to the local news. To her surprise, the weatherman reported that a hurricane was headed their way, predicted to come ashore several miles south of St. Augustine that very evening as a category 3.

"Chelsea, have you heard anything about a hurricane? Maybe we should listen to the news more often."

"No, I haven't. But, we've been busy not having fun and not buying vacation property. We really should pay more attention to the weather. This is peak hurricane season."

They arrived at the yacht at one o'clock. Jason yelled for permission to board. Chelsea heard Gina yell back, "Permission to board, PI Longfellow."

Jason and Chelsea climbed on board and took the stairs to the upper deck. Chelsea looked up at the sky.

"Jason, it's getting very dark in the middle of the day. There's a huge storm front coming in, and the wind's picking up. I'm not so sure we should have left the condo."

"No worries, Darling. I'll protect you. The safest part of a structure is the middle of the building, in a bathroom if possible…get in the tub, or something like that."

"Jason, Dearest, I'm not sure that applies to a boat."

Jason entered the cabin first. He ducked to avoid hitting his head. Through the door, Chelsea saw Gina sitting on a heavily cushioned round leather sofa in a stunning purple bikini. Gina rose and offered her hand to Jason in greeting, apparently unaware of Chelsea just outside the door. Chelsea noticed a very friendly smile on the young woman's face and the lustful look in her eyes. Jason took Gina's hand.

Gina said, "Hello there, big fella. Glad you could make it. I'm looking forward to helping you pick out some nice swimwear for the wife."

Chelsea walked quickly through the door and stood next to Jason. Gina looked up, a startled expression on her face. Chelsea glared at her. Jason dropped Gina's hand like a hot potato.

"Hello, Gina. It's *the wife*. I heard your phone conversation with Jason, and the secret of the swimwear was out of the bag. We discussed it, and I decided it would make more sense if I came along to pick out the bikini myself, since I'm the one going to wear it. Jason would look kind of silly in a string bikini. And, I'm just not sure that I can trust my husband…to choose the right swimwear."

Gina stomped her foot and huffed, a pouty look on her face. Then, she put on a forced smile.

"Well, it's just great to see you again, Mrs. Longfellow. You don't exactly fit into my plans for this afternoon, but…wait a minute."

Gina's frown turned upside down. She offered her hand, a lecherous grin on her face.

"If I remember correctly, you already rejected my proposal of a wife swap during your earlier meeting with Mark and me? Perhaps you'd be interested in the proverbial ménage-a-trois, without my husband? Mark's well into his sixties, and as you can see, I am not. He also drinks a lot, and he lacks a certain…enthusiasm…or ability to stay conscious…in the bedroom. Maybe you would be willing to share your husband's enthusiasm with me, to help me through these difficult times? I'd make it worth both your whiles, I promise."

Chelsea did not accept Gina's hand in greeting.

Jason, grinning from ear-to-ear, "Well, Gina I'm flatter…"

Chelsea said, "Jason, shut up. Gina, I'm sorry you're going through such a difficult time. I know gold-digging must be tough, what with the millions of dollars, the yacht, Orlando the deck hand and all. I feel for you, and I'd be happy to share my husband with you. Which part do you want, an arm, one of his legs, an ear, perhaps a foot? I started my nursing career in emergency medicine, where I sometimes assisted with ER surgeries. Amputations were one of my specialties."

Jason said, "Uh, Chelsea. Remember, we're here to interrogate her about murder, not to commit one. You came along to prevent yourself from murdering me. I was just going to say that I am flattered, but I love my wife and would never touch another woman."

"Perhaps I misjudged you, Jason. You do have some survival instincts."

Gina sat back down on the couch. Chelsea enjoyed the scared and confused look on Gina's face. Just then, Chelsea heard Orlando yell from the deck below.

"Gina, you and your friends need to help me tie down the yacht! It's getting a might windy out here. Where did your other friend go? She didn't fall overboard, did she?"

Gina yelled back, "Can't you take care of it? I have guests. Just do the best you can. I'm sure we'll be fine."

Chelsea stared down at Gina, who looked even more uncomfortable.

"So, Gina, I like the purple swimsuit you're wearing. Are there any others you plan to model for us?"

"I really don't think that will be necessary, Mrs. Longfellow."

She got up again and walked over to her purse, resting on a shelf behind the couch. She took out a piece of paper and handed it to Chelsea.

"Here's the name, address and phone number of the boutique where I buy my bathing suits. I think it would be best if you just went there yourself. You could try on the suits and find one in your size."

Chelsea took the piece of paper. "Thank you, Gina. I think that's a wise decision."

Jason said, "Yes, a wise decision. I'd like to keep all my parts intact."

Gina sat down on the couch again. Chelsea took a seat several feet from her. Jason followed his wife. The conversation died completely. It was obvious to Chelsea that Gina wanted them to leave. Chelsea sat patiently, waiting for her husband to start interrogating Gina about Rip Thornton's murder. Chelsea began to get impatient, stood up, and started pacing around the cabin. She noticed a framed photo on one of the shelves behind the sofa and picked it up.

Chelsea said, "What a nice photo of you with Mr. Moneyman, and who's this other woman? She looks a little like you."

Gina's facial expression suggested she was nervous, and a little drunk. She tried to feign boredom.

"I really can't say. That's obviously Mark and me, and this yacht, but I honestly don't know who that woman is. I don't even remember that photo being taken. I guess we really should slow down on the morning and afternoon martinis."

Chelsea sat the photo back on the shelf and looked around some more. From her current vantage point behind the couch, she noticed something shiny on the wooden floor to her left.

Looks like wet footprints. Small feet, maybe a woman. And, there's a wet towel on the floor next to that closed door. I'll bet that's the master bedroom. Surely this woman wouldn't be hiding someone at the same time

she invited Jason to check out her bikini collection. She did mention a
ménage-a-trois. Who knows what this little bitch had in mind for my
husband.

Chelsea saw that Jason was still struggling to find a subtle way to interrogate Gina. He stood, walked over to Chelsea, picked up the same photo and examined it.

He said, "Gina, are you sure you don't know who…"

Orlando Cerveza came running into the room, yelling and flailing his arms. Chelsea heard the sound of howling wind follow him through the door.

Cerveza yelled, "The weatherman got it wrong. The hurricane is now supposed to hit Jacksonville as a category 3, and it's arriving early. The wind is picking up fast. We need to get the boat secured and get out of here, NOW!" He ran back out of the cabin.

When Orlando had burst into the room, Jason dropped the framed picture. Chelsea watched as it hit the wooden floor with a crash, broken glass flying in all directions.

Jason said, "I'm sorry, Gina. Orlando startled me. I'll clean it up."

Jason bent down and started picking up the pieces of the broken picture frame. Chelsea saw that the base had separated from the frame, exposing the back of the photo.

Jason, in his official PI voice, said, "Hey Chelsea, there's writing on the back of this picture."

He handed the broken picture frame and photo to Chelsea, who took it and looked at Gina.

"Gina, are you sure you don't know who this woman is? According to the writing on the back, her name is Constance Conover. Does that name ring any bells?"

Gina, looking up at the ceiling, "No, never heard of her."

Chelsea looked at Jason. "Jason, does that name sound familiar?"

"Wait, what? Why are you interrogating me? Aren't we supposed to be interrogating Gina?"

"Jason, remember your new toy truck? What did you find in the hidden compartment?"

Jason looked puzzled, "A revolver, twenty-two caliber, and some *ReallyRealtor* brochures."

Chelsea, frustrated, "And…? What else?"

"Uh…the truck wobbled, and almost killed us? Is that what you're talking about?"

"Well, that part sucked, but no, that's not what I'm talking about. There was something else in that hidden compartment, something that appears to be important to this case. Think, Jason."

Jason placed his hand over his face, clearly frustrated.

"Can you give me a hint?"

"The name Constance?...Conover?…Doctor Constance Conover? Oh, for Heaven sakes. You found a car registration in the hidden compartment with the name Dr. Constance Conover on it. The truck's previous owner was Constance Conover, the woman in this picture."

Jason said, "Oh, yeah! Now I remember. But, what's that got to do with anything? We're supposed to be interrogating Gina."

"Think, Jason. Dr. Constance Conover is in this photo with Mark Moneyman and Gina, on this very boat."

Jason started to come around, like a dimmed bulb slowly getting brighter. He grinned and touched his nose, signaling he finally got it.

"We also found a twenty-two-caliber revolver and some *ReallyRealty* brochures in the car. Could this have anything to do with why Mark Moneyman was trying to shoot us? And Rip Thornton was shot with a twenty-two. Is this the same gun? How did it get in my truck? What's the connection? Oh God, this is so confusing."

Chelsea sighed. "Welcome to the party, my husband PI, although I'm not sure you really get it yet. A typical man, you can only think about one thing at a time, no ability to multitask. You're totally focused on interrogating Gina, who is not being all that helpful. This photo provides new information, that there is some connection between this Constance Conover and Mr. and Mrs. Moneyman. I'm not sure who this woman is, what her connection is to the Moneymans, or how the gun and *ReallyRealty* brochures play into the case. But, we're getting there."

Gina looked worried, gazing at the ceiling again. She said, "I remember now. That picture was taken at a boat show, where Mark's yacht won first prize. That woman in the photo was one of the judges, and Mark wanted to get a picture with her to mark the occasion."

Chelsea shook her head. "Gina, Gina, Gina. How did you ever convince Moneyman to marry you? I'd think a gold digger like yourself would be a much better liar."

"Chelsea, have you seen her in a bikini?"

Chelsea, focused on the case, decided not to react to Jason's comment. *Will kill him later.*

Chelsea removed the photo from the broken picture frame. She stared at it for a moment. Then, she walked around the couch to where Gina was sitting, gulping down another martini. Chelsea showed Gina the photo up close.

"Gina, who is this woman really? Come on. I know you know. Tell us, or I'm going to tie you to the mast and leave you there when the hurricane comes."

Gina looked at Jason. "PI Longfellow. You wouldn't let your wife hurt me, would you? Please help me. I really don't know who that woman is."

"Chelsea, maybe she really doesn't know. We can't just tie her to the mast and leave her to die, can we? That wouldn't be nice. Look at those sad eyes. I think she's telling the truth."

"Jason, first of all, I don't believe for a moment that you're looking at her eyes. Second, she knows who this Constance Conover is. Third, we need to know who she is in order to solve the case. Would you rather I tie you to the mast?"

Gina said, "PI Longfellow, please don't let her hurt me."

Jason, obvious fear in his voice, "Gina, I'm not the boss of my wife, especially when she gets all mad and…stabby. Maybe you'd better tell her who the lady is." To Chelsea. "You don't have any surgical instruments on you, do you?"

Jason walked over to Chelsea and looked at the photo again. Then he looked at Gina.

"The woman looks kind of like Gina. I'm wondering if maybe it's her mother. Gina, is this your mother?"

Chelsea shook her head. "No, Jason. It's not her mother, unless she had the baby when she was five. The two women in this picture are not all that different in age."

Jason got that childish, stubborn look on his face that Chelsea was so familiar with.

Chelsea said, "Now you've done it, Gina. Jason has shifted into full blown PI mode. You're going to regret this."

Jason stood directly in front of Gina, giving her his fiercest stare. Chelsea spoke up.

"Jason, stop it. You're not scaring her, and you look like you have to go to the bathroom. Just ask your questions."

His interrogation began, "Okay lady, is Dr. Constance Conover your mother? Your aunt? Your babysitter? Your lover? Your mechanic? Your housekeeper? Your yoga instructor? Your physical trainer? Your physical therapist? Your family physician? Your gynecologist? Your beautician? Your dentist? Your pharmacist? Your chauffeur? Your cheerleading coach?..."

"Really, Jason? Cheerleading coach? Are we back to the cheerleader fantasies?"

"Sorry, Chelsea. Just trying to cover all the bases." Back to Gina, "Your life coach? Your next door neighbor? Your husband's lover? Your plumber? Your exterminator? Your gardener? Your veterinarian? Your fortune-teller?"

Gina caved. "Dear God. Make him stop! Please make it stop! She's my sister. Dr. Constance Conover is my sister!"

Chapter 26

In the main cabin of the Vacation Vaccination, Jason and Chelsea were standing in front of Gina, who was sitting on the couch. Chelsea still held the picture with Dr. Constance Conover in it. Gina had just revealed the identity of Dr. Conover. Jason was exhausted from his strenuous interrogation.

Jason said, "See, Chelsea. I knew I could get it out of her."

Gina took the picture from Chelsea, looked at it and placed it on the couch beside her.

"Yes, Connie is my older sister. She works at Mark's company, VaccinesRUS, and she has developed a vaccine for a disease common to Florida called West Nile virus. It came here from Africa back in the late 1990's, and it's transmitted by mosquitoes. It normally causes aches and fever, but it can also cause inflammation of the brain. This vaccine can save lives. I'm very proud of Connie."

Chelsea said, "Jason, you look exhausted. I'll take it from here."

Jason saw Chelsea look down and give Gina the death stare. Chelsea said, "Jason just bought a used truck that apparently belonged to Dr. Conover…your sister…and we found a hidden compartment in it containing a twenty-two caliber revolver and a bunch of *ReallyRealty* brochures. We're investigating the murder of Rip Thornton, who was also a *ReallyRealty* realtor. He was also shot with the same caliber revolver. I can't help but wonder if there's a connection."

Not to be outdone by his wife, and in spite of being exhausted, Jason chimed in.

"Chelsea and I have found several dead realtors while looking for vacation property here in St. Augustine, and a number of them were also from *ReallyRealty*. Then, your husband shot at us with a twenty-two revolver, the same caliber used to kill Rip Thornton. And you say this West Nile virus comes from mosquitoes? When Chelsea and I went canoeing the other day we got attacked by mosquitoes, which made Chelsea mad enough to want to kill me. We've also heard something about mosquitoes and a realtor conference in Miami. Based on all these clues, I can't figure out if your husband killed Rip Thornton and those other realtors, or the mosquitoes had something to do with it. It's very confusing. Can you help us?"

Chelsea shook her head. "Jason, I'm pretty sure that a mosquito did not shoot Rip Thornton in the head, or bury him on the beach. I'm not sure what mosquitoes have to do with anything. It is reasonable to suspect that Mark Moneyman might have killed Thornton. We heard something about a realtor that couldn't sell Moneyman's beachfront mansion, and the multi-millionaire was furious. That sounds like a motive. Then, there's Moneyman's revolver."

Jason sensed the tension in the room, with all the questions flying around and the wind continuing to howl louder and louder outside. The boat began to rock and bounce as wind-swept waves crashed against it. Everyone had to grab onto something to keep from being tossed around. They all heard a voice yelling at Orlando outside the cabin, and Jason saw Mark Moneyman come stumbling through the door. Moneyman stopped and stood next to Jason.

Moneyman said, "Gina, Dr. and Mrs. Longfellow? What the hell are you doing here? We need to secure the boat and get to shelter. Hurricane Bertha is about to flatten St. Augustine."

Jason went all PI and authoritative, looking down at the top of Moneyman's head.

"Well, if it isn't Mark Moneyman. What are you doing here? I thought you were at a vaccine conference. You pulled a gun on us last time we were on your yacht, and then took a shot at us from your fancy yellow supercar. I've since found a twenty-two caliber revolver and a bunch of *ReallyRealty* brochures in a hidden compartment of my new truck, previously owned by your wife's sister, who also works for you. What do you have to say for yourself? I'm thinking seriously about making a citizen's arrest for the murder of Rip Thornton, a *ReallyRealty* realtor…YOUR *ReallyRealty* realtor I presume. And, how did you get mosquitoes to help you commit murder?"

Chelsea, yelling above the increasing din of the raging hurricane, "Jason, still with the mosquitoes? I'm not convinced that Mark Moneyman is the killer. He might have a motive, if Rip Thornton really was the realtor he hired to sell his beachfront property. But, why would he hide the murder weapon in a truck owned by Gina's sister? They're family."

Moneyman pulled a twenty-two caliber revolver out from under his jacket and pointed it at Jason. Jason whimpered.

Moneyman said, "I have no idea what you're talking about. I'm here to secure my yacht before Bertha arrives. I didn't kill any realtor, although if Rip Thornton is dead I'm not unhappy to hear it. That bastard couldn't sell rice to a Chinaman. And, as you can clearly see, I didn't hide my handgun anywhere. Now, if you people don't stop asking stupid question and help

Orlando and me secure the boat so we can get to shelter, I'm going to do more than just show you my gun. Get it?!"

Jason said, "Mr. Moneyman, Chelsea was asking you stupid questions, too. Maybe you could point your gun at her."

"Thanks, Jason. You'll be sleeping under the tires of your new truck tonight, if we survive this mess."

Gina stood up, and the group started to move towards the cabin door. Jason heard movement from behind them. He turned and saw a woman appear from the direction of the main bedroom at the back of the cabin. She looked like a slightly older version of Gina, wearing a black bikini and aiming a shiny stainless steel twenty-two caliber revolver at them.

Jason said, "Wow! Nice bikini. Chelsea, do you like that one?...Wait! Does everyone in Florida own a twenty-two revolver?"

Everyone else stopped and turned to look at the new intruder.

Chelsea said, "Idiot!" Then, to the woman, "Dr. Constance Conover, I presume? I thought I saw wet footprints leading to the back bedroom. It never occurred to me that it might be you."

"Chelsea, she's got another twenty-two caliber revolver from the looks of it. Now I'm really confused. Mark Moneyman has to be Rip Thornton's killer. A woman would never shoot a man in the head. According to my online PI course, women usually kill by poisoning."

"Oh yeah, Jason? Mention the word *bikini* one more time, hand me one of those revolvers, and I'll show you how wrong you are."

"But, Chelsea, that's how I know they're sisters. The younger one has on a purple bikini, and her older sister, with the gun, has on a black bikini. The bikini sisters. Iron clad evidence."

"Idiot."

"Chelsea, that's *PI* idiot."

Gina came to life, "Connie! I told you to stay back there. Now the PI and his wife know you're here in St. Augustine. And, they found my handgun in your old truck. I told you to toss the gun in the swamp. What are the odds of this idiot buying that particular truck? We have no choice but to kill them."

Jason said, "Chelsea, isn't that sweet? Gina wants to kill us, to keep her husband from going to jail for the murder of Rip Thornton. Now that's a great wife."

Chelsea pointed at Gina.

"Jason, as much as I don't like him, Mark Moneyman didn't have anything to do with Rip Thornton's murder. Didn't you just hear Gina say the gun in the truck was hers?"

"But, he took a shot at us with a twenty-two revolver. This is the third time he's pulled a gun on us in the same caliber that the killer used to shoot Rip Thornton in the head."

"My poor, confused husband, I don't think his pulling a gun on us has anything to do with Rip Thornton's murder. I'm guessing it's just that you're so annoying. There are lots of people who want to shoot you, right now myself included."

Constance Conover continued to point her gun at everyone. "Move, dammit. We've got to get off this boat and find shelter. The wind's getting stronger. If we stay here we're going to die."

Jason watched as Dr. Conover started moving slowly around the group of people, in the direction of the cabin door. Jason stood frozen in place as Chelsea moved in front of her, blocking her exit. Everyone struggled to maintain their footing with the bouncing of the boat.

Chelsea said, "You're not going anywhere, Lady, until you answer my questions. I think that you, not Mark Moneyman, killed Rip Thornton. I don't know about the deaths of the other realtors. Confess, and I'll move out of the way."

Jason moved closer to Chelsea. He bent down and looked at Constance Conover, his eyes focused on the revolver.

"Chelsea, let her go. The hurricane…we need to get out of here. I don't think she killed Rip Thornton. Why would she? Mark Moneyman had the motive; Rip Thornton couldn't sell his house. And, my keen observational skills tell me that there are no bullets in Dr. Conover's revolver; I can see into the chambers. How did she shoot Rip Thornton with an unloaded gun?"

"Jason, you had better be looking at the gun, not the bikini. I don't know what her motive is yet, but I'm sure she's the one who killed Rip Thornton. Mark Moneyman has an alibi. He was out of town at the time of Thornton's murder."

Moneyman, still holding his revolver on Jason, said, "She's right. I was out of town at the time of Thornton's murder. He is the realtor I hired to sell my beach front house, and I was furious with him. But, I didn't kill him. I couldn't kill anyone."

Jason said, "But, you shot at us on the race track."

"I have a temper. You pissed me off when you came on my yacht, accused me of murder and flirted with Gina. You are very annoying, and I wanted to make you go away. But, I didn't shoot to hit you. I shot over your head. I didn't even hit your stupid little clown car."

Jason looked at both guns pointed at him, and then heard the howling of the hurricane. Everyone in the cabin was clearly terrified.

Gina screamed, "Damn you, Mrs. Longfellow! Get out of the way! There's no time. We need to get to shelter, NOW!"

Jason fought against his panic, trying to be the reasonable PI guy like he'd seen on TV. He held out his hands in a welcoming gesture.

"Calm down everyone. I've gathered you all here today to reveal the murderer. Thank you for coming. Mr. Moneyman, you need to confess so we can get out of here. I know you murdered Rip Thornton. Did you know he was gay? Have a problem with gay realtors? Just admit it, and Chelsea'll move out of the way."

Constance moved her gun, pointing it directly at Jason's head. Jason stepped back, and his eyes crossing momentarily. He shook his head, trying to clear the fear.

Dr. Conover said, "Shut up about Rip. Or, I'll shoot you in the head. That damned man! He didn't act gay with me. Why did he have to be like that?"

Jason whined. "But, Chelsea's the one in your way. Why are you pointing the gun at me?"

Chelsea said, "Thanks, Jason. I thought you said the revolver wasn't loaded."

"I don't think it is. But, what do I know? I got my PI license online."

Jason was impressed when Chelsea continued to push Dr. Conover. Chelsea looked her in the eye, at which point she turned the gun back on Chelsea.

Chelsea said, "So, you do know Rip Thornton. Why did he have to be like what?" To Jason, "See, I'm thinking I'm right about Dr. Conover here. She did know Rip, and she seems to have had feelings for him."

Jason shook his head. "Nonsense. She might have known him, since they were both in Miami. But, how could she have feelings for him? He was gay. He and Rock were partners. I'm sure Mark Moneyman's the murderer." To Moneyman, "Confess! Tell us how you killed Rip Thornton, and we can all escape to shelter before Bertha blows us away."

As if on cue, a strong burst of wind rocked the boat, and everyone struggled to stay on their feet. Jason, out of his mind with panic, fell against Chelsea and almost knocked her to the floor. She grabbed his arm to right herself.

Moneyman yelped, "Shut up! I told you, I didn't kill anyone! I wouldn't mind shooting you and your wife, though. You're going to get us all killed if you don't let us off of this boat."

Chelsea, still staring at Constance Conover, "Jason, you're wrong. Dr. Conover is the killer. Confess, Lady, and I'll move out of the way. Confess! You know you want to. It'll take a load off of your mind. There's your old truck with the gun, the *ReallyRealty* brochures…that my idiot husband somehow managed to buy. I don't know your motive, or how you met Rip or managed to get him up here to St. Augustine. But, I know you killed him."

Jason couldn't believe it. "Chelsea, are you daft? Mark Moneyman has the means…he's a multi-millionaire with a twenty-two caliber revolver, the motive…Rip couldn't sell Moneyman's beachfront mansion. As to an alibi, just because he says he was out of town when the murder took place doesn't make it true. He's supposed to be at a vaccine conference right now, but he's standing here aiming a gun at my head. Help me!"

Jason put his hands up in front of his face, as if to fend off an incoming bullet.

"I know all the facts, Jason, but I'm telling you that this woman killed Rip Thornton, not Mark Moneyman. I can see it in her eyes."

"She did not. Moneyman did it."

"Did not. She did. Look in her eyes, Jason. Her eyes, not the damn bikini. Someone, please loan me a gun, just for a minute."

"Did not. He did. And, please don't give my wife a gun."

"She did it. She killed him."

"No, he did it."

Gina, totally losing it, "For God's sake, would someone shoot both of them, so we can get out of here! Their arguing is making me crazy, on top of the fact that we're all gonna die!"

Jason took his hands down and pointed at Moneyman. He started up again.

"Mark Moneyman did it. I'm the detective, and I have the facts. Chelsea, just accept…"

Constance Conover started visibly shaking, and screamed, "Stop it, both of you! I can't take any more! You're driving me crazy with all this bickering. Don't you care that we're all going to die in this hurricane? You're both insane!"

Chelsea stood fast. "Then confess! Why did you kill Rip Thornton? How did you kill him? Be sure to speak clearly and use simple words, so my husband the idiot PI can understand you."

Constance lowered her pistol and started to sob softly as she spoke. Jason felt sure he was about to be proven correct.

Constance said, "I give up. It doesn't matter. It's too late. We're going to die anyway. I met Rip when Mark and Gina first hired him to sell their beachfront house. I was staying with them at the time, and working for Mark's company, VaccinesRUs. Rip had just moved to Miami."

Jason interrupted. "So, you met him. So what? He was gay. He lived with Rock Handsome, another *ReallyRealty* realtor, as his partner for two years before he moved to Miami."

Chelsea interrupted. "I think what Jason is trying to say is, why do you appear to care so much about him if he was gay? You sound like you were in love with him. I'm guessing he was one of those guys that swung both ways? He was very good looking. Maybe the two of you fell in love? The first time I met Rock Handsome, I couldn't help but check out that buff body and tight butt. I actually fantasized that he might be bisexual."

Jason said, "Wait. What? You fantasized about our realtor? How can that be, when you're already married to this hunk of a PI?"

"Jason, you're not the only one who can check out bikinis."

Constance, impatient, "Do you want to hear my confession or not?" Everyone stopped talking. "So, like Mrs. Longfellow said, Rip and I fell in love. I didn't know he swung both ways…wouldn't have ever suspected it since he did such an excellent job of swinging my way."

"But, you didn't kill him, right? Mark Moneyman killed him. I have to be right. I'm the detective."

"Jason, shut up and let her finish her confession…as in…confessing to the murder."

Mark Moneyman said, "Would you two shut up and let her continue? How do you ever catch the bad guy? You never stop yammering."

Another large wave hit the boat, and Jason leaned on Chelsea for support again.

Constance continued. "Rip and I hit it off right away, and we moved in together. I thought marriage was a forgone conclusion. We had lived together for two years, when he started acting distant."

Jason interrupted again. "Was it because he had a fight with Mark Moneyman, which is why Moneyman killed him?"

Constance said, "Mrs. Longfellow, your husband has some real problems. Which part of *I'm confessing* doesn't he understand?"

"He's OCD, likes things to be simple and orderly, and doesn't like to be wrong. He'll start counting stuff any minute now. Please continue. You and Rip were living together."

"Yes, and he started acting strange. I asked him what was the matter, but he wouldn't discuss it. Then, one day I heard him talking on his cell. He didn't know I was in earshot, and he had it on speaker. He was declaring his love to some man. I couldn't believe my ears."

"I don't understand why you are confessing, when Mr. Moneyman clearly killed Rip…and what about the mosquitoes?"

"Jason, shut up. You're just wrong. Let her finish."

Constance continued. "I told Gina, and the next time she and Mark were in St. Augustine on the yacht Gina did some snooping. She found out that Rip was bisexual, he and Rock had been an item and had lived together for two years. After that, I confronted Rip about it. He told me that Rock had forgiven him for moving to Miami and wanted to get back together with him. He was considering it. I was furious, jealous and confused."

"So, that's when you told Mark Moneyman and he decided to kill Rip?"

"Jason, for God's sake, shut up. Somebody, please feel free to shoot my husband."

"Yes, Dear."

Constance said, "That's when I decided to kill Rip Thornton. No man was going to treat me that way. I talked to Gina about it. She already hated Rip, because Mark had hired him to sell their house, they needed the money, and Rip was a really lousy realtor. They hadn't had a valid offer in two years."

Chelsea said, "They needed the money? I thought Mark Moneyman was a multi-millionaire?"

Gina looked at her husband, and then said, "Mark's company had made him a fortune, but then he signed off on a couple of vaccine projects that failed. He also made some bad investments. I tried to tell him not to get into day trading, but he wouldn't listen. He insisted he could save the company that way. It was like a gambling addiction. He burned through our money like wildfire. That beachfront mansion was worth a fortune, and we desperately needed Rip to sell it to keep the company afloat. We're also going to have to sell this yacht soon."

Jason saw Moneyman look down at the floor, a sad expression on his face.

Constance continued, speaking louder to be heard over the roaring wind. Jason listened intently, still doubting her confession.

"So, Gina and I both had our reasons for hating Rip. We came up with a plan. She invited Rip to St. Augustine, to stay on the yacht with them for a few days. She told him that she and Mark wanted to discuss a new idea for marketing their beachfront house. Rip wanted to make the sale as much as they did; the commission would have been substantial. So, he agreed. What he didn't know was that Mark was going to be out of town that week, meeting with investors to try to drum up some money to keep the company going."

Gina, impatient to finish the story, said, "Constance wanted to kill Rip for going back to his previous lover, a MAN. I wanted to kill him because he hadn't sold our beachfront property. We needed to get rid of him so *ReallyRealty* would assign the sale to another realtor. So, the two sisters did him in together."

Constance finished, "Rip stayed on the yacht the first night. We told him Mark would be back next morning. That night, we drank a couple of pitchers of martinis and turned up the music real loud. I went to the bathroom and got Gina's revolver. I came back to the cabin and shot Rip in the head. Early next morning, Gina and I wrapped him in a rug, put him in my truck, hauled him to a remote place on the beach and buried his body." To Chelsea. "I can't believe your idiot husband found him."

Jason said, "So, that's why he was dressed in street clothes. He didn't ask you to bury him, so he could escape before the tide came in. He was dead. Geeze. Thanks, Chelsea, for just burying me in the sand, alive and stuff. I wouldn't have been able to dig myself out if you'd shot me in the head."

"You're welcome? Maybe we could go back to the beach and try again. As I said, Constance and Gina killed Rip Thornton, not Mark Moneyman."

Jason had a thought. "Wait a minute. Not so fast. Constance, you hid the murder weapon in the secret compartment of your truck, but where did you get the twenty-two revolver with no bullets you're holding on us now? And, what were all the *ReallyRealty* brochures about?"

Chelsea said, "Jason, just give it up. She did it."

Constance sighed. "You really don't get it, do you? I shot him with Gina's gun. But, it doesn't matter. This is Florida. Everyone in the state has at least one twenty-two caliber revolver and some people have several, along with 38-specials, nine-millimeters, forty-fives, AR-15 rifles, shotguns and the occasional rocket launcher. When we say *stand your ground*, we're not messing around. I just bought this one yesterday."

Jason said, "Chelsea, another thing to add to my list of things in Florida that's dangerous…pretty much everyone. They're all armed to the teeth."

Chelsea said, "Jason, you're from Virginia, you have your own CCW permit and your little gun, and you're far more dangerous to yourself than any of these Floridians. Remember the poop tank incident?"

Chelsea returned to Constance Conover. "So, you hid the revolver in the truck. You traded the truck in for another vehicle in case there was any evidence of the body, like blood, hair, DNA. You must have forgotten about the revolver?"

"Yes, I screwed up and forgot the revolver. We were so rushed and stressed out. Then, your husband ends up buying the truck. And, he finds Rips body. Go figure."

Chelsea said, "Jason does have a special talent for finding dead bodies. Both crimes and clues seem to seek him out, which is handy for a PI. Especially when he doesn't have any idea what he's doing. Jason did bring up a reasonable question, though, God help us. What were all the *ReallyRealty* brochures about?"

"Hey Chelsea, that's my question. I am the PI, after all. What about those brochures? Do they have anything to do with all the dead *ReallyRealty* realtors we've found since we've been in the treacherous state of Florida? If we're gonna buy property here, we should also be looking to get burial plots."

"Jason, the brochures. Stick to the brochures."

Another wave hit the boat, and Jason grabbed hold of Chelsea to study himself yet again. Everyone else stumbled, but managed to remain upright.

"All right. Do the brochures have anything to do with who killed all those realtors? At first I thought it was dueling realtors, fighting to the death for a sale. Then perky Debbie the realtor tried to puree my face with a hand-held mixer…but…I'm not a realtor. So, that doesn't fit. Then, there's the issue of mosquitoes; mosquitoes at a realtors' convention in Miami, mosquitoes that bit one of the realtors showing us a beachfront house, and then Chelsea and I got attacked by mosquitoes on Jesup Lake. Are there killer mosquitoes here in Florida? That would fit with all the other stuff here that tries to kill you."

Chelsea turned to Jason and punched him hard in the arm. "Now we're back to the mosquitoes? I told you, my hallucinating husband, those realtors and buyers were killed by bullets, blunt force trauma, electrocution, and Debbie tried to puree your face with a hand-held mixer. I thought we agreed that mosquitoes don't generally shoot people, toss electric blenders into the tub or hit someone in the head with a blunt object. Stop with the mosquitoes. Please! What about the realtors' brochures?"

Chapter 27

Mark and Gina Moneyman, Constance Conover, Jason and Chelsea found themselves gathered together in the main cabin of the Vacation Vaccination. The beginnings of a hurricane raged around them as Dr. Conover confessed to murder. Both Conover and Mark Moneyman still held twenty-two caliber revolvers on the group, mainly pointed at Jason. Chelsea blocked the door, determined to prevent anyone from leaving until Dr. Conover finished her confession.

At this point Chelsea thought Conover appeared to be immobilized with fear.

Conover said, "You two make a helluva investigative team. You won't stop bickering with each other until the suspect either shoots herself, shoots you or confesses. Gina, I'm sorry, but I'm going to tell them everything. I can't take anymore."

A huge gust of wind hit the yacht and threw it violently against the dock. Chelsea grabbed hold of Jason for stability. He stumbled and grabbed onto the bikini-clad Dr. Conover. He let go when Conover stuck her gun in his face and Chelsea slapped him in the back of the head. Chelsea watched as everyone else bounced around, banging into things, grabbing for something to hang onto, going down on their knees. Chelsea heard Orlando yell from the deck below.

"I'm outta here. You people are crazy. This boat's goin' down, and you're goin' with it. See ya' all in hell." They heard running footsteps as he fled the yacht.

The boat righted itself, and everyone was able to stand again. Chelsea released Jason from her death grip.

Gina yelled, "Connie, talk faster. This crazy bitch won't let us leave until you've told her everything."

Chelsea looked at Jason. "Are you sure that gun she's holding isn't loaded? Gina's right, I'm not budging until we've heard the whole story."

Jason nodded. "I'm sure?"

Chelsea looked at Constance. "Go on Constance. The sooner you finish your story, the sooner we can get to shelter."

"After I found out about Rip, I was furious enough to kill him. A woman scorned…FOR A MAN... just imagine! Gina was angry at Rip; because of his incompetence he couldn't sell their house. The more we discussed it the more our anger grew to include all realtors. As Gina already told you, I am one of the lead scientists in Mark's vaccine company. I came up with the perfect plan to get revenge on lots realtors at once."

Chelsea said, "Please tell me it doesn't have anything to do with mosquitoes. If my husband is right about that, I'll NEVER hear the end of it."

Chelsea closed her eyes and grimaced. She had a feeling she didn't want to hear this part. Jason elbowed her in the arm and grinned.

"Sorry, but it kind of does."

Jason thrusted his hands above his head. "Yes!"

Chelsea shook her head and sighed. *Someone please go ahead and shoot me.*

Constance continued. "I've been working on a vaccine for the West Nile virus, a nasty little virus that migrated to Florida from Africa back in the nineties. The virus is transmitted by mosquitoes, and it normally causes headaches, malaise and flu-like symptoms. But, in a lucky few patients that are infected with an especially high titer of virus, it can get into the central nervous system. Then, it can cause serious effects like meningitis, encephalitis, tremors, disorientation, coma and convulsions. At VaccinesRUs, I developed a recombinant vaccine for West Nile that appeared to be effective at preventing the disease. Unfortunately, it came with a unique side effect that we discovered in the first clinical trial."

Jason started doing something that Chelsea thought might be his bizarre version of a happy dance. He was obviously excited by this explanation.

Jason said, "Let me guess. When a mosquito bit one of these infected patients, that mosquito became insane and killed people, thus killer mosquitoes…"

"Jason, there's no such thing as killer mosquitoes. For God's sake. Would you please let her finish?"

The hurricane continued to roar outside at an ever-increasingly loud pitch, now very close to landfall.

"Thank you, Mrs. Longfellow. Your husband has a screw loose."

"Actually, all his screws fell out a long time ago. Please continue."

"So, like I said, in those patients infected with high levels of West Nile virus, the virus crosses the blood-brain barrier and gets into the brain. A recombinant vaccine is one that you build in the lab protein by protein, instead of just using the killed virus. We screwed up. Our recombinant vaccine stimulates immune cells like a normal vaccine, but it also binds directly to the West Nile virus. This forms a vaccine-virus complex. In patients infected with high virus titers, this vaccine-virus complex *also* gets into the brain. We called this the *angry virus* complex, because it attacked the amygdala, the part of the brain where the emotional center is located, and caused a rage response. The patients became agitated, to the point of turning homicidal. The effect appeared to turn on and off with no clear scientific explanation."

Jason said, "So, no killer mosquitoes? Disappointing. But, what's this got to do with our investigation? A few people with high levels of West Nile virus that got your vaccine went bonkers. Not a great vaccine, but I still don't understand how this explains all the dead realtors."

Constance said, "You seem to understand something about vaccines, so you're not completely hopeless."

Chelsea said, "He's a good pharmacologist, but that's his day job. It's the PI thing that he sucks at. That and buying vacation property."

"Thanks Chelsea. I think?"

"But, he does have a point. I don't understand how this explains the dead realtors."

Chelsea had trouble hearing Constance, yelling over the hurricane level wind, waves and boat banging into the dock. Everyone was hanging on tight to something to keep from being knocked over by the bouncing and rocking of the boat.

"This side effect was a deal breaker for the development of that vaccine, although we chose not to tell anyone about it. We figured we could build other recombinant vaccine constructs until we found one that didn't drive the patients bonkers, as you so aptly put it. However, it gave me an idea as to how to get revenge on local realtors. Rip planned to attend a conference of Florida realtors at the Convention Center in Miami. He was happy to let me come along. As part of my vaccine research, I maintained a colony of mosquitoes infected with West Nile virus in my laboratory at VaccinesRUs."

Jason perked up again. "Aha! There are killer mosquitoes in this story."

"Jason, shut up!"

"On the opening day of the convention I made an excuse to go to my lab first, and then meet Rip at the convention center late morning. That way we would take separate cars. I picked up a cage full of the virus-infected mosquitoes, and I snuck the cage into the venue in a large box disguised as part of a realty booth display. I took an elevator to the fourth floor above the convention center atrium and released the mosquitoes into the large room. Then, I fled the building by a back entrance and called Rip on my cell. I told him that I had a problem at the lab and couldn't leave. Later that night, he told me that several of the realtors complained about mosquito bites, which seemed strange inside the convention center. That was step one of my glorious plan, lots of realtors infected with West Nile."

Chelsea said, "And, infecting a whole convention center full of realtors with West Nile virus wasn't enough revenge for you?"

"Not really. West Nile doesn't usually kill, and I wanted a more severe punishment; something lethal. After all, Rip killed both our relationship and Mark's company."

Jason sounded sad. "So, no killer mosquitoes. I could have sworn…"

He was interrupted by another huge blast of wind that rocked the yacht. Chelsea was beginning to think she'd made a mistake by forcing them to stay on the boat so long.

Gina screamed, "We're gonna die. Talk faster!"

Chelsea said, "Step two. What was step two?!"

"That part was easy. We had originally assumed the vaccine would work, so we got ahead of ourselves and developed an oral form; easier to administer an oral vaccine to patients than a needle stick. The realtors' association had placed fancy flowing fountains full of tropical punch throughout the convention center, as part of a subtropical Florida real estate theme. Later in the week I smuggled several vials of the oral vaccine into the convention center with Gina's help, and we dumped some into each of the fountains. Vaccination by tropical punch. Then the virus, and my vaccine, combined to do their thing. In a few weeks, a certain percent of the infected realtors came down with the *angry virus* syndrome, had a psychotic breakdown, and either attempted to kill someone, or died themselves from convulsions. Even better, the ones who had psychotic breaks were usually hanging with other realtors, so that's who they attacked. I do feel kind of bad, though. I guess I got a little carried away. Killing Rip probably should have been enough."

Chelsea said, "D'ya think?"

Jason, a big grin on his face again. "See, Chelsea. I *was* right. Mark Moneyman might not have killed Rip Thornton, but if it hadn't been for the mosquitoes none of those other realtors would have died. The mosquitoes *were* responsible for those deaths. I'll bet a good defense attorney could create enough reasonable doubt…murdering mosquitoes…that Constance and Gina could get off with a minimal sentence."

"Reasonable doubt? How do mosquitoes explain the bullet hole in Rip Thornton's head? Or, the fact that his body was buried on the beach here in St. Augustine? Rip's murder is a slam dunk. Not to mention the fact that these two crazy sisters turned virus-infected mosquitoes loose at a realtor convention, and then vaccinated the people without their knowledge. The only reasonable doubt here is whether or not I'm going to strangle you in your sleep tonight." Yelling to the group, "Now, can we please put down the guns and get the heck out of here before we all get blown away?"

Chapter 28

Constance Conover had just finished confessing to what Chelsea thought was a ridiculously complicated murder plot that Conover and her sister Gina had carried out. Conover still pointed a gun at Chelsea, who blocked her exit from the yacht. A large wind-driven wave crashed against the side of the Vacation Vaccination, jolting everyone on board again. The unloaded revolver flew out of Conover's hand, landed on the floor and went off with a bang, the bullet imbedding itself in the ceiling a few inches from Jason's head.

Chelsea screamed, "Unloaded?! You said the gun was unloaded?!"

Jason said, "Sorry, Chelse…" and fainted, his body slowly lowering itself to the cabin floor.

As he lay there smiling, Chelsea just knew that he was dreaming of bikinis. The rest of the crowd stampeded through the cabin door, trampling Jason's body in the process. Chelsea was tempted to leave him there. But, good wife that she was, she stayed behind and threw a pitcher of martinis in his face to revive him. There was also the fact that she couldn't drive that monster truck he had just bought.

"I don't know why I care, since you almost got me killed…again… but get up! We have to get to shelter before we find ourselves in Hurricane Bertha's version of the Wizard of Oz."

Jason struggled to get up off the floor. Chelsea pushed him out the door, down the steps, off the boat and into his truck. She had to shove him up the three steps and into the driver's seat.

"Jason, wake up. You know I don't drive a stick, and you've got to get us out of here. This may be a great off-road truck, but it's useless against a category three hurricane."

"Where should we go? Are there are any hurricane shelters nearby?"

"I don't know, and everybody else is gone. You passed out, and they left without us."

"But, I almost got shot."

"You said the gun…pointed at me…was unloaded! You're lucky I didn't leave you there on the floor."

Jason paused, then said, "We need to head back to the condo, go into the bathroom and hide in the tub. The news lady said that's the safest place."

"That's as good an idea as any. Get this thing moving."

Jason drove through rain, hail the size of golf balls and wind gusts in excess of eighty miles an hour. The palm trees were bending in the wind, and palm fronds filled the air like berserk birds. As Chelsea looked around them, the visible buildings were still standing, but a few roofing shingles had broken loose and also taken flight. Chelsea was amazed the truck had not gone airborne.

"Jason, you need to hurry. If that hail breaks through the canvas top of this thing, it's gonna hurt. And, according to the weather station on my cell phone, Bertha is still off shore. The one-hundred-plus mile per hour winds aren't here yet. Get us home, NOW!"

"I'm doin' my best, Chelsea. I can't see anything for the rain and hail. Aren't you glad I bought this awesome truck? We can drive through these deep puddles, and it's heavy enough that we're not blowing away. The red rocket wouldn't have made it."

Just then, the wind ripped the cloth top off of the truck, and the driving rain and hail pummeled them. The pellets had gotten smaller, but the hail still stung. Chelsea covered her face and head with her hands and arms as best she could.

"This feels strangely familiar, Jason. Couldn't you just once buy a car with a top that actually works…you know…protects you from the elements."

"What are you complaining about? I have to sleep in here again tonight."

"Actually, I said under it, not in it."

"Oh, goodie."

They reached the parking lot, and battled the fierce rain and howling wind to get into the condo. When Jason turned the doorknob the door violently blew open, almost flying off its hinges. Once inside, Chelsea struggled to help him closed it again.

"Jason, head for the bathroom. I get to be on top in the tub, so you don't crush me."

"You always want to be on top."

"Deal with it, Jason."

The wind roared and the rain and hail pounded against the roof for the better part of an hour. Chelsea was sure the walls were going to collapse. Finally, it all stopped abruptly. They climbed out of the tub and looked out the front window.

Chelsea said, "Looks like a couple of palm trees came down. That one just missed your new truck. Too bad."

"Chelsea, I'm gonna have to borrow your hair dryer. My truck's interior looks a little damp."

"It looks like a freakin' aquarium. First you need to open the doors and let the three feet of water run out. If you want, you can get in the driver's seat, and I'll plug in my hair dryer and toss it to you."

"No thanks. I'd rather not find another dead body, especially my own. Come to think of it, have you been bitten by any mosquitoes or taken any vaccines lately? You seem to be scarier than usual."

"That's because you're even crazier than usual. Murder by mosquito? Victims with bullet holes in their heads, electrocuted, bludgeoned to death? Those must be some bad-ass mosquitoes."

"Come on, Chelsea, you heard Dr. Conover. Mosquitoes were responsible for some of the realtors' deaths, kind of, maybe, possibly. A mosquito might not have pulled the trigger, but…I was right, so deal with it."

"Jason, go sit in your truck, I'll plug in my hair dryer, and you can dry out the interior…kind of."

Instead, after the water ran out through the open doors Chelsea took a couple of towels from the condo, placed them on the seats, and they headed back to the marina. The hurricane had left an obstacle course of fallen trees, partially flooded roads and all kinds of debris. Chelsea saw two alligators swim by in the flood water, but she didn't mention it to Jason.

Chelsea hung on tight. "Jason, slow down, or we're not going to make it. There's debris everywhere, and deep water. I hate to admit it, but this jacked-up truck does have its advantages."

"I told you she's a tough old lady. Maybe I should name her *Hurricane Jane*."

"Or, maybe you could just watch where you're going and get us to the marina alive."

To make matters worse, Jason phoned the police on his cell. Chelsea panicked when he needed both hands to dial, and steered the truck with his knees. She screamed when the truck veered sideways, heading towards the sidewalk. She calmed down again when he placed one hand back on the steering wheel. He put the phone on speaker.

"Hello Officer, this is PI Jason Longfellow. I wish to report a murder, actually several murders. The killers are sisters, and they're probably on their way to the St. Augustine Marina to escape in one of their husband's yacht, the Vacation Vaccination."

"Hello, this is Officer Hathaway, St. Augustine Sheriff's Office. Can I ask what murder you are referring to?"

"The realtor murders. Rip Thornton was shot in the head and buried on the beach. We found him when Chelsea thought I had an extra hand. Then there's several other realtors. We find another dead realtor every time we look at a new property."

"Jason, you're confusing the poor man. Let me speak to him."

Officer Hathaway said, "You must be that crazy PI they've been talking about here at the precinct, the one they're calling the *Realtor's Curse*. It's my understanding that you're the main suspect."

"I know some people think that, apparently including my wife. But, I didn't kill anyone. It's those damn Florida mosquitoes. Haven't you noticed that pretty much everything in Florida wants to kill you?"

"Jason, stop it. You'll have the officer so annoyed he'll shoot you on sight. *Maybe not such a bad idea. That revolver was NOT empty.*

Officer Hathaway said, "So, you think you've solved the case, and the killers are about to make a getaway by boat? You do realize we just went through a hurricane. Even if you know who killed Mr. Thornton and those other realtors, I doubt their boat is in any shape to go anywhere. And, from what I've heard, I think it's highly unlikely you've solved the case anyhow."

"But, I have. Or, we have. My wife, Chelsea, has been on the case with me. It's all about a gay man who swings both ways, a crappy realtor who can't sell a beach front mansion and a bunch of mosquitoes. The motives are the usual, money and jealousy…and the mosquitoes? I don't know what their motive is. I guess it's hunger?"

Chelsea finally got a word in edgewise.

"Officer Hathaway, this is Jason's wife, Chelsea. I realize he sounds a little confused, but that's just his normal state. We really have solved the case of Rip Thornton's murder, and the other realtors, too. Gina Moneyman and her sister Dr. Constance Conover confessed to killing everyone. And, Jason's right, the two of them are probably headed for Mark Moneyman's yacht, the Vacation Vaccination, at the St. Augustine Marina. That's where they confessed before the hurricane. I'm guessing now that the hurricane's over, they'll head for parts unknown in the yacht. Jason and I are driving to the marina to head them off. It would be great if you could meet us there. They're armed and dangerous, and we could use all the help we can get."

"Ma'am, everyone's armed and dangerous in Florida. All of our officers are busy rescuing people after the hurricane, but I'll send someone as soon as I can. Be careful. Since they're armed and dangerous, if my officers don't get there in time just let them go and we'll send the Coast Guard to deal with them."

Jason mumbled. "To hell with the Coast Guard. This is my case, and we're gonna bring them in. And, Chelsea, my ass is wet. These towels didn't do the trick."

Officer Hathaway said, "What was that? I didn't hear you. Say again."

"It was nothing, Officer Hathaway. I was just about to choke my husband…I mean my husband was just choking on a soda. Thank you, and hopefully we'll see your colleagues at the marina."

Jason disconnected the call and put the phone in his pocket. Chelsea grabbed for the oh-my-god-bar and screamed as he turned into the marina parking lot a little too fast and ran his right front large knobby tire halfway up the back of a parked VW Beetle. He took the truck out of gear and let the front end roll back down to the ground.

"Whoops! See, Chelsea. I told you this thing would be safe on the Washington Beltway. It really can run over top of the other cars."

"You need to leave a note on that car with your name and phone number, so you can explain what happened and give them your insurance information later. Otherwise you're going to end up in jail for a hit and run. It should be easy for the police to match your tires with the gigantic knobby tire tracks you left on the back of that VW."

"Wow! You are getting the hang of this detective thing."

"No, what I'm doing is going into the poor house. We'll have to pay a sizeable deductible for this damage. When you add it to the damaged motorcycle, lost kiteboard equipment, purchase of this stupid truck and all the other stuff, we're not going to have any money left for a down payment on a vacation property. You're hopeless."

"Yeah, but this is a great adventure. I don't see a police car. Let's go catch the killers."

Chelsea leapt out of the truck and ran down the dock gangway. "Follow me, Sherlock."

They reached the dock where the Vacation Vaccination had been parked, and Chelsea pointed to the yacht as it moved away from them. Gina was slowly driving it through the marina towards the Intracoastal Waterway.

Jason winced. "I don't know what they did with Gina's husband, but he's not going to be happy when he sees his yacht. The channel through the marina is narrow, it's still windy, and she's bumping into every yacht secured to the dock. I'm guessing the damage is going to run into the six figure range."

"Jason, that's not important. Those two women are murderers, and we have to stop them."

"Boy, Chelsea. You're really getting into this PI thing. I ought to hire you as my assistant. I'm just not sure how to pay you, or how that would even work, other than I know I should be the boss. What d'ya think?"

"I think we need to stop these women. We can worry about how to organize my new PI firm later."

"Wait, what? Your new PI what?"

"Focus, Jason. How do we capture those two women?"

Jason pointed to the cluster of boats from the boat club that had refused his application.

"Let's check to see if there's a key in any of those."

"Oh no, Jason. You already almost destroyed one of that poor man's boats. Plus, the police are coming. This is not the time to steal a boat."

"Come on Chelsea. Let's go for it. I'll do better this time, I promise. Besides, I don't see any alternatives, do you?"

She looked around. "Unfortunately, I do not. But, Officer Hathaway did say that we should just let the Coast Guard handle it."

"Nonsense, the Coast Guard's busy with search and rescue. Remember? The hurricane? You almost crushed me in the bathtub? This is up to us. PI Jason Longfellow capturing the bad guys!"

Chelsea said, "You mean PI Chelsea Longfellow and Associate, don't you? And, stop complaining. At least I shared the tub with you. Pay attention. These are bad *girls*."

"Wait, what? Now I'm an associate?"

She followed Jason to the cluster of twenty-three-foot Cobia boats, fitted with double 150 HP Yamaha outboard engines. They frantically searched for one with the key still in it.

"Here, Chelsea. Here's one with a key. The dock hand probably abandoned it when Bertha got here. Thank you, Bertha."

They jumped into the boat. Chelsea untied it while Jason fired up the engines. Chelsea hung onto the seat, not surprised that he started out by crashing into a fifty-foot yacht on the first turn.

"Ouch! That'll leave a mark."

"Jason, slow down. We'll never catch them if we sink."

"It's Captain Jason, and no worries. I'm getting the hang of it. It's still a little windy from Bertha."

Crash! "That's gonna leave another mark."

"Now it's *Captain*? So, you're done with the PI thing? Thank God!"

"A person can be many things, Chelsea…doctor, PI, Captain…"

"Lunatic…"

After several more crash marks, Chelsea was relieved when they reached the Intracoastal Waterway. She looked downstream and saw the Vacation Vaccination.

Jason said, "Moneyman must not let Gina drive his boat very often. She's going really slow and swerving all over the place. The pitcher of martinis probably doesn't help. I'll catch her in no time."

Jason shoved the throttle forward. Chelsea barely grabbed hold of the seat in time to avoid being thrown overboard.

"Jason, if you kill me, I swear I'll haunt you until your dying day."

"Sorry, Dear. I forgot to warn you to hold on. So, be sure to hold on."

"Thanks a bunch. I have a bad feeling about this."

Jason had that insane look in his eyes. Chelsea had seen it before, the last time they were following Mark Moneyman's yacht up the Intracoastal Waterway.

"Jason, I'm getting that feeling of déjà vu all over again."

Chelsea looked at the speedometer. They were doing 40 knots when Jason came up behind the huge yacht, their boat bouncing around violently in the large wake. Chelsea was hanging on for dear life, sure that severe neck pain loomed in her future.

"Okay, Chelsea. This time I remembered to tell you. Hold on. We're gonna pass her, get in front of her, and force her to stop. Then, we'll call the Coast Guard, and hold the two sisters until they get here."

"But, Jason. Remember the last…"

Jason shoved the throttle all the way forward and guided the twenty-three-foot Cobia around to the left of the fifty-foot Vacation Vaccination, Chelsea still hanging on with everything she had. Chelsea saw Gina turn and look down at Jason from the helm of the yacht. Gina shoved the throttle all the way forward.

"Jason, look out!"

Chelsea was deafened as the massive engines roared and rocketed the giant yacht forward, creating an enormous wake. She screamed and her feet left the deck as the center console Cobia flew over the top of the first giant wave, bow up, and then the bow dropped and hit the second wave, bow down. The Cobia dove into the water, bow first like a submerging submarine, the engines pushing them straight to the bottom of the Intracoastal. Chelsea and Jason were washed overboard along with everything else not fastened down. Chelsea floated nearby as the Cobia rapidly filled with water and sank to the bottom. She found herself treading water in the middle of the Intracoastal, looking around for her husband, terrified that she'd lost him. Then, she saw him treading water nearby, and her terror turned to anger.

She yelled, "Jason, I'm over here! Are you all right? If you are, I'm going to kill you. We need to swim to one of those docks, get out of the water and call the police."

Jason looked sad. He didn't say anything, just swam along beside Chelsea to a nearby dock. Chelsea ended up standing on the dock with Jason, drenched and traumatized.

"Well, Jason. Talk about déjà vu. You did it again, only this time you sent that poor man's boat to Davy Jones's locker. That'll cost us dearly. If you're going to keep doing this, we need to get some kind of PI disaster insurance. And, I'm going to double your life insurance again."

"Come on, Chelsea. You wanted to catch them, too. You know you did. But, what's this thing about *PI Chelsea Longfellow and Associate*? I'm being demoted to associate in my own company?"

"I think it's a good idea. Once we look at the books for *your* PI firm, I'm guessing the finances are going to be well into the red…red ink bleeding everywhere. You should probably declare bankruptcy. I might have to start fresh with my own PI firm; a chance to turn a profit."

Jason looked sad some more.

Chelsea had stored her cell phone in a Ziploc bag, and it was still dry. Jason's was going to need several hours in a bed of dry rice. Chelsea called the police and the Coast Guard, told them what had happened and gave them her location. An hour later, a Coast Guard cutter pulled up near the dock where the PI couple were currently trespassing.

Chelsea watched as the Coast Guard boat sent a small motorized dingy to collect them from the dock. They were met on board the cutter by a Coast Guard officer. Chelsea found that most men in uniform were physically fit and quite attractive. This officer was no exception.

"Welcome aboard, folks. I assume you are Dr. and Mrs. Longfellow? I'm Lieutenant Maxwell Gonzales. I understand you've had quite a day for yourselves. You solved several murders and sank one of the boat club's boats in pursuit of the killers. I'm happy to report that we stopped the Vacation Vaccination an hour ago just up the Intracoastal and arrested the two ladies on board. Apparently they are sisters, they were screaming at each other when we stopped them and one of them confessed to the murders. The police have taken them to the St. Augustine Sheriff's Office for further questioning, arrest and processing."

Jason, excited, "See, Chelsea, it's okay. They got them. We cracked the case."

The Lieutenant continued, "Unfortunately, Officer Hathaway insisted that I should also place the two of you under arrest and deliver you to the St. Augustine police for questioning. A squad car is waiting for us at the St. Augustine Marina. It seems they still suspect you, Dr. Longfellow, of having something to do with the murders of all those realtors. They apparently find it hard to believe that you could appear at the scene of so many crimes without having anything to do with any of them. Then, there's the issue of stealing a boat from the boat club and sinking it in the Intracoastal."

The Lieutenant looked more closely at Jason. "Say…aren't you the guy we rescued in the middle of the ocean after your trying to kiteboard on a day with twenty-five-mile-per-hour winds? Well, no matter. I'm just here to deliver you to the police and I'm out of it, thank God."

Jason and Chelsea ended up at the St. Augustine Sheriff's office. Chelsea was placed in a holding cell, and the officer told her he was taking Jason to an interrogation room. They were questioning the two of them separately. At 7:00 PM a police officer released Chelsea. At that time the officer told her that there would be no murder charges filed against either of them. He explained that when the Coast Guard caught the Vacation Vaccination, Gina was at the helm, flying down the Intracoastal. The sisters were arguing loudly, and Constance fell apart and confessed to Rip Thornton's murder. Chelsea was surprised to hear that the Coast Guard had found Mark Moneyman tied up and locked in a lower cabin, the sisters concerned that he would rat them out.

The police officer further informed Chelsea that once in custody, Gina and Constance completely crumbled and confessed to everything, the murder of Rip Thornton and the use of West Nile virus and the vaccine to prime the realtors for aggression. Mark Moneyman, furious with his wife, apparently knew nothing about the murders. He had hired a lawyer to defend them, even though they'd locked him in a cabin. Any suspicion had been completely lifted from Jason. Chelsea was further relieved to hear that the owner of the boat club declined to press charges against Jason for boat theft, as long as Jason paid for the boat, now resting comfortably at the bottom of the Intracoastal.

Chelsea filled in the details for Jason when he arrived.

Jason said, "No jail time is good. They interrogated me extensively because they couldn't believe one man had found so many dead bodies. Apparently it was some kind of record. The trip to Florida wasn't a complete loss. At least I made my mark; I set a record for something.

***

That night, Jason and Chelsea were sitting on the couch in their rental condo, sipping wine and discussing the day's events. Chelsea was exhausted.

"Well, Chelsea. I solved the case, and we're not in jail. I'm going to take this as a win."

"You solved the case? You have a funny definition of solving a case. You were adamant that Mark Moneyman killed Rip Thornton. Wrong. He was a blustering old fool, but I knew he wasn't a murderer. He had two chances to kill us, and both times he missed us with his revolver on purpose. I suspected his wife, Gina, all along, and when her sister showed up and you found that gun and those realtor brochures in that stupid truck, that clinched it for me."

"You have to admit that the gun thing was confusing. Gina had a twenty-two revolver, Mark Moneyman had a twenty-two, and Constance had two twenty-twos. In Florida it seems like all Gods chilluns got a twenty-two. If we move to Florida, I'm gonna have to trade my 38-special in on a twenty-two. You know, when in Rome…"

Chelsea, frustration in her voice, "Jason, I don't think you have to worry about moving to Florida any time soon. We no longer have the money for a down payment on a vacation property. Your escapades…let's see…damaged motorcycle, destroyed kiteboarding equipment, run over VW Beetle, sunk brand new twenty-three-foot power boat, complete with twin Yamaha 150 engines…not to mention the purchase of that stupid jacked-up truck that a person has to levitate to get into. That pretty much ate up our vacation property fund. You suck as a PI, but you suck even worse at buying real estate."

"But, we caught the bad guys…ladies."

"Maybe, but even though I heard Constance Conover's confession, I still cannot believe that we found a dead realtor at almost every property we visited. I was actually beginning to suspect you of being the real realtor murderer. Then, there's the peppy Debbie, who tried to puree your face. You're a crime magnet and a half, or at least a dead realtor magnet. I'm afraid to go anywhere with you anymore."

"Chelsea, let's be fair. I did help solve those murders. I found Rip Thornton's body and the bodies of several other realtors, victims of the looney sisters. I also helped get a confession out of Constance Conover, even though you blocked her exit from the yacht during the hurricane."

"Yeah. I would have never dreamed that our bickering with each other would force a confession out of someone. If we're going to keep up this PI thing, we should remember that for the future; apparently it's an effective interrogation technique. I also have to admit that it feels good catching the killers. For a guy who hates chaos, you create it wherever you go. It's a unique approach to detecting, I'll give you that. Annoying the bad guys…or women… to the point of insanity. It's a good thing I thrive on chaos. I guess we make a good team."

"Thank you, I think? So, you actually enjoyed our little adventure? And, you want to continue doing the PI thing with me? We did have quite a time, what with motorcycling, kiteboarding, canoeing in Jesup/Alligator Lake, and chasing the bad guys on the Intracoastal."

"Yes, Jason, I enjoyed catching the killers. But, you still can't quit your day job. At this rate, even with both of our day jobs we're going to go broke. Next time, maybe we could come up with a client to pay us for our hard work, rather than spending our own time and resources chasing the killers. I think that's a much better business model."

They raised their wine glasses in a toast, "To catching the bad guys."

"So Chelsea, are you really disappointed that we can't afford a vacation home in Florida?"

"I would have liked to have a place here. In spite of all your disastrous attempts to have fun, St. Augustine is a beautiful place. The beaches, the downtown area, the local parks, the weather…it's a very nice place to be. But, I guess I'll get over it. Maybe someday, once we pay off all the stuff that you managed to break, we might still be able to buy a condo in Florida. What about you? Are you disappointed?"

A big grin on his face, "Actually, I'm quite relieved. Florida really seems to hate me. What with the searing sun, alligators, sharks, poisonous snakes, hurricanes, dead realtors, horny manatee, people armed to the teeth, gigantic boats on the Intracoastal and rust…it's just too dangerous!"

"And mosquitoes, Jason. Don't forget the murderous, gun-toting mosquitoes."

ACKNOWLEDGEMENTS

I would like to thank all the dedicated people that I worked with over my 40-year career with the FDA and industry in the high pressure area of medical biotech and drug development. I thoroughly enjoyed working with you and learning from you. An incredible amount of time and effort goes into ensuring that the drugs and biopharmaceuticals licensed in the US are safe and effective, and this is due to your efforts. I've always wanted to write murder mysteries, and it is the result of working in this industry that I got the idea to write Medical Biotech Murder Mysteries. During my career, I did risk assessments for new products, to determine if they were safe and effective to develop for the US market. In my books, I examine a potentially humorous side to risk assessment. I imagine absurd things that could potentially go wrong with biotech development, and work them into the plot of a murder mystery. With medical biotech, doctors and scientists produce products that act through your DNA, immune system, and cells. What could possibly go wrong?